I0817692

Praise for

A SWORD OF BRONZE AND ASHES and ANNA SMITH SPARK

'Weaves a spell that will consume you.'
Barnes and Noble

'Literary *Game of Thrones*.'
Sunday Times

'Spark blends Celtic mythology and grimdark fantasy into an enthralling tale of female power. [Her] poetic prose gives the adventure a mythic feel that enhances its folkloric and folk horror elements. Balancing the violence of war with emotional depth and thematic explorations of motherhood and legacy, this gripping outing is a testament to Spark's power as a storyteller.'
Publishers Weekly

'Anna Smith Spark has done it yet again with this cracking read, and I hope there are many more stories to come in this multi-layered and captivating world.'
Out of This World SFF

'It is a mind-blowing book. I don't think I've ever read anything quite like it. It's a story about the ragged, tearing wound you get when high myth gets stitched to the grind of mundane life. It's incredible.'
Adrian Tchaikovsky

'Lushly poetic Heavy Metal mythology.'
Peter McLean, author of *War for the Rose Throne*

'Fusing together a Tolkienesque level of worldbuilding with Celtic folklore, *A Sword of Bronze and Ashes* is hauntingly beautiful…a masterpiece.'
Shauna Lawless, author of
The Children of Gods and Fighting Men

'Anna Smith Spark's unique poetic literary fantasy delivered an *absolute experience.'*
Grimdark Magazine

'Anna Smith Spark wields a shining sword of beauty and destruction. Her books aren't there just to be read; they have to be consumed with all of your soul.'
Spells & Spaceships

ANNA SMITH SPARK

A SWORD OF BRONZE AND ASHES

BOOK ONE of THE MAKING OF THIS WORLD RUINED

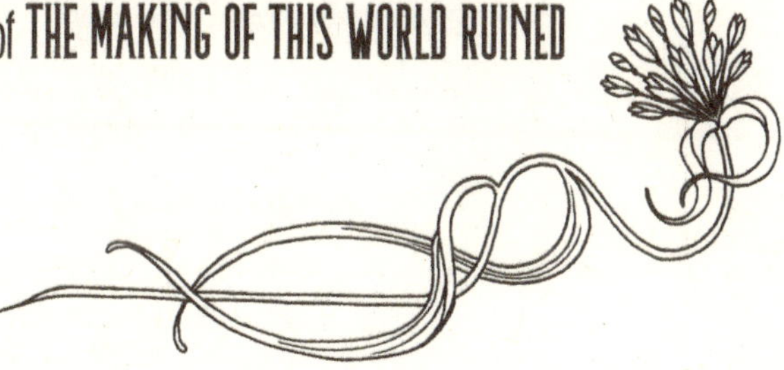

This is a FLAME TREE PRESS book

FLAME TREE PRESS
6 Melbray Mews, London, SW6 3NS, UK
flametreepress.com

US sales, distribution and warehouse:
Simon & Schuster
simonandschuster.biz

UK distribution and warehouse:
Hachette UK Distribution
hukdcustomerservice@hachette.co.uk

Thanks to the Flame Tree Press team.

The cover is made by Flame Tree Studio, working with the fine and wonderful artist Broci who created the cover and inside illustrations especially for this book. The art is © Broci 2025. The font families used are Avenir and Bembo.

Flame Tree Press is an imprint of Flame Tree Publishing Ltd
flametreepublishing.com

A copy of the CIP data for this book is available from the British Library and the Library of Congress.

1 3 5 7 9 8 6 4 2

THIS SPECIAL EDITION ISBN: 978-1-78758-999-5
Paperback ISBN: 978-1-78758-839-4
ebook ISBN: 978-1-78758-841-7

Printed and bound in Great Britain by Clays Ltd, Elcograf S.p.A.

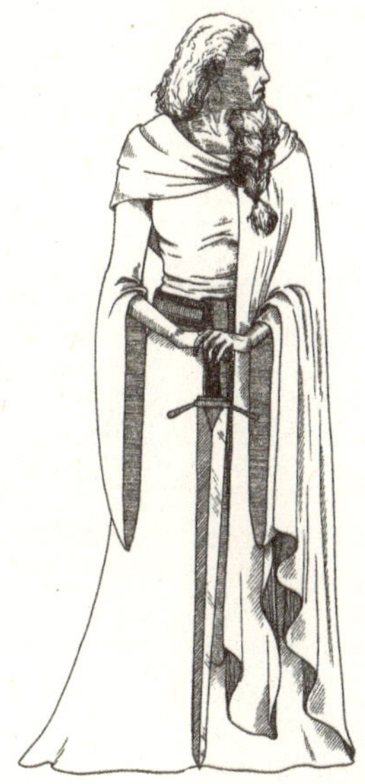

ANNA SMITH SPARK

A SWORD OF BRONZE AND ASHES

BOOK ONE of THE MAKING OF THIS WORLD RUINED

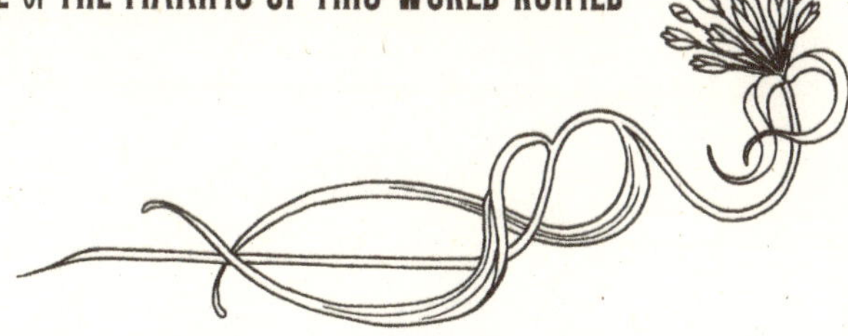

FLAME TREE PRESS
London & New York

CONTENTS

To Jude, Randa and Ryllis

CHAPTER ONE

A fine morning, damp and fresh and clean with the sky new-made pale, after long days of bitter heat. The wound of the sun's rising fast-faded, the stars fled even in the farthest west. Wind stirs the aspen leaves and they sing and shiver; the cobwebs spread like hair, rain-wet and jewel-bedecked. A magpie chatters in anger. The hedgerows smell musk-rank.

A fine morning, yes, and pleasant to walk out in to bathe in the newness, to bring the cows in from the meadow for milking. Three crows called as Kanda made her way down the hillside: three crows called from the left over toward Mal Anwen, whose peak was black with pine trees and gray with cloud-mist; a pigeon cooed in answer from the right over toward Mal Eren, whose peak was gold with gorse flowers and bright with a single shaft of white sun. The lush wet grass was delicious beneath Kanda's bare feet.

The cows – three of them, one brown, one black, one, the best and the most treasured, roan with black horns – were down in the river meadow in the valley bottom, where the grass was so good, the milk they gave was almost pure cream. How good the milk was! If she went away from the farm for even a few days, to visit Dellet's sister who lived in Aranth by the headman's hall, Kanda missed and longed for the taste of her own cows' milk. She had to scramble where the hillside fell away steeply, her feet rushing to get ahead of her. Two sheep leapt up startled from their sleep behind a hawthorn, baaed at her as they shambled away waggling their hind legs. Another crow rose up from the grass, and the sheep baaed at it.

The steep bit here was thickly planted with hawthorns, very old and twisted. Planted, surely – they were too regularly spaced, too neat and too few and too many all at once, to have grown up here naturally. In early summer Kanda could sit for hours at the top of the hill looking down at them white against the green hillside. In autumn she could sit for hours looking down at them blazing berry-red. The river lay below them as a dark shining pattern of skin-smoothness and rush-gleam. She could hear the cows now lowing, the two that needed milking and the roan that had been allowed to keep its calf. She called, "Kye kye kye." The crows and the pigeon and the sheep answered her. The river answered her, singing.

Just where the hillside flattened abruptly to the water meadow and the river, she passed the remains of a building. Small, much smaller than a house, a round circle of drystone walling waist-high with an entranceway facing the river, the stones worn beautiful smooth where the cattle liked to rub their chins against them. Too narrow to have been made big enough to stand up in, unless it was a house for a child. A bee skep, it would have looked like when it was standing. Kanda broke off a sunweed flower, placed it in the center of the ruin as she walked past. Five flowers there already, one fresh, the rest slowly fading.

"Warm sun and cool rain and good earth," Kanda said. "And three healthy children. My thanks to you."

In this place, a man was buried. A hundred years ago or a thousand.

He had lived all his life in the valley of the Wenet, or had lived far off, or homeless, or loved to wander, had happened to be passing through the valley when he died. Someone had buried him here, taken care to raise a cairn over him in this beautiful place, so his bones lay at peace here giving the land his blessing.

One of the cows lowed, and she said, "Yes, yes, kye, not to forget you. My kye, they also give thanks to you. Poppy most especially gives thanks to you for her fine son," she said laughing as the cow lowed again.

She reached the river, stood on the bank looking down at the water. Shallow, the water barely ran to her knees when she paddled in it. The bed was reddish stones. Tiny fish darted away in panic at her shadow, just as the sheep had run from her slithering down the grass. "Sorry, oh fish," she said. In the deeper places there were trout. On the other side of the river the bank was heavily wooded, rising steeply to the high wild hills that ran away south almost to the headman's hall of Aranth two hours' walk away.

"Kye kye kye." They came nosing up to Kanda, smelling of grass and muck, blinking their great black eyes and swishing their tails against the flies. "But the trout like to eat the flies, kye, and my babies like to eat the trout," Kanda told them. The roan calf snorted, skipped into the river with exactly the same showing-off joy as her youngest, Morna, looked surprised at the cold, somehow, even, in exactly the same way Morna always always always did. "Oh Strawberry." Kanda regarded the roan cow its mother. "What do we do with these babies, eh? Come and be milked now, kye, for my babies' morning porridge."

The calf came back out of the water, butted up to its mother. Kanda stared at it. It had a white flash on its red forehead.

"Strawberry? Come here?"

It didn't have a white flash, she'd helped the cow birth it, it had never had a white flash. A trick of the light....

Starting between the horn buds and running down, tapering as it ran so that it looked like—

"No." She felt very cold suddenly. The crows started up calling and she felt sick. The cows pressed around her close and she was frightened they would trample her. "Oh. No."

Something was coming floating down the river. A dark thing. A big thing.

She knew that shape also.

"Oh. No."

The crows stopped calling, and the pigeons stopped. The cows pressed around her so close she was really frightened.

The dark thing caught on a rock in the stream still far enough away she could pretend she didn't know what it was. She could leave it; it could be anything.

But the river water began to run fast now, churn up in foam. Deeper, wilder. And the water was red.

She tried to push the cows away. They were so warm under her hands, she felt the muscles of them, the bones of their shoulders. The lovely way the bones and flesh rolled when they moved. They tried to press around her, butted their heads at her chest, pressing tighter and tighter. Kanda's hand went to her hip. The warm muscle, the bones, the heavy warm sweet breath. She was frightened now that she might…she might kill them.

"Kye kye kye. Time to be milked." Her voice shook. "Come and be milked for my…my babies' porridge."

Absurdly, with the cows following her close as dogs or children, she found herself walking up the riverbank toward the…. When she reached it she splashed into the water. The cows finally left her alone, stood on the bank looking at her. They lowed gently, and she thought: they are grieving.

The body was on its back, face staring at the sky. His head was toward the woodland side of the river, knocking against the rock he'd caught on; the light coming down through the thick summer leaves made him green, shimmering as if he was still moving. He had bled heavily: he was very pale, with pale drawn-back lips. His eyes were open: blue eyes. The whole left side of the face around them was gone in blood. At his left shoulder, too, a great black stain of blood.

Kanda gave a cry so loud the birds in the wood burst up in fear. The very trees shook so that their leaves rustled in fear of her cry. The cows lowed and stamped and fled. Only the red calf with the sword marking on its forehead lingered, stared at her from the riverbank.

Three times, Kanda gave her great cry. Then she began to run up the steep hillside toward her home and her children.

Her eldest, Sal, was in the sheep field. She saw the girl as she ran up, a black figure against the sky, the light behind her making her shine as her name meant *shining* because that was what she was to Kanda. She was fifteen years old and her hair like Kanda's was brilliant red. But the blood was in Kanda's mind and even knowing it was Sal she had to hold her right hand tight clenched to her chest as she drew near. Sal said, "Mother?" in a puzzled voice.

Kanda could barely speak, her voice choked in her mouth as though she had swallowed fire. She gasped, almost crawling up the slope. "Sal," she tried to say, but her voice was like a raven calling, or like a wolf howling, or like a war trumpet. "Sal!" she screamed at last, "Sal! Where's your father? Where are your sisters? Where are your sisters, Sal, where are they where are they?" and now the raven and the wolf were gone, her right hand clutched at the girl with love until she winced in pain, pulling her away from the slope and the hawthorns that ran down to where a man was dead by a warrior's violence. "Where are they?" Kanda screamed.

Sal understood something terrible had happened. Was happening. "In the house. Morn and Calian are in the house. But Father is…he's gone to the high field. He went out just after you left…." The girl looked at her mother. Kanda looked back. "I'm a fast runner," Sal said. "Faster than you, Mum. I'll go."

"No!" And then Kanda said helplessly, "Yes. Go as fast as you can." Sal began to run at once, on up the hill where the grass grew coarser and rougher, sheep scattering before her. A crow flew over her head for a moment, and Kanda shuddered. "Sal! Sal!" The child turned back, her face even at a distance was wild as a beast's because she knew something terrible had come. "When you find him –" if, Kanda's mind screamed helplessly, if you find him, if he and you are alive still, "– when you find him – not the house – the – the—"

"Where, Mum?" Even out of breath and terrified: scorn for her mother's stupidity.

"In the – the—" Nowhere, Kanda thought, not a barn or an outhouse, not the road toward Dryl, not the river bridge.

"There's a place in the woods across the river," Sal shouted. "Calian knows it. The Camp. We'll meet you at the Camp."

The camp…. The crow was gone from near the child, her hair was bright as beech leaves in autumn. "The Camp," Kanda said. "Yes. Go!"

She herself ran to the house. It lay just beyond the sheep field, on a little ridge in the wider sweep of the hill so that the door looked out onto the view of the valley and the wooded hills beyond. Facing south, so it could bask in the sun. An apple tree grew beside it, and a garden full of green stuff; behind it there was a line of aspens. The younger girls had heard her shouting, they came out of the door toward her. They, too, were frightened. They rushed to their mother. So small still.

Calian, who was twelve, said, "I was looking after Morna properly, I was, I was. But…in the house…." She pointed back but didn't look back. "Mummy?" she said.

Morna, who was four, said nothing.

"Stay here." Kanda stood them under the apple tree. "Put your hands on the tree trunk, don't let go. Stay there until I come back." They might laugh, or run away, or want to go with her into the house, but they didn't, they stood just as she had said, very grave, shaking, their left hands clasped together, their right hands pressed to the tree trunk.

Kanda drew a deep breath. Went into the house.

It was clean and warm, just as she had left it, the table where Calian had been getting the breakfast together, Morna's two wooden dolls sitting in a corner on a scrap of green cloth. A pot of water was boiling on the fire, and she thought: it will boil dry, or crack. She thought: the house will burn down to ash. She thought: what did I think would be here? Nothing.

She went through into the sleeping place. She thought: it's lucky, I suppose, that they were all dressed. Her right hand was hurting her so much now that she had to clench it into a fist.

At the far end of the sleeping place there was a niche in the wall. In the niche there were three things. A wooden bowl, small as a child's food bowl so that she could hold it in her two clasped hands, carved of blackthorn wood. A lump of white stone no bigger than a pebble, a piece from a quern long broken. A cup of ill-fired clay, patterned with her own fingerprints. She gathered them up, put them in a leather satchel. Back in the day place she took bread and a cheese from the shelf. From a peg at the door, she took the children's cloaks. From a niche above the door that neither her children nor her husband knew was there, she took a smooth yellow human finger bone.

The girls were still standing with their hands pressed on the tree trunk. They looked so small. They were crying.

"It's not here," she said aloud. "It's gone." In the house suddenly she felt calm, none of this is real, there's not a dead man in the river, they'll laugh at me for forever, for making them all run away from the house into the woods. When I'm an old woman my grandchildren will say, "Tell us the story of Grandma making you run to the wood, Granddad." She thought: I'll bring Morna's dolls for her. She turned and her back was to the open door and somehow the light streamed in.

A shadow fell on the beaten floor before her, reached across toward the hearth fire and the sleeping place, and it was not the shadow of a farm woman.

"Where is 'the camp'? Where?"

Calian was crying again now. "Here. Somewhere here. I don't know."

"Where is it?" Try to stop herself screaming. "Cal, you have to know. Sal said you'd know."

"I don't.... We haven't been there for ages...I—"

"Think!"

A child's righteous fury: "I can't think with you screaming at me!"

"Mummy!" Baby Morna was crying. 'The woods' was not the woodland on the other side of the river. They went west, along the heights with the river valley beneath them, the flank of the hill rose and fell, there was a dip in the hills and a wood, whitebeam and hornbeam and aspen and elm and birch and hazel and ash. The river ran down from the west, which Kanda did not like because the dead man had come down the river. I should have thought, when Sal said the woods. I should have thought. And now Calian was lost, saying she didn't know where the camp was, and Morna was so heavy to carry, and crying, and the fresh cool morning had turned to gray rainfall. Before them, above them, the dark top of the mountain Mal Anwen was still hidden in the cloud. A long time, she had feared that mountain. Kanda thought: we should not be going west.

"Kanda!"

Her husband's voice. Dellet's voice. He came out of the wood then, her husband, his face so beautiful then that she wept. Sal was beside him.

"I couldn't remember," Calian said, "I'm sorry." Kanda almost fell into her husband's arms as he took Morna from her. "Take the baby, Sal," Dellet said. "I need to help your mother." He said, more gravely, "What is this…what's this all about? Why have you got—?" He could see Morna's yellow cloak half falling out of the satchel. "Kanda?"

Keep calm. Make them. Kanda said, "We have to hide."

The man and the three children stepped back, lowered their eyes. The man said, "Do as…as your mother says." Kanda took his hand like she did when they were first courting, he had Morna on his arm, in her other hand Kanda held tight to Calian, Sal held Calian's other hand. Courting couples and children walk sweet hand in hand. They went through the trees one after another, winding through the trees like a dance.

"The Camp," said Sal, pointing, Calian embarrassed because they had been so close all along. A bank of earth, a round dip beyond it, bramble and nettle in thick tangles, the tree canopies reaching close.

Safe, hidden: Kanda began to breathe more easily. And she could no longer see the cloud-capped peak of Mal Anwen. She thought with a sudden horror: but the river, the River Wenet, the river flows down from Mal Anwen.

A shriek: Calian had put her foot in a hole, twisted it. Rigid-faced with pain-shock. Oh Calian, Calian, clumsiest of my children. A howl broke out of the child, pain note on and on. Kanda stared around her, blind with fear. Baby Morna opened her mouth to howl back at her sister. Kanda clasped her hand over Calian's mouth. Gave Morna such a look that she, too, baby thing, was silent.

"Get down," Kanda whispered. "Get down, now." They sank down all together into the tangle of undergrowth, wet, scratching, stinging. The children's eyes vast with fear but they made no sound, they did not take their eyes off their mother.

Calian's ankle was bleeding. Kanda eased her hand from the child's mouth, placed it over the cut instead. Her daughter's slender bones, so warm her daughter's skin. Her daughter's heartbeat through beside Kanda's own heartbeat. The terrified eyes softened. She touched each of their hands in turn, first her husband and then her three daughters. Do not be so afraid, my loves. My loves. All that is in me, all that is good – do not be so afraid, my loves. Simply do as I say. A blankness came into all their faces, like dumb beasts, they nodded. Lies, and trickery, and a good thing.

Later, when they had been hidden long enough that Calian's cut had healed to a black scratch, she began to try to tell them something. "Is it thieves, Mother?" asked Calian, and she nodded, "Thieves, yes."

Every winter there would be people on the roads who would steal if they had to, "Give her a loaf and a cup of beer, Sal, yes, but – keep an eye on her, don't let her in the house and don't for one moment let her alone": and she, the last beggar, had two infant children with her. A great gang of men had come last spring to steal sheep and cattle, every homestead for five miles had had to keep urgent watch, gather together to defend themselves, old Dall and Ben and kind young Susa two months off her wedding day had been killed. Even here, yes, even here, so beautiful and peaceful, they understood fear and violence. But some things…Kanda looked up at the green summer leaves, touched the wet rich leaf litter at her feet. "We need to stay here for the day and the night, at least, my brave, brave children." Dellet, whom she had not married for his cleverness, nodded, nodded. Sal half knew, Calian half knew, that this was different and lying. But Sal and Calian knew also to be kind to baby Morna, whose name meant *golden* because she was golden-bright for all of them. "It's like that time last in the spring when we had to hide over in the caves up at Mal Eren, Morn, remember?" Sal said.

"That was kind of fun," Calian said.

"Yes. And now you must be silent, all of you." She gave them all some bread: it was stale and hard and she'd never been any good at baking it, so chewing it kept them quiet. They crept along a little farther, to where the undergrowth was yet thicker but had fewer thorns, a dark green tangle already in summer crusted with seedpods delicate as the curl of Morna's fingernails. And, oh joyous, a fallen tree still alive and growing verdant, its canopy a tent to hide in, a join in its branches where they could sit. Kanda gave them some more bread and some of the cheese. She rested her head on Dellet's shoulder, listened to his heartbeat and his breathing, drank in the smell of him. He rested his head against hers; the children wrapped themselves close around them both. "Traveler's-joy on an old hawthorn," Dellet called the way Sal had always wrapped herself around him.

Again, Kanda thought: there is no danger, there's not a dead man down in the river, they'll laugh at me for forever: "Tell us the story of Grandma making you hide in the wood, Granddad." But her right hand burned, and her mouth tasted of blood.

And the day passed in the greenwood somewhere between fear and boredom. Enlivened only by the need to piss. "Hold it in." "I can't." "You can hold in a poo, Mummy –" yes, I know, child of mine, beloved, I've been doing so since I was down with the cows, "– but you can't can't hold in a wee." "I can't hold in a poo. I need a poo, Mummy." It was easier when you were terrified, beloved children. And very well done, Calian, for raising that idea in Morna's head. "I need a poo, Mummy." "I need a wee, Mummy." I do too now, thank you. "You have to be silent, both of you. I mean it." "You can't be silent if you fart, Mummy." "Look, children, just…just …." "It stinks, Mummy!" "Well…yes. Obviously." Calian, you play climbing in the manure heap, ruined that good shawl your grandmother knitted you. I should have left you too terrified for speech, beloved children. "You have to be silent, children. Please. Please." "But it stinks." "But I scratched my leg on a stick." "But I need another poo." "But this is boring." "But I'm hungry." "But I'm thirsty." "But Morna's being annoying." "But I need another wee." And all the time her right hand burned, and her mouth tasted of blood.

And at last the long day drew toward a sweet gold summer evening in the greenwood, and they fell asleep because they were exhausted from fear and boredom both together to sleeping. But Kanda did not sleep.

She stood on the threshold, looking in. The Hall was dark, windowless, a low roof. The walls were made of woven hazel packed with straw and mud. The roof was dried bracken. The floor was beaten earth. A bronze cauldron hung from a tripod but the metal was cracked beyond use or repair, the cauldron was empty save for dust and cobwebs, the hearth beneath the cauldron was cold and dead. Rain had leaked in, lay in a puddle near the hearth. The Hall was empty. Not even bats or owls would come here. Not even crows. But at the far end of the Hall there was the sound of something moving. A clink of dry pebbles.

The threshold stone before her was worn down to the sea-sky-stone colorlessness, smooth and pitted, deeply worn with use. It had once been perfect black. Three things, once, she had seen buried beneath it. Ten times a thousand times, she had crossed that threshold stone. She was afraid to cross it. She must cross it. She said the words that must be said on crossing, held the doorway to steady herself, stepped.

Crossed.

The air rolled with a blare of trumpets.

She said the words that must be said.

A crystal bell sounded.

A horn rang.

Three things, she had once seen buried beneath the threshold. She herself had brought one of them.

She said the words that must be said.

The walls of the Hall were made of silver. Columns of white porphyry held up the roof of gold. A thousand columns, so vast was the Hall. The floor was made of diamonds. Rich hangings whispered in the breeze. The Hall had great windows of oiled silk that filled all the air with color, dancing. Outside the windows white lilies and red roses and golden honeysuckle, sweetest of all flowers, grew and bloomed. Always, forever, night and day, they were in bloom. The blazing hearth fire was pinewood and applewood; the flames rose blue, the fire made no smoke. Over the fire hung a bronze cauldron so large two men could not wrap their arms around it. It was patterned with birds in flight, deer running. The handles were in the shape of serpents' open mouths. The tripod it hung from had wolves' snarling muzzles for feet. Steam rose from the cauldron, scented with meat, herbs, wine. The cauldron's name was Helle, that is *Health*. It was never empty.

The Hall was filled with people, tall and strong, dressed for peace, for dancing, feasting, in red silk, green silk, black silk, yellow silk. Each wore a crown of gold on their shining hair. Each wore a jewel on their smooth forehead. At the far end of the Hall was a dais, on the dais was a throne. The throne was carved of the same black stone as the threshold. Like the threshold it was worn and pitted. Very old. It was without ornament or adornment. Although it was made of stone, the air around it felt warm. The throne's name was Thalle, that is *Hope*. On each side of the throne three swords hung from the silver wall. They were not made of bronze, there was no word in any language for the metal from which they were made. Patterns in their blades moved, flowed like the waves of the ocean, sometimes the patterns moved like water rushing in spate in a mountain stream. They glowed blue, silver, black, green.

She knew well those swords. Her sweat and her blood were soaked deep into the leather hilt-wrapping of one of them.

A man sat on the throne. He did not wear a crown, for he was not a king. His hair was white as snowfall, his skin was black as night, he was as wrinkled and twisted as the tree that grows in the wind on a high mountain, for he was very old. His eyes were red as berries. His face was kind as the spring sun.

The name of the Hall was Roven, that is *Peace*.

The man had no name that she had ever heard him speak.

As she walked the length of the Hall Roven, every man and woman present went down on their knees before her.

When she reached the dais, she stood before the old man. His eyes filled with tears to see her. He stood, slowly, for he was very old, his hands trembled with the effort as the leaves of the aspen tree tremble in the wind.

He wore a green robe that fell open at the front of him as he stood upright. His belly and his breasts were that of a pregnant woman.

"You have come home to us." His voice trembled also like the aspen leaves. Often, in the fields, she had thought she heard him in the leaves when the wind blew.

And this was the first time since she stood before the threshold, she thought then, that she had thought of the farm.

She said: "I have come home."

A great cheer rang around the Hall. On his thin shaking crane-like legs, the old man too knelt to her then. The air spun with light and dancing, gold light, white light, a movement in the air unseen yet visible, as the current of the water is seen and unseen. A sheen on the air, a shiver like a note of music, joy painted in drifts of light in the beauty of the Hall. The horn rang.

The beast from which that horn came, she had hunted.

Light moved as music moves, moved visible as the summer wind. As the ice is melted in the fields, the spring flowers unfurl, the birds and the beasts find ease after cruel winter frost. Light, a pillar of light, a tree trunk with branches spreading.

A woman. Her face was the face of a bird, long-beaked. From her golden hair there sprouted a deer's antlers, a golden bird with the same long beak perched on her antlers while a squirrel with golden fur sat among her antlers grooming itself.

The woman took the sword from the wall. Held it out.

The leather of the hilt-grip was marked with the print of her fingers, so long had she held it. The metal gleamed. Like raindrops in the blade.

"Take it," the woman said.

The old man said, "You are come home. Take it, then."

CHAPTER TWO

"Mummy Mummy Mummy."

Her right hand burned. Her mouth tasted of blood. Rain-sodden leaves pressed over her face. She could smell her own sweat, stinking, and her family's sweat and piss. It was near dawn. She thought: I slept! Anything could have come for them while I slept!

"Mummy Mummy Mummy. Can we go home now?"

I…I don't know. All of it struck her with the shock of falling into icy water. "No. We can't go home, little one."

Morna said, "I want to go home."

Kanda said with a snap, "We can't go home." She saw the child's face collapse, the wail of pain come. "I'm sorry, I…. We…." The other wind blew, the real wind, it smelled of smoke and blood. "We need to…to walk, to go…to go somewhere, little ones."

"Go home," Morna said.

"Go home," Sal said.

"Go home," Calian said. Calian, who was the fiercest of the three, the one she feared, the one she loved the least, Calian said, "This is the most stupid thing."

"This is not," Dellet said to his daughters, "a stupid thing if your mother says it isn't." He was very angry, his voice shaking, a rare thing that made the girls shrink back silent. But he too was confused, turned to Kanda. I don't understand what's happening, his eyes said to her. I'm frightened, wife.

Trust me, husband mine. Please, trust me. But the other wind blew strong with the hot metal smell that she had once loved. She thought of other things. She put her hand on her husband's arm, squeezed him tight. Strong muscled arms from a lifetime of farmwork. For the strength of his arms when he embraced her, the tenderness with which he worked that strength on the land, that, in part, was why she had married him.

"Be silent. All of you." They were: silent, still. For a little while, Kanda sat in the green tent of a fallen hornbeam, soaked with muddy rain, her hands pressed tight to her husband's arm. Drinking in the faces of her three daughters: Morna, her unexpected late child, her skin the same dark rich brown as Kanda's, her hair pale as elder blossom, still the fine silk of babyhood; Calian, twelve, her hair chestnut-brown, her skin bronze like her father's, wildest, strongest, legs and arms made for strength; Sal, shooting up thin but then she'll stop growing, soften, surely, her mother's skin, her hair her mother's autumn-beech-leaves-red. At fifteen Sal was almost full-grown, in some of the villages she'd be married off by now. I had thought – hoped – lied – that I would see her grown, married, that she at least I had hoped – lied – I would see with a life, happy, a baby of her own in her arms.

She put her hands on her husband's chest, felt her husband's heart beat once, twice, three times. A hundred times. His name meant *good man*, because, he always said, his parents couldn't think of a better one. This, she thought, I had wanted to be my home.

She let them go.

"I want to go home, Mummy Mummy Mummy."

"This is stupid."

"This is so stupid."

So they came out of the wood, walked back toward the farmhouse, because Kanda could not keep them any longer from going back. But when they see, she thought... So they came out of the wood, walked back toward the farmhouse. Thus they saw with their own eyes what their mother knew had come, had sought to spare them seeing.

The grass was green, the sky was pale, the sun was rising pale in rain. In the east the peak of Mal Eren was dark against the dawn, soft gentle mountain; the valley fell steep before them with the river hidden but they could hear the river; the woods beyond were still and calm and morning dark. Mal Anwen rose in the west unclouded, pine forest and above the great spear of its highest peak. The rising sun struck the black stone of its peak and made it gold. A flame at the top of the mountain. Birds sang, the sheep were in the fields, a fox barked. A single beam of sunlight broke over the line of the hills. A fine day for growing, for living.

Sal said, "Oh." For there in the turf before them a trail ran off in the direction of their home, and the trail was rotted and black. The good turf was as the vilest parts of a mire in the bitter winter, dead leaves and dead insects trapped there, dead slimy stinking earth. Beside the track, as wide apart as the stride of a tall man walking fast, there were patches of burned stuff where the soil was cracked open hard and white.

Sal said, "Oh." She pointed: a sheep came lumbering toward them, but the track was between them and it, and when it reached one of the burned places it bleated in pain, fell down, its body seemed to wither like dried leaves and it was dead. Sal said, "Oh," and pointed, and there were two crows dead on the good turf dried and withered, and a pigeon dead and wet and rotted next to them.

A column of smoke rose from the direction of their home. Five faces watched the smoke for a moment. Even baby Morna knew somehow what it meant. More smoke rising from the direction of the next farm along, where Ben, whom the children called 'Apple Tree' for reasons no adult could understand, had lived.

Calian pointed then, said, "Look." She began to run to where she was pointing; Kanda with a cry like a heifer ran following, "No, no, come back." Don't look, don't look.

"Stay there," Dellet shouted to the other children, "Sal, keep hold of Morna. Calian, come back, come back."

And he was running, Kanda heard his breath panting, he hated running fast, not natural, he'd say, I'm a man, woman, not a horse.

Calian was a fast runner, leaping over rocks and holes and hummocks, leaping over a clump of heather and a patch of gorse, and she was there looking down at what she'd seen before her mother and father could catch her. She made no sound beyond the gasp of her breath from running, did not look away or flinch, but she pressed herself against her father as he toiled up after her.

A circle of stone walling, too small for a house, identical to the circle of stone walling in the water meadow but that the walls were lower, worn down almost to nothing. Someone indeed had placed a posy of flowers in the center of the circle, blue speedwell that did not grow here on the hilltops. Kanda looked at the blue flowers because she could not bear to see what her child was seeing.

"It's Cythranath," Calian said. Ben Apple Tree's daughter. Laughed at mercilessly for her outlandish name.

Her arms were flung out clutching the wall, her left hand just inside the entranceway. The peace hand, the left hand: if she had got one step closer, Kanda thought, she might, might have been saved. She was on her front, all her wounds were to her back, she had been killed running away. She did not see her death, at least. She was in her night shift, her hair plaited up for sleeping, her bare feet were scratched raw. Her right hand held a butchering knife, a big solid thing of flint. It was bloody. She had fought back, then. That too was something.

"We should bury her," Calian said.

"No! Don't touch her!"

Dellet said, shocked: "Kanda?"

"You mustn't touch her, Calian."

"I know what they'll have done to her, Mum, if we turn her over, if that's what you mean."

Dellet said, "She should at least have the sun on her face." The two of them bent together. Calian gave a shriek and leapt back, clutching her right hand. "It hurts!" Her fingers were red where they had touched Cythranath's shoulder.

"I told you not to touch," Kanda said. "Wipe it on the grass, quickly. Quickly, Calian. That's it, yes. Now hold the stone there, the wall. Don't look at me like that, do it. Put your hand flat on the stones. Just there, wait, move your hand a little, there, where the red vein runs in the stone, put your hand there. No, look, there, put your hand there, there, Calian, where the stone has that line of red. Yes, there. That's right. Now hold your hand flat. Flat."

"Mum—" Calian said in bafflement: "It's stopped hurting."

"Hold it there a moment longer. Just to be sure. Yes, well, that should be long enough. Now let me see." A great weight rushing out of her body, breathing again her heart beating again, as Kanda saw that the skin was clean.

"You must never touch anything they have killed, Calian. Never. Promise me."

Calian, tears in her eyes, said, "*They*?"

"The— They—" In her mind she said the words that must be said. She thought: they will have to know, now. She said: "Not here, not now."

"*They*?"

"Leave your mother be, Cal-flower," Dellet said. He put his hand on his daughter's shoulder, squeezed it tight. "Just do as she says, yes?"

"You tell me, Dad."

"I don't know anything here, Cal-flower. But do as your mother says, hey? Your sisters are back there where we left them, and we shouldn't be leaving them."

"Wait. Just…." There was a loose thread on Calian's tunic. She unraveled it, snapped it off, draped the thread onto Cythranath's hair. 'Be at peace, Cythranath.' The tunic was brown, Cythranath's hair was brown, but the thread seemed to stand out there vividly even as they walked away, a gift of kindness and love that might ease the woman's death.

Kanda squeezed her daughter's hand. "That was well done, Calian. All of it."

"So you'll tell – when we get back to Sal and Morna?"

"I— Not—" She said at last: "We need to go somewhere safe."

Calian said, "*Safe*?" When they reached Sal and Morna she caught her baby sister up in her arms and hugged her tight. Which was not a thing Calian the fiercest and least loved of Kanda's three daughters often did.

In the sky far above them, a bird sang as it leapt up toward the sun.

Safe. Safe? Safe! The sun was in the sky now and the rain had stopped, it was around the time of day that Kanda had found the body in the river yesterday. It is true, Calian, nowhere here is now safe. Kanda tried to think and tried tried to think. She looked to the east where Mal Eren, the summer mountain, was gold with gorse flowers where the bees would be drowsing thick. She looked to the south across the river, where the wooded hills stretched. She looked to the north, where the hills ran bare of trees, turf for grassing and then heather and peat bog, then sea, cold and gray and pitiless wild, beyond that. She looked to the west where the sun would set this evening and by then her children might or might not be still living, where Mal Anwen the winter mountain rose clear of cloudcaps, its peak a spearhead. Her right hand burned. Somewhere safe.

Calian said, "The tree." Calian looked at her mother and her eyes were full of wisdom.

She understands, Kanda thought. She doesn't know, but she understands some of what is happening. She....She sees me, Kanda thought.. Or...no.... She sees...like me.

The least loved of my daughters. Because she is the most like me.

Dellet said, "The tree?" and Sal said, "The tree?" but Kanda said, "Take us there, then." As they walked through the beautiful green hills, they did not see a single living thing. Once they came upon another track of rot, burned places, perhaps it was fresher than the track that had passed them last night. Kanda was afraid they would have to cross it, for they could not cross it, they must not, but Calian said, "They are avoiding the tree, you see?" The track turned away at a right angle from the way Calian was leading them, and then away again, they had been avoiding the tree. Calian led on up to a little hollow in the crest of the hill, perfectly circular, boggy and waterlogged. Dellet had to carry Morna while Sal and Calian held on to each other, the mud sticking and sucking at their feet, the music of the water and the mud beneath their feet delicious. The water that welled up was clear and good, with a reddish tint. Kanda wetted her finger, tasted the water, it tasted of metal. That was good. In the center of the hollow a rise of lush green grass to bring them dry-footed above the wet, a little island in the bog of the hilltop. In the center of the island, a single great ancient tree. A rowan tree. Beneath the tree there was a large flat stone, big enough for them all to sit on. Both the tree and the stone were yellow with lichen.

A crow sat in the tree, looked at them without fear. As they sat down, another came to join it, and a third, and a fat pigeon. Far overhead, a kite was circling. Kanda traced her hands over the stone, felt, as she had known now she would, the pattern carved there, a circle winding its way into its own heart, like the circuit of a city wall. She breathed out a great sigh as another weight fell from her.

"The tree," said Calian. "You see?"

"I've never been here in my life before," said Dellet, puzzled.

Even as he spoke, Sal screamed.

There were four of them. Fool, fool, all this time they must have been following! The four stood on the far side of the bog, nothing but the wet mud between them and her family. Perhaps the length of two men lying stretched. A sword blade could not reach that far. But an arrow could, or a thrown spear could, or a curse.

Kanda's family stood with their backs to the rowan tree. The crows called in the tree. Her husband and children saw at last what she had tried all these long years to keep away.

The leader was a man, strong-built and tall, long golden hair falling over his shoulders, his face hidden by his bronze helmet. His red eyes blazed even in the daylight. His leather tunic was soaked and crusted with blood. It was he who had made the burned track.

Beside him was a woman, her long braid of hair white and shining. A noose, Kanda thought. She was tall, slender, elegant in the way she stood; her eyes were big and beautiful and flower-blue. Her face was flayed raw, stripped of lips and nose, ears and eyelids.

The third figure was cloaked and hooded. Gold glimmered at his throat, his wrists, he wore a neck ring, many arm rings. His hands showed curled around the hilt of a great sword. His right hand was the dark brown of old cured leather, it had a thickness to it, a plump heavy wetness to the skin. On his left hand the cured skin was torn open, shriveled over the stumps of his finger bones. His body was bent oddly, one shoulder raised very high. There was a wrongness in the way he held his head. It was he who had made the rotted track.

Behind them, respectful of them, stood a young man in the simple dress of a farmer, with a brown beard and brown hair. He carried a spear in his right hand; in his left he carried a well-made flint knife. He was Ben Apple Tree's son, Cythranath's twin brother, called Saem.

"Stay back. Put your hands on the tree, all of you." Kanda stepped forward to the edge of the water. It was deeper now, not bog-mud but a true pool of sweet water, clear and bright.

Reflections in the water. A column of greasy fire, a column of shining silver, a shapeless thing like a rotten sack. A young man, a movement on the water making his face blurred. The blade of a sword, that seemed now forged of gold.

Kanda said, "You cannot cross the water! You cannot approach the tree and the stone! They are safe here. Begone."

The man Saem shook his spear at her, so that Morna screamed. The wind blew, made ripples on the water. The faceless woman took a step forward, a sword out in her hand, but when her foot was about to meet the water she trembled, stepped back. Her sword blade rang as if another sword had struck it.

"You cannot cross the water," Kanda called to them. "You cannot come here. Begone, then."

The man in the bronze helmet raised his head, his chin jutting forward, as a herald gives the command for war. He said in a sweet noble voice: "Ikandera Thygethyn. My lady. Strangely but well met. Greetings." His bronze helmet was patterned with figures dancing. The sight of it almost made her retch.

The faceless woman said in a voice that was thick and muffled because she had no lips to shape the words: "Come to us, Ikandera! Come! If you but come to meet us, we will spare your children."

Saem shook his spear again, like the fool he was. Kanda turned her eyes to him. "Saem, I have known you since you were a boy. You should not be here with these."

"He wishes to be here with us," the faceless woman said. "Look how he holds his spear. A true man, we have made him."

"They have killed your sister, Saem," Kanda cried out. "Calian my daughter buried your sister herself."

Saem shook his spear. His voice came sad and weak. "I killed my sister, woman. I, Saem, killed her, and her body is such now that it cannot be touched to be buried. Such is the power in my hand now!" And the faceless woman laughed. Spittle ran down her chin when she laughed, because she had no lips.

"They will kill you, Saem. Your sister is buried, Calian my daughter buried her and let her spirit go free in peace. There is still time to run away, Saem." Kanda clenched her fists where her hands were burning. "Be gone from here, all of you. The tree and the water and the words once spoken protect them here. So be gone."

The faceless woman stopped her laughing. The man in the bronze helmet shook his head.

The cloaked figure stepped forward. A dark stain spread in the water at his feet. He too trembled as the water touched him. But he did not step back. He said in a dry whisper: "Ikandera. So long I have sought you. Little did I think to find you here in this pitiful place." And his voice was filled with yearning.

Kanda took one step forward herself, into the water toward him.

Dellet her husband roared like a bull then.

Dellet was across the water, smashing at the cloaked figure with his fists. The woman's white sword and the man's red sword rushed hungry to meet him.

All the children screaming. Screaming. Screaming. Dellet's strong kind arms red with his fresh blood. Kanda had nothing, not even an eating knife. Punches, kicks, teeth and nails...but he would die and she would die and then the children.... The wounds on Dellet's body were black and stinking.

Calian's voice rang clear and sweet as music: "Mother!" Calian had a sword in her hand, stained green and black with age. It was wet from where it had lain in the water, there were leaves stuck to it where it had lain beneath the tree. Calian threw it. Kanda caught it. She let out a great cry of joy as her fingers clutched around the hilt. She gave her great war cry, she leapt forward across the water, she met her enemies.

Kanda's sword clashed against the faceless woman's white blade. The woman too shrieked with joy. White fire crashed around them, the shock of it crashed through Kanda. So long. Too long. A vast shape rising before her, tall as the sky, all she could see. Arms of white fire, wings of white fire, a sword of fire, a crown of gold flames. She saw it with her eyes closed and burning. She tried to raise her sword, her arms were on fire, her sword was melting, glowing, the bronze glowed and dripped. She could hear her children screaming. Through the pain she lashed out, felt the blade meet and open long-dead bloodless flesh. "Dellet!" she screamed. "Dellet, get away. The children, Dellet!"

The faceless woman's blade took her in the shoulder. Pain opened inside her like a child ripped from her womb. The woman laughed. "You have forgotten how to fight, Ikandera Thygethyn."

The faceless woman's white sword struck her, and the man in the bronze helmet's red sword struck her, and the pain from each was blinding. A thousand soldiers all around her, all screaming, driving onward ever onward, one mind crying out to kill. In the opposite ranks her enemies are ready, but how can they be ready, when her army comes on and on to kill? The world is spinning, she hears her army cheering her, her soldiers flood around her, her enemies are dead or dying or fleeing. She screams her war cry that rings so loud it breaks men's armor, breaks men's skulls to spill out their brains to leave them dead and broken. The lofty walls of many fair cities her war cry has shattered; Erelene, bride of cities, in the far north where the snow lies piled in summer and in winter, Kydana in the dry wastes, city of the wise whose towers were once built of dragon bone, Inakanassos in the Forever Morning, that never had fallen in war to any till Ikandera Thygethyn cried her war cry. She screams her war cry now once, twice, three times, the battle fire bursts from her head. Her sword is molten metal. All there is about her is death.

"Mother!" a voice was screaming. Screaming. Screaming. "Mother!" And a child, a little child, a baby, was crying in terror. And the living man whom she loved – she could hear his weeping.

Kanda lowered the sword. The woman lay dead, her faceless face cut open, her arms hacked almost from her body, her neck shattered. The helmeted man lay dead in a pool of crimson blood. The third crouched beside him, bent and splintered.

Saem, still living, unharmed, held his spear shaking, shaking, vomiting up his terror, bleeding out his terror from his living human eyes.

Kanda's voice shook. "Cross…cross the water, Saem. Go…go to Dellet and the children. Now." She shouted, "Now! Cross the water to safety, Saem."

Saem made a strangled croak, dropped the spear, fled. Not across the water, back away as he had come, following the rotted trail and the burned trail of the dead things. The dead woman got to her feet, pulled her body back together. The scarlet blood flowed back into the dead man's body. More slowly, more painfully, he too rose to his feet. Spat blood into the filthy water. The third crawled, folded, unfolded itself.

"So you have not forgotten how to fight, Ikandera Thygethyn," the woman said. "We will be waiting."

The three of them turned, went back along their filth trail. Two of them walking stiffly. The third crawling, crumpling, slowly reshaping itself.

Kanda threw down the sword. It was ruined, notched and marked, corroded, melted. Her right hand burned. Her mouth tasted of blood.

She splashed back through the filthy water, sank down exhausted against the rowan tree.

The children clutched at their father, did not look at her. Morna had wet herself and soiled herself in her terror. Sal, like Saem, had vomited.

Her husband did not look at her. He was wounded, she stepped toward him but he drew back and bared his lips like a frightened wounded beast. "Not yet. Don't touch me…quite yet," he said.

"You're wounded." Pain in her voice enough that her husband met her eyes for one moment before he drew again away from her.

He said, dazed, "It is nothing…. They…did not hurt me." His wounds were black and dry, bloodless, they would fester. They would kill him. Kanda threw out her arms to him, grasped his hands knotted from a life of farmwork, calloused, ugly, gentle hands. He cried out in fear, tried to drag his hands from her grasp. "Don't touch me!" The light leapt between them, this too she could still remember! She heard beasts, birds, the wind in the corn before the harvest. She felt spring rain on her hands and on her husband's hands, his wounds drank in the good rain, rustled like the corn in a summer wind. Fled out of him.

He broke away from her with a cry of horror. Fled with Sal and Morna and Calian to the safety of the rowan tree. The stone was between them and their mother, Dellet had the little folding knife she had given him in his trembling hand, Sal had caught up a stick of rowan as if it were a spear to guard them. Morna held Sal's legs as she'd held Kanda's legs when she was frightened.

Only Calian said after a long while, "But she defeated them. All three of them. She saved our lives. She healed Father. That's what she did."

CHAPTER THREE

They sat and looked at the water. Morna fell into a gray terrified sleep. As the child slept the water surrounding them began to clear, the filth ebbing in time with her snuffling breath.

Sal said, "So you tell us, Mother. You tell us now. What are they?"

Kanda said to them slowly, "They were once ordinary men and women. What they are now.... A long time, longer than any of them can remember, they have been walking this world. For a long time they were far away from here, so far away they were only stories. Now they have come here to kill. They will have found our house by now, they may be waiting there hoping that we return so they can kill us, or they may have destroyed it. Every farmstead they find, they will destroy. Everyone they find, they will kill. The cattle, the sheep, the birds in the trees, they will kill if they can. They are....

"The woman's name is Ysarene. That is: *Hunger*. The man's name is Geiamnyn. *Burning*. The third...the third is only nameless and emptiness and nothing."

There are no words, she thought, for what they are. At least, when I look on your faces, my beloveds, I cannot find the words. But what else, after this, needed saying of them? Anything they find, they kill.

Only Calian, the wildest and least loved of her three children, only Calian asked: "Why? Why do they kill?"

They are....

There is pain in the world, my children. You have seen animals die, you have seen us kill animals that we raised. Susa was killed by cattle raiders two months off her wedding day, she hadn't realized it yet but she was pregnant. Your grandfather had a stroke that took away his speech, he can't walk or move his right arm, his wife and his daughter tend him more closely now than I need to tend Morna. There was a beggar girl on the road last winter with two infant children, we gave her bread and beer but I wouldn't let her in the house because I thought she'd steal things. There is so much pain in the world, children. You will suffer pain, your hearts will be broken, you will sicken, you will miscarry a child or see your beloved die of fever, there will be a hard winter then a cold summer and you will starve. It is not right, but it cannot be avoided.

No.

They are evil, my children. The men who came to steal our cattle were evil. I myself turned that beggar woman away. Some people are evil, the evil inside them rots them out until they are no longer men. That is all I can say.

No.

Kanda said, very slowly, "They are – they were – men. Soldiers in an army. Nothing more than that. They fought for conquest, for the wealth and glory of their kingdom. They triumphed in many battles, those battles that they lost they fought again and were revenged. As they won greater renown as warriors they attracted others to their banner, men and women from the lands they had conquered, whose cities they had razed, whose fields they had burned. They offered comradeship, wealth, power. A young man, say, who had lost his family in the sack of his village, who had not been able to save his children or his old parents – in his despair, they offered him comradeship. A way to prove he was a man still, with a man's strength. And so, though they had killed his family, he joined them. Like poor Saem has."

Kanda said, "Do you understand?"

Sal shook her head, wordless. Morna was a baby sleeping. She had not married Dellet for his subtle wits.

Calian said, "I think I understand, Mother."

"They wander the world killing, destroying, because…because they no longer know what else to do, to be. They were once men and women, but now they are something else, they do not know what it is to be men and women now."

"But someone will come," said Sal. Not quite a grown woman yet. Or perhaps Kanda and Dellet had raised her too well. "To help us."

"Who will come?" said Calian.

"The…the headman in Aranth. He will come with his warriors. They feast in his hall, he gives them swords and arm rings."

Dellet said, "Yes! Your uncle makes cups and platters for the headman's hall, there are thirty warriors who feast there, fierce as wolves, he says."

"He told us about them, about the feasts in the hall, when we went to Aranth in the spring," Sal said. "I watched some of them on the practice ground, they were so strong! Thirty of them!"

Dellet said, "We fought off the cattle raiders when they came, men I've never seen before or since from all away across the hills, we came together to defend all this valley and the hills around, from Mal Eren to Mal Anwen. I drove off three men with my billet hook, that day, I could do that…I…."

Calian looked at her mother.

Dellet said, "There must be…someone left here alive. Hiding. Yes, they will be hiding, we can gather together, Garv at the farm at Stone Point, he killed two men that day, he…."

Sal said, "Thirty warriors at Aranth who wear the headman's arm rings…."

But there was smoke, if Sal had been able to see it, on the southern horizon. It rose from beyond the wooded hills, in the direction of Aranth. The headman's hall there was well made. It would be a long time burning.

"What can we do?" Sal said at last, and bent her head.

Oh my children. So long have I hoped this would not come until long after you and your own children were at rest.

Three crows cawed in the rowan tree, the pigeon shat on the grass beside Morna sleeping. Kanda said in her most loved voice that was firm and cheerful, "Well, my children, my husband, right now we can rest and eat." From the satchel, she took out three of the things she had brought from the house. The wooden bowl, the piece from a quern long broken, the cracked old clay cup. She put them on the flat stone as if it was a table, carefully, reverently she placed them there, as the cups and platters had once been placed with reverent hands for a feast in the Hall Roven that is *Peace*. She went to the water, but she thought of filth in the water where the three had despoiled it. It was clear now with a patter of raindrops on it, but still from that water she would not let them drink. She took up the broken sword and cut her finger enough to draw blood there. The middle finger of her left hand. It hurt. More than a great wound, it hurt. She let three drops of her blood fall onto the tablestone in the center of the pattern carved there.

In her mind, a trumpet blared. In her mind, she said the words that must be said.

The wooden bowl was a gold platter, piled high with roast meat.

The quern was a silver platter, piled high with fresh bread.

The cup was a horn of sweet milk.

And that was the real reason why the milk from their cows was yellow with cream and her children had never known what it is to go hungry.

Kanda's family looked at the tablestone, and they looked at Kanda. They did not look with fear now. They sat together, Morna still snuffling sleeping, to eat.

After they had eaten, they sat awhile longer in silence. A good quiet now, contented with the food, resting, drawing strength from sitting all together hugging each other close. Kanda's head was on Dellet's shoulder, Sal's head was on Kanda's shoulder, Calian sat on Dellet's lap, Morna slept with her head on Kanda's lap.

We cannot stay here forever. We must…I must…. Kanda thought: at last it is come. She thought with exhaustion: but never had I thought that I should have to take them with me.

Whatever was in her face then, she had not hidden it well enough. Sal had been watching her, she realized. Sal said what must come at last. What Dellet her husband begged her with his eyes again and again but begged her also not to tell him, what Dellet could not bear to say. Some words cannot be spoken, and these words could not be spoken, but these words at last now must be said.

Morna opened her blue eyes wide as the sky, clutched her fist into Kanda's dress.

"Well, then, Mother," Sal said. "So, then. What are you?"

What am I? What, indeed? I'm your mother, Sal-my-heart. What else?

Kanda took a long deep breath.

"Once long ago….

"Once….

"Once long ago and far away now there was a great Hall all made of gold and silver, and it, it was, it was named Roven. That is: *Peace*. A place of joy, a place of comfort and great happiness. No grief dared enter Roven's fair walls, no pain, no anger, there was no sickness there, no hunger, no thirst. There a Lord sat in his splendor, wisest, kindest; there a Lady spread wide her arms to care for the weak and the frightened. A beautiful place. A wonderful place.

"Six Swords there were once in that Hall of Roven. Six warriors, poets, singers of the old songs. They were brave, great-hearted; always farther, always onward they went. Golden ones, shining; glorious in war and in sport, in words and in the deeds they did.

"In the first bright morning of the world the Lord of Roven summoned them to him, from the play of sunlight on water, from the snow that falls pure and clean, from the wild high places and from the rich tilled fields, from the stones of the earth, from the wood of the trees, he made these Six to stand before him. He clad them in shining armor, into their hands he placed matchless shining blades. Each night they feasted in the Hall Roven, whose walls are of silver, whose roof is of gold. Each day they would ride out across the world.

"The world was new then, new in its first morning. Yet there was darkness crouched there, evil and cruelty, suffering and pain. Perhaps, when the world was but water, waves rolling forever onward, there was no darkness in the world. Although even that, I do not believe. At the moment the first stone rose from the water to make the world that men live in, from that first moment there was cruelty in the hearts of men. But those Six, those warriors of Roven, against darkness and cruelty and suffering their Lord bade them ride out. As long as stood the silver walls of Roven, as long as the sun struck each morning on the roof of gold – they rode out rejoicing."

So far away. So lost, so fair. And now she was weeping.

"Six warriors, six poets, and I was one of them. I was the best, I was the bravest of them all.

"Six mighty warriors, and five of them they bowed to me."

Such words. Such memories. Such wonders before her eyes as she said these things.

She said, "That is what I am, my children."

CHAPTER FOUR

The benches set for feasting. The harper Muss, that is *Music*, playing to them on his harp of gold. Rustle of silk, laughter, six voices joined in song. In the horse field the next morning early, shivering, frost crisp on her breath. Bare feet sunk in green green pasture. Smoke rising where a woman is baking bread. She calls: her horse, Henef, that is *Swiftest*, comes to her from out of the morning mist. A black mare, mane plaited with red ribbons. The Queen of Horses. At Henef's side the stallion Dol, *Mighty*, pure white; their piebald foal Liae, *Joy*. She leaps into Henef's saddle, the horse does not need telling, they ride as one out through the earthworks that encircle Roven, the long spiraling passage through to the outer gate. The gates are open – they are always open. She rides through them, turns her horse to gaze back in farewell. The gatekeeper Benethal waves to her, sounds his horn to give her fair passing. His name is *Safe Place*. She rides through the winter country, along the bank of a wide river where the reeds grow up as tall as a man. The reeds glitter with frost rime, they hiss in the wind whispering. She turns away from the river, crosses a field, the floodwater crunching under her horse's hooves. Beyond the field the slope of a hillside rises steeply, the low sun and the frost streaking it black and green and silver. At the top of the hill there is a single oak tree, on the lowest branch of the tree there is a great green globe of mistletoe. She stops there, looks back to see into the distance, to the east behind her the Hall Roven, its golden roof, sweet smoke rising, to the west dark mountains, wild forests, unknown things. She raises her sword to the sky, shouts with joy, the wind catches her red hair, sends it streaming free.

A voice answers her shout, another rider comes bright to join her, a man, tall and strong as the oak tree in his glory, his skin rich and dark as oak bark, his hair the pale gold of new spring leaves when the sun strikes them. He rides the horse Dol and all its horse trappings are brilliant scarlet.

"Wait for me!" he shouts.

"Catch me!" She rides, he rides, his horse is stronger but hers is swifter, far and fast they run with their gilded hooves kicking up the damp earth. On and on they run. His cloak is red, hers is silver, the colors stream behind them and seem to dye the winter air. Where they cross a bare field black and silver they are the only colors, white horse, black horse, and all the brilliance of these two the man and the woman.

"Where are the rest?" she says when they have raced a long way and have stopped to water their horses beside a fine sweet stream that must run at last to the river that runs near the Hall Roven.

Her companion looks to the east: "Erenan is embroidering a girdle, Gallyn is swimming in the river, Kestre is playing her harp, Morren is sleeping."

She laughs. "I never believe that you truly see that far when you look, Palle."

"You doubt my eyes?" He looks to the east again. "Erenan is choosing a new skein of blue thread, Gallyn is shouting that the water is cold as if that is a surprise to him, Kestre has broken a harp string, Morren is sleeping."

The trees are drear and lifeless, though the stream is sweet and its banks thick with rushes that are dried gold in the winter sun. Henef and Dol stand quiet together, heads touching, their breath plumes out white. A skeletal leaf and a dried reed stem are tangled in Henef's red ribbons: little offerings, they look like.

"Erenan has made a mistake in her embroidery, Gallyn's clothes have fallen in the river, Kestre cannot find a new harp string, Morren is sleeping," Palle says.

"So they should have come out in the frost with us," she says. She laughs: "Apart from Morren."

Henef bends to drink again. She watches with pleasure the water droplets that fall from Henef's mouth. Listens to the good sound of the horse drinking.

Palle watches the horse also. He says, more seriously: "Morren—"

A trumpet calls. A horn is blown, off in the east at Roven.

Henef raises her head, snorts eagerly. Dol whinnies and paws the ground with one gilded hoof.

She jumps to her feet. Palle jumps to his feet. Palle shouts, "Now Erenan is strapping on her sword belt, Gallyn is buckling his armor, Kestre is calling for her horse to be saddled, Morren is donning his helmet. Now the horses are running! Now the Six are riding! All but you and I!" Palle shouts, "They are riding, and the enemy is come! And you and I are not there to help them!"

They mount their horses. Without needing to be told, the horses begin to run.

Faster than thought is Henef Queen of Horses. Dol's hooves break the ground open, as he runs sweet water bursts up from his hoofprints. In the time it takes to string a bow and shoot an arrow, they have ridden a greater distance than an arrow can reach. Through the woods and the fields, across the river that parts before them. In the time it takes to saddle a warhorse, they have reached the battlefield, three fields stretch before them, the first two are frost-rimed grass and crows and sheep dung, in the third the battle has been joined and four bright figures struggle against a mass of writhing warrior men. Hunger reeks from the battlefield, an army come in rage to despoil the beauty and peace of Roven, hating, howling, swollen with desire to kill. Too many to count, all white and silver, wielding bronze two-handed swords, ashwood spears tipped in bronze. Faces set. Faces cold. Faces dead. They come against Roven as the winter comes now, batter themselves against the walls of Roven. Howl to break the bones of Roven deep and splintered, tear the life of Roven rootless from the earth. The Six of Roven born of light and fire and flowers, the Lord of Roven in his rain-soft peace – and the darkness comes now, hungry against

Roven, like winter storms it comes to choke Roven's light. So few, so tiny, her four companions, Lady Erenan, Lord Morren, Lady Kestre, Lord Gallyn. Their battle line is shorter than a single spear's length, the enemy boils over them. Blue mage fire crackles in the air. A stink of burned metal. Yet they hold, the four, push forward, drive the darkness back and back.

The darkness comes like winter storm but the gates of Roven are open, the gatekeeper Benethal stands easy, for the people of Roven have no fear of any enemy while the Six are there to defend.

Her sword flashes out in one great cry from her. Palle is close behind her, his sword flashes out. So bright the blades that the frost is melted, the trees seem to stir with new leaves, the birds sing. Two Swords of the Six: she is the strongest, the greatest and most renowned, and her companion is after her the greatest. Together side by side they are as the sun returns after an eclipse. Dol and Henef leap, the two horses come down beside their companions, she and Palle each take ten of the enemy with a single sword stroke.

Gallyn's voice calls out, "What took you so long? Been idling?"

Morren's voice calls out, "Now you're here, can I go back to my warm bed and sleep?"

Erenan's voice calls out, "Be quiet, you two. Ignore them."

Kestre is silent, only concentrates on the battle.

Now the Six are joined, nothing can stand before them. They are six stars that blaze in summer noonday. Six suns risen in one sky. Six Swords that are beyond even light. The enemy falls before them, for all their killing hunger the enemy cannot place a wound upon one of the Six, for all their cradling armor the enemy cannot ward the blows they are dealt by the Six. And she is the heart of them. Blue mage fire crackles, whips around her, lashes her face: like soft rain, it feels to her. Like flies buzzing against her face. She cuts the enemy down, wounds, kills, but where she can drives the enemy off with the flat of her sword as a shepherd drives his sheep. Soon indeed the enemy is not fighting but fleeing, and the Six dance in pursuit. And the enemy are like dried leaves, and the Six are like the wind.

Blue mage fire. White mage fire. Dead-fish white. There is a holly bush in the far corner of the field, it is thick with berries, its shadow spreads deep around it. She cuts enemy warriors down and their blood flows toward the holly bush and the shadow moves and the branches move. And there is something crawling out of it.

A beast rears up at her. It is as tall as city walls. Five human heads each with five gaping mouths and five rows of teeth, the body of a dog, the tail of a serpent, the forelimbs of a monkey, the hindlimbs of a goat. It has the hide of a boar, flea-ridden and louse-ridden. It reeks like a sick man's shit.

Kestre screams. Morren shouts, "That is disgusting." Gallyn shouts, "Kill it."

Palle and Erenan turn their horses, charge. It strikes Palle a blow to the head that sends him sprawling. Erenan meets it, cuts it, but the wound is not deep. Erenan pulls her horse around snorting and squealing in revulsion. The snake tail lashes, knocks the sword from Erenan's hand, leaves a long angry welt across Erenan's face and hands, the horse's flank.

She and Morren charge, Kestre and Gallyn behind them. "Get to Palle," she shouts to Gallyn, for she can see Palle lying still, one leg bent back, twisted, one leg trapped beneath his horse's weight. "Ward Erenan," she shouts to Kestre. Erenan turns and turns ducking beneath the beast's reaching arms, stabs at it with a knife.

Her sword is hot in her hand. Glows new-made as from the bronzesmith's mold. The beast closes its right fist around Erenan's neck, smashes at Kestre with its left. Gallyn curses as Erenan's horse stamps down next to Palle's head. Kestre drives her sword into one of its five human faces. She hears Kestre's sword grind against bones and teeth. Morren shouts a war cry, severs its left arm at the shoulder. Gallyn shouts, "Watch out!" The snake tail whips around Morren, throws him from his horse to fall on top of Palle. Morren's horse, panicked, rears, kicks. She circles, rushes the monster. Huge human teeth close on her. She chokes on spurts of its blood. Erenan sinks her knife to the hilt into the thrashing tail. Kestre drives her sword into its belly.

She swings her own sword. With one blow, she severs all five of its heads. The darkness howls, and it ebbs, and it runs.

The gate is open as it is always open when they return to the Hall Roven. The windows are lit, the feast is laid, the people gathered. Meat is piled on golden platters. Wine is poured in silver cups. Men and women rise together as the Six enter. She walks at the head of the Six, the greatest of them, the most honored, the other five follow behind her. They bear no wounds, all is healed, they are clean and dressed for feasting. She kneels before her Lord, holds out her sword. The Lady herself takes the sword, hangs it on the wall where it can rest. She takes her seat at the high table. The harper Muss, *Music*, strikes up a tune. Her voice, clear and uninjured, rises to join her companions in song. The Lady herself sings in a voice that is a thousand blackbirds singing to greet the morning. Her Lord sings, his voice is frail and old, thin as the blown grasses, but as he sings the milk runs from his breasts and the unborn child within his womb kicks. When the feasting is done she sleeps in her chamber which has walls of pearls and yellow roses; its windows look out upon an orchard where the trees are always both in fruit and in blossom. Apple trees, pear trees, cherry trees, almond trees. In the farthest corner from her window there is a bee skep, for she loves to hear the bees drowsing. In the center of the orchard is a fountain, the water runs sometimes blue, sometimes silver, sometimes green, sometimes red.

She is awoken the next morning by the call of a trumpet. She and her companions meet in the hall where the table is set with bread and milk and honey, fruit from her orchard. The Lady herself comes to give them their six swords. Evil has come upon a distant city, the people there are suffering, beg for aid against monsters and dragons and evil things.

"Please," their messenger begs.

She says, "You do not need to ask."

Their horses are already saddled, their armor and their helmets waiting. They kneel as the Lady comes to place their swords in their hands, shining. In gray thin winter sun they ride out through the gates, their cloaks wrapped tight around them, brilliant color in the winter landscape. The gatekeeper Benethal waves to them, sounds his horn to give them fair passing. Winter floods spill over the fields, freeze in the hollows. Geese pick across the ridges where the plow tracks are crusted with ice. Willow trees, bare branches trapped in the frozen river, tugging. A hawthorn with black branches; an apple tree scaled with lichen, gleaming like yellow storm clouds; there are still apples in its branches, paler yellow, the color of the winter sun. They ride together eager, fearless, Six Swords sworn to glory and to all that is brave and strong and good.

"I want to kill a dragon!" Gallyn says.

Battle is joined. A fair city with walls of brass, drowning and beset by an army of such monsters, the defenders thin and starved, struggling to keep any last hope. On a hill above this fair city she draws her sword, calls to her companions: "For Roven!" They charge. Six tiny figures against an army. A dragon is there indeed. Other, worse things.

But when they charge, the army breaks.

She is at their head as they charge. The lodestar, radiant beyond radiant.

CHAPTER FIVE

Kanda's family sat breathless, eyes huge. Wonder on their faces: when Kanda held out a newborn child to them – "Your daughter, your sister, you see how beautiful she is" – she had not seen wonder on their faces that she saw now.

Sal said at last, awed, dazed, "You were—"

Calian said at last, "You are—"

Morna said, "Again! Tell us again! The beautiful hall and the garden and the lady with her lovely horse!"

Dellet her husband looked at Kanda. He looked at the floor. He said, "You were.... And now...."

He said, "And us, Kanda? Wife? If you were all that...?"

He said, "What are you doing, Kanda, living with the likes of us? What are you doing here? Being my wife?"

Lord Palle: *Calm.* Lady Erenan: *Summer Harvest.* Lord Morren: *Golden.* Lady Kestre: *Song.* Lord Gallyn: *Great Leap.*

Over the baby's cradle she had whispered their names over and over. Heard their names in her children's infant babbling. Her children's first birth cries had sung their names. In the meadow calling the cows to be milked, in the birds circling as the sun sets, in the scent of running water, she had seen them.

More painful than any sword wound, to think of them.

Time passes. Even in the Hall Roven, whose name is Peace, whose walls were silver, whose roof was gold. Great indeed was the power of the Lord of Roven, but even he...even he could not hold back time. He grew old, weary. And we, we six warriors, we....

The darkness came to Roven, like the winter it came, until at last we Six could not drive it back. Those three you have seen, and others like them. For the first and the last time the gates were closed, but the gates could not hold them. The earthworks were overwhelmed. As when a dam breaks and the cruel floodwater rushes in. The silver walls fell, the golden roof was burning. The hearth was extinguished, despoiled so that never more could fire be kindled in it. The tables were cast down, the plates and the cups broken. The Lord of Roven lay in his blood, a spearcast had torn the life from his limbs. His own dogs gnawed at him.

A spearcast! The man who killed the Lord of Roven, he did not dare come close to meet his gaze.

The Lady was thrown ruined. We Six....

Memories:

The last battle there. Erenan is lost. Palle is fighting. Gallyn is wounded. Kestre is dead. Morren is fighting.

Morren's face is contorted with hatred.

If I had only.... If I hadn't.... If I'd known.... If I'd tried.... If I....

Gallyn weeps cradling Kestre's body. Palle is weaponless now, swinging his hands still trying, wounds on every part of him. Kanda's mouth is rank with blood, her hands aching, her sword blunted. The fields are full of fire. The river runs red. The sky is stained red. She knows: this is the end of everything.

Before, in peacetime, Erenan shouting at Gallyn, Gallyn shouting at Erenan. Kestre begs, "Please, please, stop it, both of you. What's wrong with you?"

"Nothing. Ask Erenan. She started shouting. I have no idea." Gallyn throws up his hands. "I'm going out for a walk. Ask Erenan."

"Pathetic, both of them," says Morren. He's been watching it all.

"This is your fault," Erenan says. "Always, it's your fault, Morren."

"What? Oh, please. I said – I don't even know, something about

Gallyn – and you, shouting suddenly— You can't blame me for this, Erenan." Morren says in fury, "You always blame me, Erenan. She always blames me, doesn't she?"

Erenan shouts, "I don't always blame you, Morren. Or if I do, it's only because it's true."

She can hear Gallyn outside the door crying. So young, somehow, Gallyn is. Erenan is listening, her face is so…bitter. "Listen to him. How can he—? His life so— And I—? When Eliusa won't— When—"

"What did you say to him?" Kestre says, and she's angry. They are angry, she thinks, like children, all of them. "You hurt him." Kestre runs out, follows Gallyn to comfort him.

"We are the Six!" Palle says. "What would our Lord think, seeing this, hearing this? What would all the people of Roven think?"

"The people of Roven!" Erenan says. "I know what at least one of them thinks."

"Oh, well done, Palle," she says. She's been trying to keep her temper. "Well done."

"They would think we are heroes still!" shouts Morren. "How dare they think anything else of us?" His left arm was broken in their last battle, poison got into it, it pains him despite all the healing his companions and their Lord himself can give. "They have no right to think us anything but heroes."

Erenan says, "Is it only our Lord's thinking on us that matters? What he wants, what he thinks?"

"We are the Six!" Palle says again. "That is what matters."

"Is it?" Erenan says. Erenan is crying. She herself is crying but she cannot understand why. "Ask Gallyn what matters," Erenan says. "Ask the people of Roven."

"We are the Six!" Palle says. Pleads to them.

"We are the Six," she says. She is crying, and the words hurt her deeply, and she can't say why they hurt. Now she has children, she can understand why she hurt, she thinks, looking back.

Later that day. Or the next day, she can't remember.

Morren shouting: "Good riddance!"

Palle and Kestre shouting: "You can't leave. You can't go."

Gallyn shouting: "I'm sorry."

Erenan saying nothing. Her back is set to them. Riding away.

She isn't watching Erenan. She's watching the shadows in the distance that Erenan rides toward. She sees them move. But Erenan is riding away into the morning sun.

That evening she stands before the Lord of Roven. She is alone here with the Lord of Roven. The rest of the Six are gone. Through the skin of her Lord's belly she sees the baby kick. He puts his left hand on his belly. The peace hand, resting there gently, holding his child's hand through his skin.

"Would you like to touch?" he says.

She puts her hand on his belly, almost touches. Beat against her hand: one, two, three. She draws her hand back. Too strange a feeling. She thinks: I am one of the Six Swords against the darkness. But her hand is trembling.

Her Lord looks grave and sad at her. "The Six are not happy," he says. "Are they?"

She says, "I am happy, my Lord."

He ignores her change of words.

She says, "You made us to fight the dark, my Lord. That is what we are."

"Yet you are afraid," he says, "to feel my child kick."

"I am the greatest warrior of Roven, my Lord," she says. "I fight the darkness. I…." She says, "I am happy, my Lord. I swear it." But she's so afraid her hands shake, and she can't touch where the baby kicks.

The darkness came to Roven. I fled from it. In the dark, alone, grieving.

All light fades. All things end. That is all I can say.

Kanda took her husband's hands in hers. "Dellet: I love you. Truly. From the first moment I saw you, I knew you were a kind man. For so long I wandered the world alone. But you…. Love, pleasure, children, life. We argue, I shout at the children, the roof leaks, my favorite plate gets broken, I sit up awake five nights running with a screaming puking baby cursing you that you can't feed it – yes, that would be you, Calian. All this you gave me, Dellet. I was lost and alone and grieving. Here with you, I found my peace."

So terrible, that ending, Roven fallen in fire, her Lord dead. And yet…if it had not ended as it did, she thought, I would not be here with you and our children, Dellet. Nothing can last forever. And that is a bitter thing, but a good thing in the end.

CHAPTER SIX

It was past noon now, the sun high in the sky, the rain had stopped, the sky had cleared, they had eaten and rested, secrets had been told. So it was time to try to go on.

She felt good for having told them. It was not that she had lied to them before: this was her life, a farmer, wife, mother, plain ordinary woman (she had never flattered herself even in the days of glory that she was beautiful), sagging stomach and breasts from three children, spreading hips (the milk her cows gave was pure cream and it happens to us all as the years pass), red hair full of gray now, wrinkles round her eyes from laughter and shouting in rage at three children (yes, she shouted at them, once she'd hit one of them – not Calian, astonishingly, but Sal despite and because deep in her heart she loved Sal first and best, and she'd cried in Dellet's arms for an hour afterward), if she'd had such a thing as a mirror she'd have seen two thick hairs sprouting beneath her chin. She'd dropped Morna's favorite doll so its nose broke then tried to pretend it wasn't broken; her attempts to explain that Sal would soon start bleeding from her woman's parts had been… dreadful; she'd got so drunk at the Eve of Sun Return Feast six years ago she'd not been able to cook for the children on the day itself. She told the girls she wanted them to go out into the world to do wonders, in secret she dreamed only of them settling down in the valley and giving her grandchildren. Her greatest delight in life was walking over wet grass to fetch her cows in.

Kanda the farmer: not one moment of that was a lie. An easing thought now, a scar she had not known ran so deep.

And the memories now. Oh, in her heart she saw it. I was glorious! I should be proud. And I should speak of my glory, inspire my children.

She stood up, dusted herself down as if she had been doing housework. She thought: and I never thought I should have to do it in an apron and farmer's dress. Calian had made her the apron as a Sun Return gift. The stitching was terrible.

"Right then, you lot. We need to get going then." The mother's voice when she was trying to get them doing something they hated. Digging a new privy. Mucking out the pig pen. She gathered together the bowl and the stone and the cup like she was tidying up a picnic. "Right, you lot. Come on."

"The bad people are gone, Mummy?"

"They.... We can keep away from them, Morna, yes. So that's, I mean, yes, they are gone, yes."

"They are gone, Morna," Dellet said, with a look at his wife.

"If we go north a little, we should come to the droveway. That should be safe." Kanda said, suddenly realizing: "You knew this place was here, Calian."

"Of course I knew it was here. I've been coming here for forever."

Sal said, "I've never been here before. Or Dad, and he's lived here since he was born."

"That would be because your sister runs wild and refuses to keep to where she's told," Dellet said.

"Thank you," Kanda said to the tree and the stone. They splashed through the mud, drew a frightened breath, all of them, as they crossed onto the dry grass. No poisoned trackways, the land spread before them vast and empty so they would see. I would know if they were near, Kanda thought. Bees were buzzing in the heather and Morna pointed to a butterfly, which was a good sign. "Stay close to me," Kanda said. She took up the broken sword, held it before her ready to fight.

Sal said, "You're shining. Shining gold."

Yes, child. I shine gold. I was as a torch against the night, once, in the first morning of the world.

"Stay close to me," Kanda said.

They went down the hill going north, crossing low stone walls and low ditches that had once been field boundaries, Dellet said. The rubble of a house, no roof, the doorway empty, the yard grown up with nettles.

Kanda shivered. "We should not go near," she said, but Dellet said, "No, it's well, I know that house, the woman who lived there left to go to her daughter across the river, the family have a good house there now. There's no sorrow there." They went past and Kanda felt better, yes, a memory of common life and common kindness lingered in this place. Across another old field boundary, then a stretch of dry high ground with patches of bare soil showing, no insects here, no birds to be seen, Kanda held her sword ready, eyes darting back and forth as the eyes of a hawk dart. Told Dellet to hold the children very close. A scramble down a steep slope, a high valley in the hills, the ditch and bank of the droveway ran east toward Mal Eren, west toward Mal Anwen. The clouds had come back, heavy with the promise of evening rain, around the spearhead peak of Mal Anwen.

Two kinds of way cross the high hills north of the Wenet River. The droveways are for flocks and herds to be taken to feasts or to market. They are good ways, made by human hands, they are safe. Rabbits had made burrows in the banks of the droveway, the ditches had pools at the bottom, boggy enough for marsh plants. Someone had taken cattle down here only a few days ago, from the cow muck. Kanda lowered her sword a little.

"The caves on Mal Eren," Sal said. "We can go there! Good idea, Mum!"

Good idea, Mum! So hard it is, Kanda thought, for them to keep it fully in their minds.

"There might be some others there," said Dellet. "The caves are a good place."

The caves are a good place, yes. The best place I think of to keep safe.

Sal started off that way. "Come on, then."

Sal and Dellet and Morna began to walk east, their heads raised with new confidence.

"There'll be others there," Dellet said again, "I know it." The grass of the droveway was so good and green, that way. Sal had to step wide over a huge patch of cow muck.

Calian said, "No, Sal, Dad. Not that way. Wait."

Kanda said slowly, "No. We go west. To Mal Anwen."

"Mal Anwen is a cursed mountain. Don't go there. You come from...from the south where the land is safe, Kanda sweetling. Promise me, my love, soon to be my wife, promise me you will never go there."

"Why would I ever go to Mal Anwen, Del-my-heart? Two days it would take me to walk there, I should think, at least. Two days away from my beloved? From our bed?"

"Don't joke, Kanda mine. Please: I know it sounds stupid. I do. But: promise me: you'll never go to Mal Anwen."

"It's just a mountain, Del-my-heart. All right, I promise: I will never go there. I will never walk for two days to climb a cold wild rain-swept mountain."

"My grandfather knew a man once who almost died on Mal Anwen, Kanda. There are things that .... 'When thunder breaks the stones of Mal Anwen,' my grandfather would say, 'that is a sign the world will end.' There are...when I was a child, I had nightmares about being lost on Mal Anwen."

"Well that's just foolish. It's just a mountain. There are storms there all the time, I should think. Thunder can't break anything anyway, it's a noise. All right, all right, I said I promised. Never, I swear, will I walk for two days to climb a cold wild wind-swept mountain, and never most especially during a thunderstorm. Now come here to bed, Del-my-heart."

Once, twice, three times, Del-my-heart, have I already broken my promise not to go to Mal Anwen.

"West, then." Dellet's voice was dry and quiet. "The mountain. So." He turned, came back very slowly toward Kanda. "I won't ask why," he said. "I wouldn't understand, I expect, if you told me." He walked past her, without looking at her, Morna in his arms. His bitterness stank around him. Not even anger at her, a couple quarreling. Despair at her. He went fast, as if he would run now that moment to reach Mal Anwen. He said, indeed, without looking back: "Well, what are you waiting for, Kanda? Come on yourself, then."

He squared his shoulders. Stopped walking. He did not turn around, but he said, pretending it was to himself, "Well, I suppose, at least we know where we're going." He walked on more slowly. "Hard to get lost, as well, I'll grant, when you're headed for a mountain. Let's put you down now, Morn birdy. A good track here you can walk.

"I said you can walk, Morn birdy. Look, Morna, sweetling, you're four now. You weigh more than a yearling sheep. I can't carry you all the way to the cursed mountain.

"All right, all right, Morna. I can carry you some of the way to the cursed mountain. That tree there, you see it? I'll carry you as far as that and then you can walk a bit."

Kanda hurried to catch up with them. Dellet still ignored her. But now he was only angry. Morna said, "Mummy can carry me!" and Dellet said, "Your mother can't carry you, birdy. She needs to have her sword to keep us safe, remember, see?"

Kanda touched his arm. Thank you, husband.

"I've never been this way," Sal said after a while. There was a sense that Sal and Calian were trying to find things to say to make it all seem right. The sky was scudding clouds of a cool summer day that was good for working but made the farmer wince for the harvest, the track was very fine to walk on with the high banks giving shelter and sweet with weeds: talk, chatter like birds about little, like it's all well in the world and we are walking to Aranth to market, like our lives are not overturned, like our mother is not a stranger suddenly, like our parents are not arguing. "I don't think I've ever been this far west." "It's raining on Mal Eren, look, so it's probably lucky we're not going that way." "It is raining." "So Mum was right." "I can carry Morn for a bit, Dad." "Dad said she should walk." "It's beautiful country here." "We should see the river again soon the way the track's going." Little birds, little bees, chattering.

They stopped to eat the last of the bread and cheese in Kanda's satchel. Sal said, "I'm so thirsty, Mum." Kanda could only say, "We'll find a stream soon." They all looked at the satchel Kanda carried and tried not to look at it, but not one of them said anything. What happened didn't happen, what was in the satchel was the things Mum kept in the house as old luck tokens, important things but nothing more.

"There's a hawk, look." "It's too big for a hawk, it's a kite." "Says you." "Oh, there's a rabbit! Bun bun bun! Look, Morn! You see him? Look at his darling tail!" Exhausting themselves chattering.

The droveway ran down into a dip in the hills where there was a stream running, the banks and the ditch stopped to let the stream run down across the track. Mint grew in the water, and tiny yellow flowers.

"Wait." Kanda squatted, placed a flower by the water, touched the water with her fingertip. The danger was great, where the bank of the droveway was broken. But no, this was a safe place, the water was a guard, and the water was cool and sweet. "You can drink," she said. They washed their hands and faces. Rested a little again. On the other side of the stream the bank and the ditch were good and strong.

Sal said, "Look at the sunlight there, look, Mum!" To the north the gray sky was pierced with great beams of silver, making the wild moor silver in turn where it met the earth. Before them in the west cloud shadow rushed dancing across a smooth curve of good grass. On the banks here where it was sheltered there was whitelace growing taller than Morna, feather-leaves and lace-flowers, that looked like the cloud shadow on the grass did. But the sun was slowly sinking lower, their own shadows grew late-afternoon long. Already in the farthest east the twin stars Irulth would be visible, the two stars that marked the first changing into night. Beyond the high banks of the droveway, there came the soundlessness of things creeping. They walked on such a little way and the night was coming in too sudden, the mountain still so far off stood out black before the setting sun. Too sudden the western sky was all afire, a great bar of red light. Red light reflected too from the peak of Mal Eren behind them, clear now of raincloud, so that it gleamed like a sword against the twilight.

Once, twice, three times before Kanda had gone to Mal Anwen. But never before had she taken the droveway across the high hills; each time before she had gone from the farm down into the valley, walked along the bank of the Wenet. The track narrowed a little, turned sharply to skirt a rocky outcrop, the ground here was briefly damp where another stream ran down from the rock. The track straightened, widened. Another track crossed it here, running down from the north. Narrower than the droveway, a gash in the turf bottomed in gray stones half covered in leaf litter; one might think at first it was a dry streambed.

Never had water run in that streambed. Two kinds of way cross the high hills north of the Wenet River. The droveways that are for flocks and herds to be taken to feasts or to market, good ways, made by human hands. And the henket path, that is *death*.

The bank and the ditch were strong here, to protect the droveway.

Outside the ditch, something stood waiting for them.

A joke thing. The body was wood, a woman's torso roughly carved twice life-size, wrapped in a thick black cloak. It was all rotted and damaged, the wood swollen and stained by water, charred by fire, the cloak was torn and wet. A horse's skull on a spear shaft rose in place of the woman's head. The left eye socket and the left side of the jaw were smashed in. Silver bells were tied on tattered ribbons around its waist. It had been given crude wooden arms and legs, a giant version of Morna's jointed dolls. The arms were tipped with sharp flint.

The girls screamed all three together. Dellet screamed. The stink of the thing was enough to make Morna gag and retch. Dellet threw his hands over the child's eyes, pressed her face into his shoulder almost to smother her, so she would not see or smell it.

The faceless woman Ysarene's voice called: "Do you recognize her, Ikandera Thygethyn? You should. We dragged her from the mire that marks now the charnel house of Roven. She was burned in the fire when we burned Roven then she was drowned in the flood. Her head was missing, so we gave her a new one. You should recognize that, too, Ikandera Thygethyn. Do you recognize it?"

The horse's head turned toward Kanda, champed its teeth.

Kanda said, "Yes. I recognize it."

She could smell where Morna had wet herself in terror, and that human smell of a child's body gave her some strength.

Ysarene's voice called, "So, Ikandera? Now you see, will you come with us?"

Kanda could only whisper in answer, "I— I— Is Geiamnyn there with you?"

Laughter. "Geiamnyn and the other whom you are thinking about are not here, Ikandera. They are gone south across the river. That man there with you, he has a mother himself, who lives in the shadow of a war chief's hall, does he not? Geiamnyn and the other you are thinking of when you ask about Geiamnyn, they are pleasing themselves there, Ikandera Thygethyn."

"But you here," Kanda said, her voice shaking, "you and this thing you have made, you cannot cross onto the droveway. So go, join Geiamnyn and that other one."

"All you say is 'go', Ikandera Thygethyn. 'Go', 'flee', 'we are safe here hiding'. You did not used to be so fearful, so hiding, Ikandera! You used to stride out boldly to fight." The monster, the *hodden*, raised one absurd wooden arm with a smell of mold and maggots, a trailing patter of black damp.

Ysarene called laughing: "And are you so sure you are safe there, Ikandera Thygethyn?"

The hodden creaked forward on its rotten plank legs. It made a horrible gobbling neighing.

There was a place in the high bank of the droveway where a notch had been worn in the soil. There was a place in the ditch where a crow lay dead. Thus the hodden stepped across from the henket path, onto the droveway.

Kanda came to meet it. The broken sword was out, the sword met the stone hand with a stroke so mighty chips of stone flew up. It towered over her, the length of its wooden arms was twice the twice the length of her sword blade. She spun back, hacked low at its legs. Her sword caught its left leg and sank into it, sending out a shower of rotten wood dust. It neighed, its teeth clacked. A flint hand came down heavily against her shoulder, pain blossomed, she twisted away dragging the sword out. She tried not to hear her family's cries as they saw she was bleeding. She staggered, struck again. Harder! Harder! A shower of wood dust that made her choke. Splinters of rotten wood in her mouth. Now Kanda gagged and retched. The hodden lumbered forward, smashed Kanda sideways. She grasped its arm, the wood crumbling under her hand, driving splinters into her skin. The whole left arm creaked, snapped hanging broken. The flint hand jerked to catch Kanda's leg. It smashed her aside again. Harder, hard as flames. She fell against the bank of the droveway, the world about her spinning. Its cloak trailed over her, her skin crawled where the wet cloth touched, sickness in her so that she could not see or think. Die, she thought. Sink away into sickening death.

Ysarene's laughter. A thousand children butchered in that laugh.

Staggered upright, hands raw, itching, clutched at the cool green grass of the droveway bank. Groped to see. Her sword trembled like a willow leaf.

The hodden made its gobbling neigh of triumph. The hodden was not trying to kill her. It was trying to reach her family.

Run at it. Tear it with her bare hands if she must. Bite it with her teeth. You cannot, must not touch my children. Sweet human scent of her children's fear-sweat. Dellet shouting, useless, "Keep back! I'll kill you!" Dellet howling as he hit at it, the filth crawling over him.

Stagger, run, crawl if she must, on her belly on the earth, lamed, bleeding from her shoulder, the sword blunted. But the earth was green and good. The smell of her children's terror gave her strength. Struck it, cut off its right arm with the ease of cutting a dry branch. Gritted her teeth. The hodden neighed, spun around. The bells at its waist were all ringing. Its cloak swirled out spreading dank water. Its flint hand met Kanda's sword, the impact of it made her bite her mouth.

The blood in her mouth was human blood, and that too gave her some strength. She spat blood at the hodden. It staggered now. Its horse head turned jerkily toward Kanda.

Drove her blade into its carved breasts. Where if it were a living thing its heart would be.

The sword went in with ease, as cutting unarmored flesh. Blood poured out.

Ysarene screamed in fury. In Kanda's mind, distant, a woman's gentle voice.

A fury of flesh and breath beside her. Kanda screamed herself because Calian was there shrieking, stabbing at the hodden with a pocketknife.

"No! Don't touch it! Don't let it touch you!" Pulled Calian back, or trying, Calian like a wildcat twisting free. Calian stabbing, hewing at the thing over and over. The hodden's legs crumbling away.

"No. No, Calian, leave it. Leave it now." The night had come down while they were fighting. Things unseen moved outside the ditches of the droveway. Something seemed to slither unseen through the gap in the bank.

"Run!" Kanda screamed.

The hodden neighed as they fled.

CHAPTER SEVEN

Thus along in the dark, fleeing, breath gasping, feet slipped and bruised on grabbing rocks. The high banks of the droveway cradling them, the tread of heavy feet and the thunder of a horse's hooves following them. Dry rustling sounds and wet soft sounds of something crawling following them. Once, they heard the gobbling neigh of the hodden, which made all five of them scream. Kanda had thought to go east back to the ruined farmstead they had passed: it had felt safe there. But instead they ran into the unknown darkness, into the last faint glow of twilight where the sun had set. And on, and on, running, they fled as water runs in rainstorm, without thought. All their mouths choked with rotted wood dust. Dellet carried Morna, a lump that must be stone-heavy, her piss and shit and tears streaming down him. Pain in Kanda's shoulder, her dress flapped wet around her legs, tripping her, sick-wet, it made her roil with horror, it was like a hand pulling her back. Sal was a fast runner with her long thin legs like a crane running; Calian was a fast runner, spent her days wild on the high hills swimming in the pool of the Wenet; they ran and they gasped in pain and they could not run and the darkness howled ever closer behind them. As well outrun a storm swept down from the hills. As well outrun the sunset. As well believe they could outrun old age and death. Slowing, stumbling, beyond hope. Only madness kept them running.

Dellet failed first. Morna in his arms was too heavy, although he would have failed sooner if he had not been holding her. He staggered and his legs died beneath him. He fell on his knees like a tree broken. "Morna!" he screamed.

Kanda pulled his arms. The child clung to her father's body, seemed one with it, she could not pull Morna away. "Get up." She was so exhausted she was not sure her words made a sound. "Get up, get up, curse you, curse you, Dellet, get up. You filth, you disease, you monster, get up, get up, get up. Dellet!" she screamed. "Curse you, get up!" The darkness was a void before them, from which white bared teeth gnashed. "Get up, Dellet," she pleaded to her husband.

The darkness was a wall before her.

The darkness was a storm wave breaking.

"Mum!" Sal cried out. "Mum! There's a shieling, Mum! A shelter, Mum!"

The girl's voice was joyful. Hope. No – absolute certainty – in Sal's voice that they would be safe. It caught Dellet up; he staggered upright with Morna clutched in his arms. Ran without seeing toward Sal's shouts. Kanda ran after him. The darkness was a halter around her trying to pull her away from him, but she ran against it. "Get back," she gasped to the darkness. Sal's voice drove the darkness back.

They must leave the droveway, cross the bank, jump the ditch. There, off the droveway, shining in the utter dark, stood a stone house like a bee skep. A larger version of a grave cairn, its doorway gaped open like a hole in a skull. Sal stood by the doorway shining with the light of the house, her red hair was a hearth fire, her brown skin was rich brown earth when the sunlight breaks. She held out her hands, called them in.

Calian shouted, "Go, Dad! Get inside! Inside, Mum! Now!" pushed her father in. Calian ran in, Sal ran in, Kanda ran in. The darkness snapped at Kanda's heels, teeth caught her dress and tore it, hands grasped her ankles pulled her back. The roar of the dark rang out. Kanda spun to face the dark breaking over the shieling. The stone walls creaked. The dark rushed in at the doorway.

Kanda held up her sword. The walls of the shieling held firm, though the stones were screaming. The light of the shieling held.

The dark could not enter the doorway of the shieling. All around the stone walls it howled and raged, scrabbled at the stones, gnashed its teeth and beat its fists against the open doorway. But it could not enter., and they were safe.

A shieling is a drovers' way house, a shelter for people crossing the high hills. Kept up by all who dwell in the hills, or by…someone keeps the shielings tended, dry and strong and clean against rain and snow and wind. Large enough to fit ten men, perhaps, to ensure no one passing in need of shelter must be turned away. The floor swept clean, a hearth well kept, a stack of well-kept turf for burning, the stone benches around the walls to sleep on laid with dried bracken. Above the doorway a branch of heather hung, the dried flowers the purple of a soft evening. Beneath the threshold, a man lay sleeping, who had been chosen after his death as a good man to guard this place.

Kanda sank down with a gasp of pain. The darkness roared outside the doorway still, fingernails clawing at the stones, the hodden neighed. Inside the shieling the sound was muffled. As a vast storm batters the harbor wall while in their safe houses the fishermen sleep. When she could finally draw breath, Kanda said, "Thank you, Sal. Well done."

"I…I just…saw it," Sal said. "And I knew…."

"Yes." Last traces of light in Sal's face. Kanda kissed her daughter's forehead. "You knew, of course." She shook herself, trying to put herself and her family back to their real lives. Maybe…a mother talking to her children when she's ignored the clouds gathering for a rainstorm, they've all had to run laughing for cover, blaming her for keeping them out just a little too long. "So…well now…. Let's get the fire made, shall we? Calian, could you bring the turf there? Sal, look in the crock there, see if there's meal there that's edible?" Poor Morna lay hot and red and silent in Dellet's arms, eyes open and staring past up into the roof. "And we'll get Morna…." A great wash of exhaustion spread over Kanda, she rubbed her eyes, "We'll get Morna…we'll just…." She tried, so hard: "We'll get the fire going; Calian, see if there's some meal in the crock, some oil…."

Calian spat out, "Shut up! Don't you speak to me! You bitch! Bitch! Bitch!" She almost struck her mother, wedged herself as far away from her mother as she could against the shieling wall. Which wasn't very far, so even in the danger and the wonder she looked… like what she was: a child, angry and rather stupid with it.

Silence.

"There's meal in the crock, yes, Mum, and oil," Sal said. "It's a bit stale I'd guess but fine. I'll get the fire made, then I'll make some meal cakes." Sal said, joyful: "And water, Mum, there's a skin of water here! Fresh and sweet!"

"Good girl, Sal." Dellet peeled Morna from him, put her carefully down on a sleeping bench. She lay very stiff, gasping, "It's all right, Morna duckling," Dellet said. Morna sighed, nestled into the bracken. It had such a lovely smell, dried bracken for bedding. Dellet stroked the child's forehead. "Sleep now, Morna duckling, Morna my littlest heart." He looked at his tunic all covered in her muck. "Here's some good water for you, sweetling one, you drink it for Daddy, hey? That's good. So Sal-Sal is making you meal cakes." Morna sighed, closed her huge eyes. "Good girl, Morna duckling. There, now. Right, then, Sal, let's get this fire built, shall we? You start on the cakes."

He did all this without looking at Kanda once. But Sal said, "No, Dad, Mum's arm." Dellet grunted, he finally looked at Kanda but he didn't look at her face.

"It's fine," said Kanda. Fleeing, it had soaked her dress crimson. In the safety of the shieling it was healing quickly, by the time the meal cakes were ready there would be nothing left but a scar.

"That thing near took your cursed arm off. I saw it." The healing did not make it better between them. Made it worse. "Near took your cursed arm off," Dellet said. Dellet built up the fire, Sal made a little shriek that made Dellet drop a turf-sod: "There's a pot of honey here with the meal! Oh Morna, Calian, good water and honey with the meal cakes!" The fire settled well made, Sal got down to cooking.

Dellet said, "That.... That name the...the woman called you. *Ikandera Thygethyn.* That's your name?"

A pause. How to answer? He looked at Sal and she looked at Sal and they sat quite close together but they would not touch.

Kanda said, "A long time ago that was my name, yes."

Dellet said nothing, she saw him turning the words in his mouth. He did not like the feel of them on his tongue.

Kanda said awkwardly, "It means: *Great Warrior.*"

"*Great Warrior.* You want us to call you that, then? Your real name?"

Kanda said, "No."

"It's your name, isn't it?" He meant: that woman, *Hunger*, enemy of life that tried to kill him and his children – it knew his wife's real name, when he did not.

Kanda said, "My name is Kanda, Dellet."

There is nothing I do not know about you from before I met you? Nothing all these years we have been married you have kept secret? Every corner of your mind, every thought you have, everything you have ever done, I suppose, Dellet, I know? I am not Ikandera Thygethyn now, that is no longer my name, that woman has been gone for a long time. I let her go long ago without regret, Dellet. Not once since we married have I spoken that name, or looked back with regret.

Our farm, our children, your hair on the pillow beside me in the morning – those things are my real name, Del-my-heart.

But she could not say it, because he was so bitter at her. Awkwardness because the children were there.

Dellet got up. "I'll settle Morna properly," he said. "Try to scrape the shit off her and me. Poor tiny thing. Poor duckling lamb. Look at her." He sighed very deeply. "I suppose tomorrow will be worse. Won't it?" He said gently, "You should try to rest...Kanda. I'll do what the children need tonight. You rest."

He touched his wife's hair gently.

Thank you, Del-my-heart.

The meal cakes were cooked and cooled ready to eat. Sal had scraped out crystallized lumps of honey with a stick snapped off the branch above the door. "He won't mind, will he? It'll make him happy, in fact, I expect." Before she offered the meal cakes, Sal came over to Kanda. "Mum: I'm worried about Calian...."

Dellet said, "Didn't I say, Sal, that I'd see to you children, that your...that your mother needs to rest?"

"No, it's fine, Dellet. It's fine, Sal. What about Calian?"

"Talk to her, Mum. Please."

Kanda said, "She doesn't want to speak to me."

"Just talk to her, Mum."

The girl was hunched up, her head pressed into her knees. She raised her head at her mother's approach. Her eyes were red with crying.

"Calian?"

"You shouted at me! You shoved me away from it! Bitch!"

"I—" Kanda too lashed out, two cats fighting: "You stupid child, Calian! It would have killed you. Another moment and you would have been dead. What did you think you were doing?"

Calian screamed, "I stabbed it! I hurt it! You saw I did! I had the knife, and I stabbed it, and I broke it. You saw I did! What are you, jealous I hurt it too? That I'm a warrior as well, that I'm not weak? That you're not the only one who's strong? I can fight, I can kill too!" Calian shouted.

Memory: the first time she herself had met Ysarene. The sickness she had felt, the fury that Ysarene had woken. *Hunger*, ah, yes, that is what Ysarene is. Kanda and Kestre had been out questing, sixty days they had been away from Roven in the northern plains. Midwinter: the snow lay knee-deep and the horses plodded through it weary. All was white snow blindness, snow silence, their faces and hands bitter and cold-eaten, raw and cracked. A long quest, a thankless one at times, if in the end as it must be a victorious one. A long ride home still ahead of them. Kestre said, "Perhaps the next quest we are sent on will be to the south where even the winter is warm, do you think?"

The snow stopped falling suddenly. Almost as if it was a lamp put out: gone, and the eyes blink. Kestre reined in her horse. Pointed. Two figures stood very black in the snow, blocking the road ahead. They had not been there when the snow was falling. One of the figures was thickly cloaked and hooded, snow covering its cloak so it was like it was made of swan feathers. The other was dressed in light armor, a woman with long fair hair, and she had no snow on her.

The woman stepped daintily forward, another young woman warrior as they were. Kestre looked to greet her pleasantly. They saw her face, and a shock and a sickness went through Kanda, a cry broke from Kestre, for the woman's face was maimed as a cruel man might maim a rabid beast. Flayed, without nose or lips or ears or eyelids.

"Get away!" Kanda cried out in horror.

"You are hurt," Kestre cried out in anguish. "Tell me, who has done this to you? Can you speak? I will help you, whatever you need. If a man did this to you, friend—"

"Help me, will you?" the woman said. "Oh, I will hold you to that, Lady *Song*. I will make you sing and sing to help me." She raised up her hands, and they were blood-covered, she was bloodied on both arms to the elbow, she drew her sword and it was vile with blood. "There is a town near here," the woman said, "and I have killed every person in it. Do you know why I did that?" The woman said with a laugh of great happiness and pleasure, "I did it because I could." She said, leering at Kanda, "There is another town but a little way farther. Will you two fine bold warriors not come to enjoy yourselves with me?"

Kestre drew her sword, charged at the woman. Snow fell thick suddenly, and the woman was gone. Kestre spun her horse around and around, flailing out with her sword. "Where has she gone? Where is she?"

The cloaked figure seemed to watch Kestre, though its face was hidden. Kanda found she was staring, and she felt frightened.

A weight on Kanda. Her horse reared. The woman squatted behind her with her arms wrapped around Kanda's back. She laughed in Kanda's ear: "I am free to do anything I want. I can do anything! I pity you very much!" Kanda shrieked, her horse was rearing and bucking, the woman laughed as she rode Kanda's back.

The woman jumped away. The two strangers were gone, the road was empty, the snow fell feather-soft. No tracks in the snow, but where the other had stood the snow was stained black. "What was she?" Kestre shouted. "What happened to her? Why did she say these things?"

Kanda did not speak, for sick rage filled her, if she opened her mouth she would vomit it up.

Whisper, laugh, shudder, fear: *free, are you? Because you are free?*

"Oh!" The memory was too horrible. Her body was tense. Where am I? So much bitterness in my mouth. Calian. That is who I was angry with. Why do my children have to ride my back also? I was— Deep breath: and then shout furious: "It could have killed you, Calian! Killed you killed you killed you!" Hands raised to strike the child. Shaking. Just do as I say. Just stop, Calian. "You stupid reckless child! It could have— Never do that— I told you not—"

"It was killing you!" Calian shouted. "And I hurt it! How do you think I knew the sword was there, by the rowan tree? Because I found it! In the bog there, I found it and I practiced with it! So when that thing came, I could hit it." Calian shouted, "I helped you! Are you, what— Don't you want anyone else to be able to fight like you?"

"Calian, if you speak one word more to me I— I'll—"

Hunger. Rage. Deep breath. Deep breath. Deep breath. Just stop. Oh my sweet Calian, fiercest and least loved of my children, you struck it deep and well; then your sister found this safe place. You helped me. Thank you.

Kanda said, "You struck it well, Calian mine. You did."

Stiffly: "I know I did."

Deep breath. Clench hands. Unclench. Deep breath. Kanda said, "If I.... If I had two swords here now, Calian, I'd give you one to use."

She heard Dellet about to speak, fall silent. She heard Dellet let out a sob. She heard Sal make some little noise of hopeless comfort to him.

Calian said, "I've still got Dad's knife. I cleaned it, see? While you were getting the food, I've been sharpening it."

Silence.

Dellet said, "It's yours, now, Cal-flower."

Calian said, "Yes. It is." Kanda leant her head on her daughter's shoulder. Felt the child's heart beating as fast as a frightened animal, still rage-tense. Calian said, "Tell me…tell me about what it was like, Mother. When you were that great warrior. Tell me about…about Roven." She meant, awkwardly as any child: *I'm sorry, Mum.*

Roven. The last tongue to speak that name had been Ysarene's. It had dripped poisoned from her mouth. The girl's sweet child voice now made it music again. The sound hung in the air, made them all relax a little. Filled the air like a sleeping child's breath. A charm, Kanda thought, a protection as great as any shield, to talk to them of those days. They will hold it in their minds, it will protect them.

Roven: it filled the air like a lamp suddenly lit.

"Eat the meal cakes, then, my loves, and I'll tell you." She looked out into the utter dark howling beyond the doorway, saw with her other eyes, she told them a tale of her past when she was glorious, that was only bright and good.

CHAPTER EIGHT

It was the Feast of the Sun in the Hall Roven. Wine gleamed dark in silver cups, the tables were piled high with roast meat. Wheaten bread, red cherries from the orchard, curd cakes fresh-baked. And meal cakes with honey, yes. The floor was strewn with flowers among the rushes, applewood burned in the hearth, warriors' swords hung at peace on the wall. The harper Muss, that is *Music*, sat in a shaft of sunlight playing a fair tune on his golden harp. In a shaft of sunlight the Lord of Roven sat on his black throne. Ten white doves and ten black crows flew in through the great windows of Roven from the gardens, and each wore around its neck a collar of gold. On either side of the Lord of Roven sat the Six Swords of Roven, three to the left, three to the right, dressed not in armor but in robes of fine silk. The Lady…Kanda, the greatest of the Six, sat at the Lord of Roven's right hand. Her hair was red as fire, her skin was brown as earth, her eyes were blue as sweet deep water, on her brow she wore a circlet of bronze. Out of good sown earth and wildfire and red autumn berries, she had been shaped. At the Lord of Roven's left hand sat the Lord Palle, the only one who could match Kanda in combat; his hair was black, his beard was plaited with green ribbons, his cheeks were painted with green paint. His name means *calm*, for he was the wisest and most thoughtful of the Six Swords of Roven. Out of the smooth calm sea and the roots of the mountains he had been shaped. The harper played; Lady Kanda and Lord Palle lifted up their voices to sing together; all those there assembled were made glad by their song.

The feast went on, the wine went round dark and unwatered, the laughter and the singing grew. At the feast's height the doors of Roven were flung open. The harper Muss stopped his playing. The birds flew away. Into the hall there ran a white hind and a black bull. The hind had a diamond tucked behind her right ear. The bull had a diamond tucked behind his left horn. The beasts ran down the length of the hall up to the Lord's table, the hind kicked up her pretty hooves, the bull let out a bellow, they brought down the Lord's table with a crash. The Lord of Roven's own winecup fell to the ground with the sweet wine spilled out black. The hind pranced, the bull bellowed, the two beasts ran out of the halls, the doors closed after them.

A long silence in the Hall Roven, save the dripping of sweet wine onto the floor.

The Lady Kanda leapt to her feet. "My Lord," she cried, "give me leave to ride out now, and I shall bring you back the diamond that shone behind that bull's horn."

The Lord Palle leapt to his feet. "My Lord," he cried, "give me leave to ride out now, and I shall bring you back the diamond that shone behind the ear of that hind."

"And I! And I!" the other four Swords cried out.

The Lord of Roven said, "Ride out, then." He bade the harper Muss play a hunting tune on his golden harp.

It may be on the morning that the Six felt a little less joyous. It was raining, the fields around Roven were churned to mud, they had no idea any of them where the hind or the bull had gone. But they put on their bronze armor, the breastplates and the fine helmets the Lord of Roven had made for them. They took their swords from the wall, they bowed to their Lord, they rode out together through the gate. The Lady of Roven who stands at the gate smiled at them. They rode south, because it was as good a direction as any to ride in.

That is not a good reason to ride south, no. But they had not had much sleep, they may have drunk a little too much wine the night before that fogged their minds a little, they had no idea in the world which way the beasts had gone. The Lady of Roven wore a cloak that blew to the south that day, so that is the way they went.

Yes, that is an even more foolish reason to ride south. Now hush.

They rode south.

After several hours riding through the rain they came to a river. It had been raining for several days, even though it was midsummer, the river was running high. On the opposite bank of the river the white hind stood; it kicked up its heels and ran when it saw them. So they had no choice but to ford the river, the water up to their horses' chests soaking their fine boots and cloaks and fine armor. And very cold and muddy and full of leaf litter that river was. Poor Lady Kanda, her horse Henef, that is *Swiftest*, kicked and bucked because she did not like the water, Lady Kanda got soaked up to her earlobes, even the beautiful red crest of her helmet was splashed. On the other side they followed downriver, until the river flowed into a wide great black lake.

A causeway ran across the lake to an island thick with pine trees. On the causeway they saw the tracks of a hind and of a bull.

The causeway was too narrow for the horses. And it is not good to take horses across such a causeway to such an island. So they dismounted, one of the Six, the Lady Erenan, stayed behind to guard their horses.

They crossed the causeway with Lady Kanda leading, squelching in her muddy wet boots. From the bank the causeway had seemed no longer than the length of a feasting hall, but they walked on and they walked on and they walked on and the island got no nearer. And then Lord Palle thought to turn around to look behind him. And the dry land, the horses, Lady Erenan – can you guess? They were all gone. Nothing could be seen but the black water of the lake and the causeway.

Now it may be that the hearts of the five rejoiced at this high and terrible magic. Because in the bright light of a wet day when you have not been drinking unwatered wine and singing of your mighty deeds – it may be that questing to bring back a diamond from behind a beast's ear does not seem quite so heroic a thing.

But none of them spoke this aloud, if they did.

They went along the causeway, Kanda leading, Palle at the rear. Still the island grew no closer.

At last the third of the Six, Lord Gallyn, began to laugh. "This is a fine adventure," he said. "Five of the Swords of Roven will spend all eternity on this causeway, while Erenan will be left to defend our Lord all alone. All the glory will be Erenan's alone! But let us see." Lord Gallyn took from his finger a ring of fine wrought copper, that the man he loved had given him. "He'll be angry," Lord Gallyn said, "that I've lost it. But he'll be angrier yet if I never come home to him." And he threw the ring into the lake. "Take it," he said, "and let us cross, and let us get home afterward safely, and I swear never to do anything as foolish as this again."

And – what do you think? – they stepped from the causeway onto the island.

The island was very beautiful but very silent, a pinewood with the pine mast deep and sweet beneath their feet. The smell of resin was all around them, and the smell of the pine needles – it was like the scent of the Hall dressed with greenery for the Feast of Sun Return, that glorious joyous scent. The hearts of the five were filled with happiness. Palle said, "We should not be seeking those beasts. What cruelty, to hunt them."

But Lord Gallyn who was the kindest of the Swords of Roven, formed from sand and driftwood and the babbling of snowmelt, Lord Gallyn said, "Wait."

They came to a clearing in the pinewood. There the buttercups grew as high as a man's waist. In the clearing the white hind and the black bull stood waiting, white and black against the gold and the green. Lord Gallyn went forward into the clearing, holding out his hands as one does to shy children or shy beasts. "Please," he said. The two beasts bent their heads to him. From behind the right ear of the white hind he took the diamond. He took the diamond from behind the left horn of the black bull. "Thank you," he said to the beasts. The hind kicked up her pretty hooves, the bull bellowed.

They crossed the causeway, with Erenan waiting on the other side. It was no longer than the length of a feasting hall, they could see her smiling face from the island. They rode back to Roven, Lord Gallyn placed the two diamonds in the hands of their Lord. They told the story – Muss the harper made a song of it, although Lord Palle did not quite like it to be often sung. And it was, oh, days at least, two days, three, even, before they feasted again in the Hall Roven and rode out the next morning early on another quest.

And that, my loves, that is the Tale of the Hunting of the Black Bull and the White Hind, which is among the most foolish and the happiest of the Deeds of the Six.

CHAPTER NINE

I remember. Oh, remember! It was glorious. It was wondrous. Summer sunlight in the depths of winter, fresh cool winter breeze in fetid summer heat. The sky made liquid after rainfall. The smell of baking bread. Before the first taint of sorrow came to Roven, she had ridden out on quests such as this. And this time at the beginning, when the world was new-made, she did regret.

She thought: would I go back there? Give up my husband and my children? I don't know. She thought after only a moment: no. Not for that, or for anything. She looked at her children sleeping, at her husband, she heard their breathing, breathed in deep to be part of them. Nothing can last forever. And that is a good thing in the end. If it had not ended as it did…I would not have them.

Now hush. Sleep, my loves. Sal, Calian, Morna, Dellet my husband, my love, sleep. The dark is howling outside the doorway, but here inside we are safe. I swear it to you, my loves. Sleep. And she woke to birdsong. The fire still burned, the rain had stopped, the dark had slunk away in brief defeat. Her family slept in a tangle of arms. The sky was broken with the wound of the sun. It was time to walk on now, tired and knowing now, back to what waited for her on Mal Anwen.

CHAPTER TEN

The words had created magic. A shield covered her family. They walked half dreaming, half forgetting anything beyond that they were walking to the mountain. Why are we going to Mal Anwen, Mummy? Well…if you walk all the way to Mal Anwen, my beloveds, you can have some sweet cake and I'll make you each a new dress. Does that sound good? The spell of Kanda's story wrapped itself around them, they walked happy and without complaint, even Morna strong on her stout young legs. The enemy waited, Kanda saw it far ahead of them like the shimmer of heat haze, behind them crawling across the hills like rain. The words kept her family from seeing.

And I am keeping them safe, she thought. I have thrown a shield over them, my power keeps them safe. This was something she could do easily, once, this too she had forgotten. My power ward thee and keep thee. Peace and hope be upon thee. A glow around her, that would flow from her hands to enfold those she fought to protect. For a little while, just long enough to stop some small world from ending, her shield would embrace and protect. Her family walked with their heads high, smiling into a breeze that blew cloud shadows running across the green hills, talked, babbled, bickered, sang. The hodden gnashed broken teeth far off behind them; the click of wooden limbs and with it the thud of a horse slowly walking. A shieldwall between, which the enemy could not break. Morna fell over a pebble, sat howling, her knees grazed; she was still howling when Calian leapt and skipped, somehow managed to fall grazing her hand. Dellet and Kanda ran to scoop them up, kiss it better – struggle of "No, Mum, get off," from Calian, fierce, embarrassed, "Get off, I'm fine." Morna cheered up at Calian's misfortune; Calian cried a bit because she'd been stupid, snapped at both her sisters. The hodden lifted its head, the crawling thing snorted: Kanda thought ruefully: this gift I have to keep my children safe from great evil, but not from bumped knees or wounded pride.

They did not take the droveway now but struck out straight across the moors, the shieldwall the story had thrown up enough to keep them safe. It would be a long time before flocks and herds would walk the droveway in peace, the drovers would struggle with them, the beasts would be wild or refuse to move. "A bad road, that droveway," the men would say, "ill-made; if a man takes his cattle down it, I promise you, his best cows will get thin and sick." Only in ten years or twenty years would beasts be happy again to walk it. We will make it up again, she thought, when the spring comes in we will rebuild the banks, re-dig the ditches. We will spread flowers to cleanse the track where the hodden stood. To the guardian of the shieling, we will offer the good rich milk and new-baked bread and a bronze arm ring besides, to thank him for his kindness. What a good man he must have been. I wish I could know his name.

If we live, she thought. If we live, we will do these things.

They will live, she thought. My children will survive this, if it costs me everything and more. She thought of Ysarene's laughter: I will not let her have them. Or…or that other one, empty, he will not…he will not so much as look at them again, whatever it costs me. Calian frowned, the shieldwall wavered. The hodden pricked up its horse head.

Say something foolish, children. Fall over again, or quarrel, or point out something insignificant like a beetle and then get in a rage because I can't see it. Kanda was walking at the rear to guard them, she walked faster to be among them.

Sal came to walk beside her. Unusually, Sal being fifteen, the girl slipped her hand into her mother's. "The food in the shieling," Sal said, "Mother, you did that I know, somehow, I know you did." Said in an awkward, respectful way that was not how a child speaks to their mother: "Thank you."

"I did nothing, Sal." In there, Kanda thought, with the dark roaring outside, it was all I could do to hold your hand in mine, Sal.

"But…the water. The food, the turf."

"A traveler must have slept there recently, that's all. That's why it's important that we keep the droveway mended, keep the drovers' huts and such tended and stocked if we can. We never know when someone may have great need of them." Here ends the mother's lecture; Kanda thought: oh my sweet Sal, my oldest my most beloved, *Shining*, I named you…don't you guess?

Sal was silent a little, deep in thought. At last she said: "Was that story you told us really true?"

Kanda said slowly, "It was true, Sal."

"Tell me about them. Lord Palle, Lord Morren, Lady… E-something…?"

Calian had been walking swinging her knife. She drew nearer, Dellet and Morna drew nearer. As birds come down to safety after a long flight over water, so the names of the Six gave comfort to them. Calian said, "And you. Ikandera Thygethyn." The girl frowned, thought flickered behind her eyes like a fish. Then she said, "Tell us more about them."

Kanda said, "We should be looking out for danger. Not talking." She thought: don't ask me, please. It is too painful. Once there was a time I was glorious, Sal my love, but that time ended never to return. But the names in Sal's voice drew her also. Remember! The joy, not the pain of the end. The Six Swords of Roven: joy, we were, hope, glory: the smell of my children's hair; the dew on the meadow grass; the cows' breath steam-sweet-rising; the birds like clouds in the sunset.

If one of my children dies today, she thought, would I never speak of them as if they had never been?

"Tell us!"

"Tell us!"

"Come on, Mum!"

There was a bush of ragwort alive with black-striped caterpillars; Kanda pulled off a flower, shredded the petals. So loud her heart seemed in her chest now. I can't speak of them. I can't bear to speak. But look: my children's faces! I must speak.

"The Six, then." There was new warmth, saying it. "Lord Palle I told you about last night. The calmest and the wisest of the Six. Often he would be cautious, overcautious sometimes. But a great one for jokes and games and wordplay also. Rhymes and riddles, he loved. His helmet had a double crest of gold to it, it was like…it was like two sundogs around his head. Fitting: he looked like the sun in splendor when he fought. He was the bravest and the best of them."

Calian burst out fiercely, "Apart from you, Mum!"

"I—"

"You said! Apart from Lady Kanda he was the best, you said!"

Kanda sighed. "Yes, yes, Calian, I was the best of them, the greatest of the Six, it's true." She threw the ragwort flower away. "But apart from me, Lord Palle was the greatest of them. He was the best of them."

"Apart from you."

"Lady Erenan. I told she waited with the horses while we crossed the enchanted causeway. She was formed from sunlight and summer blossoms and the water of the mere. She was the weakest of the Six in the strength of her arm, she could not walk without two sticks to hold her weight, but she was the best rider of them – of us – and of us all she was the most fearless in battle. Her helmet was worked with green enamel, set with jewels above her eyes and on the cheek guards. She could be quick to anger; I made her angry sometimes and regretted it. Of all of them, of us, she had the greatest, fiercest sense of honor and justice.

"Of all of them, she was perhaps my dearest friend.

"Lord Morren. Yes, Morna: Morren, like your name, yes. The most beautiful of the Six, he really was like a gold statue – and he knew it. But it was impossible not to think well of him. A young man in the flower of his manhood, the best dancer, the best poet, a good swordsman, but he did not like fighting. I would tease him sometimes that he would grow fat because he loved feasting far more than he liked fighting. Even his helmet was inlaid with gold figures of the people of Roven dancing at a feast.

"Lady Kestre. She was formed from birds' feathers and the wind in the trees and green wheat. Her helmet was inlaid in silver, with a white crest, but she hated to wear it: she had long golden hair that she let fly free around her like a war cloak. Like Lord Morren, in her heart she hated fighting, she would weep sometimes over her sword when we were called to ride out. But in battle she would throw herself into the thickest part of the fighting, she would be first to draw her sword, the last to sheath it.

"Lord Gallyn: *Great Leap*. The youngest of us, still a boy, the most joyous and I think to the people of Roven the most beloved. His helmet was crowned with a silver stallion, but to me he was more like a young bullock in his first summer. Sometimes he and Lord Morren quarreled and did not speak to each other for days. Erenan would be the one to reconcile them. She'd be so angry at their quarrels, they'd make it up between them to stop her being angry at them. Even in his anger, though, Lord Gallyn was the kindest of the Six.

"I remember once he rode ten miles out and ten miles back to bring Morren a message from a certain fair lady. Even though he and Morren had quarreled and weren't speaking."

With the story last night already in their memories, speaking the names aloud made the shieldwall so strong Kanda was surprised her family couldn't see it glowing around them. Ah, that is good. It was good for a long time, hours, a hotter brighter day with the sun on their backs. So warm the grass steamed. Mal Anwen drew near, as it had not the previous day's walking. Whether that was a good thing or a bad thing, Kanda did not know. It gleamed gray as new slate roofs, in its crags and its great spear-shaft peak she saw a moment the towers of a far-off citadel, towers and turrets and great gates calling to her to hurry to them. Memory! So precious that memory, her greatest glory. She almost turned to smile at her companion, heard a familiar voice cry in joy: "Look, Ikandera! There, there we shall ride! The city awaits us, Ikandera!" They had kicked their horses fast, raced toward the citadel laughing. As she rode through the gates such a cheer was raised for her; they threw flowers before her horse's hooves, red flowers and dark and white; the high turrets of the citadel were as smoke before her, or as cool gray autumn mist. Such memories! Such memories indeed! She heard the hodden neigh, the shieldwall weakened, a frown crossed Calian's face. No more memories. Keep the shield here now strong. There's a nettle, Morna, you're about to walk straight into it – and there was a shieldwall for a moment on the child's skin. Kanda's heart leapt in triumph. Calian relaxed. From pain, I ward thee. From grief, I ward thee. From my own grief, I keep thee safe. This power I have, my beloveds. All is well here, all is good.

But the spell must end soon. At her greatest Kanda had been able to hold the shield only a little while. The day was hot even in the shelter of the spell-words, Sal and Calian bickered good-naturedly, finally like any siblings they started properly arguing and then: "This is stupid I want to go home, why can't we just go home and never mind the stupid stupid mountain. She'll never let us go home again, Sal, you'll see, my feet ache because of her stupid walking. I'm not going to move until she says we can go home and stop walking." Calian was sitting down cross-legged.

Kanda sighed. Dellet said, "They need to stop walking, Kanda." He sounded cross too, more confused than her salmon-swift daughters as to what was happening.

Something slithered at the far corner of Kanda's vision; if she let the shieldwall weaken even a little she would see it clearly but they would see. But they must rest, yes. Calian, she thought, could go on the farthest, if she let the shieldwall drop so they could remember why they were walking, Calian could run all the way to Mal Anwen beside her mother, ahead of her mother on her fast legs. Calian's eyes were bright when she looked at her knife. The shieldwall held, though the effort was exhausting.

Kanda said, "Look, now, all right, there's a place here we can sit to eat some more of Sal's good meal cakes. Just for a little while, quickly, okay?" A sheltered place, thick with heather, so a good place, surely, she thought, a safe place, the bees drowsed in the heather, there were more black-striped caterpillars in a clump of ragwort.

"Look!" shouted Morna. "Wherties!" A fine bush of whortleberries, already ripe, grew in the dell. Morna and Calian-who-was-refusing-to-walk-farther ran to pick them.

"Be careful! Be careful, girls." Morna stuffed her mouth full. A terror seized Kanda and she shouted, "Don't eat them!"

Sal said, "Don't be silly, Mum. Look, they're just whortleberries. Here," Sal said, giving her mother a few berries. They were beautiful and ripe. Kanda ate and her exhaustion faded, she felt as refreshed as if she'd slept and eaten a fine meal and bathed herself. She smiled at her oldest daughter, who was ensuring Morna drank from the waterskin she'd borrowed from the shieling. Thank you again, Sal. She unpacked the last of the meal cakes from her satchel, along with a few battered remains of the cheese. "Right, then, who wants to eat?"

"Me me me me me me me!"

Tomorrow, Kanda thought, we will reach the mountain. Tonight, perhaps, if we go fast.

Calian shouted, "Argh! Caterpillars! Argh!" Morna-purple-with-whortleberries grabbed one, rather damaging it, "The itchy ones! No!" The hodden neighed. A man was laughing. Her family, even Calian, did not hear.

Soon, Kanda knew, they would hear and see. A light seemed to flash around the mountaintop, that also they did not see but soon they would see. Her right hand burned; in her mind she saw the skin stained red. A flock of birds flew over ahead, wheeled in the air together, she should see beauty in it, and a sign of safety that the enemy was distant still; Dellet, who loved birds, pointed it out to the children, who were not interested – Kanda saw the shape the birds made as a sword.

Despair swept over her. Had to blink to keep back her tears. The shieldwall would break soon. I thought you would be dead and at peace, children, before this day came. A lifetime, I thought I had left. To watch you grow, to see you blossom, lead good lives, have children yourselves.... I would die now, happily, if I knew you would live good long lives. But I wish…all I want in my life is to see you grow and blossom, my beloveds. I hear the fires in the fields grow closer. I see the shadows fall, I feel my heart fail: cold and slow my heart beats. Tomorrow, or tonight, battle will be joined. I will die happily, my beloveds, if my death saves you to live even only for a little longer. But it breaks my heart to think of dying before I see you grown up.

"You're not eating, Mum," said Sal. "There's a last meal cake left, if you want it? It's a bit burned, that's why no one's eaten it."

"And some cheese," said Calian, "except that Morna dropped it."

"You have it."

Calian said, "Morna's leftover cheese? There is no way I'm eating that. You always eat Morna's scraps anyway. Oh but you can't give Mum that, Sal, it's burned black. Why'd you even bring that one, you should have thrown it away. I'll throw it to the birds."

"No, Calian," Sal said. "Mum needs to eat properly. Keep her… keep her strong for…. Mum needs to eat. Morna, go and pick her some more berries."

The light flashed again on the peak of Mal Anwen. Calian saw it this time and her hand went to her knife. She half drew it, then she blinked, puzzled. "What's…what's that?"

Dellet, who was looking directly toward the mountain, said, "What's what?"

Darkness crawled in the green hills toward them. There was a stain spreading red on the grass very close. On the horizon in a band of cloud armed figures were fighting. The circling birds had fled. Battle would soon be joined. Calian stood up, her knife in her hand. "We should get walking, Mum."

Kanda got to her feet. "Yes. Quickly now. Come on."

I hear the trees cut down, I hear the fields burning, I hear the whetstone on the blade, I hear death.

CHAPTER ELEVEN

Memory. Walking. Seeing it as she walked.

Winter had come to the Hall Roven. The first great cold of winter: snow lay thick around the high banks of the earthworks, the gatekeeper Benethal stamped his feet and blew on his hands to warm them, his hood crusted white. The birds gathered in the roof of the Hall for shelter from the cold, ravens, crows, wood pigeons, hawks, red kites; deer shivered in the pinewood; wolves ran in the white fields leaving black footprints. But inside the earthworks the snow did not settle, inside the Hall itself the hearth fire burned warm and without smoke. The Lord of Roven wrapped his cloak around him, went out to the gates to set one foot on the snow there, poured offerings of wine and oil and the very last of the year's milk. "A kind winter, Lady, grant us that, on this the first cold day you bring." The Lady's face was changeless but the earth at her feet drank up the offerings gladly; for a moment a warm summer wind blew. "Thank you, Lady. The women in the Hall are even now weaving your new spring cloak."

When the dusk fell all the people of Roven went to the gate to watch the night fall on the first snow of winter, the sun's death over the white cold, and the Lord of Roven made offerings of a side of roast beef and ten loaves of wheat bread. When the last of the gloaming had fled the sky, the people of Roven lit the winter fire before the doors of Roven, scattered wheat on the flames, leapt the flames. Lord Gallyn, whose name means *great leap* – no matter how high the fire burned, he could always leap higher, though his cloak was scorched and singed and marked with smoke. The snow came faster, thicker, the white flakes like a swarm of bees. When the snow met the fire it hissed. All the people of Roven cheered the snow falling, although still the snow did not settle inside the great earthworks. The spell for a kind winter – and a night of fun.

Gallyn leapt so high his heels seemed to touch the peak of the Hall's roof. All the people cheered. But Gallyn gave a great cry, fell down almost into the fire, ran with all the people staring after him to the open gates.

A dead man on a dead horse rode through the snow up to the open gates.

The gatekeeper Benethal shouted warning, held out his ashwood spear to bar the way. The dead man held his horse steady outside the gates with the snow thick covering him. But Gallyn pushed aside Benethal's spear, crossed beyond the gate, took the horse's bridle.

"Let him pass," Gallyn said. "Let him come inside the circle of the fire where it is safe."

Lord Morren said, "This is madness. We leap the winter fire to keep such things as this far off from Roven, not to invite them in."

"Let him pass," Gallyn said again.

Lady Kestre said, "Let him pass. Make a space at the fire for him."

Benethal looked from one to the other. He put down his spear, crossed beyond the gate to join Gallyn. He held out his hand to help the dead man dismount. He said, "Welcome. Let us take your horse, give it a place in the stable out of the cold. You yourself come now to the winter fire, warm yourself. You are safe here, friend."

The dead man dismounted, Benethal led the dead horse away. The dead man was cut and injured, so that Gallyn and Kestre between them had to help him walk. He came into the circle of the fire light. All the people gathered were silent, staring, hands moved in signs against evil; yet Gallyn and Kestre helped him as if he was a frightened child. His shield arm and his sword arm hung limp and useless. His throat had been cut.

Gallyn said, "Can you speak?"

Nervous laughter at that, it was so horrible. Morren laughed nervously. Erenan laughed.

A noise like stones grinding together, that made the dogs howl, as the dead man spoke. "Dead and maimed, I rode here with my horse dead under me. My throat is cut but I must speak. Raiders have come from the west in their black ships, my wife is dead, my children taken. Through the snow and the dark, with wolves running at my horse's heels, I have come to beg the Six of Roven to ride out." He pointed to the west. "Five hours' ride, no more, my village lies burning. Please," he said, weeping dead tears. "I beg you. Help them. I am dead, my children are lost, but some may yet live."

There was a great terrible silence. A long time, it seemed: time enough for a child to die, a life to fall ruined, just time enough for two tears to fall. The dead man slumped forward into the fire. The flames rushed up to give him peace.

Their horses were saddled, the Lady of Roven came to press their swords into their hands.

"We shall bury him with honor," the Lord of Roven told the Six. "Now ride. Ride!"

The Six did not need telling: faster than the wind they rode, faster than thought, faster than breath. The wolves and the deer started up in terror at their passing, their horses kicked up the snow that was piled as high as a man's waist. The clouds cleared, the moon rose white and brilliant, a new moon with the old moon held in her arms for safe keeping. A good sign, that, for the first great cold of winter. The frozen world stretched before the Six in beauty that would have moved Kestre to song and Gallyn to laughter and Palle to verse, had they not seen such horror and known more horror was to come. They rode through the sleeping fields where in spring the wheat would grow, through a wood of pine trees sweet-scented, through a wood of birch and ash trees bare like reaching fingers, the trunks of the birches whiter than the snow itself. As they rode the moon fell behind them, the twin stars Irulth were ahead of them, red star and bronze star, they were a gateway into which the Six rushed. They rode through a wild place where there were neither trees nor fields, between the stars now a light seemed to be shining.

Kanda reined her horse and said, "There. That is where the raiders are." A village burned like a vast winter bonfire, the flames made the shapes of men with spears and axes.

Kestre said, "I am afraid."

"How many times have we ridden out?" said Morren. "How many victories have we won?" He drew his sword and tossed it high in the air. "When the sun rises, we will have won another victory. The winter fire will still be burning when we ride home again."

"Raiders," said Palle. "Slavers. Morren is right: they will run, I expect, when we come against them." But Palle's voice was uncertain.

"I am afraid," Kestre said. She drew her sword. Its hilt was worked to look like a skylark's wings. She kicked her horse forward. The flames in the shape of men turned to meet her coming. Her sword was like the skylark's song. Kanda and Morren rode after her, and Palle and Gallyn and Erenan after them.

The village was small, undefended, six roundhouses thatched with turf, a handful of barns, a byre with walls of heaped thornwood. A communal oven stood in the center of the village, with a shrine next to it. The turf houses gave off thick black smoke as they burned. A man's body was huddled in a doorway, Kanda looked in through the doorway, closed her eyes, said, "Don't look," to the others. The byre was empty; nothing moved, nothing lived. Before the oven there was a pool of dark blood, with a broken spear shaft floating on the surface.

"Poor wretches," Palle said.

Kestre said, "Shush. Listen." A sobbing noise, and a gasp, and silence. The Six looked around then, and then Kestre said, "The oven?"

Kanda went to look, stepping carefully over the blood. Inside the oven, crouched tight, was a child. A boy. Very young.

Kanda lifted him out into her arms. He hit at her, tried to fight, screaming.

"You're safe now, little one."

"Where did the raiders go to? Is there anyone else left?" That was Erenan, who was not good with young children, but Kestre said, "Hush, Erenan. We won't harm you, little one. I promise."

The boy looked at their swords with blind mad eyes. Kestre sheathed hers, held out her hands to him wide open. "No danger now. We won't harm you, I promise you. My sword is gone, see?"

The boy said nothing. Kestre touched his face, very gently. He sighed, blinked.

"They put you in the oven?" said Morren. His face was filled with rage.

The boy reached his arms out toward the oven. "Mummy…safe… Mummy said…."

"That was a wise thing for your mother to think," said Kanda. "Now look, little one, here is some water, see, my friend here, Gallyn, you see his fine helmet, he will give you some water, and my friend Palle here, he will give you some bread to eat."

The boy stared at the men and at the bread and water with terror. But Gallyn drank some water, Kestre and Erenan drank from their waterskins, and then the boy drank. But he would not eat.

"What's your name, little one?" said Palle.

But the boy would not answer either. He only pointed to the oven and said again, "Safe…Mummy said safe."

There was silence. Erenan and Morren itching to get off to find the raiders. "Where did they go?" Erenan said. Her voice was angry, impatient, the boy shrank back in terror, his eyes grew blind like the eyes of a dead thing. "Please," Erenan said, more gently, "please, boy, little one…we have to know where the…the bad men went."

The boy said with eyes as dead as the dead man and the dead horse but with a voice that was bright and happy: "Kill the bad men?"

Erenan made a choking noise. Tears in her eyes. Sickness in her face.

Palle said after a moment, his face too sickened, "Yes, little one. I expect we will have to kill them."

The boy said, "They went the sea way. They had Denall with them. I heard him shouting." He said, "I will come. See them dead."

Erenan cried out in anguish, and Kestre had to comfort her like a child herself.

A path led on west out of the village toward the sea. The Six made an offering of bread and water at the shrine – a cow skull on a pole, with seven gray stones piled around it. The stones had been dislodged and the skull was crooked. Gallyn and Kanda carefully reset them. "Why bother?" said Morren, impatient for battle. "There's no time, there are people still alive who need helping." The boy sat on Erenan's horse, his eyes seemed to lighten a little when the shrine was whole again. He pointed. "The sea way." They rode past the stream where the village got its water, there was another shrine there, a wooden post as tall as a man carved with a bird face, there too the Six drew up their horses, made offering. "Let someone be left alive, we beg you." And Erenan cut a lock of her hair, dropped it into the water, said, "Let this child live and be healed, I beg you." They crossed the stream, rode west long enough for the sun to wound the darkness in the east. The boy indeed twisted round to look back at the sun rising with the smoke of his village black against it, making Erenan shout at him for frightening her horse. He cried with joy, "The village is mended, look!" and then he was silent, seeing the truth that the sun shone on his village and on the snowfields and nothing was mended. He twisted around often to stare behind him, certain that this time the sun would have mended his village. Erenan did not shout at him.

They came to the sea, a high cliff looking down over a beach of sand that was pale as the snow in the early morning. A fine place these villagers had lived in, with the sea and the fields and the sacred stream. A ship was drawn up on the beach above the tideline, a camp set a little farther up still where the snow lay showing the sea did not come. A very safe place, the cliff cradling the raiders, the wide bay beyond. A single narrow path wound down the cliff to the beach, so steep and poorly made and narrow that one man could hold it.

Kanda counted: five crude tents, each big enough to hold perhaps three men. Two more men at least sleeping on the ships.

A slave pen at the far end of the beach with the camp between it and the path. There was a shape by the pen, something crouched. Kanda squinted. It moved and she realized it was a huge dog.

They could not get the horses down the cliff path. Erenan cursed.

"You stay with the boy," said Morren.

From the beach, a baby wailed. "Denall…" the boy said.

Erenan snorted. "This is not some pleasure quest, Morren. I will go down there and fight. With the boy safe on my horse with me." She turned to Gallyn with a smile. "*Great Leap* – will you leap with me?"

Gallyn laughed. "Erenan, I will leap with you."

Erenan drew her sword: its hilt was the gold of wheat ready for harvest. She wrapped her shield arm tight around the boy. Gallyn drew his sword: its hilt was red roses. In his shield hand Gallyn grasped Erenan's horse by the bridle. The two kicked their horses, rushed, leapt their horses out over the cliff.

Into the morning sky they leapt, the seabirds rose screaming all around them, between the pale sea and the pale sky their horses trod the air and their horses' gilded hooves were gleaming. On the pale snow-sand they landed with a crash louder than the waves breaking. They gave their war cry. They charged together into the raiders' camp.

"Erenan is indeed fearless," Morren said. "And witless, I think."

Palle said, "The poor little boy."

Kestre said, "I will not ride my horse over that cliff for anything." She dismounted, ran down the path to join Erenan and Gallyn, Morren and Palle and Kanda at her heels.

There was a guard at the foot of the cliff. It would have been wiser perhaps for the raiders to have set a guard at the top of the cliff. The guard was sleeping – the village had been brewing the winter ale, it seemed, when the raiders struck. It would not have mattered if the guard had been wide awake awaiting them with a sword and a shield and a strong helmet – with one blow Kestre killed him, one blow so great it struck his head from his shoulders. His head flew almost into the sea. Men and women were staggering from the tents, dragging out their weapons. Erenan struck them down, rode her horse over them. The guard dog at the slave pen bayed, strained at his leash – he was vast, as big as a pony, a demon hound with red eyes and blood-slaver dripping from his knife-teeth. The slaves screamed. Gallyn kicked his horse toward the slave pen. The dog leapt into the pen, worried at the prisoners like they were sheep. They screamed and screamed, the boy saw and was screaming. The seabirds came down to tear at mauled flesh. Gallyn was at the slave pen shouting, the dog came to meet him with its muzzle raw-red. It snapped its leash, sank its teeth into the horse's throat. The horse was screaming, and then the horse was down and dead. Gallyn flailed in the snow-sand, the horse trapping him. The dog mounted the horse's body. Its teeth snapped shut.

A woman ran toward Kanda, wailing, an axe in her hand limp and useless. All the left side of her face and her body was soaked with blood. She fell at Kanda's feet wailing and groveling; her body came apart as meat as she begged. Kanda raised her sword, lowered it, raised it, struck. The body shattered. The begging stopped.

"She was mine!" Erenan shouted. She rode her horse over the woman's body, made her horse rear and kick to trample the woman's broken flesh. Kanda ran to where the dog was mauling at Gallyn, Gallyn was striking the dog with his sword, cutting it and cutting it. The dog howled, like the woman its body was breaking. Gallyn shattered its jaws, put out its eyes, hacked off its ears and its legs. It fell dead over him, over his horse's body. He hacked at it hacked at it hacked at it. Kanda joined him. They cut it until it was torn to fragments. It was like shredding meat or crumbling old bread.

The boy they had rescued cheered them on to cut it harder.

The slaves were screaming in fear.

Sick-brained slaughter. There were sixteen raiders. In less time than it takes to saddle a horse for battle, in less time than it takes to mix water and flour to make bread – in less time than it takes to kiss a child's forehead when it is sleeping, it seemed, the Six killed every one of the raiders.

Butchered them. Dead and rubble, and so far beyond dead.

Nothing would be left, Kanda swore in her heart, to bury, not one bone would be left unbroken to be buried. The gulls would feast on a slurry of human meat.

Kestre said, "Stop." Kestre cried, "Stop! Stop!"

The others of the Six did not hear her. No, that is not true. The others of the Six heard her and ignored her, fought on and on against the raiders, poor wretches driven by poverty and greed and cruelty to become an enemy, fought on hacking and rending at bodies long defeated and dead. The boy cheered. The slaves screamed.

Kestre began to sing:

"The cows are come in, and the fields they are sleeping.
The cows are come in, and the evening wakes.
The cows are come in, and the children are playing.
At the table the bread and the beer, the fruit, the good meat.
Come in now, come in now, out of the evening.
Come in now, come in now, from the fields that sleep.
Come in now, with the children about you.
Come in now, come in now, rest, eat, sleep."

A child's lullaby. A song for kneading the bread dough, for weaving a warm good blanket.

"Stop," Kestre said.

The others of the Six put down their swords. Looked at what they had done there on the snow-sand beach.

Kanda knelt and put her head in her hands. Erenan sat fixed on her horse with the boy in her arms, perfectly still but for her hands that shook. Palle stood on the shore staring into the sea as if he would drown himself. Gallyn stood with his horse dead, he sank down, buried his face in the horse's mane, wept.

Only Morren said after a little time: "We have killed slavers who destroyed a village, we have rescued children from worse than death. There is nothing that we should be ashamed of."

And Kestre turned her back on him.

The seabirds wheeled overhead, feasted and glutted. The tide came in, heavy gray waves that beat like war drums on the beach. Blood and ruin washed down into the sea, traced patterns there in the gray water. The snow began to fall white over red. Kanda knelt and vomited in shame and horror, Erenan was beyond weeping, Gallyn was beyond weeping, Palle wept, Kestre wept. The baby cried again, and the boy leapt from Erenan's horse faster than Gallyn and Erenan had leapt. He ran across the killing, hurled himself at the slave pen, he shouted with joy: "Denall! Denall!"

In the slave pen there was a woman with a baby in her arms, and five children. The woman was the boy's mother. Every child from the village was alive there, though three children and the woman were injured. The prisoners drew back in sick terror from the Six, who must seem more monstrous than the slavers. Kestre alone had the courage to look at the prisoners: she knelt before them, before wounded children and a wounded mother she had saved, she bent her head as before her Lord at Roven, "We will not harm you," she said. Morren snorted at her words. But Kanda and Palle and Erenan and Gallyn joined her, they sank down as before their Lord at Roven, they held out their hands to show the woman they would not harm her. Morren snorted, but then he came also, he too knelt there in the snow-sand with the incoming tide washing over him.

"You have saved us," the woman said at last. "They were planning to sail on this tide that is coming in now. They…I…. What they did…." The woman looked at the ruin on the snow-sand, she looked at the baby she held, at a little girl injured who was trying not to look at the ruin trying not to look trying not to look. "Thank you," she said. But her voice was uncertain. As well it should be, after what the Six had done. Only Kestre could meet her gaze as the Six stood.

"We will take you back to your village," said Palle. "If you wish it?"

The woman paused. "I…."

"We can take them to Roven, perhaps," said Gallyn. "That would be better, surely? One woman and these children, and the village…."

The woman took a last long look at the ruin of the beach. She said, "I do not think I want to go with you to this *Roven*. I will take the children and we will go back to the village." She began to walk fast to the path up the cliff.

"Wait," Gallyn called to her. "We will help you rebuild the houses, purify the shrine there. Help you bury the dead."

"At least let us tend to your wounds," Erenan called. "We can heal you."

The woman did not turn around. "Healing…?" She clutched her son's hand very tight. "I need to wash my child's skin clean where you have touched him."

The snow fell thicker as the Six rode back to Roven. When they passed the shrine at the village stream they stopped to make offering, but a shadow seemed to come over the water, the carved post seemed to turn its back on them. They rode on. They skirted wide around the village. The vile killing smoke was gone now. Gallyn, who was walking, limping where his horse had fallen on his legs, said, "I smell a cook fire."

"I hear a child talking," said Erenan.

They had ridden fast going; now returning they went very slowly, agreed it was because of Gallyn. Yet none of them wanted to stop, although the snow was so thick they should take shelter.

"I have never felt as I did on the beach there," Kanda said after a long time.

"I felt…happy," said Kestre.

"I felt as I did when I dance," said Gallyn.

Night came dark around them, a blizzard, yet they rode on. Forever, it seemed, they could ride.

"My sword was like sunlight in my hands," said Palle.

"My sword was like a kiss," said Kestre.

But Morren cried in grief and shame: "I do not understand what we have done wrong."

When they reached the gates of Roven they hesitated. The gates were open, as they always were open, but their horses drew up as if a barrier was there. The gatekeeper Benethal stood in the gateway. "Who goes there?" he called. "This is the Hall Roven. You outside the gates, state your business here."

"We are the Six Swords of Roven!" Kanda cried. "Benethal! Do you not recognize us?"

"I…I recognize you, yes, lady. Come in, come out of the snow and the night. I'm so sorry," Benethal said. "How foolish of me…. This snow, I think, it must have been…. I'm so sorry, so sorry…."

They stabled their horses, a long time they took over their horses. They went into the Hall itself, they knelt before their Lord of Roven on his throne Thalle that is *Hope*. Desperately, with hunger, they looked at the throne.

The Lord of Roven said, "You have rescued the village children from the raiders?"

Kanda said slowly, "We have, my Lord."

The Lord of Roven was silent a long time. He knew what they had done. He held his hands over the swell of his pregnant belly. His robe hung open, Kanda thought she saw the unborn child within him kick.

"Remember this," the Lord of Roven said. "Remember how it felt when you saw what you had done. Remember how it felt to do it.

"Come here now," he said.

One by one the Six mounted the dais and the Lord of Roven embraced them. The Lady of Roven came to stand beside her Lord, she too embraced them.

"You know what evil is, now," the Lord of Roven said. "Try to find something good in that if you can. Rest now. Tomorrow you will ride back to the beach and you will bury those you killed and raise a cairn over them. Then you will go to the village, you will rebuild it with your own hands though the woman and the children there will spit at you and shun you. You will heal them, though they shun you in revulsion. And then return here to me. And perhaps then you can forgive yourselves for what you have done this day."

It took the Six all winter to rebuild the village. Every day the snow fell thick, a cold wind blew. Three times the houses of the village collapsed just as the Six thought they had finished building them. Three times they had to purify the shrine in the village, for the cow's skull turned away from them in disgust. Every day the woman and the children spat at them and shunned them. Until at last the houses were built and furnished, the shrine made holy, Gallyn and Kestre had brewed beer, filled the storehouse with grain and apples and cheeses and salt meat, Kanda and Palle had led two fine pregnant cows and ten fine pregnant ewes and two fine rams into the byre, Morren and Erenan had helped with the calving and the lambing, they had sown wheat in the fields, built a bridge over the stream, tended the cherry trees and the hazel trees and the vegetable garden back to green life. Good earth banks they raised around the village, and a good strong gate. At last the village was remade. When all was done, the Six went down to the beach where they had raised a cairn over the raiders they had slaughtered, wretched men and women driven by need to cruelty and an evil death. Thin and pitiful the raiders had looked when the Six had returned to the beach to bury them, their clothes were ragged, their weapons cheaply made, as damaged and patched as their ship. One bore on his forehead a slave brand, one had on her back the marks of a slaver's whip. One had the bowed legs that come when a child grows up starving. The Six had buried them with care, now they knelt before the cairn, offered bread and meat, unwatered wine, made gifts of their warm cloaks. Kestre said, "More kindness here in grave offerings than the raiders ever had in life." They could not go back to give offering to the raiders living, they could only make grave offerings.

The Six returned to the village just as the sun had reached the summit of the sky. Kestre cried, "Look!" From the direction of Roven a man came riding. The dead man who had come on his dead horse to beg the Six's aid. Horse and man alive and well. He caught the woman his wife up in his arms, he kissed the children his own sons and the other children who were his children now also.

At last the Six dared to meet the woman's gaze as she bade farewell to them.

On the first day of spring, the Six Swords rode back through the gates of Roven, Benethal greeting them joyfully. In the Hall a feast was laid for them, the Lord and the Lady sat in splendor, the plates were piled high, the cups filled. Six voices rose in song. When the dawn came the Six went to their chambers, Lady Kanda slept in her chamber with walls of pearls and yellow roses, its windows looking out upon an orchard where the trees were always both in fruit and in blossom.

But a shadow was there in the hearth now, and a shadow in all their eyes, or so it seemed to Lady Kanda. That evening was the first time she was afraid to raise her left hand, her peace hand, to her Lord in greeting. The flowers and the fruits of the orchard were false, unpleasant to her. The food in her mouth that evening had a fetid taste.

CHAPTER TWELVE

The way you killed the raiders, that sick killing: that was what you were like when you were fighting at the island, that's what you looked like. Horrible. Frightening. No, no, my loves, that was different, that was fighting to protect you against things that deserved no compassion. Ysarene, Geiamnyn, they were like those raiders once, perhaps, an eternity ago, then they deserved compassion, but now they deserve nothing but death. And the end…it had a happy ending, in the end, you see? Laughter on the wind, in the whortleberry bush and the ragwort, Geiamnyn's laugh – he liked that story.

The hodden neighed in the distance. Calian heard it, her face pricked up like a hound's, frightened but keen.

Kanda thought: what am I doing here remembering the past? The past is rubble. The darkness came, the Hall Roven fell, and we Six …. That grief cannot be healed. But my children here now are alive.

The hodden neighed. Geiamnyn laughing. Calian turned her head, shivered, her hand strained at the pocketknife. So fierce she looked. Kanda thought: no, Calian, no more fighting. Her own right hand burned. She said, "Get them up, Dellet. It's time we got on."

Dellet got the children up quickly. Kanda said, "I'll tell you another story, little ones, as we walk, hey? Winter had come to the Hall Roven. The first great cold of winter: snow lay thick around the high banks of the earthworks, the gatekeeper Benethal stamped his feet and blew on his hands to warm them, his hood crusted white. And the Six Swords of Roven woke that morning to find a dragon curled before the gates.

"The green dragon had sworn to burn down the Hall Roven, take the Lady back to his hoard, kill the Lord of Roven and the Six.

"Gallyn could not wound it; Palle could not wound it. Kestre could not wound it.

"It rushed toward me spewing fire.

"With one blow of my sword, my loves, I struck off its head."

She thought: that deed that has no shadow on it, the story of the Six Swords of Roven and the Green Dragon. That was glorious! That was a great deed of arms well done! Why have I not told you that story before, beloveds?

But the story had taken longer than she thought to tell it. When she closed her real eyes, the slopes of Mal Anwen were suddenly very near.

Sal said, "Mother – Lord Morren…?"

"Yes?"

Sal said, "He—?"

"What?"

Sal frowned. "Nothing." She said after a little: "What is it that's on Mal Anwen, Mum?"

Ah. Calian knows already, I think. My poor husband, he refuses to know. Kanda said, "Something of mine that I need."

Sal said, "Oh. Yes."

And they must get on quick, hurry to what it was waiting. Run on with strong new legs from the rest here, new strength in them from the story, the shieldwall around them was strong and held. Memory of the child's face when they killed the raiders, his cry of joy when they freed his mother, memory of the work rebuilding the village, the houses better than they had been, larger, warmer, better lasting; they had ridden past the village later – a year later, or two years, or three, time in memory is shifting as the sea – they had ridden past, Kestre had said, "I recognize…?" Morren had said, laughing, "You should do. That roof there near took the skin off both my hands." The houses well kept, all occupied; the orchard and the garden verdant to overflowing; two fat porkers in a pig pen. "We didn't build that, I don't remember?" said Erenan. A hulking youth went to throw slops to the pigs with the proud look of the pen's maker: one of the children they had rescued, rushed up into youth like a sapling tree. A newborn baby wailed. A child sang a rude song. Think what you like about what you did that day – yes, we did terrible things. But look at this village now, the people in it prosperous. More prosperous, and the village better, than it had been before the raiders came, because we remade it. That house there, I remember struggling to raise up the house posts, the first one we built and we hadn't the trick of it, and then we got it, the work went quickly, not the most elegant of houses, to be sure, but I can be rightly as proud of that house as of anything I've done.

Morna said, "I'm cold, Mummy." It was cold, the wind blowing shearing-knives as the people round here said. Mal Anwen was lost in cloud. Dellet let out a groan as the black rainclouds rushed on the wind toward them. Helplessly, Kanda watched a black line of rain hammer down faster than a man could run.

"There's some trees down there," Sal said. The view ahead was cut off, the rain was like a wall.

"Hurry," Calian shouted. The rain hit them.

Again, Kanda thought: I have such mighty powers, never have I been defeated in battle, but I can't stop little things like the rain getting down the neck of my children's tunics. The great deed of dragon slaying seemed a tiny thing indeed beside Morna falling over in the mud and somehow pulling Sal over with her, Calian cursing the rain in words Kanda had no idea the girl knew. The rain was icy, Kanda would not have been surprised if it blew hail or snow. It hurt almost as badly as hail. In four footsteps their clothes were soaked black and they were wet to the skin. They waded toward Sal's trees, of course down a steep slope that had turned into a river, of course Morna slipped in a hollow with water up to her waist. Kanda tried to think, it'll wash the mud off, at least. When they reached the trees they were stunted, one indeed was dead, hardly any shelter, and oh joy! the trees of course grew by a stream that was now a river, and a steep slope rose on the other bank. There were a lot of nettles for Morna to fall in.

Kanda, slayer of nettles! The children's teeth were chattering. Kanda hacked at the nettles with her sword to try to make Morna cheer up a bit. Dellet squashed the children up closer and closer together under the best of the trees. He was standing so that he himself had water pouring down the back of his neck. He had the brilliant idea to hold his cloak over the children's heads a bit like a tent. Unluckily the cloak was so sodden the water leaked through on them somehow worse than the rain. The stream rushed over their shoes. Calian was uncharacteristically horrified when she saw a drowned mouse.

"It will stop soon," Kanda said in her most loved voice that was firm and cheerful. "I'm sure it will."

"That's the worst thing you can possibly say, Mother," Calian said. "It'll rain all day now, you'll see."

But we have to get on. We have to get on. And the danger— Because he knew her face well, even just the set of her shoulders, Dellet said, "Rain like this will slow down anything, I expect. Wolves don't come out in weather like this, I don't suppose those... things will. That wooden thing, it'd be washed away! And that man and that woman didn't look like the kind to like getting soaked to the skin. Might get mud on their armor and their fancy hair, couldn't have that, could they? And you said, you said, Kanda, that they couldn't cross water: well, we're back on an island again here, aren't we, under a tree? Three trees." Another gout of water went down the back of his neck. Kanda saw him screw up his face but keep silent because the children hadn't seen he was keeping the water off them.

Kanda smiled at him with her heart almost breaking. You are the glorious one, Del-my-heart, not me.

"It'll stop soon, Calian bird, it's summer rain, it'll stop, then we can get on to the mountain, we'll be safe there, your mother promised."

That made her heart bleed. That's how I felt, Del-my-heart, that day on the beach when I lowered my sword at Kestre's song. But the confidence in his voice, the trust he had, his face so grieving yet so certain.

"It's stopping," said Dellet. "See?" He pointed. "To Mal Anwen, then. We just need to…wade…swim…go round this stream. That's right, Morn, littlest lamb, Daddy will carry you. Oh goodness!" he said, as water sopped out of Morna's tunic all over him as he picked her up.

Promise me, Kanda, love, that you will never go there; when I was a child, he says, shaking, when I was a child I had nightmares about being lost on Mal Anwen.

Dellet said, "Come on, then. Yes, I know it's a mire, Cal-flower. Just…walk carefully. Come on, girls. Look, on the bright side, that wooden thing couldn't take one step in this…. And that horrible lady…mud all over her."

After a long time walking they came to the remains of a farmhouse, far out in the middle of the wild moor. A circle of wooden post stumps with the roof and the wattle long rotted, a tumbled stone wall beyond for a field had one gatepost that was made of a single stone as tall as Kanda's shoulder. It was crusted with yellow lichen, cattle or such had rubbed themselves against it to wear it down in one place. A path led toward it, raised and dry above the new-made mire. The spearpoint of Mal Anwen was framed by the house's roof.

"Who'd have a house out here?" said Dellet, puzzled. "Odd-looking place, too. This isn't right, is it, Kanda?" He called to the children: "Don't go anywhere near it."

"Obviously, Dad," said Sal. "It's a pile of rubble."

The posts shivered. Grew. They stretched up taller, high enough to hold a roof. Good strong wood. They had faces carved in them. A rustle of dry branches – willow withies snaking up between the posts, plaiting themselves into the wall frames. A cow lowed – a strong smell of manure as the daub worked itself into the withies. A seabird called – whisper of sedge, smell of salt and mudflats as the sharp cutting reeds grew up as thatch for the roof. A stone and a post outside the door, as was proper; the stone was topped with a bell, a crow's wing hung from the post. A leather doorcurtain unfurled itself over the doorway. Smoke began to rise through the roof. From inside the house there was noise: a dog barked, a child shouted, someone was using a quern: a woman, she began to sing in time to her grinding.

"The cows are come in, and the fields they are sleeping.

The cows are come in, and the evening wakes."

Kanda felt her arms ache from hefting wooden posts. The pain of a splinter under her thumbnail, the scratch of rushes on her cheek. I don't remember we built a house so tall or so big.... The doorcurtain twitched, a pair of eyes peeped through. A child's giggle, the woman broke off her song, called to the child, "What is it?" The quern stopped, the woman said, "Hang up my apron, will you? You stay there, Ty." The doorcurtain opened.

The woman was similar in age to Kanda, broad-hipped and strong-armed with black hair in a braid down her back. She wore a rosy pink dress embroidered with yellow flowers at the neck and the wrists, a string of blue stone beads around her neck. There was a smudge of flour on her cheek where she had been working the quern, and a sheen of sweat on her forehead. Alarm flashed across her face as she saw Kanda's sword, then she smiled nervously, then she smiled more kindly as she noticed baby Morna, then she said, "Good afternoon. Greetings."

Dellet said dumbly, "Greetings."

"Travelers?" The woman said loudly, "The men are out in the fields, my husband and his three brothers, but the fields are very close, they'll be home anytime now." She gave the crow's wing a push to make it swing. That established, she looked quizzically at the children. "You look like you've been outside for days. You're soaked through," she said in astonishment. "Have you been in the river?"

"The rain—" Sal began. The house and the ground around it were bone-dry.

"You must be frozen," the woman said. "The poor little child there, look how muddy she is." Her voice had reproach in it for Kanda, good mother, are you, letting your little one get soaked through and muddy to the waist, children get sick so easily don't you know? The child, a boy a year or so older than Morna, pushed out through the doorcurtain beside her, whispered something. The woman thought a moment, then she nodded. She set the crow's wing swinging again, then she said, "Well, this is my husband's house, but I think I can speak for him. If you put that sword away, woman, you and yours had better come in."

Inside the house a fire burned bright in the hearth, a cauldron stood at the fire with soup cooking in it. A loom stood near the fire to get the best light, a fair-haired girl knelt at the loom weaving red cloth. The dog sat beside her, it jumped up as Kanda entered, growled with hackles raised and teeth bared, sank back to the ground at a word from the girl. There were baskets and crocks full of hazelnuts, walnuts, honeycomb, berries; strings of onions and mushrooms, dried fish and bunches of herbs hung from the roof struts. A wolfskin lay on a great bed dressed in red blankets, smaller bed-benches were pushed back beneath the wall posts. A shield and a leather corselet stood on a panoply with a tallow lamp burning beneath.

"Water," the woman said. She held out a clay cup. Kanda drank, Dellet drank, the woman drank. The woman dipped her fingers into the cup, scattered water drops on the fire. "That's done now," she said. "You've drunk our water, you won't harm me, we won't harm you. My name is Gella. This is my son, Ty. My husband's sister, Garn. My husband is called Ethr, his brothers are called Marei, Karh, and Rit."

"I am called Kanda. This is my husband, Dellet. My children, Sal, Calian, Morna. Thank you for your water."

"Sit by the fire," the woman said. "Get dry."

They sat. Morna stretched out her hands. "Oh that's good, Mummy." The wood was well seasoned, almost smokeless, it gave off a faint scent of apples. Every now and then it hissed and spat blue sparks, which made Morna and Ty grin with delight.

"The men will be home soon," Gella said. She gave Kanda and Dellet and Sal each a cup of sweet mead. "When the men are home, we can eat."

"What's cooking?" said Calian.

"Meat stew!" Ty shouted. "Yum!"

"We've been lucky this year," Gella said. "Those barrels there are all full of salt meat."

Garn hummed as she worked the loom. The loom weights clinked together nicely; she made a song of their rhythm.

The doorcurtain swished aside with a breath of warm wind with it. Gella said, "Ah, here are the men." Kanda and Dellet got to their feet to greet them. Three huge solid men, thick and tall and gnarled like old tree trunks on a barren hillside, thick red beards plaited and tied with pebbles, long plaited red hair. The first, Marei, wore a bronze neck ring, the second, Karh, wore a necklace of black pebbles, the third, Rit, wore a necklace of cow's teeth. They nodded greeting to Kanda and Dellet and the children. Kanda thought that Marei looked at Sal in a way she did not like. Sal smiled back at Marei.

"Where's Ethr?" said Gella.

"He's in the field still," said Marei. "He said he'd be in soon enough. The light's still good, he said." Marei nodded to the cauldron. "He said to eat, not to wait for him."

"Drink some mead," Gella said. "Then we'll eat."

Garn hummed as she worked the loom. How fast her fingers worked, how fast the loom weights clicked! Her weaving sword flashed fast as a real sword in battle. All this time when her brothers had come home, she had not looked up.

"That's good mead," Dellet said. "Your own brewing?"

"We traded metal for it," Karh said.

"Metal and stone," Rit said.

"Stew," said Gella. She served them all clay bowls of rich stew fragrant with herbs, juicy with tender meat. Bone spoons to slurp it up with.

Morna said, "This is the best thing I ever ate."

"Mummy's the best cook, that's why," Ty said.

"Better than my mummy," said Morna.

"Morna!" Dellet was laughing. "It is delicious, though, thank you, Gella."

"Is Garn not eating?" asked Calian.

"She'll eat later," said Gella. "Won't you, Garn?"

Garn only hummed.

Marei was sitting next to Sal, smiling as she ate the stew. "We must fetch out the winter cloaks, Gella," Marei said. "Lend them to them. You'll sleep here tonight, I hope?"

"Meal cakes?" said Gella. "To sop up the liquid?" Ran and fetched them from a crock behind a wall post. "These are a little stale, I'm afraid," said Gella. "The meal is stale."

They were stale. And a little burned.

Calian said, "But these look just like— Taste just like—"

Garn hummed at the loom, and then she began to sing:

"The cows are come in, and the fields they are sleeping.

The cows are come in, and the evening wakes."

"Eat up this good food, Calian," Dellet said.

Calian took up a spoonful of stew. She looked at the meat in the stew. "What meat is this?" she said.

The fire burned blue and cold, without smoke because it was not burning wood.

Rit is *hateful.*

Karh is *ruined.*

Marei is *grief.*

Gella is *wasting.*

Garn is *wolf bitch.*

Ethr is *walls fallen.*

Ty is *take sick.*

The doorcurtain opened, Ethr came into the roundhouse in a gust of warm wind. Strong-built and tall, long golden hair falling over his shoulders, his face hidden by his bronze helmet. His eyes, red as embers, blazed even in the firelight. His bronze armor was soaked and crusted with blood.

Garn stopped singing, stood up from the loom. The wolf at her feet raised its hackles, bared its teeth, blood dripped from its red tongue. Her long braid of hair was white and shining, she was tall, slender, elegant in the way she stood, her eyes were big and beautiful and flower-blue. In the light of the fire her face was flayed raw, stripped of lips and nose, ears and eyelids.

The sword was there, but Kanda could not find it. Human flesh choked her throat.

Geiamnyn said, "You have drunk a cup of our water, Ikandera. You cannot harm us. We only want to talk with you, Ikandera. I dream sometimes of the old days when we would talk together."

He took off his fine helmet with its golden figures dancing, placed it carefully on the panoply raised to himself. The lamp before it burned human fat, rank and stinking. He turned his face to Kanda, the firelight bright on it. Kanda gasped, for he was as beautiful as she remembered. Geiamnyn's skin was white-golden, there was a light in it so that it shone itself like the morning sun. His hair was brighter clearer gold than any ornament, a golden crown or a golden throne would look tawdry beside Geiamnyn's flowing hair. His lips were red as roses, full for kissing, his face was the face of a man just out of green youth. Obscene, it looked, above his filthy blood-crusted armor. His red eyes blazed grotesque from that perfect face.

"You cannot harm us, either," Kanda said, her voice shaking. "You are bound by the cup offered just as we are bound by the cup taken, Geiamnyn. 'My husband's house,' the woman said." Talk? Once, she thought, she had found such pleasure simply in looking at him.

Geiamnyn said lightly, "You threaten me with such things, Ikandera? Do you hear that, Ysarene? Ikandera Thygethyn thinks to threaten me with old bindings! She'll threaten me with an oath truly sworn, next, do you think?"

Red rage. "You are bound!" Kanda shouted. "All of us. You cannot harm any of us."

Ysarene spat, cuffed the wolf on the side of the head so it let out a growl. Marei leapt up with an axe in his hand, Karh drew a long knife, Rit a wooden club studded with stone flakes. Geiamnyn's hand went to his sword hilt. But the air hissed, a scent of metal, Geiamnyn's hand shook. His beautiful face filled with pain, as if he was wounded. He groaned. Ringing of bells, lap of fresh water. Marei and Karh and Rit lowered their weapons. Geiamnyn let his hand drop.

"I am bound by the cup offered," he said. His face filled with rage, his eyes blazing. He cursed, turned with a growl to Gella and struck her on the mouth hard enough to draw blood on her lips.

"Stop!" Kanda shouted.

Gella wrung her hands. "I'm sorry I'm sorry I'm sorry, husband."

Kanda thought, If I had not drunk from the cup offered, I would put my sword into that woman's hand now, show her how to use it. She said to Geiamnyn: "If you touch that woman again, Geiamnyn, I will break the bindings."

"Shut your mouth, you, woman, bitch, stop that sniveling," Geiamnyn said to Gella.

"I'm sorry I'm sorry I'm sorry, husband," Gella said.

Kanda wanted to vomit. Leave, flee, now. The girls should never see this. She said, trying to keep her voice steady, "So now let us talk, then."

"I'm eating first. If you'll hurry up and bring me some food, woman." Geiamnyn unbuckled his sword belt, threw it to the ground at Gella's feet. "Pick that up, then, woman, bitch." He lounged by the fire. Very fine he looked by the firelight. "No, the food first, then the sword, I'm hungry, the food quick. And a drink. No, woman, first the drink." Gella hurried, mumbling on and on, "I'm sorry I'm sorry I'm sorry, husband." Calian was watching and Kanda knew Calian was thinking the same: I would put my pocketknife into that woman's hand now, urge her on to use it, cheer her on. Geiamnyn drank a cup of mead, ate the stew. "Good stew, isn't it? My wife here, she's a stupid useless bitch but she's a fine cook."

"I didn't eat any of it," said Kanda.

"Lying, lying," Ty sang. He was showing Morna his toys, little carved dolls like the dolls Kanda had in her satchel; now Kanda looked at him knowing, his skin was pallid, his cheeks fever-flushed.

Gella poured Geiamnyn a second cup of mead. A beautiful silver cup. He raised it, smiled, drank it off in one go, threw it down into the ashes of the hearth. Gella scurried away with it, ran to mop up the spilled dregs.

"Do that later, woman," Geiamnyn snarled. "I'm trying to talk to my guest."

"I'm sorry I'm sorry I'm sorry."

"Shut up, woman, bitch."

Kanda said through clenched teeth, choking, "So talk, then."

The burning eyes glared at Gella, who fled into the shadows behind a house post. Geiamnyn turned his face to Kanda and smiled; he was fine and beautiful and calm and kind. "We did not know you were living here," Geiamnyn said. "Truly, Ikandera, we none of us knew. Even the other, he has been looking for you a long time, but he had no idea you were here when we came here. If we had, we might have left you alone."

Kanda thought: lying, lying.

Geiamnyn said, "*Great Warrior.* A farmer's wife, a mother, stinking of cow shit! Look at you with your sagging breasts and your gray hair!"

"We'd have left you alone, Ikandera," said Ysarene, "because it would have been too amusing to watch you living out your days like this."

But Geiamnyn spat. "We'd have left you well alone, Ikandera, because it is too disgusting to see what you've become."

Blink back the pain. Laugh at him. "This is all you wanted with me, Geiamnyn? To laugh at me for my life? My hair is gray, my nails have muck under them. My breasts sag. And? Yes?

"I wet myself sometimes when I laugh too hard, Geiamnyn, I have stretch marks from my armpits to my kneecaps, every other month my bleed is so heavy I should strap a cauldron between my legs. You forgot to mention those things. I'm sure my husband could tell you more about me, if you ask him. I sweat in my sleep so the blanket needs washing, I snore, I fart in my sleep, sometimes I piss and fart when I come."

"She defeated the hodden," said Ysarene. "Her and her daughter."

Geiamnyn turned disgusted eyes on Sal. His eyes were curious now. "So?" Sal drew back, flushing with fear.

"Not her. The other, the younger. Calian, is it?"

"*Eagle*." Geiamnyn said, "That is a fine name for her, Ikandera."

I did not name her that. I never wanted to call her that. Dellet's father's name, that's all. We argued about it for months. Kanda opened her mouth to find something to speak.

Calian had been sitting quiet by the fire with her head bowed. Now she leapt up. "Don't you speak my name, you *Burning*," she spat at Geiamnyn. "Or you, *Hunger*. Say my name again or look at my sisters, and I will kill you myself."

"Calian!" Kanda got to her feet beside her daughter, put her hand on her daughter's shoulder. "No. Sit down. Now, Calian. This is enough, Geiamnyn. I am a clapped-out old woman, my body is fat and ugly, my days are wasted with ungrateful children, while you are a mighty warrior and strong and beautiful. If that is all you wanted to say, good, fine, you're welcome, I'll leave you now, go back to my cow shit."

"Leave?" Ysarene said. "Leave, Ikandera?"

Geiamnyn said, "You can't leave yet, Ikandera. Your little girl is so happy here, playing with my sniveling disease of a son. Look how happy it makes my useless bitch of a wife to watch them."

Calian screamed. Threw herself at Geiamnyn.

"Calian, no!"

We are bound, we have drunk from the cup offered.

You are a child, Calian.

Calian had the bronze sword in one hand. The pocketknife in the other.

Calian struck Geiamnyn in the chest. He staggered back, a howl of rage bubbled out of him.

Not rage: pain.

Geiamnyn was bleeding.

"I have not drunk your filthy water!" Calian shouted. Her sword danced in her hand, her knife flowed in her hand, her sword ripped into Geiamnyn's chest, her knife ripped into Geiamnyn's face. "Beast, monster!" Calian shouted.

Geiamnyn fell back, crashing into the cauldron on the hearth. The firedogs clattered against his legs. Calian stabbed at him.

Ysarene flew at Calian. Marei and Karh and Rit were up before the doorcurtain with axe and knife and club. The wolf rushed at Dellet.

Kanda was bound by the cup received, and could do nothing.

Geiamnyn stumbled, swaying, Calian screamed at him. His feet kicked up the hearth fire, he roared in pain as he went down with the flames around him.

His sword – Gella had hung it on the panoply. Kanda threw herself toward it. The wolf was there, its teeth closed on her wrist. "You are bound!" Kanda screamed at Geiamnyn, Ysarene, at the wolf. Blood poured from her wound. But wounds opened also on the wolf's flanks.

"They cannot harm you, Calian," Kanda shouted at her daughter. "If they hurt you, they will be hurt themselves worse." Kanda thought in despair: you cannot be harmed, my love, please.

Ysarene grabbed at the sword on the panoply. Her hand met Kanda's hand over the sword hilt. They clawed at each other, wrestled to hold on. Wounds opening on both their hands. Breathing together in pained gasps. The panoply toppled sideways with a great ring of bronze. Weak, sickly child's wail. Ysarene hissed in triumph as Kanda's grip on the sword hilt failed.

White pain. Red pain. Kanda's fingers closed around Ysarene's flayed face.

Revulsion. So strong Kanda fell back.

Pity, in a great sickening rush over her; pain in her face, pain in Ysarene's face.

I never asked, you never told, Ysarene, the name of the one who did that to you. She was down, choking on pain and bile, Ysarene was on her, smashing at Kanda with Geiamnyn's sheathed sword, struggling to draw it.

You are bound. If you kill me you kill yourself, Ysarene.

White pain. Red pain. Kanda spat blood and broken teeth.

Fire rising from all around them. The house burned. Kanda threw up her left arm, warded off the sword, jolt running down her left shoulder, pounding at her lungs and heart. Ysarene fell over her, the scabbard between them. Pushing. Pushing. Kicking. Gasping. The scabbard pressed down over Kanda's throat.

"Die, beast, monster!" Calian was screaming.

Gella's voice came beside Calian's. Two lovely voices in sweet chorus, women's well-song at the first dawning of the spring. "Die, husband, cruel, worthless, die, leave me in peace."

Geiamnyn's voice came weak, begging, frothed with his blood. "Die!" Calian screamed. Marei and Karh and Rit came at Calian with bronze axe and bronze knife and stone-tipped club. Calian swung her sword, cut Marei's right arm at the shoulder. Marei went back with a cry of confusion. Gella grabbed up Marei's axe, almost too heavy for her to hold, brought it down on Geiamnyn's breast. Again Calian swung her sword, cut Karh in the left arm. Karh dropped his knife.

Kanda thought, with joy: they cannot harm you, Calian.

The wolf mounted Kanda's body. Kanda braced herself, sucked down her own blood, pushed, kicked, tore at Ysarene. They rolled all three together, writhing together. Kanda was uppermost with Ysarene beaten under her, Ysarene was uppermost with Kanda panting weak. Wolf howl of frenzied enjoyment. Red pain. White pain. Bitterness.

Kanda's flailing hands met Geiamnyn's sword hilt. Thrust it back, slammed it with every part of her being into Ysarene's throat. Slammed Ysarene away backward, kicked her flying to smash against the burning hearth. Tore the sword from the scabbard, ripped it deep into the wolf's flank.

More pain than the mind could conceive of. Her own body slashed open, gutted, burning. The skin of her hand eaten by the heat of Geiamnyn's sword hilt.

Shake the sword from her hand like shaking off a slug. It clung to her, wanted her to hold it. She cursed, threw it off with the vomit rising in her throat. Staggered to her feet.

Wood creaking. Long deep groan as the house posts bent, split. The roof was burning, fire pouring up the walls. The doorcurtain burned: it did not burn with flame but with pain itself.

Geiamnyn lay sprawled on the great bed over the wolfskin, his chest cut open from his navel to his throat, his white flesh and his beautiful golden hair burning, the wolfskin burning under him. Gella shouted, triumphant, "I'm free of him!" But already Marei, Karh and Rit broken by Calian's sword came crawling toward him, flowed into him, his cut throat bubbled.

One of the house posts collapsed into rotten wood dust. The walls were rotting, falling.

"The doorway!" The lintel was breaking, clots of rotting, burning thatch coming down. Dellet ran for the doorway, pulling Sal with him; he cried out as he reached it as blue pain-fire leapt over him. "Get through!" he screamed. He threw his arms around Sal to keep the worst of it off her, no different to the rainstorm, pushed her out through it. Calian had the light of victory in her eyes, she pulled Gella toward her: "You and the boy, come on. Come on." Gella hesitated. Her hands reached, hopeless, toward Geiamnyn her husband. Dellet wrapped his arms around Calian, dragged her out, "Come on, Gella! Come on!" Calian was screaming. Sal came running back into the house through the pain-fire: "Morna! Morna!" "I'll get her, Sal, get out." Sal howled, "She and the boy hid under the bed."

"Get out," Kanda screamed. Dragged Sal away. Pain-fire, all her wounds wailing. Wet rotten leather from the doorcurtain stifling her face. "Get out!" She threw herself and Sal through the doorway, fighting her daughter who clawed to get back, get Morna away. "Get out. I'll go back—" Rotting leather, raw uncured hide bloody and rotten, flapped in her face. Push it aside. Push the pain-fire aside. Reach out—

Ysarene shrieked with laughter.

The house fell.

They stood on the wild moor with the earth a mire around them, rainclouds black overhead. The house was a pile of rubble, a circle of wooden post stumps with the roof and the wattle long rotted. A single human skull lay within the circuit of the walls, half buried.

Morna was gone.

CHAPTER THIRTEEN

"Bring her back. Get her back. Get her back. Make her come back, Mum."

I don't know

How to make

Her come back

Calian.

I can't

Get her

Back

Sal.

I don't

Know

What

To do

Dellet.

"Bring her back. Make her come back, Mum."

CHAPTER FOURTEEN

"There wasn't any time. That's all that happened. It could have been any one of the girls, or you, or me."

"She'd crawled under the bed with…with that…boy. She was hiding, and the bed was on fire, and that…Geiamnyn's body…was on the bed. I tried to grab her, but she was so frightened she hit my hand away. The…the boy was so frightened he bit me."

"Ty," Calian said, "his name was Ty, that boy. His mother was Gella. That's her skull there in the ruins, I think."

"There wasn't any time. It could have been any of the girls. It just happened to be Morna. It could have been you. Or me. That's all. The house was falling down, and there wasn't enough time to get you all out." And Dellet went over to the stone gatepost, punched it so hard the skin of his fist burst.

Calian said in a dead flat voice, "Is she under there somewhere? Her…bones, I mean." She shouted then in fury, "Are they all dead? The monsters? Are they dead? Tell me they're dead and gone?"

No more words worth speaking. But words must be spoken, truths must be told. Kanda said, "Geiamnyn and Ysarene are not dead, no, Calian. You see my wounds here, healing? So will Geiamnyn and Ysarene heal. They are gone, but they are not dead, just as they were when I fought them on the island." They were in the rainstorm, in my mind as I walked to the roundhouse, in the story I told of the raiders, they are here now in our grief.

"I killed him! Gella and me!"

"You cannot kill him, Calian."

"I killed him. Can't you accept that? While you sat there gibbering on *talking* to him."

Shame. "I— I couldn't—"

"But Morna is dead?" Calian threw the sword down at her mother's feet. "You take this useless thing, rubbish, rubbish, rubbish, it can't harm that monster but Morna is dead. You use it, be *Great Warrior* while Morna is dead."

"You keep it, Calian. You found it on the island, you used it to rescue all of us but Morna when I could do nothing."

"I don't want it. Rubbish, useless, vile stupid useless useless. Break it, smash it! What's the point of any of it, anything, if those monsters can't be killed but Morna is dead? You didn't do anything. You *talked* to them. Useless rubbish useless useless."

Kanda said, "You are alive, Calian. You and Sal and Dellet."

Dellet said nothing. Traced his finger over the bloodstain on the gatepost.

Calian said, "I wish you were the one dead."

Kanda could only look away from her daughter at that, but then she found Sal's eyes on her, and she could not look at either of her children or at her husband. But Dellet said slowly, "Cal-flower, Cal-my-heart, you are alive and Sal is alive, and that is all there is I can say." He said slowly, quietly, "This is not your mother's fault, Cal-flower. You can't blame her. Those monsters...." He said, his voice breaking, "The cattle thieves who came last winter, they killed Ben Apple Tree, they killed poor Susa two months off her wedding.... Cattle and sheep die every winter, don't they, Cal-my-heart, sickness comes and people die, hungry years and people die, the sweat-sickness in Aranth, you remember? Susa's sister who died in childbed and the baby died with her...."

"And?"

"And nothing, Cal-flower."

He drove his hand hard against the gatepost, opened his mouth to scream, then he shook his head, took his hand away.

"I'm going home," Calian said. "Away from her." She walked five paces, her body so full of anger she was like a red fire herself. She stopped, ran back, threw herself into her mother's arms howling.

"I killed him. Beast, monster – what he was doing – to that woman – what he said to you— I killed him and he still killed Morna and I thought I'd killed him I couldn't kill him he'll go on and on and on and on."

"That is what they are, Calian." Kanda stroked her daughter's hair. What can I say? Your father is right: you are alive, and there is much pain in the world, and…nothing. "We are alive still, Calian," Kanda said.

They sat quiet a long time together. After a long time Sal got up, gathered a few rough flowers, placed them in the rubble of the house. After a long time Dellet got up, said, "I'll bury that skull. Gella's skull, if that's who it is. Poor woman."

"I'll help, Dad."

"No, Cal, lass, you— Thank you, Cal, lass, Cal-flower."

"We need to get on," said Kanda. "We can't stay here."

Dellet ignored her entirely. "Dig the earth deeper, Calian, that's it. If we had a stick or something, at least…."

"The sword," said Sal. The first words she had spoken since they entered the roundhouse. "We can use that." She too had begun digging at the earth with her hands.

"No!" said Calian. "We use our hands."

"We have to get on," said Kanda. But she too joined them digging.

"That's deep enough, Sal, Calian," Dellet said. "Well done, you two." Kanda reached for the skull but Dellet picked it up quickly, placed it in the hole. "That's done, then. Well done, you two. Easier now to shove the soil back."

When it was done Kanda said, "We have to get on, Dellet. We can't stay here. Please."

Her husband finally looked at her. "I know that."

"Press the earth down better, Sal," Calian said.

Kanda said, "Why are we going to Mal Anwen? Sal? Calian?"

"We could put a stone on it, perhaps," Calian said. "A grave marker. What do you think, Dad?"

Sal said, "Because…." She said, the second words she had spoken since they entered the roundhouse, with even some faint hope in them: "There is…armor there. Or weapons. A sword. There's a sword hidden on Mal Anwen. You put it there."

"There is, and I did." Kanda said, "I am called Ikandera Thygethyn. *Great Warrior.* I was once the best and bravest of the Six Swords of Roven. On Mal Anwen I buried my armor, my helmet, my sword, yes.

"With that sword, and with that sword alone, I can kill the monsters, Sal, Calian.

"Morna is dead, our house is destroyed. And that is why we must go on to Mal Anwen."

Such a cruel reason to go there. To be revenged. To kill.

Three times before she had gone to Mal Anwen. Once she had gone to bury her sword. Once she had gone in terror to check it was still buried. Once she had gone to laugh with relief that it was buried there.

Calian said, "Wait." Ran back. Took up the sword she had thrown down as useless junk.

It looked right as she held it. A shadow on her face, the same sorrow that would come over Kestre when she took up her sword, for now Calian understood more what a sword meant. The girl's face was reflected in the sword blade. The sword was whole. New-cast bronze.

Made for her, that sword.

A shadow and a chill on Kanda's skin. A happiness, also. Pride. You are a warrior born, Calian. I wanted a quiet life for you, for all three of my children, but it seems you have chosen a life of your own.

They walked through the dark now, and they were not afraid of the dark. The moon was new and thin but bright. It was easier going without Morna. Once they heard the hodden's gobbling neigh. Calian held the sword steady, the sound faded. Calian was the shieldwall now, the warmth and light protecting them. Out of sight in the darkness hooves, footsteps, something huge and heavy shambling; Ysarene laughed, once, sang far off in her lovely voice, "I'm sorry I'm sorry I'm sorry." Calian raised the sword; the sound was gone.

Kanda touched her daughter's hand. "On Mal Anwen, Calian, we will fight them together side by side."

"Leave me alone," Calian said.

"It will be the greatest pride of my life, Calian mine, to fight beside you."

"I said leave me alone."

Dellet said, "Best leave her for a while, as she says."

They walked on, until Sal stopped, cried out, "What's that?"

"What, Sal?"

"Don't you hear?" Sal turning and turning, trying to find something, she looked…she looked like a cow when they had taken away the calf. "I can hear Morna," Sal said. "Listen!"

They were silent but there was nothing.

"I heard her cry," said Sal. "Her angry cry."

Silent, silent, silent.

"I…I thought I did…."

"That *Hunger*," said Calian. "Taunting you." She brandished her sword.

Listen.

"It's gone," Sal said. "Thank you, Calian."

"I'll kill that *Hunger* with a thousand sword strokes," said Calian. And then she frowned, a sick look came into her face. In the darkness she saw her face reflected in the sword.

Sal squeezed her sister's hand tight. "It's all right, Cal." The two girls walked on together holding hands, Calian's left hand in Sal's right.

Kanda tried to walk with Dellet, take his hand. We used to go on night walks together hand in hand before the children came along, all night we walked sometimes. Talking about the future, sometimes. Children's names. You wanted a son.

Dellet said, "You promise me, Kanda, you swear it, you can kill that man *Burning*?"

What could she say to that? *I'll try, Dellet, I'll try my best to kill him and not let him harm our other two children?*

"The only reason we are still with you, Kanda, is because you.... I'd take the girls and run a thousand miles away from you, if I didn't think...." He said bitterly, "I should never have gone into that house. I should have taken the children to Aranth that first morning."

"If you had taken them to Aranth, you'd all be dead now, Dellet."

"I know that. That's the only reason I haven't told you to leave us alone." In the darkness, she could pretend she couldn't see him and he couldn't see her seeing him.

"That woman.... That boy...." Dellet said: "Calian was like the sun, in there."

"She was."

"I always knew she was too fierce to be a farmer," Dellet said. "Like the sun. Magnificent." He said, "She's a special one, isn't she?"

"She is."

"And Sal...."

"You know, Dellet. What she did in the shieling."

"She thinks that was your doing. I didn't tell her otherwise. Like the sun, both of them."

They'd be there soon. Kanda said, "We should stop. Rest, eat. There is danger still, up there on the mountain." Thinking of the sun, she said, "I would rather go there in the light."

"We're not going into a house again," said Dellet. He was trying to be funny, light with her. Kanda felt such happiness toward him.

"No. We're certainly not," she said. She looked around until she found a good place, where the ground was good thick turf. "Calian, take your sword, cut a circle around us in the earth."

Calian stared at her like she was mad. Then she nodded. She set the sword point into the earth, plowed up a circle around them. Kanda said the words.

Rustling of leaves. Smell of green things.

Surrounded.

"What's that?" Dellet cried out, afraid.

Calian said, "Trees, Dad. Young rowan trees." Her voice was full of wonder and delight. But she did not sound surprised at what she had done.

Kanda said, "Open the bag, Sal." Dellet gave his wife a glare of anger, and then he shook his head. "Well, well, Sal girl. That's a lucky find, isn't it? There must have been more than you remembered left." Oatcakes, a rind of cheese, the waterskin half-full.

"I'm not eating those," said Calian.

"No, no, Calian," said Sal. "These are fine. These are the ones I made." She said, with something almost like happiness her voice, "Um, you can tell they're the ones I made because there's one of my hairs baked into this one."

Dellet gave his wife another glare of such anger. Then he laughed, and Kanda laughed. "You can tell you learned to bake from your mother, Sal."

"Put aside a portion for Morna," said Calian. Sal nodded. They poured water too for Morna. "She would have loved these trees," said Calian. A pause. Calian plucked a sprig of rowan, laid it by the food offering. Gray caterpillar twig, the leaves just unfurling from the bud in little long-snouted beast heads.

Calian broke off another twig, placed it beside the first, then a second, then a third. The third was bigger than the others, the leaves open wider and a richer green. "She's not dead, is she, Mum? It was her that Sal heard."

"I don't know," said Kanda.

I want her to be alive. But I don't want her to be alive. Not with them.

"Don't," said Sal. "Don't talk about it, Calian. That boy.... It was *Hunger* tricking me. I didn't hear Morna, I heard the wind, or a fox, or something. That boy...that woman...."

"You talked to him," said Calian. "Mum. You watched him hit Gella, heard how he spoke to her, and then you *talked* to him."

I was bound. I couldn't do anything else.

I was trying to humor him. Stop him getting worse. He stopped hitting her – ignored her completely – once I was talking to him, didn't he?

I've seen and heard him do far worse to a woman, Calian my love. He is evil, poisoned, that is what poisoned men do.

No.

Kanda said, "Yes, Calian, I knew what he is, I saw what he did to Gella, and then I sat and talked to him. And now Morna is gone."

Calian hissed. Rearranged the twigs. Got up, walked to the edge of the circle, sat with her father in silence. Sal stayed beside her mother, but she looked over at Calian, and then at the three twigs. The leaves on the twigs were autumn leaves, glorious red.

Sal said, "Those things he said to you about how you look. The things you said to him."

"Yes?" Sal was silent. Kanda said very gently after a moment, "My hair is graying, Sal. My breasts do sag. When my bleed is heavy…." Ruined a dress once, in public, half the farmers from the valley there for a baby's naming, Sal and Calian had punched their mother they were so embarrassed. Kanda pulled up her skirt to show the lines on the skin above her knee. "Geiamnyn is young and beautiful."

"They were such horrible things he said."

"Everything about Geiamnyn is horrible, Sal. He is poisonous. Poisoned. But everything he said then was true, Sal. Yes, I admit, it would be a fine thing to be young and perfect forever. But I'm aging and I've borne three children. What should I look like?"

One battle between them she remembered vividly. One of the great moments of her life.

Geiamnyn stood on the battlements of a high citadel, the world in flames behind him. Tyren, the ghost city, once beautiful beyond human imagining, it was built by giants, its houses were roofed in metal, it had been ruled once by a line of blind mad gentle white-bearded kings. The throne in the king's hall was made of shadows. The king cast no shadow. The crown of the Kings of Tyren was made of a single diamond, and to look at it too long was to see the whole course of one's life and death reflected. Geiamnyn had come to Tyren with an army sick with plague, rank with famine, his soldiers had torn the houses apart with their fingernails, butchered everything within. Geiamnyn had hanged the king from the highest tower of the citadel, the noose he used had been plaited from human skin. "My army is starving!" he had shouted. "Now they will feast! My soldiers are paupers! Now they will be rich!" Geiamnyn had burned the granaries, despoiled the rich country around Tyren, taken every scrap of wealth for himself. He ate gold and drank silver, shat precious stones. His soldiers ate the bloody dust.

"Who will fight me?" Geiamnyn shouted from the battlements of the citadel, smoke rising stinking behind. "I have destroyed all that lives in Tyren! Who will dare to fight me?" Stroking himself. Gasping on his violence.

Kanda and Palle stood beneath the battlements, the last two in Tyren who lived. Palle said, "I will fight him."

But Kanda said, "I am the stronger of us, Palle. I will fight him." So Kanda drew her sword, shouted up to Geiamnyn, "Come down, then, Geiamnyn, murderer, killer, sickness. I will fight you, and I will win." Geiamnyn stared down at her from the battlements. She saw that he was afraid to face her. His soldiers cheered the challenge met. He shouted, leapt from the battlement like a star falling, their swords met with a crash.

Not the first time they had fought. Not the last time.

The greatest time, the greatest battle of Kanda's life.

Geiamnyn's sword was like lightning. Kanda's sword was like gold light. Geiamnyn was grown so vast with his pleasures that he blocked the sun from the sky, the earth was dark night where he stood. Kanda was the strongest of the Six Swords of Roven, her strength and her skill at their noontide height. The walls of Tyren shook at the force of their battle. Geiamnyn cast Kanda back to fall to her knees – the walls trembled, stones fell shattered, cracks opened in the living rock. Kanda cast Geiamnyn back to stagger against the battlements of the citadel – the battlements fell in rubble around him like rain. Geiamnyn glowed with white light as they fought, his beauty was such it was dazzling, so beautiful he was that it was painful to look at him. Kanda glowed with all the light of glory, youth, righteous fury at Geiamnyn's sickness. He averted his eyes from her in pain at her splendor, the fire in her face that was pure and good.

Palle stood staring. Second of the Six Swords, the greatest and the strongest, save for Kanda only: his mouth hung open in wonder. Geiamnyn's soldiers stood staring. So glorious, so terrifying the battle that many sank to their knees, wept.

Geiamnyn struck Kanda, cut her, her blood ran hot and red. Yellow flowers and blue flowers grew in every spilled drop of her blood.

Kanda struck Geiamnyn, threw him back against the battlements, cut him. His blood was dry and rotten. Blight grew up in every spilled drop of his blood.

Geiamnyn struck Kanda in the face, set her ears ringing, her head spun so that she could not see. Geiamnyn's face ran with pleasure. He stank of his pleasure, he raised his sword high to finish her, his beauty was such that through her closed pained eyes he shone.

Kanda struck Geiamnyn in the chest. He did not have his fine bronze armor then, he wore a corselet of studded leather that gave before Kanda's stroke.

Geiamnyn fell back, his chest cut open from his navel to his throat. Just as one day Kanda's middle daughter would cut open his chest. His blood was dry, the blight that chokes down the wheat just when it is ready for harvest, the dust that is left in a dried-up stream. Kanda raised her sword, cut off his beautiful head.

Kanda stood before the broken battlements of Tyren, her sword raised to the sky. She held up Geiamnyn's head by his golden hair that was so fine and so shining. She shouted out her war cry. Once, twice, three times, she shouted. The broken stones reformed themselves. The burning towers rose from the rubble. The metal-roofed houses sprang up safe and strong. Geiamnyn's soldiers fled howling in terror from the city of Tyren. All but a handful, who knelt to Kanda, begged her to forgive them. "Queen, Wonder, Lady Who Outshines the Sun," they pleaded to her, "forgive us, redeem us, let us stay here in Tyren that shall be called ever after *City of the Bright Lady* and *City of Sunlight* and *City of Peace.*" Kanda shouted out her war cry for the fourth time and the fields around Tyren were rich with crops growing. At her fifth shout, the sky was filled with birds returning, swallows, swifts, wise ravens, white doves. At her sixth shout, the copper-roofed houses of Tyren were clean and well furnished, food cooked on the hearths.

For six days the people of Tyren feasted Kanda the Bright Lady. Then Kanda and Palle rode away together back to Roven.

"When you stood before the battlements in your victory, that was the most wonderful thing I have ever seen," Palle said.

I do not think I could fight like that now, or shout like that.

She thought: well…it would be nice if the bleed wasn't quite so heavy, and if I didn't fart so much, and if I didn't wet myself when I laugh, although that's a war wound from pushing out three fat babies so almost I should be proud of it. But the other changes, though, I don't regret.

CHAPTER FIFTEEN

It was dawn, and they must go on. In the darkness before dawn they had heard Morna crying, Ysarene's laughter. The boy Ty had shouted, "Come to play, Morn-Morn." Don't listen. Ignore it. Morna is dead. Accept that she is dead. Walk away and on. Sal clutched her hands to her ears. Calian raised her sword high, and the sounds were gone. The wound of the sun was the color of rose petals, softer than breathing, and Kanda felt it like a breath on the back of her neck. The sky in the west before them was blue shadow, cool to look at, the last stars clung there; against the indigo sky and the stars the dawn birds were wheeling, swifts come from the far south where the winds are red with sand, rooks flowing from their nests at the foot of the mountain. A single great star hung gold over the spearpoint of Mal Anwen. The sun mounted clear of the eastern horizon, Kanda felt its rays on her back, she turned to see the sky pale fire behind her, she turned to see the sun strike the spearpoint of Mal Anwen, free of cloud, turn it to pale fire itself. The dawn flowered on the slopes of the mountain, the pinewoods there were bathed in the dawn and warmed by it, a dancing rushing stream from the height of the mountain was a stream of silver and a ribbon of sunlight, the pine trees were perfumed black. A rock face flashed black toward the peak of the mountain, it was a mouth there carved smiling. Her shadow and her family's shadows fell long toward the mountain.

Sal said with wonder, "Mal Anwen is beautiful, Mum." Sal said firmly, "We'll rescue Morna, Mum. Get her back safe. I know it."

Kanda thought: you and Calian, yes. You two, now, if anything in the world can be done for Morna, you are the ones who will do it.

"We need to go over to the right, the northern slopes, there, you see, that rock face there?"

Calian squinted. "The gulley…there's…a stream running down? There, you mean?"

"Where the trees are thick, and then the gulley, yes, that's it, Calian." A deep cleft in the mountainside, where a stream had cut the rock deep. Thick pinewoods on either side of it, the gulley itself was a narrow valley really, itself thickly wooded, at the top of the gulley the stream burst out from the solid rock. At the mouth of the gulley, perhaps a third of the way up the mountain, the stream poured into a round lake that sat in a flat lap of rock. The soil was too thin there for pine trees, the lakeside was all grass and heather and gorse, the lake was bearded with wild irises.

"Elelan Mere," said Dellet.

The water of the lake was brilliant blue, Kanda remembered. So clear the stones at the lake bottom were visible. The name of the place meant: *joyful lake.*

"They mined copper up by the mere," Dellet said, "long ago now. That's what my grandfather told me. You can see the scars there, the workings, you see there just to the left of the lake, where that patch of gorse is? No, the left there, Calian. See it now? Merchants would come from a thousand miles to trade for the copper, my grandfather said. But the mine workings were so small, he said, the tunnels so narrow…they must have used children, he said."

"I didn't know that." Kanda shuddered. The caves and passageways there had seemed at first a safe hiding place. "We don't need to go near the mine workings. We keep to the right of the lake."

"Copper is for bronze," said Calian.

"Yes?" Then Sal said, "Oh. Yes."

Dellet said, "It looks near, but it must be an hour's walk still. Stop yakking, girls. It's odd," he said, "but I don't feel tired in the slightest. That magic you and your sword worked, Cal-flower…."

Calian said, "Thank the trees, Dad."

There was another terrible moment when they found another mass of whortleberry bushes, Calian began delighted, sang like a sparrow: "Hey, Morn, wherties—" broke and stopped and looked like she would cut the bushes down with her sword as an axe. The berries shriveled, the leaves withered, the earth was dry and cracked. Calian breathed out very slowly, like she was counting in her head to calm her breathing. "Wherties," Calian said. The berries were ripe and fat, the leaves glossy, the earth soft.

"Cal—"

"It's all right, Mum." She pointed, "Look, a hawk! No, a buzzard? No. Not a kite, I don't recognize—"

It hung in the air very close and low, absolutely still. The blur of its wings was so fast they seemed still.

"A gyrfalcon," said Kanda, awed. It was gone so high upward, straight up, circling, and then it was still again far up against the sky.

Kanda said, "It lives in the north, on the ice. I have never seen one wild before. Because they live in the far north they are so used to the cold they can fly higher than the stars. They can look down on the sun and the moon. They have seen behind the sun and the moon."

"It's racing! It's…. Look, there, the— A crow, look, it's going to catch that crow!"

A darker, smaller shape. The crow called in panic, dived, circled. The gyrfalcon rushed like cloud shadow. Struck, struggled, it tumbled in the air and its prey was twisting alive and liquid in its grip. "It's going to lose it! No! Hold on, falcon, hold on!" It came down in the whortleberry bushes near them, unafraid in a mad beating of falcon and crow wings.

"Oh," said Calian. "Oh. Oh."

Kanda looked at Sal, questioning. Sal shrugged.

The lake. Force through dark trees damp and resin-running, the day was hot, the trees and the earth steamed. Stink so strong, green, living, wet mold rot that was not blight but was whole and good. Great deep softness of pine mast beneath their feet. Between the trees the ground was bracken, waist-high, luminous against the shadows and the black trunks. Squirrels ran in the trees, arguing. "*Ratatatusk*," the squirrels shouted. The sky was lost in the treetops. Slide down the bare hills running, breathe deep, swim into the cool shadows of the pinewoods, climb the mountain's deep roots.

Sal said, "It smells like winter."

Calian said, "Next winter, we could decorate all these trees." In her eyes the gyrfalcon was still flying. She had put the sword away in her belt. They wound their way up and had to scramble over a fallen tree wallowing in the bracken, the sunlight burst in in a thin line of silver where the canopy was broken, "It's like a wall of light," Calian said, in the light a thousand insects were dancing. They wound their way up and had to scramble over a long hump of rock erupted from the bracken, thick with moss and yellow lichen, "It's like a bit of the mountain's bones," said Calian. "Like the way you can feel Morna's backbone through her skin."

Each time, Kanda said, "Look carefully, Sal, Calian."

"Carvings!"

On the fallen tree trunk, circles within circles. Ripples in a pool on a calm day when a pebble is dropped in. On the hump of rock, zigzags. Lightning. Storm waves.

"This isn't a bad place at all," said Dellet.

Kanda said, "No."

Force through dark trees damp and resin-running, wade through bracken, trip, scramble, the sky opened before them suddenly, the lake before them too blue. Dead rock around it, a lip between the trees and the water, then yellow irises, then the riot of heather and gorse. The water was utterly still, like a skin.

Kanda said, "If you kneel on the bank here, you can see the mountain peak reflected in the center of the lake. But don't touch the water."

"Why not?"

Sal said, "It's poisoned. No fish."

Calian said, "*They* poisoned it?"

"No, no. The mine works. That made the lake and made the water blue." At the far end the mountain's flanks rose very sheer, with the scars of tunnels and pits.

Sal shuddered. "It's like.... It looks like it's diseased. Like that beggar man with leprosy."

"You remember him?" Well, Kanda thought, I suppose it's not a thing a child forgets.

"When was that? I don't remember."

"You weren't born, or maybe you were a baby, Cal."

"Be grateful you didn't see him," Sal said. She stared at the workings, itched her face. "It's horrible," she said.

"You can find the tools the miners used," said Dellet. "My grandfather brought one back. Used it sometimes himself, it was that well made. Stone axes. To hack metal out of living rock." He shook his head in wonder. "Ruins of where they lived, too, little huts, they lived in. And graves." He frowned. "This, here, this is the bad place. The mines, not the mountain."

They went right around the lake, Sal staring off at the workings for as long as they were visible. "It's pleasant walking on the flat for a while at least," Dellet said, "hey, Sal?" The stream came down to meet the lake, tumbling over stones in a tiny waterfall, its banks were deep in cress and mint, this was where the yellow irises grew. The stream water was not poisoned, it was cold, sweet. The stones of its bed were brown-gold, streaked green with waterweed fur-soft. A dragonfly hung a moment over the stream, so large they could hear its wings. It dived, circled, dived, vanished. "It hunts just like the gyrfalcon," said Calian. There were more carvings on a stone by the stream, round cups in the rock with rings rippled around them. They climbed beside the stream. The gulley was very steep. Sometimes they had to climb in the stream itself. That was hard, funny at first splashing, just for a moment, until thinking about Morna came back. Then their boots and their clothes were soaking, Sal slipped and cut her leg. The gulley was much steeper and harder to climb than Kanda remembered it.

"You'll get your sword," said Sal, "then you'll kill those things, and you'll get Morna back."

Her blood was washing in the stream, she'd smeared mud on her face, her hair was damp with sweat. She ran up the streambed like a wild goat. Kanda said, "Yes."

Dellet grunted, but said nothing.

The gulley widened, flattened a little, a narrow valley, yes, with high sheer rock walls topped in pine trees, the stream cutting deep through heavy green stuff. Calian shouted because some of it was thorny. They had to splash through the stream and wade through the green stuff, it was colder up here on the mountain, more exposed, the rock walls fell away so that they were scrabbling up the flank of the mountain with the stream running fast away from them, soon going higher they would come to the place where the stream burst out from the innards of the mountain. A great mass of birds was wheeling around the mountain's peak.

A movement in the green stuff ahead of them. Sal cried out, "Oh no. No."

Kanda said, "Hush."

A deer.

A white hind.

She leapt the stream, as fast as the gyrfalcon perhaps. The same white sudden wild flash of movement and yet of utter stillness.

Calian said, "Oh. Oh."

It was time. Kanda looked where the hind had leapt and there was the stone she had set there the first time she came to Mal Anwen. Round, smooth, black, a cup mark on its flat top.

"I have to go on alone now. To fetch the sword. You must stay here, you— You three."

"I'm not staying here, you're not going on without me, Mum."

Kanda gave Sal her stern look. "I must go alone, Sal."

"Listen to your mother, Sal," said Dellet. "I don't like it either, but…if that's what she says now, you do it."

She thought Calian would be the worst. *I'll come, Mum, I'll help you, defend you, I fought with you twice, Mum. You bitch, Mum, you think I can't fight like you can, you're wrong.* But Calian had seen the stone that Kanda had left, Calian knew, Calian nodded. "I'll protect them, Mum," Calian said.

Kanda went to the stone. No lichen, no moss, no insect litter or bird droppings. The print of the hind's dainty foot beside it, the only trace the hind had left. "I need to borrow your knife, Calian."

Calian said nothing, knew, passed it.

Kanda set the knife to her right palm, cut deep.

"You can't do that—" Dellet began. As disgusted as Geiamnyn had been by her gray hairs.

"Hush," Calian said.

The blood must go to the stone in offering, and then the stone must go with a clatter of stone-on-stone and stone-in-water, the stone must go to the stream. Roll away fall away far down the mountain into Elelan Mere.

"Stay here. Whatever happens."

Calian sat where the stone had been with her sword on her knees. Her face was reflected in the blade. She looked so old and so young. "Go, Mum," Calian said. "I'll protect them."

The cut in Kanda's palm was very deep.

She went on up the gulley only a little way, a few steps, a short spear's distance. Her family was gone, she was alone on the mountain. Three steps, four, five, six steps. Seven steps. Eight steps. Nine steps.

Another stone. The blood must go to the stone in offering. But this stone would not go to the stream. She turned, all the country she had made her home lay spread before her, the rolls of the hills were like the roll of a bed coverlet over her children sleeping, the curve and rise and crags and valleys were like the flesh and bone and hair of Dellet's body sprawled open to her arms for love. The River Wenet and her own valley was a thin, frail, sliding thing.

She smeared her blood on the offering stone.

She said the words.

The beast rose up from the stream with bared teeth.

As tall as a man, faceless, shapeless, a little, a very little, like the figure of a man sketched out of clotted blood. A mouth on what might be its head, a mouth on what might be its belly, a mouth on what might be the mound of its sex. Wolf teeth bared three times with slaver dripping. No eyes but it looked at her hateful. No hands but it had claws that could grip her throat, tear her open to rip her heart from her chest.

The mouth of its sex spoke to her: "You have returned. You swore you would not return."

"I need my sword now."

The mouth of its head spoke to her: "No."

"I know, my friend. But I need the sword now."

"I swore," the mouth of its belly said. "I promised you."

Old bindings. An oath truly sworn. Promises made, promises broken.

I swear it, my Lord of Roven. On my right hand and on my sword, I swear.

I promise myself to you, Dellet, I shall be your wife and you shall be my husband.

I promise, Del-my-heart, that I won't go to Mal Anwen.

You promised she'd be safe, Mummy. You promised you'd protect us.

I promise I'll never leave you for one moment, never, ever, babies, little ones.

You promised, Mummy, you'll play with me when you've finished the washing up, you said!

"Give me the sword, my friend," Ikandera Thygethyn said.

The beast hissed at her. Growled. It had no eyes and no face but it stared at her in pain.

"I need my sword. This is a different time now." Ikandera Thygethyn said, "I created you. From my own blood that I spilled here, I formed you. I gave you a mind, a voice to speak, I gave you claws and teeth and fierce strength. I gave you a treasure, I bade you keep it safe here on this mountain. I created you, so now I command you to give me that which I once trusted to you to guard."

"I don't know what to do," the mouth of its belly moaned. The beast cowered, writhed in pain. "I cannot give it to you," the mouth of its sex moaned, tormented. "I don't know what to do." The mouth of its head wailed, "You made me swear I would never let you take back your sword. *If I beg for it, plead, weep; whatever the reason – do not give me back my sword*, you said."

Its shape twisted. It grew vast. Its three mouths opened in chasms. Wings unfolded. Its claws were long as spear shafts.

Teeth ripped into Kanda's hands. Worried at her, burrowed deep. Red pain. White pain. Mauling her, holding her frozen, too much pain to think. Its bulk, like a tower crashing over her, its mouths dripping poison. Impregnable, the guard she had set over her sword; implacable, its one purpose to keep the sword hidden.

All three of its mouths howled in fire: "*Kill me, if I ever try to take back my sword. Swear it to me.* That's what you said."

Kanda fell, rolled, bloody hands scrambling in the earth. One arm struck something, jarring bruising pain in her bones over the tearing pain in her skin. Rolled, crawled backward, insect crawling panicked helpless. Fire in her eyes in her hair, breathing fire, drowning. She thought: I am killed by my own hopes. The beast reared, its claws pounded her body, caught her, threw her over and over, trampled her down relentless. Smash of stone-pain into her hip. She gasped in air briefly, briefly before the fire flowed. Grind against stone-pain hard to steal away her gasped breath. Claws flaying her back open, claws breaking her arms and her legs.

Once, when she first came to the valley, Ben Apple Tree's youngest son had fallen into the Wenet swollen with fast floodwater, been washed away and drowned with the river knee-high and the bank within a child's easy reach.

She could open one eye almost, enough to see the beast in a circle of fire, like a shape seen with fists pressed into closed eyes, red and black and black and red. Children's game: *don't do that, Calian! You'll, I don't know, you'll push your eyes into your head and die or something.* It drew back, raised itself on wings beating the air to hurt her, drew ready all of its clenched teeth.

Beg to it. Like begging a child: *I know I said never. But this is, this is different. You don't understand: when grown-ups, sometimes, when they say things….*

It lunged. Fell upon her. The weight, weight of her blood clotted, bore her down, sank her into the earth. Her mouth was full of soil and rock shards. Cut the inside of her mouth. Spat, gasped, choked, and its heat was tearing her to pieces. Withered her from her bones out. She clawed back. Tiny against the vastness. Its fire washed over her, warm and pleasant, stinging her face sweet. Her fingers dragged over it hopelessly. She tried in despair to bite at it. She threw soil and rock shards at it.

I know what I told you. But this is different. I didn't mean…. If I really needed it….

Her hands must be a sword, then. Her fingers dragged at it. Sank in. Grip into it. Grip it like breaking soil. Tear it apart like tearing meat. You remember, Kanda, on the shore, what you did that day? Geiamnyn's favorite tale of the Six of Roven. Do that to it. You made this thing and you held it to that promise, and now you must destroy it for keeping faith.

Her hands were swords. Her hands were axes to break the black earth. With teeth and nails she met it, beast fighting beast. She devoured it. She rent it open, she made it nothing. A ruin beyond repairing. A chasm, a void in the world where it had been. A howl of grief that rang hollow. A hiss, a whisper of fear, of sorrow. Nothing.

Nothing.

Nothing.

Her blood smeared on the offering stone, an ache in her hand where she had cut her palm deep. A tumble of rocks, green stuff growing. The stream ran fast, as thin as a child's wrist. She walked on, four steps, five, six. A sheer face of rock, at the height of her shoulder the stream burst out from the mountain's innards, rushed down the rock. A pool where it had eaten the rock away with the weight of its impact – such a strong, terrible, relentless thing, a stream! All the rock face and the pool overgrown with green stuff, moss, lichen. The wet stone gleamed like new metal. A cup mark and a ring mark carved in the rock face at the height of Kanda's eyes. A zigzag, like lightning or like a deer's antlers, was carved at the height of her sword belt.

"I'm sorry," she said to the beast she had created and betrayed.

She placed her bloody hands on the rock face. The blood must go to the stone. The stream flowed over the rock face: the stone must go to the stream and the stream must go to the lake. The lake was called *Joyful* because of the riches it had created out of children's toil, and she had not known that when she came here to hide the sword.

She pressed her hands hard against the rock face. Pushed. The mountain roared like thunder. The mountain roared and broke. The rock face opened in a doorway. The stream was the path. At the end of the path was the sword that waited.

She said the words that must be spoken.

She stepped through into the mountain.

Thus did her world end.

CHAPTER SIXTEEN

Gentle darkness, and the stream was the light for her. A tunnel as wide as her arms outstretched, the roof just higher than the top of her head. She remembered, now, how easily she had opened the rock. Walked her way singing into the mountain.

Just dark, and the water. She had not remembered that the way was so long. Her family behind her – had they heard the battle? Seen something, shadows, flashes, felt the ghost-breath of claws and fire and wings? They would be frightened, Dellet would mutter beneath his breath, cursing, poor man. Calian would grip her sword, want to be part of it. Start to her feet and Sal would say no, stay, she said. Morna would— She thought: Morna was not born, years and years before she was born, when I last came to this place. I thanked him then, my guardian beast, for keeping the sword so well.

The passageway turned sharply to the left, to the right, to the left, to the right, to the left again. Zigzag. Maze. If she had had time, she remembered, she had wanted to make a labyrinth to fill the mountain. A long curve in the dark that was pleasant to walk somehow. The stream was the light, the walls were glossy as glass. She could almost see her face reflected. Her hands as she traced the wall.

Narrowing. The roof closing down, the walls closing in. Bent double, arms clasped at her sides: this had been easier then. Her knees creaked. The bending made her fart. Seven, eight, nine steps, doubled over, her back aching. Walking in the streambed; the light was blotted out by her splashing shuffling feet.

Hit of stone-smell damp-smell. The tunnel opened into a cavern. She had not made the cavern. Huge as a feasting hall, more splendid than any feasting hall for it was roofed in gemstones, floored in gemstones, columns rising from the floor and columns falling from the roof. The walls of the cavern were lined with figures: dancers, leapers, tumblers, mumming, spinning, wandering. Faceless, shapeless; many-bodied, many-headed, or without form: it was from these she had found the idea of her guardian, his shapeless bodied shape. They glittered, gleamed like wild water, cast in stone they flowed alive like water, changed their shape. They were marvelous beyond any power of making, even the Lord and Lady of Roven could not shape such things. The mountain itself had created these things.

Water spread ankle-deep on the cavern floor. It was as still as the lake *Joyful*. The water was absolutely clear.

Veins of copper ran all around the cavern. She felt the metal like blood pumping. Yes, she thought, the copper for Calian's sword has been hacked from this mountain.

Like a baby being born, she thought, the way the copper was ripped from the bowels of the mountain. Why they mined it using children.

The mountain stirred at her presence here. Hush, sleep, I have not come to tear your riches from you. I came here once before, remember, I entrusted you with something. You did not want it, I do not think. I have come to reclaim it. Do not be afraid. Sleep. She waded through the still water. Her tread did not make ripples. She walked through the water as through across dry rock. The dancers on the walls, the leapers, the tumblers – they did not notice her passing.

At the far end of the cavern was a second passageway, tall and wide enough for three men to walk abreast. She had not made this passageway, but some human hand had shaped it. Her hands traced patterns carved into the walls. There must once have been a way in to the cavern that she had not found. Thirty steps, the passage curved to the left, ten steps, the passage curved to the right. Six steps, and she came out into a small chamber, round and domed. The ground here was dry rock. A shaft of light came in from a single crack in the rock high in the center of the domed roof. She had taken the three offering stones from here. The last, the fourth, remained in the back of the cave.

Her mouth tasted of blood. Her right hand burned.

She crouched, pressed her bloodied hand to the stone.

The stone sang with joy. Beneath the stone, her sword sang.

She lifted the stone, rolled it away across the cave floor. A dark pit beneath, she reached in, a heavy bundle wrapped in leather that was awkward to pull out. She was trembling as she undid the binding cords, so eager her hands slipped on the knots, she thought for one terrible moment she would not be able to get it untied, would have to drag it as it was out of the passages, ask Calian if she could borrow her sword. She thought absurdly of cutting the bindings with Dellet's pocketknife. The wrapping was tough leather from a bull's hide, the binding cords were deerskin, they would not easily give. She wrestled with the knots and hurt her fingers doing it. She hated the feeling of unpicking knots.

The knots untied. She took one long trembling breath. Her heart was singing. She did not want to open the wrapping, because this moment was so wondrous.

She folded back the leather. Her armor lay there, and her helmet, and her sword.

She gripped the sword, lifted it, drew it from its sheath.

The cave was filled with light, with singing.

She thought: mine. The sword cried to her: yes!

She put on the leather corselet. She put on the helmet with its great plume of red horsehair. She put on the sword belt.

She stood, held the sword. Her heart was overflowing.

Ikandera Thygethyn walked through the passageway, the passageway was floored in gold and walled in diamond. In the cavern the water boiled as she walked through it. The dancers and the leapers and the mummers danced and leapt and tumbled for her. Their cheers filled the air. Silver bells and silver drums and silver war trumpets. She walked through the narrow tunnel she had made and the tunnel was as wide as a roadway. She could have run the whole of the distance in two heartbeats, so fast her feet did not touch the ground, but she made herself walk slowly, carefully, counted her breathing, every little while she had to stop to remind herself all this was real. How long she had dreamed and feared this time would come!

What will they say, she thought, when they see me?

If they did not know where I had gone, she thought, they would not recognize me. She had feared that she would feel wrong after a lifetime of farmer's dresses. But the armor and the helmet were like her own skin back around her.

Ikandera Thygethyn stepped through the doorway out of the mountain. She said the words and the doorway closed. The stream burst through a crack in the sheer rock face. The stream faltered, ceased to flow.

Oh. No. She thought, no. She put her hands on the rock face and the stream burst out stronger, faster. Clean sweet water. Wash away the copper-poison in *Joyful Lake*.

The shattered remnants of the guard beast lay at her feet. Dried blood, gently crumbling. A feast for the birds and the insects, and the blood would nourish the soil. The plants here would grow strong. Flies buzzed, birds swooped to catch them, the dragonfly hunted. The gyrfalcon, she thought, would be hunting somewhere overhead. Out of my blood, she thought, I created the guard beast, I gave it life. I knew, she thought, it knew, that this day would come when I destroyed it. I made it, she thought sadly, just weak enough I knew I could destroy it. And the sword, she thought, the sword must be protected. If Geiamnyn had come, or that other one, if they had found it....

If Calian, she thought, had come wandering here and found it....

She stepped down the mountainside. The sky seemed heavier, darker blue and it was much later in the day. A hot day, as it had promised, a purple tinge to the edge of seeing. The air smelled heat-tired. Fear seized her that they had gone, given up on her and abandoned her on the mountain, days, months, years past. Winters come, winters gone. She stared around as if to see time had passed in lifetimes, the mountain itself changed, reshaped by snow and wind. She was changed. All must be changed.

She thought in panic: I never went back down into the valley of the Wenet back to a young farmer whom I loved and who loved me. I came here to give up my sword but I did not give up my sword. The world before her was Dellet's coarse body, his bones, his fat, the trees his thick hair. She thought: I did go back to him, I did give up the sword, I did, I did. I didn't want to have to take it back, I set the guard in all the honesty of my heart filled with love for the life I could lead with him. She went farther down the mountain, desperate where before she had been glorious, only a few steps sick and terror-trembling – they were there, sitting, waiting!

Dellet sat on a rock looking out over the landscape, gazing, yearning. He was looking far off in the direction of their house. Sal sat next to him, her head resting on his shoulder. Her red hair ran down his back. It was as if Kanda was seeing herself sitting quiet with her head on her husband's shoulder. The helmet was suddenly very heavy, the armor awkward and stupid to wear. Her heart ached.

Calian stood with her sword drawn. A sentry, a guard over them. She too was looking away over the land falling before them, but her body was set like a wolf.

Calian saw her first. No: Calian felt the sword, saw her mother only afterward. For a moment Calian's face was a wolf also, snarling, her own sword raised, her body poised to leap into the fight. For too many men, Kanda thought, that wolf's snarl would be the last thing they saw before they died. Kanda said, "It's me," just as Sal said in wonder: "Mum?"

All the world was silence.

Dellet said, in wonder, "Kanda?" He said, "I thought you'd look… frightening." *Stupid*, she heard as well, hiding behind *frightening*. And *wrong*. And *not like my wife*. "But you look…."

Reflected in his eyes, Kanda saw herself.

Dellet said, "It sounds mad, but... When I think about you, in my head you've always looked like this."

CHAPTER SEVENTEEN

Bronze helmet trimmed with silver, the cheek pieces worked with silver spirals, circles within circles within circles, twisting and flowing without beginning or end. Eyes, mouths, eddies in deep water, birds wheeling. No nose-guard, open to show her face. It rose to a tall point at the crown of her head, a teardrop of bronze, from the top of the point the red plume erupted, the horsehair long to hang down her back. It was thickly lined in red silk and red leather, the chin-strap was red leather worked with silver and gold.

Black leather corselet, plated in bronze, with a war skirt to her knees. The laces of the corselet were red leather, bright against the black.

Sword belt of black leather studded golden. Bronze scabbard worked with silver, flowing lines so the scabbard was like liquid.

Black sword. The hilt was undecorated, the grip black leather molded to the grip of her hand. The pommel was the head of a snarling beast with red eyes and silver teeth. Black fire ran down the blade.

CHAPTER EIGHTEEN

Calian looked at the sword for a long time. Held her own bronze sword up to meet it. Calian's sword looked like a flower, beside Ikandera's sword. "It's.... You can kill them with that?" Calian said. "That sword can kill them?"

Kanda moved the sword through the air. The blade was bright and very silent. "Do you think this sword can kill Geiamnyn, Calian?" she said.

"It feels like...like being in ice-cold water," said Calian. "Jumping in the river in midwinter, maybe. Being near it. When you move it." She said, "It...it eats the light in. With that sword...I think you could kill anything."

"You killed a dragon with it," said Dellet. Awed. Loving.

"I...." Anguish came over Kanda. So quick, after the joy! But she could not lie to them. "Not with this sword. That was another sword I used then. I did not have this sword then."

"You had two swords like this?" Calian was a young girl, not a warrior, when she said that, more like Morna than Sal.

"Not...not like this." Remember. Oh, remember! She saw it there, in Calian's sword, perhaps, or in Calian's fierce eager face. "The Lord of Roven formed me from good sown earth and wildfire and red autumn berries, first of the Six; the Lady of Roven set a sword of gold and silver and water and starlight in my waiting hand. Iath, that sword was called: *Kind Strength.* That sword killed a dragon, saved five children from slavery, was never drawn when questing after the White Hind and the Black Bull. That sword...." Tears in her eyes, her voice choking. Remember! That day, when the Lady held out the sword for me, the best, the most beautiful day. "That sword...." Darkness. She closed her eyes, too painful, too empty. Time passes. All must pass and change. I said that to Sal only a few months ago when Morna broke something, a cup or a bowl, most things get broken if you like them enough to use them, I said, that's how life is. "That sword…."

Dellet said, "It's all right, Kanda, love. Whatever it is."

Kanda said, "What are we doing standing here talking? We should leave here, find somewhere to rest. You've been sitting out here for hours in the heat. What am I thinking?"

"Kanda, love…."

"We're fine, Mum," Calian said. "But the other sword, Mum? *Kind Strength*?"

"Iath was broken and I have this sword instead," said Kanda. "That's all. And this sword, Calian, can kill anything, can kill Geiamnyn and Ysarene, where the sword Iath could not."

I cut off his head with Iath, held his severed head high in triumph – he deserved that, his victims had suffered enough they needed to see it, it was a shameful thing to do but still after everything I rejoice in it – I threw his head down in the dust for the dogs to eat. And still he lived! Five days he lay rotting, mauled, flyblown, the crows pecked and shat over him. And he got up in the darkness, crept away in his rot, healed himself back to being beautiful and fled away. He laughed when next I saw him: "That pretty sword, too pretty to harm anything!"

But this sword: this sword will kill him.

"I can believe it, looking at that sword," said Calian. She shivered.

"We can fight later, if you want," Kanda said brightly and quickly. "Try you against it, see how you manage."

Calian said, "I— Maybe. No. Yes."

They began to walk down the mountain back toward the lake. Harder and easier going, slithering down the gulley with the stream dancing with them. The water sang, helped their going, washed their bodies fresh. Late afternoon now, hot heavy summer's rot-days, not quite building to break in storm. Kanda felt the sky and the earth sing to her, joyful, you are you are you are you are Ikandera Thygethyn. And yet there was a great shame in it, a sorrow in her, my children's lifetime and more, I dreamed or feared this moment, coming here to take up my sword, my heart's dim yearning, my oath never to come here – and it is done. And now we walk back down the mountain, I am Ikandera Thygethyn, it is done. It felt the same kind of pain she felt when her children crowded round her hugging her, *love you love you, Mum*, and she felt...shame, obscure and almost obscene deep inside her, that they loved her so much. She thought: my armor is comfortable but hot to wear, my helmet makes my hearing muffled, it feels good to have my sword hanging beside me, it does not feel wrong or strange. I thought it might feel wrong.

She thought, oddly, of the time when she had first felt Sal kick within her hard enough to be certain it was the baby quickening. She had thought then: the world is changed and remade, the sun should dance in the sky, the moon and the stars should shine in midday at midsummer, every stone in the fields should cry out as I pass, "Kanda, you have a child within you! Joy to you! The world is good!" She had thought all the world would stare at her as at a creature of wonder. The world went on unchanged, she herself sometimes would be caught up with the cows and the farm, stop thinking with wonder that she was pregnant, she would think: how could I forget, for one brief moment, that I am pregnant? It should be shouted in the sky with my every step.

She thought, sadly, of the young soldier she had once fought beside, who had not understood why the world was not changed and he was not changed after he had first killed a man in battle. "*No one even noticed*," he had said. "*At the feast a girl poured me a cup of mead like...like she didn't see it in me.*"

She was silent, thinking these things, and her family walked silent with her.

The lake was coming up below them, and the water did look less blue, more like good healthy water, she could imagine fish coming to live in the lake now, a kingfisher brilliant in the pine trees, watercress and lilies and mint growing up thick. Children and young lovers coming here to swim. Trees would grow thick over the mine workings, the place would be at peace. Joyful Lake.

"We can stop here a little," she said. "Just to catch ourselves. Then—" She broke off, confused suddenly. And Dellet said, "Kanda… now you have your armor, your sword, what are we— What are you going to do, Kanda? How will you rescue Morna?"

She wanted to say with harsh bitterness: I don't know, Dellet, I find them and I kill them and I rescue Morna and I protect our children, and then I rebuild our house from its rubble because Ysarene will have ground it to dust so that not one stone is left whole, I call our cows back to life, I make our garden green again, I remake our bed, our hearth fire, our cook pots and our clothes, and then I suppose I comfort our daughters, rebuild their trust in life, when I've done that I can maybe sit at rest for one evening before the bread needs baking and the cows need calving and the fields need plowing and Cal grows again and needs new clothes and Morna breaks Sal's third favorite plate, I don't know, Dellet, you're a grown man yourself, what do you think I should do? You have lived nearly fifty years in this world, Dellet, yes the Wenet valley is a peaceful place, yes you have never traveled farther in your life than the headman's hall at Aranth and the headman there is a good man like you, but even so, Dellet, as a man who has lived nearly fifty years in this world you must know that Morna is likely dead by now, and what Geiamnyn will have done to her if she still lives, and that everything is ruined now and it's not easy and we can't go back.

But she took a long breath before she said any of it, one breath, two breaths, three breaths, held her voice hopeful, hoping: "I will kill them and I will bring Morna back to the farmhouse. That is what I will do." Her family looked at her and looked away and she thought they must see the lies. See her bitterness. She thought: it's shouted in the sky: *you're lying!* But then she saw they looked away because they believed her.

And she thought: my loves: thank you.

Sal said, "You'll find them, then? You know how to find them? I suppose you would...."

Dellet said, "Of course your mother will find them. Like a wolf guarding her pups, your mother, when it comes to you three."

Calian's eyes and Kanda's eyes met over Dellet's bowed head. Weary, shattered, but he was such a good, kind man still.

Oh, Del-my-heart, I do not need to find them. They have waited for me to find my sword, and now they will come to find me.

Kanda looked around the mountain, at the lake. At the sky. And in the north a band of cloud was coming, men were fighting in the clouds all dark and vast.

"We will stop here for the night, I think."

They will come in the night. It is better that we wait for them.

Dogs, wolves, wild beasts: but I am Ikandera Thygethyn, I will not run, they can run howling in the dark for me.

"We could go on awhile yet," said Dellet. "Couldn't we?" He didn't say, *get away from Mal Anwen.*

Calian's face and Sal's face were set grave. "The mine workings," said Sal. "We can wait – shelter there, do you think, Mum?"

Calian said, shocked, "But...the children there!"

Sal said, "Yes, Calian. The children there."

Calian put her hand on her sword hilt. Thought. Nodded. "Yes. Very well. That will be a good place."

Dellet looked at all three in bleak confusion. Then he stumped away a little into the pinewood. They watched him grope around, searching. He came back, said, "Cal-flower, can I have the use of your sword? Just quickly."

"Yes, Dad. I suppose."

Kanda thought of Sal carrying out a dead frog once that Morna had found, carrying it by the farthest tips of her fingers, her arm so stretched out she looked like she would split. There was crashing and a bit of swearing, Dellet came back carrying a stout pine branch as long and thick as his forearm.

"It's not a sword," he said. "But then, Cal-flower will tell me I couldn't use a sword to save my life. Can we make a fire, Kanda, or will that be too dangerous? Only I'd rather...." He gave the sword awkwardly back to his daughter, tried to smile, "I'd rather see you all three, rather than...I want to see your faces," he said. "Not the dark."

"We can make a fire," said Kanda.

"I'll get the wood then. There's lots of good wood. It'll smell fine, hey, girls? Like midwinter, didn't you say? And it burns pretty, does pinewood."

"He fought the cattle thieves that time," said Sal when her father was out of hearing. "He was as brave as any of them. He frightened off a bull that was coming at me once, do you remember? And he was always so...he was never worried that you were strong, Mum. He always says he wants us to be strong and fierce. 'More like your mother, less like me.' He says that all the time."

Kanda thought: I know. It breaks my heart too, little ones.

But Dellet got the fire built up beautifully, tucked in a mine passage hollowed out with rocks around to cradle it. The light would be half-hidden, they could sit sheltered with the rock to protect them at their backs, an overhang giving cover above them. A narrow place where they could not be surrounded, the four of them could hold it against many. If they could fight.

"It's a good place, Dellet," Kanda said. "A very good place, well chosen, Del-my-heart."

He shrugged and looked away. "Seemed an all right place. Sheltered." The mine passage was small, child-sized, ran only a little way back, Sal said, before it was blocked. She had found a flint knife blade, also child-sized, laid carefully before the blockage. It was too small for Sal to hold properly but she took it in preference to Calian's pocketknife.

The mine was just above the lake. A scramble up the rock face to the right of the stream gulley, and a narrow split in the rock led into a bowl-shaped fissure, the walls pitted with tunnels and shallow gaping holes where copper-bearing rock had been hacked out. Humps in the turf showed where buildings had once stood in the shelter of the fissure, to store the copper or to shelter the workers when storms came. A cow's skull had been placed carefully in the entrance to a tunnel so small only a tiny child of Morna's age could have worked it. Dellet looked sick at the tunnels. Reached his arm into one, shook his head in despair. "The mountain, and this place.... You swore to me never to come here, Kanda. Because of this place. The copper for some of the tools we use on the farm must have been mined here. This is the worst place I've ever been."

Then you are lucky beyond words, Del-my-heart.

No, Kanda thought, that's unfair. I have seen many terrible things, and this is a terrible place.

"The fire smells like midwinter, Dad," Sal said.

"It's sheltered," said Dellet. "That's the main thing. You should have that pocketknife, Sal." He put his head in his hands and wept. "My old pocketknife! Sal, oh, Sal. I'm sorry, I'm so sorry."

Sal said, her voice strong, "I have this flint knife, Dad. Don't worry about me."

They waited, they waited, they waited, but the evening came but nothing came with it. No sign or feel of Geiamnyn or Ysarene or of the other who was only emptiness. He must be near somewhere, Kanda thought. He must be. But the evening came clear, the clouds were banked far to the north. The birds sang the evening chorus. Many birds. They sang very sweet. The fire burned clear, dry wood that gave no smoke. The sword was a shieldwall for them, the helmet was a shieldwall, she was Ikandera Thygethyn, the enemy would not come. Kanda crawled a little way up the rock face, waited silent until she felt a life near and timid. A hare, stretching itself to a flat place in the rock, nibbling at the heather. Its black eyes were afraid, it could tell something was near that was a danger to it. Kanda crouched very still holding her breath, spoke calm silent words in her mind. The hare softened. Just a little. Kanda had a smooth round stone in her hand. A pebble from the mine workings: offering stone, child's secret treasured token. White, as the hare would have been in winter. She threw the stone, struck the hare hard enough to stun it. Caught it up, she had been so near to the hare it should never have come if she had not been Ikandera Thygethyn and if her children had not been hungry, dashed it hard on the rock to kill it. Brought it down and Sal sighed over it, Calian's lip wobbled, both girls licked their lips as Dellet set to skinning it.

"Is this safe? I mean, to cook it? Won't they…smell it?"

"They can wait, all three of them," said Kanda. "I want to eat. We need to eat. They have taunted me and hurt me, they can wait until I've had my fill of a meal." She sounded so firm, like Morna sometimes did with her certainty.

"It's good," Calian said when it was done.

"Very good."

"Thanks, Mum."

"Thank the poor hare."

They buried the guts and the skin and the bones in one of the mine tunnels. "I'd leave you meat, too, children," Kanda said, "but I can't spare a mouthful, I have hungry children of my own who must be fed. I'm sorry." The mine children made no answer, but she thought: they dug the copper for Calian's sword, they gave Sal that knife blade.

The evening drew to gloaming. The twin stars Irulth were in the east, one red, one bronze. "There was only the red star once," said Kanda. "The bronze star its companion rose one evening, no one could say where it had come from. It is the brighter, see, the bronze star? The red star leans on it. One day perhaps the red star will fade, leaving the bronze star alone there." Irulth is *gate*. So once there was not a gate there, and one day there would not be a gate again.

"A shooting star!" said Sal. "Look!"

"I didn't see it," said Calian. "Boo. I never see them." A little later she said, "A bat!" and Sal said, "I didn't see it. Boo again." "But listen," said Calian, "can you hear them?" "I can hear them," Sal said. Dellet said, "I can't hear them," and the girls said together, "That's because you're going deaf, Dad."

Nobody said Morna's name. She was around them like the night was around them. So there was no need to say her name.

Soon, soon, Kanda thought. Please. But then she thought: this one last night with the rest of my family – let me have that, at least, please. A small thing: one night in the wild in a mine where children suffered to make killing weapons, cold and damp! You can give me that, Geiamnyn. But it was not Geiamnyn she meant and it was not Geiamnyn who could grant it.

Sal said, "Tell us more about the Six, Mum. Tell me about…what were their names…Lord…Marron?"

"Lord Morren," said Calian. "How can you not remember their names, Sal? But I want to hear about Lady Erenan and Lady Kestre, Mum."

"Not now." I don't want to talk about them, Sal, Calian, about the past. I want to sit here with my family, I want to think of this time now, who I am now.

"Oh, come on, Mum. Tell me about…Lord…Lord Morren. Please."

"No, Sal."

"Oh, Mum."

"Leave your mother alone, girls," said Dellet. Kanda thought: he doesn't like to hear about the past either. That past.

"We can make the house bigger," Kanda said, "when we rebuild it, what do you think? Your father and I built that house together, with only your Aunt Hana and Uncle Sym to help us. And Sym wasn't much help at all, really, him being a potter. We could build it different, when we rebuild it, make a new part in it for you girls to sleep, maybe, do you think?" She shouldn't have mentioned their aunt and uncle, who must be dead now, and she saw that. "Oh, all right," she said quickly, before the pain came to all three of them, "Lady Erenan, was it?"

"Yes," said Calian, "Erenan and Kestre," just as Sal said, "Lord Morren. I mean…Lady Erenan, then maybe Lord Morren."

"So?" It was strange to hear them say the names so lightly. First we say *Aunt Hana*, Dellet's sister in Aranth who has an unfortunately large nose and brews exceptionally fine beer, then we say *Lady Erenan, Summer Harvest*, formed from sunlight and summer blossoms and the water of the mere, the weakest of the Six in the strength of her arm, the best rider of them and in battle the most fearless. "She was my dearest friend," Kanda said, "we would ride out together sometimes, race our horses for the sheer joy. I could defeat every one of the Six in combat, but I could never ride my horse as well as Erenan, never could I beat her in the race for all that my horse was the swiftest horse that ever lived. Her skin and her hair were pale as petals unfurling, her eyes were as gray as dove's wings. As I told you, she walked with two sticks, awkwardly, but when she fought on horseback no man could withstand her sword. We quarreled terribly about nonsense, the way you girls quarrel and for the same reasons. She had a woman she loved, Eliusa, a lady of Roven, who was gentle and kind and sweet as the spring. Erenan loved her deeply and she loved Erenan, but they did not marry. Why they did not marry, I don't know, that was one thing Erenan never spoke of, apart from – once, she almost spoke of it to me, and I think it was a sadness to her."

Long years since she had thought of this, Erenan's face laughing as she raced her horse across jumps and bends Kanda could never dare risk, "How slow you are on that fast horse! Henef's wasted on you, she really is!" That time Erenan had almost spoken of it to Kanda…and the anger in Erenan sometimes, that grew sharper with the years….

The fire spat and tumbled, burning branches rolled, Dellet swore. "Sorry sorry sorry. Curse it." The fire was half-out.

"What happened there, Dad?" said Sal crossly. Ash had blown up into her face and hair. "What are you doing?"

"I'm making the fire burn better," Dellet said. "That's what, Sal."

Calian said, "Umm…?"

"I'm making the fire burn better, Calian," Dellet said. "All right?"

"Yes Dad. Sorry Dad."

Silence. None of them looked at Dellet or the fire. They tried very hard not to look.

"There," Dellet said after a while. The fire was burning almost as well as it had been before Dellet poked at it and Dellet had soot on his cheek and a burned thumb. "Burning better."

"Yes, Dad," Calian said.

"And now we'd all better get some sleep, I think," Dellet said. "I'm going to try to get some sleep, anyway." He gave Kanda a glance that was something she could not understand. Grief? she thought. Anger? We should not be able to talk or sleep with Morna gone. But he wants to sleep away the time until I bring her back to him by magic.

"A good idea," Kanda said. "Try to get to sleep now, girls."

"You didn't tell us about Lord Morren," said Sal.

"No. I didn't." Sal, Kanda thought, you are still such a child in many ways.

Calian touched her sister's hand, made a face at her, Sal made a face back. "Stop it, you two," Kanda said. "This is not a suitable time or place for you to be like that." Tomorrow, Kanda thought, I have to do the hardest thing I have ever done, so please, please, girls, leave it in peace now.

"How can we sleep?" Sal said. "With Morna—"

"Sal: sleep," said Dellet. "Now. Calian: sleep. Leave your mother be. Now."

The two girls lay down wrapped in their cloaks. Dellet reached out, pulled Kanda next to him. His body was very stiff at first, awkward holding her, then he softened, held her tight, the two of them wrapped in his cloak. "Try to get some sleep, Kanda, wife," he said.

"You try to get some sleep, Del-my-heart."

A noise from Calian that was a little sound of happiness at her parents.

"You get some sleep, my loves."

Gentle breathing. Kanda lay awake listening to the sound for a long time. Dellet's snores, the girls' breath like they were tiny children. Almost a third child's breath, sleeping.

I will kill them and I will rescue you, Morna my golden one. I will rebuild the farm better than before. She thought: in one day, with a song, I, Ikandera Thygethyn, will rebuild the farm bigger and better than before.

She thought: not bigger or better. The same as before. And that was a good thing to think.

They slept, and the enemy did not come.

CHAPTER NINETEEN

She stood at the threshold. She could not bear to look in. The Hall was dark, windowless. The walls were made of woven hazel packed with straw and mud. The roof was dried bracken. The floor was beaten earth. A single weak fire that smelled greasy, burning bones and cattle dung because there was little wood for burning; no lamplight. A bronze cauldron hung from a tripod but the metal was cracked beyond use or repair, the cauldron empty save for dust and cobwebs, the hearth beneath the cauldron was cold and dead. Rain had leaked in, lay in a puddle near the hearth. The Hall was empty. Not even bats or owls would come here, not even crows. But at the far end of the Hall there was the sound of something moving.

Ten times a thousand times, she had crossed that threshold. Still, again, she was afraid to cross.

She held the doorway to steady herself. Stepped. Crossed.

The air rolled with a blare of trumpets. She said the words that must be spoken. The crystal bell sounded. The horn rang.

The walls of the Hall were silver. The columns of white porphyry held up the gold roof. A thousand columns, a forest of them. The floor was made of diamonds. Rich hangings whispered in the breeze. The great windows of oiled silk filled all the air with color, dancing. Outside the windows the white lilies and the red roses and the golden honeysuckle grew and bloomed.

A feast was prepared. The tables covered in rich cloth, set with silver platters of bread and meat. Wine gleamed in the great mixing bowl, lovely maidens in green samite held the dipper, filled to the brim the bright painted cups. Six cups for the Six Swords of Roven, each painted with their owner's device. For the greatest of the Six, as was fitting, a sword upthrust and shining, painted in liquid gold. Iath: *Kind Strength*. The sword itself hung in splendor on the wall behind the Lord's high dais. The maiden cupbearer bowed her head to it as she set the matched cup in its place at the Lord's right hand.

Now the feasters entered, talking and laughing together, a mass of color too brilliant for the eye. Crowned in flowers new-gathered from the gardens, the sweet scent of petals more beautiful than any perfume, dewdrops that glittered more radiant than any crafted gem. In they came, high-stepping down the length of the Hall, the maiden cupbearers gasped in wonder to see them in their beauty. The Lord at their head alone, his white hair combed and dressed with a silver fillet, his black skin gleaming. Beneath his sea-green robes his belly was vast and the baby kicked. Milk spurted from his breasts. Behind him walked Lord Palle, crowned with wild irises, his black hair and black beard plaited with green ribbons, his cheeks painted with green paint. Behind him came Lady Kestre and Lord Morren, side by side in radiance. Behind them Lord Gallyn walked with his husband Tobelef, an older man with silver just tinting his brown hair, a gentle man and no swordsman he, he wove the finest and most delicate of silk cloth. Then Lady Erenan, crowned in wild roses, hand in hand with her love Eliusa: Erenan had herself gone out in the dawn to gather for Eliusa a crown of violets. The harper Muss struck up the music for them. How great were the cheers for them resounding, how joyful the faces to see them.

But there for the first time Kanda saw something she had never seen before at any feast. She saw the faces watching Eluisa and Tobelef. How envious, some of the glances cast at Eluisa and Tobelef who each had the love of one of the Six. She saw Tobelef know he was envied, shrug it off with quiet confidence. A grown man in middle age; he had been married once before, been widowed before he met Gallyn. But she saw Eluisa frown, flush, she saw how the young woman's hands clenched. She saw, as she and as none of the Six had ever before seen, the pain in Eluisa's face as she went to sit far down the Hall while Erenan took her place at the Lord's dais. She saw, shocked, the look of something even like hate that Eluisa turned on Erenan and on the Lord of Roven. She saw Tobelef look once at Eluisa and then look sadly away.

No. She too turned her eyes away from Eluisa. No, I am mistaken. Enjoy watching the feast, she thought, see them in their glory, remember them! Morren got up to dance, persuaded Kestre to come with him. Many others formed up beside them, Gallyn and Tobelef among them, Muss struck up a new, fast tune. Like the wind rippling the barley, Kanda thought, as she watched them dancing. Then a shout from Gallyn, the dancers went back to their seats calling for wine, their flower crowns crooked, Gallyn alone jumped and leapt. He leapt far across the Hall to Tobelef, kissed him, leapt and spun away to throw his crown of poppies at the Lord of Roven's feet. Morren sprang up then, snatched his sword from the wall, "A sword dance!" Morren shouted. He danced alone, kicking up his heels high before him, throwing and catching the shining sword. He could throw the sword up to the highest rafters of the Hall, spin in a circle three times, catch it as it came down. He shouted for Gallyn to join him, Gallyn grasped his own sword, leapt, the two sparred dancing, strike blades with the sparks flying, whirl away spinning, jump together, strike blades. Gallyn leapt and Morren's sword swung under him; Morren ducked and spun in a circle, Gallyn cut the air above Morren's head. They threw their swords high together, caught each other's sword, threw them high. Gallyn thrust with his sword and lifted the flower crown from Morren's head. Morren clutched his bare head in mock horror, thrust his sword. Cut a long rent in Gallyn's white gown.

A long rent in the silk, and a single red drop of blood staining it where the sword had cut Gallyn's skin.

Silence. Kanda thought: this did not happen.

Kanda thought: this happened but I did not see.

Lord Palle was standing staring, blinking and shaking his head. His cup spilled out wine onto the white tablecloth, white and red as Gallyn's robe and blood. The Hall was dark, windowless, the hearth was cold and dead. In the dark at the far end of the Hall, she heard the Lord of Roven drag himself, hobble, halt, move.

Tobelef's voice rang out clear: "I wove him that robe. I can mend it, or weave him another. I never thought it was my best work anyway, it was rushed for the feast."

The walls of the Hall were silver. The columns of white porphyry held up the gold roof. A thousand columns, a forest of them. The floor was made of diamonds. Rich hangings whispered in the breeze. The great windows of oiled silk filled all the air with color, dancing. Outside the windows the white lilies and the red roses and the golden honeysuckle grew and bloomed. On the dais the Lord of Roven sat in state with his white hair combed and dressed with a silver fillet, his black skin gleaming, milk spurting from his breasts. Gallyn peered down at his wound. "It's nothing," Gallyn said, "I've cut myself worse shaving, he's cut me far worse in the practice." Gallyn said, overdoing himself: "Honestly, my husband's given me worse in bed." Morren tried to laugh along, too wide a smile too loud his laughter: "Oh, you wish, you wish, Gallyn my friend."

The harper Muss struck up a tune. Lady Kestre began to sing. Gallyn and Morren sheathed their swords, both looked embarrassed as children. The music rose, wine was poured, Gallyn and Tobelef went back to the dancing. From dusk to dawn they danced and feasted, the dawn tinted them as pink as Erenan's wild roses as they stumbled at last to their beds. Gallyn and Tobelef lay in each other's arms; Erenan and Eluisa lay in each other's arms; Morren lay in the arms of a handsome young stable lad. Yet there was a hunger and a fear and an emptiness in them all, none of them quite so easily and peacefully slept.

The Lord of Roven sat on his throne Thalle, that is *Hope*, with his hands folded over his pregnant belly, touching the baby where it kicked.

Lady Kanda lay awake, and her right hand burned, and her mouth tasted of bitter ashes. She saw her Lord in her mind as she lay on her bed unable to sleep, she saw the baby kick and it revolted her. She did not know why she was afraid. But a soft voice said in her mind, sweet and reassuring: you do know.

CHAPTER TWENTY

Kanda woke to the cloud-dawn, the sky dark but lit from within itself. The blue glow of Morna's eyes, Kanda thought, as they stared up huge after Morna's birth. The first birds were singing, just waking to sing, over them she heard an owl hoot. She lay still, Dellet's arms wrapped around her. His hair stank of smoke from his fire disaster, under the smoke it smelled greasy and unwashed and rather like cows or sheep. She kissed his hair, black turned gray, breathed in the smell. He stirred: don't wake, Dellet, she thought. Let me lie here a little longer. You lie here sleeping a little longer before you must wake. He shifted, farted, buried himself back deep in sleep.

Del-my-heart, your sweat reeks and your farts reek and your breath reeks.

But mine do too, I expect. Worse, I expect.

Del-my-heart. Del-my-heart.

He heard her thoughts, his arms folded her tight. He sighed in his sleep.

She almost thought: thank you, Geiamnyn, and you other one, *nameless, empty*: thank you for this last night with him.

She felt Dellet's arms around her and thought suddenly: Eluisa was afraid to think to marry Lady Erenan of the Six. When we were young then I did not see it. Eluisa did not feel welcome because…because we were so close to Erenan. She was envious of us.

Oh.

She thought: I should have made her welcome, told her we were happy for her and Erenan. She saw Erenan and me together close as sisters, the six of us ride out together, return together to ringing cheers, she could not see a place there for herself as Erenan's equal in life. She felt too apart. She hated us.

And Erenan: again and again she had to choose, torn between Eliusa and her duty to the Six.

Ride out on a quest, Erenan! Ride out to battle! Ride out to war! Leave off your embroidery, get up from your chamber, ride away. I'll come back, Eliusa my love, I'll come back to you tomorrow, or in a few days, or in the summer, or in the winter when the summer has long gone. Goodbye, Erenan my love, for a day or a year or two years, I'll sit faithful in our chamber and wait.

I remember once Erenan trying to talk to me. "I can't— I— How do you…you manage—?" But it was before a feast, we were celebrating another victory, I was distracted.

Be honest, Kanda: I was very full of myself because I'd fought better than all the rest of them put together, I wanted to enjoy my triumph, I really had no interest in listening to Erenan.

Then….

The last time I saw Eliusa, she lay on the bier being taken to be buried. But Erenan was not there to see. I remember Erenan's words as she rode away from us: she said she'd return, she'd try…. It was a beautiful day, I remember that, all the roses were in bloom in the gardens, the sky was the most perfect blue. There were two swans on the river with their cygnets following, and Erenan told us she had to leave, she would come back, she said, she just needed time. "You can't leave," Kestre said, I remember the anguish in her, *is this our fault, Erenan?* I remember Erenan said, "Kestre: that's why."

We waited for her to come back. Eliusa fell sick, died.

Then there was no time.

Kanda was wide awake now, hot with shame-sweat, sick at heart so she wanted to get up, fight, run, hit. She thought: keep sleeping, Del, because she could not bear for him to be awake now with her although she wanted him to wake and hold her and breathe in the smell of him. Her right hand was burning. She unfolded herself carefully from his arms, sat up, took her sword. It calmed her to hold it.

She looked toward the girls sleeping. She looked at Calian, fierce with her sword by her hand.

She saw that Sal was gone.

Not you too not you too not you not you not you. Leapt up breathless. Not you not you not you not you too. The sword was a mockery, the helmet was a mockery, Geiamnyn had left her in peace so he could take away another of her children. *Sal, Sal,* she opened her mouth to scream, but she must not scream must not scream because Calian and Dellet would wake up. Let them lie sleeping forever, never know. Better that Geiamnyn had killed them both. Better she killed them herself now in their sleep. Geiamnyn who knew so well how to hurt her best.

She had been dreaming of Roven, she remembered dully, of a dance, a feast – how could Geiamnyn have come while she had such a dream? He could have come only moments before, there would still be a trace, she could follow, seize Sal back, kill him. The mine workings were empty and silent, the sky was silent. There was nothing, no trace. She opened her mouth to cry for him: *I challenge, Geiamnyn. Will you dare to fight me?* A sound of stones behind her, she swung round already to kill him, come to gloat, come to take Calian too, but Calian my eagle, you will never dare to take, Geiamnyn. I will cut off your head, Geiamnyn, I will out your eyes and your tongue, your hands I will cut off, I would cut out your heart and eat it before you, Geiamnyn, if you had a heart. I will kill you, I will leave you for the wild beasts. With this sword, Geiamnyn, I can kill you I will kill you.

Sal ducked with a shriek from the sword. Her breath came a terrified hiss.

"Sal. Oh Sal. Oh." Hands shaking on the sword so much she dropped it, her arms too weak. "Oh Sal Sal oh Sal oh."

"What? What are—? Mum! Are you—?"

"I thought— You— Them—" Gasp. Shake. Buckle. No breathing left.

Sal said, "I just went to have a pee."

"Ah. Ah." Kanda almost fell, sat crumpled, ran with cold sweat.

"I just went to have a pee behind a rock."

"You shouldn't go out of my sight! Ever! You stupid stupid girl!"

"I went to have a pee, Mum." Sal sat next to her, held her trembling. Kanda's hand lay limp as a piece of rope. Sal took it, stroked it. "It's all fine, Mum, I'm fine. I wanted to go in private, I'm sorry. You were asleep." She said, and Kanda wasn't sure if she was trying to make her mother laugh in the way an adult might do: "I'll do it all in front of you from now on if you want."

"Oh Sal. Sal." Just strength enough in the great mighty warrior's right hand to squeeze her daughter's fingers. "Sal. Sal."

"I'm sorry, Mum," Sal said awkwardly.

"You've got…flowers," said Kanda when she could speak.

"I—" A little posy of white saxifrage. The girl had squashed them in her panic over her mother. She clutched them tightly now. "They were growing behind the rock. I…I picked them." She looked embarrassed. "I picked them for the mine children. I thought…they're pretty. They're all ruined now."

"No, no, the mine children will like them still. It's the thought, Sal. A lovely act." Starting to find words. Shake. Shake. Calm, breathe, shake shake shake.

"They're all smeared on my dress." Sal threw the flowers down. She was suddenly so angry there were tears in her eyes. She stamped her foot down, ground the flowers into the earth. "You made me crush them, Mum."

"Sal!" Kanda took a great deep breath, tried to be a warrior or a mother or anything that was not shaking and weak. "I'm sorry I panicked, Sal. I just…. I thought…. You—" Try. Try. Greatest of the Six of Roven. Look to your sword, try to be anything strong. "This is an impossible terrible thing that has happened, Sal. I…. This is the hardest and worst thing I have ever done, Sal, my *Shining*. I thought Geiam— I thought they had taken you, Sal—" Do not speak his name so casually before my beloveds, she thought. "I stood here and if he had been here I would have done things to him that…." She thought:

even to Geiamnyn, what I thought to do would have been a sickness. "I was so frightened for you, Sal."

Silence.

"We all need to pee, Mum," said Sal after a while.

Kanda tried to laugh. "We do."

"Look at these sleepies. They slept through all of that."

I'm so glad they did. "Shall we wake them?"

"No, Mum. Let's just sit here together for a bit. Look at the trees and the lake." Sal said after a while, "Cal looks different with her sword."

"Yes." You don't mean Calian, Sal, I know that. Look at the trees and the lake. Look at the birds. "Is that Calian's gyrfalcon?"

"Not wrong. Just different."

"Yes."

"It's not Calian's gyrfalcon."

"I have to have a pee, myself," Kanda said, just as Sal said, "Mum?"

"Yes?"

"Mum.... Lord Morren.... The Six, I mean.... When you talk about them, it's like....

"What happened, Mum? What was the terrible thing one of the Six did?

"What was the oath that was broken, Mum? Who broke it?"

CHAPTER TWENTY-ONE

I don't know what you mean, Sal.

Nothing happened, Sal. Things change, things pass, things end. Great indeed was the power of the Lord of Roven, but even he…even he could not hold back time. He grew old, weary. And we, we six warriors, we…. Nothing lasts forever, Sal. Everything dies, all light fades in the end. You'll die one day, Sal, I'll die, your father, your sisters. Thus the Six and the Hall Roven.

A terrible thing happened and Roven fell, yes, Sal. We were warriors – how else would it end? But if Roven hadn't fallen, Sal my love, I wouldn't have you and your sisters and your father now, would I? And that's good, isn't it, Sal, so that's all that need be said. A terrible thing happened once at Roven, but now I have you, my love.

No.

You know what happened, Sal. Don't ask me to tell you.

CHAPTER TWENTY-TWO

In the first bright morning of the world the Lord of Roven summoned the Six to him. From the play of sunlight on water, from the snow that falls pure and clean, from the wild high places and from the rich tilled fields, from the stones of the earth, from the wood of the trees, he made us Six to stand before him. Six Swords against darkness, cruelty, evil, Six Swords to protect.

As a part of our making he bound us to him with a mighty oath. To act always with honor, with kindness, with forethought, with truth. To question always what we were doing, to ask ourselves always why we did as we did and whether what we did was right. As my sword's name: *Kind Strength.* Wise strength. The dawn broke on the first morning of our making, the wound of the sun brilliant red, we knelt before our Lord of Roven, our maker, we raised our swords in homage, with one voice we swore our oath to him. I remember every beat of my heart as I swore that oath.

Long years. Golden years. How could they not be golden? An orchard where the trees are always both in fruit and in blossom, a fountain whose water runs sometimes blue, sometimes silver, sometimes green, sometimes red. A table set always for feasting, a hall that rings with music, laughter, dance, beauty. Honor and glory poured over us, every day we are celebrated, eyes widen at the sight of us, voices fall silent in deference when we speak. We are all that is good, we are the light and the wonder. We are made to shield the world from harm. And I am the greatest and most honored even of the Six.

I can't say what happened. The oath was broken, yes, one of us broke it, I can't say, I can't tell you. But that's not fair, a lie or at best an evasion, child's blame – *it wasn't me! It was him!* A long time already it had been broken, little by little, tired, angry, unthinking, all of us Six broke the oath.

Part of our being. So fierce and so glorious we shone. The Lord of Roven in his great wisdom, I think, I think he asked of us impossible things.

The battle. The last and the greatest. Ysarene, Geiamnyn, that third nameless empty one, the last time I fought all three of them. Kestre and I were alone. For already it was ending, breaking. Erenan was angry, Gallyn was angry, Palle was— Morren— Morren was—

"It is she! The savage thing, the— *Hunger*—" Kestre cried to me. "Beware of her! Don't listen!"

Yes. Close my ears to her. She smiles without lips. The man beside her, all golden, I know him also. *Burning*. He does burn so very bright. And the third, so horrible I can't look at him, the third, the shadow, I know him from the shadows cast on the walls of my chamber, the shadows that run across the orchard's green soft grass. A sick thing like a toad, he squats in the shade of an ash tree, the ground beneath him is wet. He raises a hand to me. Greeting me. Filth runs from his hand. His hand is dead.

"I found him in the mire," the woman *Hunger* says. "I dug him up from the mire. He lay in the mire and I heard him calling. Do you like him?" She says to me, "You should name him, lady. He wants you to name him."

She says to Kestre, "Lady *Song*. You know, I think, this other friend I bring?"

"Don't look don't listen," Kestre says. She draws her sword. She is least eager always to fight, the last to anger – she, Kestre, who loves better song and music, last to fury, first to peace, she rips her sword from its scabbard with a face as storm clouds, she is hot with anger, she is so cold with anger the world dims. "All three here I will kill with one stroke if I have to," Kestre says.

"I have been wandering here and there across this fine land," the woman *Hunger* says to me. She ignores Kestre as if she has never spoken.

"What a lovely place this land seems. I killed every living thing in one town, I told you. Then I found a village and I made the children there kill their parents, the parents turn on their children. I did not lift one finger myself, and they are all there dead. Isn't that a fine thing I have done?" She says, "Do you want to know why I did it?"

"Be silent," Kestre says. "You are lying."

I hear my own voice very distant from me: "Why did you do it, Ysarene?"

"You tell me, lady," the woman *Hunger* says. She says to Kestre, "Lady *Song*. Ask your friend beside you why I did it. For she knows the answer better even than I."

Kestre has her sword drawn, the blade has the smoke of battle-lust. But it is I who leap to battle, I have lain awake long nights thinking of driving my sword hard and strong into this woman *Hunger*'s face. I wound her, I cut her face already maimed, she is a skilled warrior also, her sword cuts me deep. We are not fighting, we are only hurting each other. I think I am hurting her. I cannot be hurt.

Kestre fights the man *Burning* and I have never seen her fight as she does now. She is so angry, she is filled with loathing.

The third one only watches. I feel him watch me.

I drive the woman *Hunger* back. Now our swords meet and meet, warding, blocking, neither of us can land a blow to hurt. Kestre drives the man *Burning* back, he rallies, he drives her back, she rallies, she drives him. So well met. Each knows the other's every sword stroke.

The third one only watches. The earth is dead beneath his feet. I find myself staring at him in horror even as I am fighting. Until I cannot look at my enemy to fight, and she cuts me very deep.

My sword falls from my hand. I fall to my knees. The man *Burning* wounds Kestre, she too drops her sword, falls to her knees.

I feel…fear. And I feel…relief. I look away at last from the third one there. I see my own shadow before me.

Kestre says, "We were created to destroy such as you. We have sworn an oath. We are the Six Swords against the darkness. What are you three, then? You are nothing." She raises her face to meet the man

Burning's fire-red eyes. He sneers, he tries to spit at her, he steps back away. He runs away.

The woman *Hunger* gives a cry. She runs away. She is a shape ragged on the wind, flying weak away.

The third one holds up his hand to me in farewell. He is gone as the sun dries the mire and makes it safe to walk.

"Always we will be killing these ones here," Kestre says. "Always. We swore it."

The ground where I kneel is wet with my blood. But the oath was already broken then.

CHAPTER TWENTY-THREE

Kanda said, "Don't ask me that, Sal my *Shining*. Never ask me that. Please. I beg you." Woman to woman, showing her weakness, not mother to child. She was ashamed when she had spoken, talking to her child like that. She waited for Sal to say something more. *But what happened? But who broke it? Mum? Tell!* But the girl reached down, picked up a sprig of the saxifrage she'd gathered. Looked at it a long time, then threw it away. Stood up, made a show of smoothing her skirt, dusting grass and soil off. "We should wake the others now. I'll get Dad's stupid fire going." She said then, "You won't be able to get Morna back, will you, Mum?"

"I—" I am Ikandera Thygethyn. I—

Woman to woman. Not mother to child. Kanda said, "No, Sal. I don't think I can rescue her. No. I don't think I can, no."

"You don't need to keep saying it!" The Hall Roven was a story to her. This was a real thing. Sal went running down to get the fire going, Kanda heard her cursing her father's uselessness at building it. From a distance, Sal's face was burning burning hot.

CHAPTER TWENTY-FOUR

Two battles, I remember, when the oath was already breaking.

The first was at an urgent summons from a distant mountain kingdom, beset by a vast enemy host. A fierce people bitter at the world in their mountain fastness, careless of the world beyond their border, selfish, petty, violent to each other and to strangers who crossed the high mountain peaks. Hard to think well of: I…hated them. It was not quite as it had seemed in the Hall Roven at the urgent desperate plea there, frightened and innocent, peaceful gentle simple folk beset by darkness. (It never is.) The valley kingdom bristled with swords and spears and strong armor, not all of it new-forged in panic now from plowshares; the people of the valley knew many words for fighting. (The king's son, it seemed, had done…had been…so thus the enemy might indeed be…angry…justified, even…. Oh, she was…only…a peasant girl? Yes, I…I think— I see, yes.) They had, in truth, little need for a great captain to lend them her courage, they had certainly no need to be taught battle tricks. Indeed, they had already fought one battle with the enemy, been victorious; the king's son, the bravest and best of warriors, had led the charge against the enemy. But, alas, the king's son had been killed in the fighting along with many good young warriors, and all the heart had gone out of the king his father, he had sued, nay begged, for peace. (You returned the woman? With humble apology and recompense? Oh, she left on her own…? Before you could arrange it…? I should say 'good', then…. And she was the one who, in the fighting, it was her sword that…? Well…that's…I mean…. Don't say 'good', Kanda, don't say 'good'.) But the people here were indeed innocent, they had no part in the king's son's doings, they begged him to let her go, they did not ask for this, any of it. (Did you say it to his face? Tell him what you thought of him? Well, yes, I suppose…I can understand it was…awkward, him being the king's son, yes….) They are outnumbered, mostly farmers, that is true; the enemy that has come upon on them is savage and hungry, it is not gathered here for revenge against what one boy did. That woman was a pretext only, the enemy has no interest in her sufferings. (Those who lead the enemy must have delighted in what the king's son did.) From the slopes of the far mountains the enemy came arrayed for battle, eager, hungry, these people will die here butchered if we do not help them. I curse them and I weep in anger at what I am doing, even as I fight. (To dear young Gallyn, who in his innocence sees in the king's hall only a dead boy his own age, strong and eager, cruelly slain in defense of his gentle people, I must not speak of any of this.)

The second was in defense of a village truly innocent. Hidden away in high mountains also, cut off from all the world's cruelty; they did not know metal working, nor the use of weapons; Ysarene came down upon them with a mere handful of men to butcher them. They died blank-faced with horror: what is this that is happening? The Six came to teach and lead them. They learned fast, being clever and resourceful, too quickly they fought back with teeth and nails and sharpened stones. And then…ah, Gallyn! to him it was a shock, that almost itself a shock – when the battle was won and Erenan had struck down Ysarene, cut out her heart, left her crushed on the killing ground – they turned their backs on the Six, cursed us as bloodthirsty, murderous, mere savages. No better than Ysarene. They drove us away with curses. They threw stones after us.

Palle and Erenan cursed them.

Gallyn cried.

I did not blame them.

CHAPTER TWENTY-FIVE

They ate breakfast of stale meal cakes, drank water from the spring. "A lot of meal cakes you made, Sal, girl, amazing," Dellet joked, tried to. Sal only glared at him. Calian was hunched and poised like a beast, eating without looking at her food, her head twitched every time she thought she heard a sound. Her sword was in her hand as she ate. "You don't need to.... It's good to be on your guard, Cal-flower," Dellet tried. "Just make sure you eat properly, okay? Don't choke yourself eating like that."

You named her *Eagle*, not me, Kanda wanted to shout.

"Look," Dellet said. He spread his hands wide in a helpless gesture. "Look, I'm sorry I was angry last night. I don't like this place, I don't like anything, this is all wrong. But you three stop it yourselves, okay?"

Long bitter silence. *But what happened? But who broke it?*

"Okay, Dad," Calian said. Her hand on her sword relaxed, maybe, slightly. Sal said nothing, bit down fiercely on her meal cake, but then she handed her father another stale cake from Kanda's satchel.

"You shouldn't hold it so tightly," said Kanda. "Hold the sword loose. Just resting in your hand."

"Oh shut up, Mum. I know that, I worked that out. I'm only holding it now tightly because I'm cross."

Oh. Well, that was Dellet's fine work ruined.

"They won't come," Kanda said after a moment. "I mean: they will come, but I'll know. We'll have warning."

"Like we did before, you mean? You won't walk up to them and give them a hug and share a meal with them this time, you mean?" Calian chewed down the last of her breakfast. Walked off, crouched against the rock face with her sword on her knees. She had found a good place to wait, an overhang protecting her from above and at the sides, a narrow space in front of her, she could hold there a long time against three or four men.

"That's…not fair, Calian," Kanda said weakly.

Sal said, "Isn't it?"

"Hush!" From far off, she thought she heard the hodden's gobbling neigh. Dellet heard it, winced in pain, Sal and Calian heard it. Were frozen. Frightened children.

"Mum?" Sal said.

Kanda took up her own sword. A sprig of Sal's saxifrage had got caught around the hilt. Put on her helmet. "Get into the mine workings, Sal, Dellet. Calian, if you—" Calian made a sound deep in her throat that Kanda knew well. "Calian, when they come: breathe deep, hold your sword loose in your hands, don't think too much about what you are doing. Calian, my eagle, that sword will hold them."

The hodden neighed again in the far distance. Again, again, quieter, farther off yet. Calian and Kanda stood side by side against the rock face. A spur of rock prodded uncomfortably into Kanda's back.

A cow, she thought, would love to scratch themselves on it.

It was a hot day again, with the heaviness in the air that hinted at storms later. The sky had that purple tinge to it that hurt the eyes. Made the world look very slightly wrong. Kanda's mouth was dry. She found to her irritation that she kept clutching her sword too tight. She could feel Sal and Dellet crouched in one of the mine workings. Hear them occasionally shifting around, whispering together, then they would be silent, too frightened to speak. Calian would frown whenever she heard them move or speak.

"They're well hidden," Kanda said, "and Sal has that knife from the mine, remember. Your dad has his stick."

A hawk screeched high up in the purple sky. A little later they saw it dive and vanish. A little later still they watched a flock of crows. A hart came to Elelan Mere to drink.

"I thought the water was poisoned?" Calian said. "Look at its antlers. But it's too far to count the points."

The hawk came again, hovering to scry and then diving. A stonechat, little dark bird with a rust-colored breast, landed on the rock near them, made a sound like flint knapping, his wife darted round to join him, they both flew off.

"You must be hot in that armor," Calian said. She shifted her sword to her left hand, flexed her fingers in her right hand, moved her sword back again.

I told you not too hold it too tight, Calian, Kanda thought.

"That helmet must be hot as anything," Calian said. She squinted out. "I haven't heard that thing neigh for ages now."

She was trying to sound like one seasoned warrior talking to another, Kanda thought.

"They'll come up the gulley, do you think?"

"Probably, yes."

"I would. If I was attacking me here." She shifted the sword from hand to hand. A hind and her calf came to Elelan Mere to drink. The stonechats were back, flitting around and calling, two others joined them, all four flitted away. A line of wild ducks flew past. The wind changed direction, bringing a scent of wild thyme from the mountain. Clouds banked in the east.

"This is boring," Calian said.

I know. Yes.

"Why don't they come?"

I...I don't know, Calian.

"I wish they—" Calian said firmly, "I hope they never come. We can stay here forever, being bored."

The wind changed again, blowing the threatened clouds far off beyond seeing. The sun was at its height. It was very hot in her helmet. Hours, Kanda thought, since the hodden last neighed. And was that smoke rising far off to the east?

This is not like Geiamnyn. Ysarene will not want to wait.

He will not want to wait, surely?

"There's a dragonfly, look. No, it's gone. I wonder what it's doing up here? Oh, and a rabbit, look there. My legs ache. We could sit down?" said Calian. "Put our swords down?"

The sun was in the west behind the mountain. The mountain's shadow was vast on the land before them. The ducks landed splashing and quacking on the lake.

This is wrong, somehow. Why don't they come?

"Mum?" said Calian.

"Yes?" It's pretty boring listening to you babbling like this, to be honest, Calian.

"I heard you talking to Sal this morning, Mum."

Sickness. Kanda said, "You were asleep."

"I was awake, Mum. The noise you and Sal made…but I think Dad was asleep." Calian said, like the child she was really, "Sal might be happy for you to lie to her, but I'm not. So who broke the oath, Mum? Which of them?"

"Your father, are you sure he was asleep?"

"He was snoring. Mum: which of them?"

Kanda gripped her sword so tight her hand was screaming. "I…I can't tell you. I can't. I— Some things…I can't bear to say, Calian. Do you understand? Of course you don't understand, but— It's not that I— I mean—"

And the words came out rushing, pouring out. A miscarriage, Kanda thought, that was what it was like as she spoke. Not things a mother should ever say to her child. Or things that every mother should say to every child, to remind them.

"I cannot forget that day. I see it in my dreams and I wake weeping.

"Geiamnyn soaked in gore drunk on bloodshed, striding through the Hall and where he stepped the Hall was burning. With every stroke of his sword he killed five, ten, twenty men. He seated himself on the Lord of Roven's throne. The throne burned. Thalle, that is *Peace*.

"I remember it so clearly, Calian mine. The throne running with fire. Geiamnyn sitting upon it in the fire laughing.

"I remember Ysarene leading her troops into the fields where the servants had fled. The trees blackened as she touched them, the crops withered, the birds of the air and the wild beasts fell dead. The earth itself howled in pain as her feet touched it. Dried and cracked open as after a long drought.

"She ate human flesh that day. Drank human blood.

"But she is *Hunger*. Even that day, she was not sated.

"And the third, who has no name but emptiness....

"There are no words for what he did that day in any human language. I would cut out my own tongue rather than speak what he did. Every day, in war, men do what he did.

"I remember Kestre. *Song*. I remember her screaming. And she could do nothing. I saw her dying. I remember Geiamnyn strode over to her dying body. Pissed on her as she died.

"They left nothing alive in that place. The oath – we were not bound to make it, nothing would have come to us if we had not sworn it. A promise we chose to make. I—"

Shuddered. "What am I saying? I should not have told you one word of this, Calian!"

Calian shifted her sword from hand to hand. "I stabbed that monster *Burning*. I cut his throat. I think...I do understand, Mum."

Calian said, "That's why you had to leave her. Leave the place we lost her, I mean. I know that.

"It's more important," said Calian, "that you kill them, than that you rescue Morna. Isn't it, Mum?"

I—

Kanda said, "Yes. It is." They will be coming soon for us, and whatever happens after, we must kill them.

They were coming soon.

They were coming soon.

It was evening.
They had not come.

Kanda's head ached, her knees ached. Calian rubbed her shoulders. "This sword is really heavy, Mum."

They'll come in the dark. With the dark as a weapon.

They won't come in the dark, because Geiamnyn will want to see my face clear in the daylight as he kills my children.

Tomorrow, they will come.

They are enjoying this, Kanda thought. Making me wait for them. I thought I was making them come to me, but they are making me wait, baiting me like a fox in its earth hiding, fearing. He will not want to wait, nor Ysarene, but Geiamnyn is enjoying this game with me. She was so tired after standing all day in the heat terrified and angry, when she closed her eyes she saw so many memories: the dragon charging and her triumph as she killed it; Erenan fighting the wild men of Escran who had mocked the Six; Morren running down the White Wolf of Rethen, a sorcerer and a shapeshifter, killing him bare-handed; Kestre's song as she walked in the snow in the woods beyond Roven; Gallyn on his wedding day; Palle on the practice field laughing, "I can never beat you! How do you do it?"; the taste of bread and wine at the feast. Geiamnyn is pleasuring himself making me remember all these things.

But the night came, but the enemy still did not come.

They are not coming. Thus: choices: Kanda opened her satchel, took out three of the things she had taken from the farmhouse. Set them on a rock before one of the mine workings, said the words that must be said. Seven drops of her blood on the stone here, because the stone was filled with sorrows, the magic must be stronger, there was no kind welcoming pattern laid here. Not flowers, Sal my kindhearted girl, but blood we must offer here to the mine children. The wooden bowl was a gold platter, piled high with roast meat, the quern was a silver platter, piled high with fresh bread, the cup was a horn of sweet milk. She set the shieldwall of her power around the mine workings; seven drops of blood she shed there in a circle to enclose her family and the mountain eagerly drank them up. She felt the mine children reach out their hands to shield her family, she saw a new gleam on Sal's flint knife. She cut sprays of heather and bracken, laid them in the shelter of the overhang, spread their cloaks. Fine beds with thick warm wool blankets, smelling fresh. "Go and bathe in the lake," she told her family. "Wash your hair and your clothes." They were hesitant, frightened, "Dad said the water was poisoned." "Just go and bathe," she said. They went, they came back clean and shining, dressed in fine warm clothes. Calian wore the leather wrappings of a warrior. Sal wore a dress of pale gray linen like a girl on a feast day. Dellet wore the woolen tunic of a farm man.

Kanda looked for the saxifrage flowers Sal had found, to make them garlands for their hair. She could not find them, but she found the wild thyme instead, picked them each a tiny sprig. In their new clothes they ate and drank as if this was a feast.

Perhaps, Kanda thought, Ysarene had spoken the truth. They would leave her alone to their laughter. Weep with laughter watching her rebuild the farmhouse, go back to mucking out the byre and milking the cows, spend lambing season with her hands up a sheep's private parts.

Almost, she thought, I would rejoice and thank them for that.

Do you hear me, Geiamnyn? I will stick my hands into cow shit, I will bury myself in weeding and pruning and mending drystone walls and baking bread. I will grow older and grayer and mutter to myself and complain of aches in my knees and say that means it's going to rain. Leave my family alone, Geiamnyn, and Ikandera Thygethyn will be an old peasant woman and you can laugh at me every day and I will be happy.

Almost.

Her right hand burned, and her mouth tasted of blood. She stroked the blade of her sword with love.

CHAPTER TWENTY-SIX

But the next day the enemy did not come. Or the next day. Or the next day after that.

CHAPTER TWENTY-SEVEN

Choices: stay here waiting, a fox driven to earth, or set out hunting.

The mine children were used to them. Guarded them. Every morning, charmingly, Sal rose with the dawn, the first to wake, plucked flowers for them. The platter was full every night and every morning with meat fresh-roasted, the plate was full of bread fresh-baked. The horn brimmed with milk so rich it was pure cream. The beds were soft and warm, their clothes warm and clean. The mine children were kind now, Kanda need only shed three drops of her blood.

Calian practiced her sword strokes with Kanda. She was very good. She refused to try herself against Kanda's black sword. Once when Kanda had offered – begged – she almost said something about the sword, but she closed her mouth on it.

"You don't like it, do you?"

Calian said, "It's your sword and it will kill those monsters. It doesn't matter whether I like it, if it can do that. But your other sword sounded more beautiful."

Kanda said, "It was. Are you sure you won't try a bout with me, Calian?"

"I'm sure, Mum."

Sal sat long hours staring out at the land before them, far off toward their home. She toyed with her flint knife blade, liked to hold it, and Kanda was certain it was as much Sal's doing as her own that the food was there, the lake water pure, their sleep soft. Sal's face was thoughtful, wistful. Sometimes she would cry silently. Sometimes she would frown, bite her lip – she's thinking of Morna, Kanda would think. Sometimes she seemed almost happy, smiling to herself. Kanda thought looking at her: Calian is my fierce one, my eagle, but you, Sal, are truly my kind strength. Kanda thought looking at her: I will not tell you to hide in the mine workings again, Sal. The enemy should fear you the most. Sal did not speak much, but then Kanda and Calian did not feel much need to speak.

Simply waiting.

Only Dellet fidgeted, fretted, muttered endlessly, bit his knuckles, hefted his stick. He had eaten Kanda's food hungrily, with relish; now he ate as if it might be poison, and ate less every meal.

He and Kanda slept in their bed, but he did not touch her. If she brushed against him, he drew back in his sleep.

"We should just go home," he said the fourth morning. "What use is this? Squatting here like cattle rustlers. Go home. Raise a grave for Morna. That's what I'll do." But he didn't get up from where he sat.

"We are waiting here to destroy monsters," Calian said with bared teeth.

Sal said almost as fiercely, "Morna is not dead. She'll come back, we'll get her back."

"She's dead and can't even be buried. Her spirit will never go free. Your – your mother, she wouldn't let us find Morna's bones. Go home," Dellet said again. "Mourn my children." He said, "You were right what you said the other day, Calian. She led us to those monsters, talked to them, ate their food, gossiped away like any drunken old woman at a wedding, you all saw her gulping down their strong mead! She gave them my Morna, let them have my Morna, wouldn't let me stay even to find her bones. You think she'll kill them? You think she'll get my Morna back? Old clapped-out bitch who lost my daughter. Didn't care to find her bones. None of you cared to stop and find her bones. I'll go home alone and mourn my child, you three women stay here in this cursed place."

He spoke quietly. Gently. He did not shout or curse or foam at the mouth.

It would have been better if he had shouted and cursed and foamed at the mouth.

Kanda clasped her hands over her mouth, ran a few paces, bent and vomited. Roast meat, creamy milk, fresh bread. Yellow bile searing her throat.

"I dreamed when I was a child that I was lost on Mal Anwen," Dellet went on in his soft calm voice, he did not acknowledge his wife bent vomiting, "and here I am, my whole life is lost and gone on this cursed mountain Mal Anwen. You women stay here with your magic, your swords, your not caring. You're not my wife, not my children. You've taken away my children, done this to them. I'll raise a grave for my child," he said, "and then I'll slit my throat over it. That's all you've left me." So quiet, so soft, without anger, so terrible was his voice.

There were no words. There were no thoughts. But a bird still sang overhead as if the world had not ended. If the world was kind, the sun should fall now from the sky.

"We have to kill the monsters!" Calian shouted. "The beasts! If it takes forever, we stay here, we hunt them down, we destroy them! Morna can be dead a thousand years unmourned and unburied, we can wait here until our bones rot – but I will wait here and when they come I will kill those beasts those monsters! They are sickness and disease, they must not be allowed to spread their filth. You be a coward then, go home to nothing. I will hunt them down, I will destroy them."

But Sal shouted over her, grasping her father's arm, pleading: "Morna is not dead, Dad. She's not dead, and I can get her back. If we stay here just one night longer, I can get her back, I promise."

Dellet said, "What?"

Kanda said, "What's that?"

"I…I mean…. She's not dead, I mean, I know it, she's my sister Morn-Morn, she can't be dead, we just need to wait, I mean…."

"Sal?"

"We have to stay here one more night," Sal said and she was crying now. "One more night. Please. That's all I mean. I….

"Just trust me. Mum. Dad. Calian. Please."

That's not all you mean, Sal, Kanda thought. What have you done, Sal?

She lay awake all night waiting. Dellet had not left his place by the fire, sat where he had sat when he laid his curse on his family. He had not moved or spoken. Only: "Tomorrow at first light, Sal, I swear it, I will go home and build a grave and cut my throat." Then silence. Calian had sat all day and half the night with her sword on her knees, her lips drawn back in a wolf-snarl that Kanda feared was fixed forever on her face. Before the light faded too weak to see, she was certain that in all this time Calian had not blinked.

Sal was awkward, would not speak further, sat chewing her lip frowning, sometimes a light like joy would strike her face, sometimes she shook, sobbed silently, trembled.

"Mum— Cal— I— No, no, it's fine, one night, please."

Once she came close, crept to press herself close to her mother. Then she was pacing near Calian's hunched wolf-shape.

This is the worst thing. The worst place I have ever been.

Ikandera Thygethyn's magic, or Sal's magic, or the kindness of the mine children, came at last, and Dellet slumped and slept, Calian slumped and slept.

Sal's magic. Kanda felt herself grow sleepy. Her head nodded. She thought to herself with a savage hate: like an old woman indeed, you are, Kanda, an old crone who has been guzzling strong drink at a feast. Stop feeling sleepy! Watch and wait!

She bent her head, pretended she was sleeping. The cruelty of her thoughts helped keep her awake.

As the first fingers of the gloaming came into the sky, Sal got up careful and silent, smoothed her dress, smoothed her hair, crept off up the mountain in the direction she said the flowers she gathered came from.

Kanda counted breaths, waited – longer, longer, not yet, not yet. Like a warrior poised to spring in the ambush – always you must wait longer than you think. She could not bear to wait longer. She was

Ikandera Thygethyn and she could stalk her prey in total silence in utter darkness. She must be patient, a little longer, wait, wait. Too quickly, she got to her feet, made herself stand waiting, hurried on after her daughter up the mountain, made herself stop and wait.

She went on fast up the mountain. Her daughter's footsteps were as clear to her as if they were made of light. Go slow. Take care. A tiny pebble moved with a roar beneath her feet. She made herself stop, counted to a hundred, at fifty she gave up and went on. A hunter, silent, intent, slow and careful.

There was a great high rock, a barrier, that she had not noticed on the slope of the mountain.

There was a mist here that was too thick.

There were voices from behind the rock, and a scent of flowers, and music: sweet silver bells. Strong magic hung in the air around the rock. Kanda choked on it. Sal's voice came muffled, she could not hear what her daughter said. A sob, a little cry of fear, and Sal was there suddenly with the mist about her like a veil. Her lips were parted, her eyes very wide, her breath came fast. She clutched a little posy of white saxifrage hard to her breast.

She cried out, "Mother?" Flinched, drew back. "Did you follow me?"

"Sal? I was looking for you."

"Get away from here, Mother," Sal cried, urgent.

In her eyes there was red fire. The mist swirled and opened.

Geiamnyn stepped smiling to join her from behind the rock.

"Don't touch her! Get away from him, Sal. Now. Get away. I'll hold him. Run, Sal. Just run."

Kanda drew her sword, edged closer. Geiamnyn too drew his sword. The blade hungered to meet Kanda. Too close, too close: "Stay there, Sal. Don't move." Like when Sal was in the field with the bull, and Dellet had said, "Don't move, don't move, Sal, love," very calm and carefully, taken one step toward the bull then another, "Just stay still and breathe, Sal, love, you can do it, Sal, love, that's it," while

Kanda in the farmhouse doorway was beating her fists on the wall and biting her fists to keep from screaming and her legs were trying to run. "It's all right, Sal."

Sal looked stricken from her mother to the monster there. Kanda took one step, her sword trembling in her hand, any moment, any moment Geiamnyn could cut Sal's throat. One step, two steps, she was close now with her sword, she said fierce, "Get behind me, Sal."

Geiamnyn arched one eyebrow. "I think your mind must be aging even faster than your body is, Ikandera Thygethyn. A moment ago you told her to run away. Make your mind up."

Kanda spat, "Be silent, Geiamnyn. Get behind me, Sal. Quickly!" But the girl stood fixed, Geiamnyn was so close he was almost touching her, she was fixed staring from her mother to the monster there.

"Really, Ikandera Thygethyn, what will you demand the poor girl does next? Stand on her head?" Geiamnyn's hand closed on Sal's wrist. Kanda saw her daughter's eyes open wide in terror, but still the girl did not move. Geiamnyn said smiling, "I won't harm her. I promise you, Ikandera Thygethyn."

So close together, Sal and Geiamnyn were standing. It was not fear in Sal's face.

"He means it," Sal said. "On his sword, he swore to me."

Kanda said, "You spoke to him?"

Sal said in a new voice, "You spoke to him, Mother. Why shouldn't I?"

I know what he is. I'm your mother. I'm wiser and stronger and older than you. She did not speak, but she saw that Sal heard all these things.

Sal said, "Geiamnyn is not as you told me, Mother. We have spoken these days together he and I, and he is…." She cast a bright shining smile at Geiamnyn.

Geiamnyn gave a little bow back to her, a gentle sweet boy's flush to his face. "Your daughter is as kind as she is beautiful, Ikandera Thygethyn," he said meekly. "Far kinder to me than I deserve, I'm sure."

Sal's smile deepened. Wise, thoughtful Sal simpered, lowered her eyes in embarrassment and delight. She sniffed at the flowers Geiamnyn had gathered for her.

"As lovely as those flowers. More lovely," Geiamnyn said.

And Sal, wise gentle kind child Sal, put her hand on Geiamnyn's hand, still smiling and simpering. And Geiamnyn, *Burning*, enemy and monster and beast, Geiamnyn closed his butcher's hand over Sal's, and he too smiled and simpered.

Geiamnyn had looked at Sal in the roundhouse. Sal had gasped and drawn back. And she, Sal's mother, had thought her daughter had been a child, frightened.

Sal said, "You don't understand, Mother." Sal said, "I know what I'm doing. I'm not a child, Mother."

Sal said, "Let us go, then." She was talking to her mother, of course, obviously, who else could she be talking to, she thought they could walk away the pair of them. And perhaps they could, because Sal was Kanda's firstborn daughter, her *Shining*, nothing could happen here, not while Kanda stood here strong in her armor. She was Ikandera Thygethyn, nothing more could happen to her not after Morna had been lost and her husband had cursed her, no more ill could come to them.

"Let us go indeed, my lady," Geiamnyn said. He bowed his head elegantly to Kanda, took up his fine bronze helmet with its golden figures dancing. Placed it on his beautiful golden head.

Sal said, "You are more beautiful than the sun itself, my Lord Geiamnyn." And Sal smiled deeper and brighter than sun after rainfall, gave Geiamnyn a look of more joy than a bird's song is joyful as Geiamnyn put his butcher's arm tightly around Sal's waist. "It's all right, Mother," Sal said. "I know what I'm doing. I do."

"You are both wise and beautiful indeed, my lady," Geiamnyn said. "A true queen. Enjoy your cow muck, Ikandera Thygethyn." His arms closed around Sal, pressing her yielding-soft to his chest.

Kanda ran at them. Her sword out to strike Geiamnyn. Kill him! Destroy him! Scream out her war cry! Geiamnyn flinched back, she saw it, she did, he was afraid of Kanda, he let go of Sal, stepped back, he did, he did! But a yell of pain from Sal. "No! Mum!"

Kanda's right hand with her sword about to strike Geiamnyn down.

Kanda's left hand had struck Sal's face.

Sal, more astonished than hurt: "You hit me."

Kanda dropped her sword, stumbled back. "No, Sal, I—" Words catching dry dust in her throat. Croaking. Worse than croaking. "I—" Her mouth and chin were wet. Hate spittle on her lips. "Sal. I—"

Geiamnyn's arms folded around Sal tighter, holding her, that was how Dellet should be holding Kanda, protecting, caring. Beneath his helmet, Kanda saw the smile of triumph on his face. He had been about to run, he had been frightened, he had, he had, he would have gone. Geiamnyn said sweetly, "I don't think she meant it, beloved. Flapping her arms like that, I've seen old women do that when they're angry, it's not her fault. But we should go now, I think, my beloved. Before the poor woman does anything worse."

The air trembled. The mist rose to drag her daughter away. Column of greasy fire, Geiamnyn's red eyes blazing. Point of bronze light, like a star, blossoming, fading. Thin and gone.

Kanda screamed out uselessly too late, without believing what she saw there, it was impossible, what she was seeing there, "Sal! Sal! Come back! What are you doing? Whatever you think you're— You're wrong. I'm sorry I hurt you, Sal," she cried, as if that was all it was.

Smoke, like mire water thrown on the hearth to destroy it. Smoke that covers the sky when a city is burning, extinguishes the moon and the stars and the sun.

Sal was gone.

There was nothing left in Kanda to vomit up over the burned earth. She fell to her knees. Her heart and her mind were gravestones.

Lie there on the mountain, her sword thrown useless beside her, her hand stained with her daughter's blood. Let the dogs come to gnaw my flesh. Let my bones rot here. Let all that I am be as ashes and dust. Three daughters I have birthed. Two daughters I have lost. The third – she will never forgive me for this now. I cannot face her. I cannot face her father my husband.

Come and kill me, Geiamnyn, Ysarene, you other who are only emptiness. I will go away, she thought, creep away into the dark and hide there forever. Sink into the filth of the mire forever hidden from the light. I will do whatever you want, only let my children go free.

A few scant days, she thought, since she had taken up her sword with such hope within her. Dellet saying with such pride: when I think about you, in my head you've always looked like this.

They didn't know I was here. We could simply have run away. But I wanted to fight them. My right hand burned for killing. With my left hand, my peace hand, I have killed my Sal my *Shining*.

I'm so sorry, my beloveds. Put out her hand to touch her sword, gentle, the dark metal so warm and good. Take it up, take it to her throat, get it ended. If this sword can kill monsters, it can kill an old farmer's wife.

I thought I could be more than I am. I'm so sorry.

Good, holding the sword like that. Despair: waiting. Calian and Dellet – they will not forgive me. What did I think I am? What did I think I could do?

A voice came whispering in her mind, kind, gentle: "Ikandera. Don't despair. Be strong as I knew you to be." Who's there? She thought, raising her head a little. I know that voice. Good memories. I was strong then, yes. "You never despaired, Ikandera. You were the bravest, the strongest, you gave me strength, remember?" Yes. I remember. "You were never defeated, Ikandera. Alone among all of us."

She sat up, dropped the sword. What was I thinking? I am Great Warrior, I do not despair. I can help my children. She put out her hand: "Are you there?" she called to the voice. "Where are you?" Speaking in her heart, her mind, for her tongue was stone-still, unable to shape words. If she spoke aloud, what would pour out would be not words but knives and stones and the rope a hangman uses. Bones, torn flesh, she was afraid she would vomit up if she spoke aloud. "I haven't the strength to stand. Help me up," she said in her mind. The well-remembered voice whispered back: "You are so strong, Ikandera. Go and find your children."

Ravaged with grief, like a creature cut to raw pieces, Kanda rose to one knee. She said aloud, panting with effort, "I can find them. I can rescue them."

Calian's voice called from down the hillside: "Mum!"

No, Kanda thought. Calian – not yet.

"Your third daughter?" the voice in her mind asked. Angry. Tenderly. The strength left her, and the pleasure in the long-remembered voice. Horror at the thought of the girl's eyes poisoned by the sight of her shame.

"Leave us alone," she croaked aloud at the voice. She fell back to a crouch with her limbs broken. Do not see me, Calian mine, my love. Calian came on with fast steps alert and alive and fierce as an eagle hunting, her sword like a flower in her hand.

"Where are you? I heard your voice. Where's Sal?" Calian called. The girl stepped on past Kanda, stopped at the patch of burned earth where Geiamnyn had stood. Fear came over the girl, she gripped her sword. "Who's there?" the girl whispered. "What has happened?" The fear was mastered, the girl caught her own reflection in her sword blade. Courage swept Calian up, drove away her fear. "You monsters: show yourselves," Calian called. "I am a warrior like my mother. I have sworn to destroy you. My mother may be afraid of you," Calian shouted, "but I am not. Show yourselves." Calian stood still, listening. She shouted, "Come out!"

The third, *empty, nothing*, stepped from behind the rock where he had all the time been waiting and watching. The hodden was beside him. Saem, Ben Apple Tree's son, was grinning beside him.

Cloaked and hooded. Gold glimmered at his throat, his wrists, he wore a neck ring, many arm rings. His hands showed curled around the hilt of a great sword. His right hand was the dark brown of old cured leather, it had a thickness to it, a plump heavy wetness to the skin. On his left hand the cured skin was torn open, shriveled over the stumps of his finger bones. His body was bent oddly, one shoulder raised very high. There was a wrongness in the way he held his head. Where he stood, the earth was rotted.

Calian grunted. Almost pleased to see him.

Despair returned to Kanda's heart. They are laughing at you, child, I hear them laughing. Run away, Calian. You are a child. Go back to your father, flee this place. What are you, child, to think you can fight monsters? Flee away, live huddled in fear in beggary and grieving, only live safe. I should never have brought you here. Forgive me, Calian mine, least loved of my three children. But her voice was a gravestone, she could not speak.

Calian moaned, stepped back. All courage fled. Yes, Calian mine. Run! Run! Flee away. Fear him. Run.

Saem hefted his spear, grunted at Calian. Fear dripped off him, also – the spear shook in his hand, his voice was weak as he spoke, trying for cruelty and carelessness: "Calian!" He brandished his spear fierce and raw: "Calian. Come to join us too?"

The third one did not move or speak.

"I'll kill you, Saem. I warn you," Calian said. That too was pretense, Kanda thought, her child talking so lightly of killing a man she had known since her babyhood. Calian's hands were too tight on the sword hilt. Saem flinched as if Calian had struck him, lowered the spear, bowed his head to stare in fear at the ground. She saw Calian's face wrinkle in disgust. Almost in pity for him, this poor wretched boy pretending false and horrified to be an evil cruel man. Saem hefted his spear again, shook it, bared his teeth.

The third, *empty*, said, "Calian…?" All the hope and pain and yearning in the world in his voice. Light and gentle. So long remembered, that voice. "Calian," he said. A spear's length, or a little more, between him and Calian. Five sword blades' length. A vast terrible yawning space between them. A killing ground between them. A vast great gathered army's death.

"Do not speak my name," Calian said. "Any of you."

The third one, nothing, only emptiness, drew his sword. Held it out hilt first toward Calian.

His sword was brother to Kanda's. The hilt was undecorated, the grip black leather molded to the grip of his hand. Black fire ran down the blade. Only the pommel differed from Kanda's sword. It was shaped as the head of an eagle, with red eyes and silver beak. The sword had had a name once, before he who was only *empty* and *nothing* took it. It had been called *Eagle's Blade*. Calien.

Calian raised her own bright sword. Rushed at the empty one.

CHAPTER TWENTY-EIGHT

Crash of metal. Swords like stars. Like flames wheeling in the air. The third, *empty, nothing*, met Calian stroke for stroke. Her sword lashed, sprang, twisted, alive in her hand, raging. His sword was a smear of darkness, rotted, oozing. It flowed, it was filth as it spreads through clear water. Disease as it spreads black and killing up the skin. He did not have Geiamnyn's strength but he had a power to him that was as filth, as dying. Kanda had seen men fall away, beg him to kill them, turn their sword before him to cut their own hearts out. He moved boneless. Like a clot of heavy blood. The heart, the throat he aimed at, to cut them open his joy. The eyes he aimed at. To put out an enemy's eyes his delight. Black fire on his blade that burned so cold it turned warm beating blood to dead ice. The pain of that blade's fire was *bitterness*.

Calian matched him stroke for stroke.

She was like a newborn creature dancing. Rejoicing in the strength of her limbs. So much beauty there in the curve of her arms, the turn of the blade like leaves, the fast careful careless placing of her feet. She whispered as she fought, the whisper growing louder, louder: "Monster. Death. You are rot and ruin. I am alive. I am life." Whisper of leaves, as the sword was leaves in spring rainfall, whisper of ripe corn in the field, whisper of reeds in the salt marsh. Her bronze-gold skin more warlike than any helmet. Her black hair her war cloak.

The swords met high above Calian's head, crashing. The swords met low, tangled in fighting limbs. They flew apart, flew together, pushed, met, flowed back. The empty one struck at Calian's heart: she blocked it, spun away, jumped at him. Her sword caught his shoulder, caught and sank in. Wounded him. Through this cloak, dark stinking mire water came oozing. Calian started, shocked that she had wounded him. Hesitated. He closed on her; his sword sucked at her throat. Leech. Rot-on-a-wound. Miscarriage clot.

Calian shouted, threw up her arms, ducked under the killing blade, came around to strike him. He had to twist, wrench himself with a noise of wet cloth tearing, on the rotted earth he made, slick with the mire that oozed from him, he was unbalanced, his arms slipped, flailed at nothing. Calian was on him, cut at him, was past him leaping to pull herself up onto the rock, just out of reach of him. He bent and staggered. Shapeless nothing. Growled in rage as he realized Calian stood tall above him.

A shaft of sunlight caught him. Fell at Calian's feet, spilled out in offering, fell on him to show him as rotted leather, rotted coarse old cloth. His bone-fingers scrabbled at the rock face, reaching toward Calian. Three finger stumps and the stump of a thumb, the fourth finger entirely broken off.

Calian stamped down hard. Creak of old bone breaking. He drew his hand back. His arms, so strong yet so weak and broken, beat helplessly at the rock.

But now the hodden lumbered forward, and it was tall enough to reach at Calian. Saem sprang forward, he was armed with a spear, he was a young man bred in the high hills, like Calian he had spent his life clambering among rocks.

There was nowhere for Calian to go. The hodden lurched and struck out with its flint blade-hands. Kanda had wounded it sorely when she fought it on the droveway: its head lolled like a hanged man, the horse skull shattered almost clear in half; its wooden body cracked open; Kanda had cut off its legs when they last fought and they had been replaced with spindly green branches that groaned beneath its weight. The bells tied round its waist jingled. Calian leapt back out of reach of its arms, it was clumsy now, collapsing, it was only mindless pain and its blades struck the rock as its arms flailed. Its stick legs creaked, began to snap. It champed its broken jaws, neighed and beat hard at the rock. Calian could skip almost between its blade-hands, like a child playing. But Saem was there with his spear. He jabbed at her, drove her toward the hodden's blades, with a grin he clambered to join her on the rock.

Calian lashed out, warded off the spear. Warded off the hodden. Saem rose up on the rock before her, leapt at her. He was a man grown, strong from farmwork, suddenly again she was only a child. His arm had greater reach, his spear had greater reach. He was grinning. Licking his lips. He roared in imitation of Geiamnyn's war cry as he thrust at Calian. The hodden jabbed at her legs.

Empty air behind her. Stranded between earth and sky on her rock.

Even now, there was no fear in her. She was like a flower blooming. A hard long painful pregnancy, and a hard long birth, Kanda had endured with her. Sal had hated her at first when she was newborn. Always the wildest. The clumsiest.

All this time, Kanda had lain in the dust hidden from them, cowering from her daughter's sight. Tried tried tried not to look at the third, that one who was only *emptiness* where his name was. I cannot watch him kill her. Some things are too terrible to be seen.

Get it over with. Give up, Calian. It will be better for you, the only thing left, if you die quickly.

Calian danced on the rock, the hodden gnashed its broken teeth, gobbled in triumph. Saem was grinning. "Bitch girl. I've watched you. Oh, I've watched you." Calian struck, wounded him. He cursed, spat blood at her: "Bitch girl. I'll stick you." Crude labored parody of Geiamnyn. His spear jabbed, caught Calian's thigh. She cried out in pain. Never before, in all her life, had someone struck her to harm her. The hodden jabbed at the back of her legs. Cut her. Blood streaming.

On broken limbs Kanda clambered to her feet. Her helmet was strong around her. Her armor was good and strong. She threw her sword into the air; the sun that showed the third for what he was, a thousand years drowned and bog-buried, the sun caught and flashed and warmed her black blade.

She spewed up stones and dead flesh. She shouted her war cry, so great and so loud the earth shook. You will die now under my sword, you *emptiness*. I will rejoice over your death.

She leapt to join her daughter.

They were back-to-back. As she and Palle had once fought, two together against a howl of darkness. Two blades that beat as one, knowing each other's movements without speaking. No thought in it. The pattern of their blades, and the pattern of light and shadow their blades cast on the world around them. Towering over the creeping figure of Saem, Ben Apple Tree's son, wretched boy, he whimpered, not fair, not fair, his face said. Shock in him at Kanda there with her sword vast as treetops, so much power in her. But you're a...she's a girl, you're an old woman. What's this? I killed my sister, his face screamed. How can you be fighting me?

Beating me?

His spear lashed hard and frantic: I'll show them these women show them show them show them. One two three four heartbeats. He yelled in fury, smashed with the spear shaft. Kanda warded him off without effort, wretched boy. I don't want to kill you, Saem.

She said it after one two three heartbeats: "I don't want to kill you, Saem. Drop the spear."

A mistake: Calian spat and hissed, furious; Saem roared in shame, drove mad with the spear into her face. Ikandera Thygethyn felt the boy's spearpoint scratch her cheek.

Calian seemed to manage him. A joy in her, beating him down. Kanda thought at the very back of her mind: did he once...? She hates him. I had no idea she loathed him like this, poor old Ben Apple Tree's son. The hodden struck at her legs. Its teeth clacked. It too tried to mount the high rock. Kanda struck down, her sword like an axe chopping, the hodden gobbled as the sword sank into its left arm. The wood splintered, the arm hanging limply off. The hodden screamed, half-woman half-horse dying. Kanda felt sick with grief. The arm snapped off entirely, dragged down by its own weight. The hodden thrashed at her with its right arm, lurched its broken neck forward trying to bite. Kanda's sword cut into its shoulder, ripped its cloak, sheared a long fragment of rotting wood. The hodden swayed on its absurd branch legs.

Not like this. She leapt down to meet it fairly. Now it loomed above her. The third squatted toward her. Black fire poured from his blade. She kicked at the hodden's legs, made it lurch backward. Whirled, her sword met the third's blade. Evenly matched, equal: a gasp in her heart as the two swords were joined and met. His fire and hers flowed together. The world was made brighter in their black light. The third, *emptiness*, pressed her, she skipped backward to keep him distant. The hodden stumbled, slapped its remaining arm against her, neighed into her face. She saw – felt – Calian on the high rock closing to finish Saem. The hodden rushed her, gobbling neighing, its branch legs snapping. The third leapt, his sword was in her face so close it was confusing: his sword, my sword. His left hand closed on her arm, the broken fingers gripping into her flesh as his sword drove at her chest. His hood fell back, showing his face.

The shock was so great her legs buckled. She almost fell. Only his hand clutching her seemed to keep her from ruin. His sword held with the point over her heart.

Pale hair vivid against his brown-cured skin. Mustached but cheeks clean-shaven. But stubble on his cheeks: he had not shaved the day they killed him. Middle-aged, a little fat around the jowls, the chin weak, the nose rather big. A bluff, commonplace face.

Hanged, drowned, thrown down in the mire: the skin of his face was wet rotten leather, the bones of his skull had been crushed by the weight of the earth pressed over him in the long years he had lain dead. His face was distorted, folded, broken. His throat was torn open, gaped like an open sack. The weight of his head had torn the skin of his neck wide open when first he had clawed and crawled his way out of the mire back to something almost like life.

His closed eyes turned, searching for Kanda. Filled with utter hate. She opened her mouth to beg him. His sword broke the skin over her heart as he pushed.

The hodden neighed. Kanda choked, smashed her arms up; the third, the nameless one, *empty*, now staggered back. Her sword was awkward but she drove hard with the flat of the blade, punched him with it in his chest so that he flopped backward. Followed up with a blow to his arm that made him drop his sword. She kicked the sword away, spun away from him, raised her sword, brought it down to cut clean through the hodden's neck. The horse skull seemed to leap at her to bite her; with a cry of disgust she struck it away. She trod down hard on the third, *empty*, *nothing*, felt with shamed delight his ribs crack beneath her heel. The hodden collapsed beside him. One of Morna's dolls dropped and abandoned. Kanda raised her sword, gripped it two-handed, brought it down like an axe to splinter the rotted wood of the hodden's torso.

It shrieked as it cleaved in half. Blood poured out and was gone.

Again she raised her sword high, sank it deep into the third's body, breaking his broken spine.

Calian shouted in triumph. Kanda spun around to see Calian deal Saem a great wound to the chest. His spear was broken off in his hand – she had cut it down; his face and his hand and his shoulder were bleeding. Sweat covered his white face. He fell from the rock with a wail, collapsed; Calian leapt down to stand over him.

"I told you I'd kill you," Calian said.

Saem scrabbled in the dirt, cowered with his face buried from her. Too terrified to beg.

Calian looked down at him with revulsion. "You killed your own sister. I buried her, Saem."

"They told me…made me…."

Calian said, "Lying, lying." She placed her sword on the back of Saem's neck. "I'll cut off your head."

Calian: no. Please.

The girl looked at her mother uncertainly. I don't want to do it. But I do want to do it so much. Tell me, Mum, what should I do? I can't do it, Mum. Is that all right, Mum?

"You get away from here, Saem, run away a thousand miles away. If I ever see you again," Calian said, "I swear I will kill you. If you look at a woman again, speak to a woman— Go away a thousand miles and…and beg every person you see to forgive you,

Saem. Go to Cythranath's grave and beg her forgiveness, then get away." She pressed the sword to draw a blossom of blood on the man's neck.

"She cursed me," Saem whispered. "She cursed as I.... She was screaming at me. How can she forgive me?"

Calian said, "Obviously, of course, Saem, she won't forgive you."

She released the sword a little, so that Saem could raise his head to stare up at her. The marks where his sister Cythranath had cut him defending herself were clear on his skin. "I curse you too. Get away with you out of my sight now."

So much relief in Calian's voice. Well done, Calian. A glimpse of peace, hope, in Calian's face. This is the right thing to do, Mum. I know it. I don't care what you think.

Well done, Calian.

Both – all three – drew a breath of sweet relief. It seems as if the world might be good still, Calian's face said. Indeed let the sun shine and the birds sing!

The third, the *emptiness*, dead and cut to pieces, killed, rent, the third said from out of his death, "If you spare his life, Calian, I too will live."

Calian spun, staggered, her sword lashed out wildly at nothing. Kanda closed her eyes in pain.

"What?" Calian screamed at her mother. "You said that sword would kill them."

The third one's dead body said tired and weary: "Ikandera Thygethyn has killed me. But if you spare that man, I will return to life again."

Kanda could not open her eyes to see her daughter.

"I have bound him to me. His life and mine. His life to my life."

"Bindings! Promises!" Behind her eyes Kanda saw her daughter press her sword into Saem's neck. Saem whimpered in terror. Cried out in pain as her sword bit. Calian bit her lip so that blood showed. She stared from her mother to that third one's broken body, she was a child, she was a warrior, she wept helplessly and defeated. Cutting,

cutting, into Saem's flesh. "My mother promised me that with that sword she could kill you!

"Curse you all!" Calian threw down her sword, fell to her knees. She struck mad at her own chest. "Get away, Saem!" she screamed. "Now, before I kill you."

The man fled on all fours like a beast. But he turned as he fled, spat behind him at Calian, "You weak pitiful bitch!"

Calian screamed and tore at her face. She sprang at the third, kicked and tore at him. Her mouth like a wolf worried at him. Tore him apart, so frail his dead body, Kanda heard his bones break under Calian's hands, his skin rip. A stone came into Calian's hands, she smashed at that third one's face. She tore her hands into the flapping rent in his throat, dragged him apart, tore off his head. Her sword came into her hand, she stabbed and stabbed until the earth beneath him was shattered. All the time, she was screaming Saem's name.

Ikandera Thygethyn had known this sick rage. The Six of Roven had felt this sick rage and its taint had never left them. Kanda fought with her daughter, pulled her off the rubble of the third's body, wrestled her fought with her slapped her face held her punched away her kicks and punches.

The child slumped into her mother's arms sobbing.

The third one, *emptiness*, groped himself back into being. Splintered bones cleaving together. Tattered fragments of ill-cured skin. He rose to his feet broken with no shape to him. Crawling, changing. The stub of his left hand grasped up his sword by the blade. He fumbled with it, held it in his two hands, moved wrong and dead away from Kanda with his bones breaking and reforming and breaking.

He too turned. His head lolled on his neck; he could not hold his head to see Kanda.

He fell and crawled away. She was left alone with Calian.

CHAPTER TWENTY-NINE

"I couldn't do it."

To say, like any wry mother, *I realized*, seemed too cruel.

"I've known him since forever, Mum. Ben Apple Tree's son. He was so disgusting, I wanted to hurt him so much. But I didn't want—" Her eyes were as vast as the sky. "I realized what it meant for him to be dead."

"What did he do to you, Calian? You should have told me he was—" *Bad? Wicked?*

Calian's voice was confusion: "Do what, Mum? He's Saem, Ben Apple Tree's son." She said after a moment, "Oh. You think he…? Oh no, no, Mum. He was always, I mean, he was hardly exactly interested in saying hello to us, but he was perfectly nice if we had to speak to him. Didn't really notice him – I mean – he was just Ben Apple Tree's son." For one moment she was free, back in the past before, her life girl-child things. Then she stiffened, clawed up her hands. "That's what made it worse. Why I wanted to kill him. He was just…a man in the valley, like the sheep and the cow, and what he said…what he did…." She took a long deep breath, tried to open her fists. "Do you think he always thought like that?"

Kanda thought: I don't know, Calian. Probably not. Or not often; sometimes, if he was angry at his sister or his father maybe, at his mother for dying, at his brother whom she died birthing for drowning even after his mother had died birthing him.

She thought: your father spat the same abuse at me only yesterday. You spit that word bitch at me yourself, Calian. There's anger at the world in poor Saem that's as justified as your anger at me.

"I should have killed him," Calian said. She picked up her sword. "I was going to. That monster – I could have killed him too. I should have. I just…I thought how horrible it would be to kill someone. Make them dead. I was so weak. I thought of Ben Apple Tree and I couldn't kill Saem and now that monster isn't dead. My fault. Stupid! Stupid!"

Kanda thought: if you had killed Saem, Calian, you would be so full of guilt and horror at yourself, you would have been poisoned forever, and that would have been far worse than that that third is still living. I'm so glad, she thought, that you were wise enough to understand. It seemed so pathetic to say it: *"It's good you admitted you slapped Morna, Calian, let's think maybe what you can learn from this," and Calian rolls her eyes. "Oh shut up, Mum."* She said it, and Calian frowned deeply, played with the hilt of her sword and knew it was a childish untrue thing her mother said.

"I just couldn't do it. He seemed so pathetic groveling and hurt. He was so frightened. I kept thinking how…how Ben Apple Tree might feel, if he knew his son was dead. How you would feel if I was dead." She said after a moment, "Not even that – just that…if I did it, he'd be dead. I'd have killed him. I couldn't do it." She said, "Stupid. Stupid."

"Never say that about not killing, Calian. Calian – you spared a man's life."

"And that thing, that *emptiness* – so will it spare a man's life?"

Silence. Kanda thought, I'm not going to answer that, Calian.

Silence. Kanda said, "Do you think, Calian – that's what makes—?"

Calian said, "Just shut up. Stupid! Stupid Saem Ben Apple Tree's stupid son."

Silence.

Silence.

Silence.

Calian gasped. "But Sal! We have to— I only came up here to find Sal. She's missing, Mum. I thought she was you, but she's not with you. You haven't seen her?" She looked sick. "What if they found Sal before they found us? Sal!" she screamed. She turned, waving her sword as if she could still fight them off her sister.

"Sal's gone," Kanda said. It came out choked, Calian didn't hear her, was searching around as if her sister was a toy dropped in the grass. "Sal! Sal! If they've hurt her.... I should have killed him. Cut him into pieces, killed him."

You promised, Mum.

"Sal's gone, Calian," Kanda said loud and clear and sharp as a trumpet. "She's gone."

"Gone? How can she be 'gone'? Where—?" Calian's voice was a howl like a wolf dying. "And you let me spare him?" She turned on her mother as if she would kill her too.

Kanda said, "Geiamnyn took her."

"*Burning*?" Calian collapsed, Kanda rushed to catch her, hold her. "But...she can't have.... She said...."

A sick cold came over Kanda. "Calian?"

"She can't have."

"She can't have what? Tell me now, Calian." Hit the child! Slap her! Shake her! Hit her face until she confessed! You know what's she's done, Kanda, strike Calian, hit her, slap her till she too is bleeding, because you can't hit Sal for doing this. "What can't Sal have done, Calian? What did Sal say?"

Calian said, utterly wretched, "I shouldn't—"

Guilty. Children's secrets. She'll be angry if I tell. If I don't tell, nothing will have happened.

"Calian. You tell me."

"She had a plan. I told her it was stupid. I told her!"

Calian's hands twisted on her sword hilt. She scratched at her hands. Kanda placed her own hands over Calian's hands to stop the girl hurting herself. "She said.... That *Burning*, she said. The way he'd looked at her. In the roundhouse. I thought she was making it up, I mean, you remember in the spring, when we went to Aranth, she was mooning over the warriors at the hall, she was sure one of them was looking at her, and of course he wasn't, I mean I thought it was just like that, I mean, I thought he'd never— She'd not—"

Aranth? Warriors? Calian you're not making...

…any sense.

"She said she'd ask him for Morna back. Like: in exchange. Like: a gift."

In the roundhouse, Geiamnyn staring, Sal starting, drawing back. And she, Sal's mother – she had thought her daughter had been a child, frightened.

"A wedding gift."

Kanda heard Calian's voice from a long way off. Stones and raw flesh in it. "I didn't think she'd really do it."

Silence.

Calian shouted, "So full of himself, that one, he must think every living thing he meets wants to rut with him." She used the word they used for cattle and sheep. She was a child, Sal was a child. "So she thought, if he believed her that she was in love with him, she could agree to go with him and then he'd let Morna go." Calian whispered, "She said she wouldn't…she wouldn't rut with him until he let Morna go.

"I told her she was being so stupid. But she…she said this was the only way she could think of to rescue Morna.

"If you weren't going to do anything, she said."

Sal shouting: "Well, I'll get it then, if you can't be bothered to do anything for us ever, Mummy." Sal shouting: "You don't care at all about Morna, Mummy, if you did you'd…." I'd do something unnecessary and wasteful and pointless. Sal and Calian conspiring together, in a corner with hurt glances, fake muffled voices fake whispering: "If she won't get it for Morna, we'll have to get it for Morna instead." And then it all goes wrong, sure as night follows day follows night again, because there was a very good reason I didn't do it get it let them have it, which they don't know because they're children.

Kanda shouting: "You're fifteen now, Sal. You're twelve now, Calian. Can't you do anything for yourselves? What do you want me to do, wipe your arses for you? Can't you see I'm exhausted?" Kanda shouting: "Look after your sister, won't you? She's your little sister, I shouldn't have to ask you to look after her." Kanda smiling: "I'm so proud of you, Sal, Calian, for doing that thing on your own, for being grown-ups not children."

But that's about small things. Child things. All the weight in the world I will always carry for you, my children.

Kanda took her daughter awkwardly in her arms. Find the words. Comfort – herself. "At least you …you told me. Sal is so strong, so…. Sal will have them all running around for her by this evening. Ysarene washing her clothes, Geiamnyn fetching her a cup of milk. Can you just imagine that!" It was wrong and false and Calian was disgusted at her thinking it would comfort her. "I don't think Geiamnyn will hurt her. It's me he wants to hurt, not Sal or Morna." And that was a worse lie, but Calian was just young and innocent and hopeful enough still not quite to know or see.

Should I be pleased I must be such a good mother, Kanda thought, because neither of them can really understand what a monster Geiamnyn is? Sal, simpering and giggling at Geiamnyn, yes, she does think he's handsome, who wouldn't? Trying to sound so grown, so confident, a warrior like her mother, I know what I'm doing, Mum. I should be proud that my children have so much courage. I should be shocked if they had not looked to rescue their sister from harm. Calian, my fierce one, my eagle; Sal, my shining, my kind strength. Warriors, her daughters, trying to do what they thought best. Planning, plotting, hoping, trying. All the strength and power they had in them, poured out to save a life. No more and no less would I myself have done. If Geiamnyn had offered to exchange my life for Morna's, Kanda thought, I would have kissed his hands and gone with him rejoicing, knowing he lied but unable to turn away from the chance. If Dellet had made an exchange, slit his throat for Morna's life back, I would have…I would….

But Sal – it's different.

The world breaks, the world is dead and cold now. But for Calian's sake – be strong!

She thought, almost with terrible laughter: then I'll sit screaming and weeping for Sal, and Calian will go off with her sword, "*I have to do something if Mum is just crying*," and Calian will be lost, all three of my daughters each gone after the last. Then Dellet after them. Then what?

Kanda took a long deep breath. "We will go together to find them both. You and I, Calian. Then you and Sal and me, together we'll rescue Morna, we'll make everything well. I – I promise we will."

Calian shivered. A brief, weak flame of child's hope. The girl frowned, trying to think her way through hope and despair both at once. "Sal was certain that *Burning* was Lord Morren once. She'd worked it out, she said. *The most beautiful of the Six, golden, a young man in the flower of his manhood. Even his helmet was inlaid with gold figures of the people of Roven dancing at a feast.* It's the same helmet, she said. She said he must be the one who broke the oath."

A desperate hope in Calian's voice now. "So if he was once your friend, he can't be…he can't be all bad, can he? That's what Sal said."

She waited for Kanda to say *yes, yes, he was Lord Morren, he was my friend once, he must still remember somewhere what he was. What we were. Perhaps, even, seeing me again…and Sal looks very like me, everyone says so, Sal's such a good kind child, he'll see, he'll remember…. Beautiful and shining and good.*

Pain on pain, endlessly rising. Kanda groaned so loud the earth shook. What did I just tell myself – three daughters I have borne, two I have lost, the third now I shall lose. The rock on which Calian had fought trembled at her groan, trembled and groaned itself and split apart. The earth groaned in answer to her, cracks opened, the mountain was breaking, again again again did her world end. The purple heather turned gray and brittle, the yellow gorse and the green grass were gray. Birds rose up beating their wings in terror at her groan, the air was cold so that Calian breathed out white frost. Kanda beat her hands on the earth, opened chasms beneath her fingers: bottomless, those chasms were, reaching down forever into the dark. Clouds came in a rush to cover the sun. Memory: Morren dying, his face astonished, the golden beauty leaching out of him. His hands raised to meet the air. *But I won't be dancing. Singing. Feasting. But all the lips to kiss, all the games to play, I am Lord Morren, most beautiful of the Six, I don't…but I don't even like fighting.* Geiamnyn standing over him, exultant. Ikandera Thygethyn at Geiamnyn's side. Ikandera Thygethyn laughing.

Many promises I've broken. Many things I've lied about or kept hidden. As everyone keeps things hidden, as everyone breaks promises to those they love. But I've never lied to you about the true things of the world, Calian my love.

Calian looked at her mother. So alike they were, Calian and Kanda. The least loved of Kanda's three children, because if Sal looked the most like her mother, Calian was so like her mother in so many other things.

Calian said, "I told Sal she was wrong about *Burning*. That it would be much harder than she thought, I begged her not to do it, because I knew she was wrong. I don't know if he was Lord Morren once or not. I don't think he can be. If it is the same helmet, it's because that *Burning* stole it from Lord Morren.

"But – your sword, Mum. Your armor, your helmet. And your name, *Ikandera Thygethyn.* It's not like the others' names….

"Lord Morren wasn't the one who broke the oath, was he, Mum?

"He wasn't the one who did the terrible thing."

Breathe in. Try to speak.

Try to speak.

"Mum. Tell me the truth, Mum."

Try to speak:

"Morren did not break the oath. He is not Geiamnyn. I told you: Geiamnyn was only a man once.

"Geiamnyn took Morren's helmet for himself, yes, it is the same helmet, it sickens me to see it on Geiamnyn's head. But Geiamnyn did not kill Morren. They fought before the gates of Roven, and Morren had the better of it. Three times, he threw Geiamnyn back. Geiamnyn fled from him."

Kanda said, "I killed Lord Morren.

"I struck him from behind, a coward's blow. I helped Geiamnyn strip off his armor. I spat on his face as he died and told him I would tear down the walls of Roven with my bare hands. I swore to him that I would kill the Lord of Roven myself.

"That oath also I could not keep.

"Morren begged me with his last breath at least to bury him, but I refused him. Because he was beautiful, Ysarene buried him.

"Ysarene buried him!

"I was the greatest of the Six, the bravest, the strongest. But what my name was then, I do not remember. Or so I tell myself. 'I am Ikandera Thygethyn,' I cried to Lord Morren as I killed him. 'And I am a greater warrior indeed than any of you Six who are so soft and weak.'

"I was the one who broke the oath and destroyed it all, yes, you're right, Calian."

CHAPTER THIRTY

It was a day of wonders. Any army gathered in the fields waiting for the daybreak, "The night is more fearful, yes, fine it would be to stalk them in the dark, bringing night terrors – but we will kill them in the day," Ysarene shouted, "so we can better see their dying faces." Their banners flew proud overhead. Ikandera Thygethyn sharpened her sword over and over, sharp as the wind, it must be, to strike off the Lord of Roven's head.

They had diced for that privilege, Ikandera Thygethyn, Geiamnyn, Ysarene and that third one without a name. That one who was *emptiness* won the game, but he gave the honor to Ikandera Thygethyn as a welcome gift. A sword, also, he gave her as a gift.

They raised up the sacrifice. On high poles, tall as the tallest treetops, they hung the bodies they had sacrificed. They beat the war drums, sounded the deep trumpets. Shared and drank deep from the loving cups. Three warriors chosen for their valor took the front wrapped in bloodied raw cloaks. They were unarmed, without armor, only the blood coated them. These three would die that the rest would fight without harm, and they gloried in it.

On the far edges of their ranks shapes moved that Ikandera Thygethyn could not yet see. Only after she had killed in this battle would she be able to see them. They did not dare come near to her out of fear of her, and that was greatly pleasing.

Such power she had, Ikandera Thygethyn. Such new great joy she felt in it.

The only grief she felt was that she could not remember what her name had been, when she had been one of the Six. If she could remember that name, how much she would enjoy mocking and despoiling it.

The sky grew lighter. The wound of the sun indeed! A day of warmth and sunlight. A summer day, with the crops almost ripe in the fields. How pleasant the sun was on Ikandera Thygethyn's skin.

Ysarene, *Hunger*, whom Ikandera Thygethyn thought of with scorn, weak and stupid, Ysarene seemed, and so pitiful in her needs, Ysarene held out to Ikandera Thygethyn the loving cup of pure gold set with pearls and diamonds and red rubies, filled brimming with wine red as blood.

"To all that is death and dying," Ysarene said, and Ikandera Thygethyn drank deep.

"We will drink better things tonight in the ruins of Roven," Ysarene said. "We will drink human blood, eat human meat." Hunger-spittle clung to Ysarene's flayed chin.

You disgust me, Ikandera Thygethyn thought to Ysarene. If someone had not already maimed you, I would do it myself, I think. Ysarene saw that, cowered. She took the cup back from Ikandera Thygethyn, drank.

Geiamnyn strode to join them, his face radiant. *Burning*. Ikandera Thygethyn thought: he is a better companion than Ysarene. But he too is so pitifully weak.

She thought with pleasure of the coming battle: how much can I show them. Teach them! She sharpened her sword again, because it must be sharp as the wind to take off her Lord of Roven's head. "I will see you grovel at my feet," she crooned to herself, running her hand down the sharp sword blade. "I will see you grovel and beg, weak old man, and then I will take your head. I will tie your head to my belt as a trophy, and when I have raised a new hall for myself, far greater and grander than your Hall of Roven, I will set your head above my seat. But your body will lie unburied and unmourned, and the dogs of your own hall will tear at it. All these things I swear, Lord of Roven." She said to Geiamnyn and Ysarene and that one who was only *empty*, she said then, "If you touch him, if any hand kills him but mine, I will have their head, and I will not make their dying easy." And Geiamnyn and Ysarene and even that empty one whom she still feared a little were afraid, and bowed their heads.

That oath, also, was broken. Through fire and blood and ruin she strode eager to the Hall Roven. But at the threshold she drew back, trembled, the sword fell from her hand and her body was as water. She pissed herself with fear. She fled. She butchered the servants, the pretty girls whom Lord Morren had loved to dance with, the cooks, the weavers, the gardeners who tended the orchards. The dogs which she had sworn would rend her Lord's body, she butchered. She watched the army sack Roven, Geiamnyn and Ysarene and that empty one gut Roven, she watched the roof fall in fire, the walls running flame. Only then did she dare cross the threshold.

A day of wonders, truly. She feasted that night in the ashes where the Hall had stood and was content.

CHAPTER THIRTY-ONE

She waited for Calian to ask her why. Always why, always questioning her about the ways of the world, that one. *Why did the raiders come to steal our cattle, Mum, when they could raise their own without risk of dying, all of us here in the valley could have spared them between us a bull and a breeding cow and a calf couldn't we, if they'd asked? Why does the headman at Aranth need thirty warriors in his hall, Mother, what in the world do they need to do, they didn't do anything when the raiders came, why not, Mum? Why didn't you let that beggar woman come in and eat with us, since you say all the time we should help people and be good?* She remembered Calian asking of Geiamnyn and Ysarene and that empty one, "Why do they kill, Mother?" truly confused and wondering so far beyond *because they are wicked and evil.* Why, what possible purpose could it serve them, to wantonly kill like this? But why are they wicked? What made them evil? She looked at Calian, waiting. Calian sat and looked at her sword a little while. Calian looked at the sky.

"I guessed it," Calian said. "When I saw your sword. When you told me the story of the oath. The way the monsters spoke to you. The way you spoke to them. I knew."

Calian said, as if talking to a younger child, "I didn't tell Dad or Sal, don't worry."

"Your father must guess." If I say it, Kanda thought, it will not be true.

"Of course Dad doesn't guess. He loves you."

Ask me why. Please. Then I can...I can lie to you. *It was a mistake. I didn't mean it. Like Morna being lost, or Saem's brother drowning, just...a bad terrible thing. I was angry, I shouted, "A curse on my oath to you, Lord of Roven, a curse on the Six!" I didn't mean it to happen like that, the words came out, we all say things, but it was an oath sworn and so it was – like...like smashing a plate, and you didn't mean to throw the plate, and suddenly it's broken, and you think, you think, I didn't...I'm sorry...but it's too late....*

CHAPTER THIRTY-TWO

She is standing before the Lord of Roven's throne on the high dais. She holds out her sword. The Lady is not there to take it. The distant sound of the bird flapping its wings where it is caught in the Lady's antlers.

She is not angry. She says it very calmly: "A curse on my oath to you, Lord of Roven. A curse on the Six. Hear me now. See me now. Here I stand, and I break my oath."

She throws down her sword. The most beautiful thing she has ever seen before she sees her children's newborn faces, that sword. A chain, a curse on her, that sword is.

The sword breaks at her feet.

Three swords hang on the wall behind her Lord's throne. They break.

One sword is with Erenan somewhere distant, Erenan is afraid, lost without her companions, brokenhearted for Eliusa, too proud and too afraid to come back to Roven. Erenan draws her sword to cut sticks for the fire, to hunt down rabbits, to build herself a shelter in the wild wood. She hears Erenan's sword break.

One sword is with Palle on the training ground, he strikes and strikes, practicing his sword work, his footwork, the hold for the shielding of a child, the hold for the warding of a gate. "They will come, the evil, I feel them, they call me, they will come for me," he whispers to himself, mutters day and night and night and day, "we must defend, we must keep the people safe here, they will come, they call me, I'm weak, I'm too weak." She hears him mutter it, she hears him strike the practice post, "they'll come, they call me, I'm too weak to defend." She hears him strike, harder, harder. "I must be ready, I must be better." She hears his sword break.

Her Lord of Roven looks at her. Milk flows from his breasts. But the baby is still beneath his skin.

She tramples on the broken sword. In the tread of her feet is ash and dust.

"Where is Kestre?" she says. "She is hiding in fear of a battle.

"Where is Gallyn? He is with his husband, whom he cares about more than he does we Six.

"Where is Morren? He is idling in his chambers.

"Where is Palle? He is on his knees weeping.

"Where is Erenan? She is driven off alone.

"Where is the Lady of Roven? She is nothing but carved wood going rotten.

"Where is the Lord of Roven who made me? He is sitting before me old and weak."

When she says this last thing, her voice finally is so angry it breaks.

"You lie," she says, "about all of this. *Peace*, you call this Hall? *Hope*, you call the throne you sit upon? You send us out, we are victorious, you send us out, you send us out, you send us out. Where is the *peace*? Where is the *hope*?

"Your child will never be born, and we will never be victorious," she says. She says the worst thing she can think of. Then and forever. "If it is born, I hope your child is born dead," she says.

She strides out of the hall to silence. The men and women gathered are too afraid to look at her. Better that, she thinks, than their eager hungry staring. Her track is marked in dust and ashes. The gates are open, she walks through them. Benethal the gatekeeper raises his horn to his lips. She hunted the beast that bore that horn. Benethal, *Safe Place*, lowers the horn unblown from his lips.

Beyond the gates of Roven are three figures, one silver, one red fire, one wet and darkness. She walks to them.

CHAPTER THIRTY-THREE

I have never felt as free as when I went from that place to join them. I have never felt such peace. I had no fear. I had no shame. I had no guilt on me. I had only the freedom from fear and shame and guilt.

They were hunger. They were burning. They were emptiness. But I....

I was a great warrior. I did not feel anything beyond myself.

Calian stood up, sheathed her sword. Held out her hand to her mother to help her up. "You are still a great warrior, but they are your enemy now. So I think we should go together and kill them."

You don't judge? You don't hate? A mother cannot ask her own child that: *do you hate me, do you forgive me?* Not easily. When Kanda took Calian's hand she felt the child flinch, a shudder run through her. Then Calian's hand closed on her mother's hand tight.

Kanda said, "I would like very much to do that."

They went a few steps, both going slowly because neither could face the pain of what they must tell Dellet. They had to step over piles of broken rock and gaping fissures in the earth. The hodden's remains lay with stones and dust over them, the branch legs both crushed, the wooden body crumbling away. They stopped over it. In all this horror, Kanda had almost forgotten it.

Calian squatted, put her hands on the rotted wood. The curved lines of a woman's hip and waist, if you knew it had once been the statue of a woman. Calian said, low and clear, "Thank you, Lady, for the sword and the peace of the island." She said to Kanda, "I thought I saw her, just for a moment, the first time I used my sword." A faint weak light glowed around the broken statue. Glowed on Calian's hands.

Calian said like talking to a younger child, "Put your hands on her." Kanda squatted beside her, reached out, drew back, reached out. The Lady's broken body glowed brighter. Kanda's hands glowed. In her mind the Lady's voice whispered clear.

Oh. Oh.

Kanda bent her head, wept for both joy and grief.

"Should we bury her?" Calian asked.

"No. There's no time for that." Her hands shook, it was too terrible, the thought of digging that grave. "She lay for a thousand years in the mire after Roven fell ruined. Let her lie now on the open hillside with the sun and the rain on her. Let her body be food for the earth."

The horse's skull was in shattered pieces. Calian lifted the largest shard of bone, looked at it. She placed the bone shard on the wooden body, began to gather the rest of the skull together. "And this? Horse's skulls are like nightmares," said Calian. "Always terrified me."

Kanda said, "She could outrun the sun rising and the wind blowing and the turning of the tide. She was the most beautiful horse. Black, her mane almost as soft as your hair. But it's true, she was wasted on me, she should have been Erenan's."

Calian said nothing.

"Leave her also. A wild animal: she does not need burying. She would not let me go near her after," Kanda said to Calian. "She ran wild and a wolf killed her. I fought it off her but it was too late."

I didn't ask, Mum, I didn't think it, Calian's silence said.

"*Henef, fairest and swiftest of horses, high-hearted, dauntless, never-weary. Henef, Queen of Mares, bedecked in shining gold.*" Kanda thought, and looked, and thought, and reached out more fearfully than she had reached to touch the Lady's body. A single tooth had come loose from the lower jaw, and here, beside it, a little chip of bone, one edge raw fresh cut from Calian's sword stroke, one edge the smooth curve of the socket of a black liquid eye. Kanda took the tooth and the bone chip, tucked them away in the pocket at her belt.

A horse's hooves thunder like a racing heartbeat. She felt them drum against her belly. Like an unborn baby kicking.

She took a splinter of wood also, put it beside the tooth and bone. It was disgusting in her hand, crumbling, rotted; she shuddered with a taste of damp and grubs. Then a tiny spark of warmth against her belly. Too quickly swallowed by her own skin.

Kanda wept only for grief. But she thought: we have freed them, they are at peace. She felt a warmth in her that she had not felt since she first saw the hodden. She thought and felt, and for the first time since she had seen the hodden she realized she could not hear crashing in her mind the sounds of war and pillage, the ceaseless rasp of a whetstone on a blade. She thought with horror: all I have done since I first saw the hodden has been corrupted by fear and shame. Well, now the hodden is gone.

They came down the mountain together hand in hand. Dellet still sat where he had been sitting all this while. Kanda thought with rage: didn't you hear the battle? Your daughter, Del, fighting, you sat there and did nothing. What if I was here now saying she was dead at that empty one's hands, Del? Or at the hands of Saem, Ben Apple Tree's son? You'd blame me for that. Dellet turned his head, he felt them coming, he knew they were come. His heart leapt into his face and Kanda thought of his wounds healing under her hands on the island.

He tried to pretend nothing had happened, sat where he had been sitting. Grunted, "You didn't find your sister, then, Calian?"

"I found her and I'll bring her back, Dad," Calian said gravely. She took her hand away from her mother, put her hand on her father's shoulder, passing strength to strength. The man sighed deeply, rested his head against her.

"I got some breakfast ready," Dellet said after a moment. "Just the leavings from last night, I can't do…and I'm not touching that bag of your mother's. Enough for…enough for three," he said, despairing. "I didn't dare hope. I wasn't going to risk making…making her…like a curse, it felt like. It was just getting something to eat, just a few scraps of old bread!"

"It looks very good, Dad," Calian said gently. A fine meal set out, food for five hearty appetites carefully set in three places.

Kanda said, "It was wise not to set food for her, Dellet. Well thought."

The man grunted. But he lifted his head, let go of his daughter's hand though it was a great effort, took up a crust, then waited with his eyes eager on his daughter's face until she had eaten something. The bread was from last night, the last leavings, but it was fresh and still warm when they put in their mouths and tasted as though it was spread thick with butter and honey. Dellet stared in wonder.

"It seems you can do magic too, Dad," said Calian.

They ate and washed themselves in the pool. The water was so clear now, fish darted in between their legs. If Kanda listened very carefully, she thought she could hear the mine children splashing in the water with them.

A thought came to Kanda: "Where's Sal's knife?"

"She was keeping it by that bush there. I think, I'll get it." Calian looked around the gorse bush, searched around the entrance to the mineshaft, even went a little into the shaft. "I can't find it. She must have taken it with her." Triumph in her voice: "I told you, Mum."

A trumpet rang.

Not a war trumpet. A joyful, dancing note, calling the guests to the hall to feast. The air shimmered before them and a man was standing there smiling at them.

He wore dark armor and a helmet of boars' tusks; his yellow beard and his long yellow hair were plaited with pebbles. His white face was the face of a man who had no blood left in him, his eyes were the blank eyes of a dead man, his throat was cut. He held a beautiful silver trumpet, its bell a firedrake with greenstone eyes and a red tongue that moved with the music. A silver bird sat on his shoulder, pecked at the wound to his throat as he sounded the trumpet.

He took the trumpet from his lips. Now the trumpet was a tree branch made of silver and gold and the leaves made of diamonds. The bird hopped from his shoulder onto the branch, cocked its head at them.

"The branch of peace," the bird croaked. It blinked black glass eyes. "My Lord Geiamnyn, mighty in strength and power and glory, he is wedding a fine fair maiden who has stolen his heart away and you are bid to attend the wedding feast. Ikandera Thygethyn and the warrior called *Eagle* and the one who is nothing but Dell, *man*, who attends them."

"Geiamnyn thinks that I will come to watch him destroy my own child?" But Kanda though in despair: I can be the old crone who waves the bloody sheet after the bedding.

Calian hissed at the bird. It flapped its wings at her. "No harm! No harm will come! My master bade me tell you he has a fine rich bride gift for his beloved that you will see if you attend. A day to the south and a day to the east and twenty paces beyond what you find there," the bird croaked. "When the horn has been blown and the blade has fallen, there is spread my lord's wedding feast."

Calian looked at Kanda, Kanda looked back at her. Neither could bear to look at Dellet.

Kanda said slowly, "Tell your master, then, that we will attend."

"Joy!" the bird croaked. "Joy!" It rose into the air with a clattering of metal feathers. The silver branch was a silver trumpet, the dead man raised it to his lips and blew. The note was beautiful. The dead man lowered the trumpet, bowed to Kanda, bowed to Calian, bowed to Dellet. The trumpet was a firedrake, black and silver with green eyes and a red tongue. It spat fire, flew away to the south. Calian watched it until it was drowned in the liquid sky. Yearning for it sang in Calian's bright face.

The dead man fell dead at Kanda's feet, five days, six days dead? Putrid, certainly, poor wretch.

Him, too, she and Calian and Dellet buried. Getting good at digging graves. Kanda did not tell them what he must have been, agreed when Calian said, "I recognize him, I think, from Aranth. The monsters must have killed him when they destroyed the hall." She said sadly, "He was one of the ones Sal was mooning over. He wasn't very good at fighting, actually, I thought that when we were watching the warriors practice."

Kanda thought: poor wretched man. She thought as she placed a sprig of green on the grave: we are alike, you and I. I can only pity you for making the same mistakes. Let your spirit go now in peace.

When the grave was dug she said to her husband and her last remaining daughter, "So. Now we must attend Sal's wedding. A day's walk to the south and a day's walk to the east and then twenty paces."

The mineshafts where the children had toiled rang with happiness compared to Dellet's face. But briefly he touched his wife's hand, briefly he tried to cross his pain toward her. "I suppose I should think of a speech to make," he said. "Never been good at that. Words and things."

"Calian can give you some help with that, I should think," Kanda said. "She's the clever one."

"Too clever by half," Dellet said. "Aren't you, Calian?"

The dark came back over him as they walked. His footsteps were the sound of a whetstone rasping on a sword blade.

When they had been walking south for several hours he said, "What did it mean: when the horn has been blown and the blade has fallen?"

Calian said, "Nothing good."

CHAPTER THIRTY-FOUR

Dreaming. At night when they slept. In the day, behind her waking eyes, while they walked south and then east.

Ikandera Thygethyn stands on the plain with the city before her and her army behind her. She stands alone in the death place between. A fine army, matchless, surely – from a stone from the wall of a ruined city, from the thigh bone of an unborn baby, from a spearhead that had killed its wielder's own father in battle, she has shaped her men. Three drops of her blood she let fall on the stone and the bone and the spearhead, she spoke the words, her army leapt up around her armed and waiting. The fine rich city shines so bright her eyes ache to look upon it. Inakanassos in the Forever Morning, ever has it been at wise gentle peace. Gardens, fountains, courtyards; palaces for its wise men, its magicians, made of solid gold and solid diamond, or of flowers, or of sea-silk that glows golden with its own inner light; the houses for those who serve the city, its workers, white marble houses grander than palaces they would seem, in any other city in the world. Smoke rises from hearth fires and forge fires, scented with spice and flowers: incense is burned in the hearth fires and the forge fires so that the whole city is perfumed. The walls are so wide five horses could ride five abreast around their circuit. The walls are planted with lilac trees, jasmine and honeysuckle and climbing roses adorn them, covering them, the city rising out of flowers and green leaves. The city is lit up, every window is blazing with lamplight, there are fires on the top of the walls. The people of the city know that she is coming, and they do not want to wait for death in the darkness, they would rather die in the light.

She draws her fine new sword, raises it high. She brings it down with a crash to rend the earth.

Inakanassos in the Forever Morning. As her sword strikes the earth, the darkness comes down over Inakanassos. Never will the light shine on it again.

Before the city walls, an army is drawn up waiting for her. A few small weak lines of women and men. Never has this city known war: they hold new-forged spears, wear new-forged armor, they have no idea how to fight. Once, she would have had to shield them all. Patient teaching: *hold your shield thus, your spear thus. Don't fear, be comforted, I am come to help you all, you are safe now, I promise it.*

On the plain between Ikandera Thygethyn and the city there is a little stream, meandering through reedbeds, a shrine stands there on the stream bank, a stone and a bell and an offering place. Ikandera steps forward to the stream, touches it with the tip of her sword. The water boils. Runs red.

She gives the signal to attack. Her war trumpets ring.

Her army moves forward. A thick mass of soldiers marching in silence. The defenders before the city cower, moan in fear as her soldiers come on remorseless toward them. Ikandera Thygethyn says the word and cold fire sears into their left flank. They have magicians with them, they too send out fire, her magic is deflected. Anger in her, as her men fall to the magicians. She speaks the words again and her fire is greater, higher, harder. One of the magicians falls dead.

Her army moves forward. Reaches the stream. The magicians of Inakanassos and the stream that flows there rise together to defend their boundaries. The stream rushes high and wild, sucks at her soldiers' feet. Her army marches across in lines as solid as the mountains. Perfectly ordered, shields locked to shields, their armor sucking all the last pitiful light out. Cold fire plays around their helmets, runs like the rain down their spears and their sword blades. The stream pulls them under, a hundred of them, more, more, drowning. The stream is bottomless and they will sink forever into its depths. She could fight the stream. She is furious that it is killing her men. In truth, she thought that she had defeated it when she made it run red. She touches the tip of her sword to the stone on the stream bank now and it cracks apart. She laughs now: her men are still dying, drowning, so many of them sucked down that the stream is choked. Over them, the ranks of her army march on. Her dead are a causeway for their comrades to walk over.

A voice whispers in her mind. Gentle and loving. She thrills at the voice. Her face is hot like the young bride she is. But the voice is warning: "Ikandera my love, take care. Look above you." She looks up in fear, then she merely sneers.

She says to her beloved, "That is nothing. I have killed dragons before, my love."

"It is the guardian of this city," her beloved whispers. "It is why we have never before dared to raise our swords against Inakanassos. Take care, Ikandera!"

"You are weaker than me," she says to her beloved. "All of you. Don't fear. Watch me, my love."

The dragon comes down at her. Gold. So very beautiful. Her men are running now, cowering, the vast mouth opens, breathing out fire, consuming her men back to stone and bronze and tiny pathetic bones. Her men are breaking, fleeing over the plain; her men are standing staring, waiting for it in the glory of knowing it will consume them. It falls on her like the sun falling from the sky, her beloved cries in terror: "Ikandera! My wife, my love!" but she only laughs: did she not only now plunge the world into darkness, put out the sun? Its flames pour over her and she stands laughing and ready in the furnace of its breath. She shouts her war cry so loud she sees the dragon flinch.

Its claws come down at her. Forelimbs as long as her body. Her fine new sword cuts into its claws. It rakes at her, claws at her, its teeth close to tear her flesh. She shouts her war cry, her fine new sword seems alive in her hand, seems to leap itself to meet the dragon's body, hungry as she is to destroy it. She strikes and she wounds it. Its pain is vast, for the sword is without mercy. Her body sings with the thought of its pain. It pulls itself up and away, circles high above her. In her mind, her beloved gasps in astonishment.

She laughs, shouts her war cry. The air shakes. The dragon jerks and thrashes in the sky, her very shout injuring it. She shouts, "Break, you worm! Come down from the sky, worm! Grovel to me! Break!" It obeys her. Half-stunned, terrified, from its beautiful golden jaws she hears it whimper in fear of her like a beaten dog. It comes down with a crash, its belly dragging on the ground. Its scales dull sick fish-belly yellow, rank with mud. Her fine new sword that her beloved gave her comes up to meet it. She sings with a new happiness deeper and fiercer than anything she had known when she was merely a servant of the Lord of Roven. As the green dragon had died so easily beneath her sword where no other had dared fight it, so does the gold dragon of Inakanassos die.

Ikandera Thygethyn shouts, and the war trumpets ring. A thousand soldiers all around her, running now, many wounded from the dragon fire, trampling across the stream, hurling themselves at the gold and silver walls. Thrown at the city, driving on, one mind crying out to kill. In the city the defenders are ready, but how can they be ready, when the dragon guardian is dead and the army comes in and on? Her men die in columns of magic thrown at them from the defenders before the walls, they are ripped apart, melted, turned back to stone and bronze and pitiful bone. Golden fire comes over them from the city, drifting. A cloud of light. Her men die in it. Burn up in it. But her army is endless, it overwhelms the defenders before the walls as it overwhelmed the stream. Her sword is in her hand, calling her on. She meets the defenders before the walls herself, it is even easier than killing the dragon to kill them.

She raises her head, watches a ball of the magicians' fire fly over her. She thinks: it's beautiful. She watches it and it seems a long time, hanging in the air, all her time is getting lost and wandering. It crashes down breaking a thousand of her men apart. She cannot see it hit, but she feels the crash through her whole body, the earth shakes. She spits blood. Truly angry now. She strides to the very base of the walls. The walls rear up like horses, and she is a beast in the darkness scrabbling at them. She is a wolf, pacing.

On the walls the defenders are writhing. Black shadow shapes, staring down. Their spears and their swords and their helmets gleam in the light of their bonfires. They are blinded by the fires, they are facing out into the dark and she is coming for them like a beast in the darkness, like a great wave in a black night sea. But they want to die in the light, as living men.

She cries her war cry. The walls tremble, the flowers growing on them wither.

With a howl of sorrow, the walls fall.

Ikandera Thygethyn stands in the rubble. Dust coats her fire-red hair. She runs into the city. Claws at dying men.

Her army halts at the circle where the walls stood. Alone, Ikandera Thygethyn destroys the city, every living thing within it she kills. She does not leave one stone of the city standing.

She thinks: this is what fighting is.

The sun sets, the sun rises, but there is eternal darkness now where once stood Inakanassos in the Forever Morning.

CHAPTER THIRTY-FIVE

One day south. One day east. If she had not been so consumed with dreams she would have seen where they walked to: they walked to the rubble of their own home. The folds and ridges of the high hills were Dellet's body, his bones, his muscles and fat. The rocks thrusting up through the earth were a baby's head crowning, clutching at life. The folds and the ridges and the rocks and the canopy of every tree were familiar, Kanda dreamed of her glory years and her feet walked without failing the trackless way back to her farmhouse. They walked along the top of the river valley; the land fell sheer to the water meadow and the Wenet and the woods on the southern bank. Kanda was confused that the trees were still green just as they had been, the landscape unchanged, if she squinted she could almost see herself down at the river with the grass dew-wet around her ankles, calling in the cows. If the body had not floated down the river that morning, she thought, she would have gone back into the house unknowing, and perhaps Geiamnyn and Ysarene would have left her alone. She thought: but no, he would never have left me alone once he knew I was here, and they would have delighted in telling him. There, that rock where the current catches – that was where the dead body had snagged. The water swirled there beautiful, she liked to look there where the current made the water fold itself, it reminded her of a horse's strong flanks galloping. The burial house there, the hawthorns just beginning now to turn toward berry-red.

The house stood as they had left it. The apple tree and the apples ripening, the garden full of green stuff, the line of graceful aspens. Calian gave a whoop of joy, sprang forward, stopped.

"What have the monsters done?" Calian whispered.

They stood far enough off from the house that the pain it rang with was not too terrible.

"Don't look any closer," said Kanda.

Dellet shuddered. "No."

They stood awhile, awkward and stupid. Calian said, "So now what?"

"*Twenty paces beyond what you find there*. Beyond the house."

Calian looked sick. "And what will be there behind the house?"

Kanda could only say, "A horn and a blade, I should think."

Dellet reached out his hand, took Calian's hand, then after a moment he shook his head, reached out to take his wife's hand. Kanda felt him tremble, draw back one moment, as their fingers met. She squeezed his hand tight. He held her hand loose.

They went together twenty paces. They counted them aloud, as they had when they were teaching the children their numbers. Twenty paces took them into the higher sheep field. There was nothing to see but the grass, sheep droppings, tufts of wool. There were no animals and no birds. It was wrong like the house was wrong not to hear the cows and the sheep. Running across the field were Geiamnyn's burned tracks and the wet tracks of that one who was only *empty*. A crow lay dead in Geiamnyn's tracks; it was almost good to see it because it had been living.

"There's nothing here," Dellet cried. "Nothing!"

They took the last step forward. A whetstone rasped on a blade.

A fine pavilion stood in the center of the sheep field. It was made of thick yellow hide, the poles of the tent were carved bone. In the evening light the tent seemed to glow. The doorcurtain was drawn back. Hand in hand together, they walked right up to the tent. Kanda stepped inside. Calian followed her close at her heels. Dellet hesitated, for a moment they were inside the tent and he was outside in the sheep field. He put one foot over the threshold of the tent, for a moment now he was in both places at once, his face was filled with fear for he knew he could not step back out unchanged. His daughter guided him inside like a mother helping an infant on its first steps.

Inside the tent a bed was made up, the coverlet richly worked in brilliant colors, a thick black fur spread over the coverlet for extra warmth. A table set with fine bronze vessels, a washing bowl and a jug of wine and a plate and a cup, and a bronze lamp in the shape of a hissing goose. A folding seat of red leather, its poles too not wood but bone. A brazier by the table for the tent's occupant to warm their hands. A stand for a panoply, with a smaller clay lamp set below it in offering.

The stand was empty. For it was Ikandera Thygethyn's war tent. Calian knew it. Kanda saw she knew. And the girl did not look horrified at the idea of a war tent.

The doorcurtain flapped closed. Invisible hands pulling it closed so that the tent's occupant might have privacy. The oil lamps sputtered into light. The brazier flickered with flames.

On the table now there was a hunting horn. It was white, bound and tipped in silver. The horn lifted into the air. It sounded long and mournful. The note rose so loudly that Calian clapped her hands over her ears.

From outside the tent there came a sound of something moving. Something heavy and huge. Loud angry breathing. Something pushed against the walls of the tent. Snorted. The horn sounded again, yet louder. A bellow came from outside the tent. The horn blew so loud Kanda was half blinded. So loud it shattered into three pieces. A roar of cow-smell and mud and breathing. The doorcurtain was snatched open. A great bellow that was a hot wind as a bull charged through into the tent.

Black, with eyes that glittered like diamonds. It towered over Kanda, bigger than any bull that had ever been seen in the valley of the Wenet. Its gilded horns were as long as her sword blade. A garland of white flowers was around its neck. It bellowed, tossed its head. It had been whipped to madden it so that its flanks ran with blood. Its eyelids and its muzzle had been cut.

Its charge overturned the table and the brazier. Bronze vessels fell ringing to the floor. The noise and the flames maddened it further, the confines of the tent panicked it. It charged at Kanda bellowing, trampling all the tent underfoot. Without thinking she threw herself at it, plunged her sword into its heavy hanging neck. Its blood was a fountain, drowning her eyes and mouth. It bellowed, its horns caught her arm and tore her open. Her feet slid glossy in its blood. It bellowed, threw its head back, stumbled to one knee in its agonies. It lowed in fear, knowing itself dying. Kanda brought her sword down fast. Cut off its head.

She fell to her knees beside it. Sodden in its blood. What cruelty, to harm such a beast.

From outside the tent came the babble of voices, the music of a harp. The bull was gone and the tent was gone. Not a sheep field but a great high hall, five, six, seven times as large as the Hall Roven. Dellet and Calian cried out in wonder, for they had never been in a place as large as this in all their lives. The headman's hall at Aranth would have been lost from sight in this hall. Its columns were the trees in a forest, its roof was higher than the sky. Banners enough for an empire's army, lords and ladies and wedding guests enough for an empire. At the far end of the hall was a dais with two thrones upon it, too far off to see the faces of the two who sat there though Kanda knew who they would be. Kanda, Dellet and Calian began to walk towards the dais. At the center of the hall, a hearth blazed, on a spit over the hearth fire a bull was roasting. The firedogs of the hearth were wolf heads that snarled and growled and bit at Kanda as she walked past them. The spit had the heads of serpents that hissed. Two women were preparing the meal. The blood of their death wounds covered their bodies and the ropes of their slaughter were around their necks. They carved the meat with stones knives onto a stone plate. The bull bellowed in pain as they carved it.

Before the hearth fire the hall was as hot as fever. Beyond the hearth fire the hall was so cold Kanda's breath puffed out white. A steward in a silk robe hurried up, offered a tray set with three gold cups. Kanda took a cup, Calian took a cup, Dellet took up a cup.

Kanda said, "Don't drink it."

Calian said, "How stupid do you think I am, Mum?"

Dellet said, "Whatever it is, does it matter now whether I drink it or not?" But he didn't drink.

There was a long table before the dais set for a thousand men to feast there. The dead women came up with platters piled high with roast meat. No one sat at the table. The women served the meat onto gold plates and the meat was raw and before the women had finished serving it the meat had rotted to nothing and the dishes were empty and waiting to be refilled. Sweat was on the women's foreheads as they hurried to refill and refill the gold plates.

Kanda looked closely and one of the dead women was Gella, Geiamnyn's last wife.

Geiamnyn and Sal sat on high thrones on the high dais. Geiamnyn was dressed in silver, his hair combed and dressed with red ribbons, a torc of green amber around his neck. Sal was dressed in gold, diamonds and pearls at her throat, on her head a bride's crown of violet flowers and starflowers and ripe wheat. The dress was too long, pooled at her feet in heavy folds, covered her hands.

She was bound to the chair with gold ropes. Her lips were sewn shut with gold thread.

"Greetings, Goodmother," Geiamnyn said. His voice was slurred, his face flushed with drink. He lurched to his feet, came down to the dais to meet them. "Won't you welcome your son-in-law to your family then? Kiss me on the cheek, hope I've already sired you a fat grandchild to bounce on your knee?" He turned to Dellet. "Goodfather, you've raised a fine eager girl here, I can tell you. And you, my sister—" He growled and spat at Calian, his beautiful face bloated with self-pity. "My chest aches where you stabbed me, you bitch-brat."

Calian said calmly, "We have come for Morna."

Geiamnyn blinked. He was so drunk he was swaying on his feet. "Morna…? Morna…? Oh, that brat child. Our pretty bridesmaid, yes. I promised, didn't I? I did." He clapped his hands. "You, Gella, wife of mine, fetch the child out." He blinked again heavily. "I killed you, didn't I, Gella my wife? This woman here is my wife now, and she's no better than you are." He shouted, "Gella, dead-bitch, bring the child out."

Dellet's sobs rang around the hall. Too good a man: never could he in his kindness imagine that another man could be so disgusting.

Geiamnyn staggered back to his throne, collapsed into it. He shouted, "Hurry up then!" He shouted, "I'm hungry, woman, bring me a plate of meat!"

The woman Gella scurried across the hall sweat-soaked, bringing a platter of raw bull flesh, running to bring Morna out. Kanda wanted to weep, remembering Gella's cry of joy in the roundhouse. *I'm free of him!*

All this time, Sal sat absolutely still beside her husband.

Gella was back in the time it took for Geiamnyn to gnaw on a piece of raw meat. Morna came neatly after her, dressed in a fine gown of pink silk. She was holding a doll not much smaller than she was, carved of ivory and dressed like a queen with a queen's gold crown on its head. She was smiling, looked plump and clean and happy. She stopped when she saw her parents, squealed with joy, dropped the doll and ran to them.

Dellet's cry of joy when he saw her was the most beautiful terrible sound Kanda had ever heard and ever wished to hear. Dellet caught the child up, kissed her kissed her kissed her, held her so that he could stare at her face, "Morna! Morn-Morn! My own!" kissed her held her, his tears soaked her fine dress.

Sal smiled. Thin, and Kanda could see it hurt her. Gestured, hands soft like feathers: *Leave. Now. Just take Morna and go.*

I won't leave you, child. Oh Sal, no longer *Shining*. I will burn this hall to ashes, I will spit on Geiamnyn's corpse, piss on him, I will see myself maimed and dead and ruined beneath his blade before I walk one step away without you, Sal, even if he kills me I will not rest but rise up dead and rotting before I go one step away without you, Sal my shining.

But Kanda said slowly, "Dellet, walk back past the hearth fire and walk out of here with Morna."

Dellet looked at his two elder daughters. He did not look at his wife. Kanda thought he would refuse to leave without Sal. Pain showed in his face as if he were dying in pain now before her. But he turned, began to walk away without looking back. Sal's eyes followed him. Like a man drinking water after a long thirst, when he thinks he is dying, Sal watched them.

"Sal?" Calian said. "Aren't you coming?"

Geiamnyn's hand closed around Sal's arm. Sal pulled her eyes away from Morna, looked at Geiamnyn, tried to smile.

"She doesn't want to leave her beloved husband," Geiamnyn said.

"Go," Kanda said. "Just go, Calian."

Sal nodded frantically, jerked her hands. *Go. Please.*

Wait. Don't leave me.

Go. Get out.

One step.

Two steps.

Three steps.

Morna shouted in her worst baby's voice, "I don't want to go home. I like it here. I want to stay here and play with Cousin Ty." She wriggled in her father's arms. Reached back toward the high dais. "I want to stay."

Dellet froze. His face was pain as if he was watching them all die. He said, "Stop that. Morna lamb. We're going home, aren't we, you and me and Calian and – and Mummy?"

"I like it here!" Morna shouted. She shrieked like a baby. Began to hit and kick. Dellet shouted, "Morna!" She hit his face, screamed in his ear. He shouted, "Morna!" His face was terrible, which made Morna more angry and more frightened. She writhed in his arms, kicked and hit at him, shrieked. He was so angry and desperate now he held her so tight she shrieked in pain, he shook her and shouted, "Stop!" so loud and so fierce she shrieked in terror. "You're killing me!" In his panic Dellet's arms opened. Morna fell and threw herself out of his grasp. There were red welts on her skin where her father's hands had held her, his belt buckle had caught and ripped her dress.

She ran to grab up her doll. She ran behind the dais sometimes going on her two feet holding the doll, sometimes on all fours.

Kanda opened her mouth to scream. Calian opened her mouth to scream. Dellet was beyond screaming or weeping or living.

Geiamnyn on his throne was laughing so hard the spittle flew from his lips. He laughed so hard he pissed himself. "It seems two of your daughters like me very much, Ikandera Thygethyn. What about you, eagle girl? You can stay and marry me too."

Sal beside him gave him one look of such revulsion it made Kanda flinch. Geiamnyn's laughter died. Fear came into his face. "Stop that you, you stupid woman. I had to sew her stupid mouth shut," Geiamnyn said. "Your bitch daughter, Ikandera Thygethyn. One night, we'd been married, and she made me do it! The things she said to me! My own wife! You should have raised her better, Ikandera Thygethyn." Tears of self-pity came into Geiamnyn's eyes. "I'm never lucky with my women…I never understand it…. Now you've stuck me with another one…. She's worse than the others, that bitch-child. Always crying at me….

"You should be feasting," Geiamnyn said uncertainly. "We should be feasting. Toasting my wedding!" A cup appeared in his hand, as big as a bucket, he drained it. Wine ran down his chin over his silver finery. He belched. "Sit down!" he shouted. "Eat. Drink to my lovely new wife!"

Gella and the other dead woman were back serving the feast now, refilling the gold plates. Kanda and Calian and Dellet were seated at the table, they too were dressed in gold and silver, crowned with flowers, Calian wore a long string of blue beads that hung down her front, Dellet a cloak of rich white fox fur lined in brilliant red. Gella came up straining under the weight of a vast stone platter, piled their gold plates high with meat. Poured them strong sweet mead from a broken jug. The meat on Kanda and Calian's plates was well roasted, so good it looked and smelled! The meat on Dellet's plate was raw, it was alive still, it bellowed on his plate. Dellet took up his cup and drank, ate up his portion of meat. His face was beyond dying. Dead as that empty one's face was dead. "It doesn't matter now whether I eat it or not," Dellet said. "So I might as well eat."

Behind the dais Morna and Ty were playing. They giggled and talked of secret child things. Gella stopped her work to listen. Her happiness at the sound of her son playing was one moment of brightness, fell like a single shaft of sunlight over the hall. She said to Kanda, smiling, "Your daughter is so lovely, so sweet with my Ty."

Geiamnyn shouted, "Get back to serving, wife! My cup needs filling, my plate needs filling." Gella ran to attend him, filled his vast cup from her broken jug. "Always she is needing to be killed, that woman," Geiamnyn said. He looked at Dellet. "You know how woman are like this." Dellet was bent with revulsion, but he said nothing, stopped eating and then went back to eating again as Gella refilled his plate. "I don't know how it happens, these useless women I find…." Geiamnyn said.

Sal sat silent, still as stone. Her eyes were stone. Calian was shaking with fury, hand on her sword hilt.

"Not yet, Calian," Kanda could only whisper. "Not yet. Wait." She looked around, judging, planning. "Where is Ysarene?" Kanda asked Geiamnyn. "And…that other one?"

"Gone," Geiamnyn said. He sounded angry. "They are bored here drinking with me. I thought it would be a fine thing for us all four to be together again at the feast, Ikandera, but they got bored, those two, waiting. Two days at least Ysarene has been without killing, you remember how she frets, going without killing. I told her you were coming but she could not wait." He drained his cup again. "And that other one, that empty one, he did not want to be here to see me married, Ikandera!" Geiamnyn was so drunk now he could barely keep his eyes open, but he skewed his head round to stare in genuine confusion at Kanda. "I thought it would amuse him. But he said…he said he could not bear it. To see me marry your daughter, Ikandera." Shook his head, blinked his eyes heavily. "All this time I've known him, I will never understand that one, Ikandera. You explain him." His head nodded onto his chest, he started, pulled himself up a little.

Raised his cup. "A toast to my bride! You, wife, smile, look happy, can't you? Joy to the bride! Drink to my wife, Ikandera!"

Sal jerked her head at her mother, and Kanda rose, held up her cup to the couple, drank. Geiamnyn clapped his hands, raised his cup to return the pledge. Rose petals and sparkling jewels fell in a shower from high in the rafters, tumbled down around Sal. "Joy to the bride," Kanda whispered. Gella hurried to refill Kanda's cup. Hurried to refill Dellet's plate.

"That bull had lived a thousand years before you killed it, Ikandera," Geiamnyn said. "I tried to kill it once. I couldn't kill it. You were always better than me at killing, Ikandera. But then you stopped killing, so now I've taken many more lives than you. But not that bull. I never managed to kill it." He seemed to want Kanda to answer him.

She said, "No, Geiamnyn. Yes, Geiamnyn."

He was so drunk and so self-pitying her answer seemed to satisfy him. "It tastes vile," he said. "Not worth the effort. My wife's a good cook, it's the meat of this stupid bull."

Calian was shaking with fury. Kanda tried to hold her, tried to hold her, but the girl's anger was so vast, her hands clawing at the feasting table – Kanda said low to her daughter, "Now, yes, now," just as Geiamnyn lurched back to his feet. Calian ran, almost flew across behind the dais to where Morna and Ty were playing. A shriek came loud as Calian dragged Morna out. Geiamnyn staggered, astonished at something so obvious, he was so drunk the sound of Morna's shrill outraged yell struck him like a blow, made him collapse back into his seat. And Calian was running running down the hall dragging Morna shrieking and yelling with her, and Kanda grabbed Dellet's arm and began to run with him. Behind them Geiamnyn was cursing: Kanda heard a crash of plates and cups as he tried to get up, slipped in the spilt remains of the feast, fell. A boy's voice screamed: Ty, poor child, calling after Morna, "Let her come back. Morna! She's my friend!"

Gella came running at them from the cook fire, knife in her hand greasy with fat and shiny with blood: "My son's happiness! You can't take her! You can't make me go back to being married to him."

Sal sat on her throne in her gold dress and her jewels. The gold ropes pulled tighter tighter around her waist, her arms, her legs. Her eyes followed Calian and Morna as they ran. She raised her hand. Her face was lit with joy and horror. *Go. Be safe. Don't leave me! Wait! Wait!*

The rope around her was tight and cutting her. But the thread sewing up Sal's lips broke. She called out, "Run, Calian!"

Gella was there with her knife, Ty dragging himself forward. Geiamnyn staggering and crawling to his feet. Calian was slowing, Morna kicked her, twisted her arm, screamed, punched. The cook fire leapt up brilliant. A bull's great bellow. The roast carved bones of the black bull juddered on the floor where Gella had thrown them as she carved the meat for the feast. They rolled and clattered as the bull bellowed. Calian ran past the hearth, gripped Morna tighter. Calian shouted, "Come on, Morna. Stop being so stupid." The bull's bones juddered and rolled and lowed in pain as Kanda and Dellet ran past them.

The boy Ty shrieked, "No! No! Morna! Come back! You can't leave me, Morna." He ran after Morna on limping thin weak legs, his arms reaching out after her.

Morna shouted again, "I like it here. I want to stay here and play with Cousin Ty. I want to stay with Sal," Morna shouted. "If Sal can stay, why can't I?"

The hall lurched around them, the high columns were trees, were shadows, were coils of thick smoke, were white mist. The wind howled in their ears, the ground they ran across was an ash pile they stumbled over, was a vast stinking midden heap.

Geiamnyn voice called behind them: "If she says she wants to stay here, she stays. You cannot make her leave here against her will, Ikandera. You know how it is."

Calian was staggering beneath Morna's weight. Calian was tiny, crushed, Morna was vast.

Gella shouted, "You cannot take her away from Ty."

Morna shouted, "I want to stay with Sal."

Calian tried to run and tried to run. And Morna was a shape as vast as the stars.

Morna struck her sister on the face. Bit her sister's hand with teeth as long as butchering knives. Tore her sister's chest with claws as long as sword blades. Crueller and sharper than sword blades. Morna was not a child in Calian's arms, she was a beast, she was a fire, she was a shapeless clot of blood. She struck and punched and cursed. Calian cried out in pain and revulsion. Fell to the ground trying to shield herself from her sister's blows. Bleeding. Dying.

Kanda drew her sword. Calian gasped, sobbing out, "No, no, no, Mum, don't. Don't."

Calian gasped, "Help me, Mum. She's killing me."

Kanda touched her sword to Morna's writhing thrashing shifting knife-shape.

One touch of her sword on her youngest daughter's body.

One sword stroke.

Morna screamed like a beast, jerked, lay still. A great red wound on her forehead. Calian staggered beneath her, clawed her way out from beneath her sister's vast body. Grabbed at her, pulled her. "She's dead," Calian screamed. She dragged Morna's tiny body. Pulled it in her arms. "Help me, Mum."

Geiamnyn's voice came from the darkness: "You can have the stupid spoiled sniveling brat of yours, Ikandera Thygethyn, and welcome to it."

Kanda let out her war cry so loud the world fell.

The ground beneath them was coarse turf, the columns of the hall were stars, Kanda and Dellet and Calian and Morna were in the sheep field, it was dark night but far off to the east the sky was red with fire where Ysarene and the one who was only emptiness were killing and burning. But the fire was not as red as the blood that flowed from the wound Kanda had dealt her youngest daughter. No fire could be that terrible and that red.

Dellet cried, "What did you do? What have you done?"

Kanda said, "The only thing I could."

Morna's lips were drawn back showing long yellow teeth. And the wound on her forehead gnashed bloodied teeth. A little while longer in that place, Kanda thought, a few days, if days and nights could be spoken of in such a place, a few days more there and she would have been lost to them beyond recall. If Sal had not chosen to act when she did. Even now, perhaps, it might still be too late.

"She's dead," said Calian.

"No. She cannot be and will not be and must not be. Not after what Sal has done for her." Kanda squatted down on her heels, touched the child's cold face, touched the warm living earth. Closed her eyes, breathed the air of her sheep field. Took her bloodied sword, placed the sword point over the wound it had made. Dellet whimpered. Calian had to hold him back. *What have you done to my child, woman, monster? Trust her, Dad, trust Mum.* The sword was wrong and cruel for healing, but she, she had once been one of the Six.

She thought of Calian's scream: "Bindings! Promises!" These terrible evil things that must be kept because they were promised. These little daily things, a child not being harmed or frightened, that were promised and could not be kept.

"Heal," Ikandera Thygethyn said. Her voice was the voice of a war leader. "Fall," she had said in that voice, and a city's walls had fallen. "Die," she had said in that voice, and an army had died in howling pain.

"Heal. Now. Your sister has given her life for this. Heal, curse you."

The wound mouthed and champed at Kanda's blade. The wound healed, faded, was gone. Morna gave a great sigh. She was warm and soft. She let out a snuffle, a snore, she farted. Dellet ran, he too was almost on all fours like a beast. He snatched her up, cradled her in his arms, kissed her sleeping face.

Calian grasped Kanda's arm, squeezed it tight. Tried to smile at her mother.

The sweat was cold on Kanda's forehead, she felt the ghost of Morna's wound there. On her hand she felt the wound's biting teeth.

If it was Dellet beside her, she would fall into his arms exhausted. Instead, bitter and weary, she turned to her daughter and said with false cheer, "So, we've come home safe with Morna. Well done to you, Calian. Well done to—"

But that she could not say.

Calian let out a bitter laugh that was a thousand years too old for her to be laughing. "We'll bring Sal back too, Calian," Kanda said. "No: she will rescue herself. You saw already how Geiamnyn was beginning to fear her."

Calian only laughed again.

The house was there before them, a dark good shape in the darkness, a short walk through the sheep field with the grass brushing their feet; if they turned away from the distant fires it was only their own house. Calian fixed her eyes on it, her sword ready. "Stay still, keep your eyes on it watching it," Kanda had told her children about wolves and wild beasts and dangerous things. Dellet went up to the doorway. The door was shut; Kanda had shut it when she left those few days ago. Dellet put out his hand to the door, drew his hand back. He looked at Kanda. His eyes were beyond seeing. His heart was beyond grief.

Kanda gasped out, "They burned it and they rebuilt it, don't go in! You must not go in!"

Dellet pushed the door open, walked into his house. "My daughter," he said, "needs to sleep in her bed." He went through into the dark house, Kanda heard his voice echo there, "Morn-Morn, Morn my lambkin, my baby heart, let's get you to bed now, shall we, come on, let's lie you down, get you comfy, shall we? Morn-Morn my lamb, my duckling. I'll just put you down on your bed, Morna, we'll get a lamp going, shall we? See you off to sleep again."

Calian and Kanda went together right up to threshold. There were no words to be spoken. *"Welcome home, wife of mine, Kanda beloved." "Welcome home, Del-my-heart, my husband."* These words had once been spoken. In this house Kanda had conceived and birthed three children. In this house she had planned or dreamed to die old in the bed she had conceived and birthed her children in. No evil could destroy these things. This is my home. I built it with my own hands. But thunder should rumble and the stones break, she thought, if she went in. Don't go in! But Kanda went in over the threshold without need for words that must be spoken, and there was nothing there buried beneath the threshold, and the house was unchanged from the time before the world was ended, and how could that not be an impossible thing?

Calian said, "Should I go in, Mum? Is it safe?"

Safe? Geiamnyn remade this house as a joke. As a punishment. Go back to cow shit and sheep shit and wiping your children's snot off your clothes, Ikandera Thygethyn. But Kanda said, "It's safe, yes, Calian," and Calian went in after her father. Kanda heard them fussing with Morna, Morna saying something half-asleep.

One thing, in all her failure, Kanda could do briefly for them. Ikandera Thygethyn stopped on the threshold. Said with all her power and strength, "Our home, my loves. Rest, be safe, sleep. Be at peace." The voice she had used for killing, she spoke in this voice once and an army turned upon itself until not one man was left alive. She went in. They were in their own house, the four of them, they slept.

CHAPTER THIRTY-SIX

Kill them. Kill them all. So many battles, so much wonderful fighting! I was made for fighting.

This is for Kestre. This is for Palle. This is for Gallyn. This for Morren. This for Erenan. This for my Lord. This for my Lady. This, the worst blow yet, the deepest, this for what I was in the shackles of Roven.

Peace? Hope? Only endless toil. So now the light of the sun, the light of the moon, the sound of running water – now even these do not escape Ikandera Thygethyn's sword when it strikes with all the power of her fierce bright heart.

She hears Erenan cry to her, "What are you doing?"

She whispers, "What I am free to do. What I want."

CHAPTER THIRTY-SEVEN

The next morning was the strangest and the least strange. To lie in her own bed, her husband beside her sleeping, Calian and Morna snuggled together with their hair entwined, Morna's head half buried beneath her blanket, two children so small and young and sweet, the light coming in yellowish through the oiled-hide window, a fly droning against the hide – noise of summer, that noise – the rooks bickering in the aspens – "Sometimes I think we should cut those trees down, that would teach those cursed birds," Dellet sometimes said – the wind rustling and whispering and making music in the aspens – "If you do I'll cry forever!" Calian said – the smell of the oil used on the hide, the smell of dampness in the north corner, the scratch of one low branch of the apple tree against another that was both music and unutterably annoying already again. To get up, stretch, feel her feet firm on her floor, think distantly that the floor needs sweeping. Pull on her dress, go into the living place, pour herself a cup of water from the face-work jug that had been a gift from Goodbrother Sym, start on getting the morning meal prepared, wince at a run of slug trail silver-gleaming in the doorway, how do they get in? To throw the door wide to the south-warmed morning, turn her face to the sky, racing white high cloud like a dog's belly, bird dropping on the doorstep, *ah come you birds of the air, eat up the slugs that dare cross my threshold,* plunge her head and her hands into the outside morning, turn back into the house with skin brighter, lift the lid from the meal crock, breathe the scent in. A jug of buttermilk, covered against the flies, and if there was buttermilk there must be fresh butter, yes, here it was almost glowing in the best blue-glazed pot. Bannocks she'll make for her beloveds sleeping; her hands trace out the plates, the cups. Get the fire going, that's it, good wood this is, quick to catch and cleanly burning. Then after they've eaten she'll go down into the meadow, call in the kye to be milked. They had rebuilt the house with everything and more and better, the crock had more meal in it, surely, more apples dried in the rafters, they had run out, she thought, she was certain, Calian had pined staring at the tree for this year's crop, "Come on, come on, fruit." So much honey in the jar it was overflowing, dark and strong with a pine scent; raspberries in a bowl as a welcome, there had never been raspberries in the garden; two whole hams in the rafters; a whole unopened cask of salt beef.

"You could have stopped up the place the slugs come in, Geiamnyn."

The morning after a defeat was like those mornings after a three-day feasting. Wandering around sane like being new-made. *That, last night, was also me.*

Calian was awake first of the three sleepers. Naturally, of course, it would be Calian. Morna slept the sleep of a child happy in her own bed after some great nightmare. Dellet slept the sleep of one who feared to ever waken; Kanda thought: if I have that power in me, let him never wake.

Calian said at once, her body already crouched for battle, her hand reaching for her sword, "Sal—" She was marked all over where Morna had clawed her. She said, "My face hurts."

"Don't, Calian." Kanda jerked her head toward the sleeping place, put her finger to her lips. The only way to manage a defeat, little one, is not to speak yet. There is a ghost in this house, little one, if you name it, it will run away. Pretend she is still here and nothing has changed and it will not run away, little one.

Dark eagle eyes met her own. Calian nodded. "Later," Calian said. Battle plans in her eyes, fires in her eyes blazing huge. She'll burn the world if she's not careful. Geiamnyn, you chose the wrong one there. You're too afraid of her already, aren't you, Geiamnyn?

Calian went to the door, went out into the morning, stretched and bathed in it, came back in. She drank a cup of water – such sweet good water! – she looked at the cup and said, "This is the one Morna broke."

"No, it isn't." Kanda said after a moment: "Don't … don't say that to your father. He won't notice if you don't say anything."

"You're making bannocks?" Girl's voice. Hungry. Always liked bannocks. Never liked meal cakes much. Also Sal cooks even worse than Kanda cooks.

"We need to eat something." The dough was a little too wet, it always was. Kanda added one tiny bit more flour, turned it out to knead on the bread-stone. Now it was suddenly a little too dry. "Great magic, that is," Kanda said. She kneaded the dough in silence, watching her hands. These killing hands. Aging woman's hands with dry aging skin. Strong careful hands making bread.

Calian said, "Dad…?" "Let him sleep. Let him…. Listen, Calian: you want to go running back to hunt Geiamnyn down. I know, and we'd go now, if it was you and me and nothing else. We'd never have left that place without Sal with us, and without Geiamnyn's head on a pole, if it was you and me and nothing else. But…."

Calian said, "Stop it, Mum. Shut up. Stop making excuses."

"Your father, Calian mine, he needs…. And Morna needs time, I think. Your father's sleeping, Calian mine. Let him sleep; when he wakes, let him have a little time of peace." Kanda thought: I need to rest, Calian. A thousand years, I need to rest.

Calian frowned. She was a child, frightened, angry, grieving, eager to do and be. "And Sal? How long can you make Sal wait?"

Silence.

Silence.

Calian nodded. She was a warrior, thinking, planning, seeing herself dealing the death stroke. Her eyes darted around the house. "How long can we stay here, even, do you think?"

"Forever, if we want to, Calian love. Forever, I expect, and we'd never know hunger or thirst or cold or sickness. Forever, if we choose, until you die an old, old woman in your own bed."

The dough was ready. Kanda said, "Pass the skillet, will you?"

Calian stole a piece of raw dough, a thing she loved doing. "I don't know how you eat that, Calian mine. Disgusting!"

"Tasty. Okay, disgusting, but I stole it. Also it annoys you every time so it's good."

"No more! Come on! I asked you to pass the skillet."

"It's a bit thick, I think, you need to flatten it out more before you cook it."

"Yes I know, thank you, Calian. Maybe you want to cook?"

"It's a bit dry, too.... That's better, look. Oh, no, wait, now it's too large to fit in the skillet. Okay, yes, sorry, Mum. We do need to prepare, I suppose, we can't just go rushing at them. Plan what we do. Get rested and strong to really fight them. And Dad...we could give Dad...a few days," Calian said. "Two days? Do you think Sal could bear that?"

Calian put the skillet on the fire, watched the bannock very carefully as it cooked. Ah, the smell was good!

"What about you, Calian? Two days in this house?"

"I suppose there's more butter and honey and cheese than we could eat in a month of feasting?"

"And ham. And eggs."

"I could bear a day, maybe, Mum. I think. One day, maybe." Carefully, carefully, Calian turned the bannock over. "That's perfect, look. One day, one night, I could stay here I suppose if I have to." She shuddered. "Two days, for Dad and for Morna, if they need it. No more than that." The bannock was done, Calian turned it out. And I am such a good mother, Kanda thought, that Calian has no idea what Sal will endure these two days.

Thus all day they went on as if all was normal. A house made for a family of four.

Dellet set about his work. Brought in some more firewood, looked over a field wall that needed shoring up well before winter, sharpened some of his work tools. "The high meadow's looking good for a second mowing," he said thoughtfully. "If the weather holds clear tonight, I'll do it tomorrow, you'll help me, Cal-bird, won't you? I should cut that branch back," he said, listening to the apple tree branches tock-tocking, "I keep saying I'll do it. Tomorrow," he said. "And that wall…just need to get the right stones." He got out his scythe for the mowing, he'd only just finished sharpening it, he put it away, got it out. "Tomorrow morning," he said, "I'll mow the high meadow. What do you say to a fish trap, Kanda, on the river where that rock sticks out to breaks up the current? We could lay in more fish this year for smoking. Tomorrow," he said, "I'll cut the wood for it." He caught Morna up in his arms, swung her round: "More fish than you can eat, Morn-Morn my duckling! My little heron, feasting on fish!" He walked to the door, turned round, walked back to sit by the hearth. "I wonder how Sal is doing?" he said, "Big for her to run, that household, but I suppose she has…she has…servants. A rich man, yes, I'd never have thought a daughter of mine could marry so rich. What a fine life she'll have. A lady, my Sal! A great lady, she'll be…." And then he was silent, staring at his own hands that had never done another man harm in all his life. "Tomorrow morning," he said, "I'll mow the high meadow." And then he ran out of the house and when he came back his hands were cut as if he had torn and smashed them against a stone field wall, and his eyes were red from weeping, but he said nothing, sat down in his place by the hearth. "That annoying noise," he said, "tomorrow, for certain, tomorrow, I'll cut that branch back."

Morna played with her dolls by the hearth – I carried those dolls all the way to Mal Anwen, Kanda thought, I might as well have left them where they were. She found a twig that seemed to especially please her, "This is his sword," she said, "can you tie it to his arm, Mum?" A bean leaf was a shield, a cabbage leaf was a war cloak. "Can Ty come and play soon?" Morna said every so often. "I told him all about our house, he said it sounded lovely, he wanted to come and play very much. But he had better toys, Mum, he had real swords for his dolls! Can I go and play there again soon? When we visit Sal again?"

"I should think so, Morna," Dellet said. He said to Kanda, puzzled, "A good thing it will be for these two, Sal's marrying so well, don't you think? That dress Morna wore for the wedding, it must have been worth more than this house."

The day drew on, meals, work, meals, work, the light fading so that work in the house was harder on the eyes, the rooks starting up their evening arguments. "I wonder how Sal is getting on?" Dellet kept saying. "Young, she is, to be married, too young, maybe, but if she's happy…." He would shake his head. "A fine life she'll lead. A great lady."

Kanda went out into the evening. Sat beneath the apple tree. That branch was annoying. Tock-tock like someone knocking two sticks together. Knocking of wood together was now a frightening thing. Calian came out to join her: "Dad's putting Morna to bed. He's very tired, he said he'd go to bed himself soon."

"Good."

"That's really irritating…. Give me a hand here." Calian twisted the branch, Kanda helped her, it came off easy, Kanda dropped it under the tree. It was a dead branch anyway, no leaves no apples. Lichen that dusted their fingers.

"Good stick, that," Calian said approvingly. They sat down together. The evening was almost done, the birds were singing their last sad evening chorus. The thin squeaks of bats. A clear sky, the stars and a pale full moon.

"Two days," Calian said. She shivered. "Tonight and one more day and another night." She bit her knuckles. "Two more nights." The bats came squeaking, and the rooks arguing.

"Can you survive another day here, Calian?"

"Dad needs another day, doesn't he?"

Kanda thought: he needs forever, Calian.

"What do they find to argue about all day and night, those stupid rooks? If Sal can survive two more nights there, I can survive two nights here." Calian looked at the sky. "It will be under a waning moon. That seems good."

"Does it? Why?"

"I don't know."

After a time, Kanda said, "You do have a choice, Calian. You and Morna and your father, you can stay here on the farm, and nothing will ever harm you."

"Morna and Dad would be happy like that, wouldn't they? Dad's been happy. Sort of. Whatever you did to him."

"The three of you could be happy."

Pause. Silence.

"The rooks argue like you and Sal used to," Kanda said. "I haven't done anything to your father, Calian. Believe me. I wish I could."

Calian said, "Listen, you rooks: you don't know how lucky you are, to have brothers and sisters to argue with. No, don't you dare shout at me for saying it. Two days, and we all leave here forever, and that will be a good day and I will be happy." She said in a very quiet low voice, "What if Sal…? What if she wants…? If she…she wants to stay with him?"

Pause. Silence. Even the rooks were silent.

Calian said, "Like you stayed."

"Don't say that. Please, Calian mine."

"What else do you want me to say, Mum?"

But they were talking almost like adults together, two warriors. They had fought side by side, and soon would again. Two Swords shining. Calian, least loved, most known and trusted. Kanda thought: and didn't we just defeat that apple tree?

"It wasn't…love, or desire, or anything. It wasn't…them. I…." She looked at her killing hands, and there were still tiny scraps of dough beneath her nails. She said very honestly something she had only ever before said to that one who had been her husband: "I don't know, Calian, why I broke my oath. I don't understand it myself now. Or, no, that's not it, I can see it still, every day that led up to it, all the small stupid things, I can see myself and I can see so clearly how it happened, the Six of us together, and it was hard sometimes being the best of them, and it was hard being so close to them – and we had such honor, such a great fierce purpose – but it wasn't…it wasn't because of that, or of them…. I can see those last years, I can see the anger I felt sometimes, I can see.... I was happier those last years with the Six than I had been before, the best years, we all knew, like...like those late summer days, they'll be coming soon now, we all knew it was the best time but we all knew something terrible would come. If I hadn't....

"No, that's not a thing to say. None of them would have done what I did. I know that.

"It wasn't something I did in anger. I thought about it for a long time first. Prepared myself."

She said, "I knew what I was doing. Every step of it."

She closed her eyes and said what she had never said even to herself: "I'll never know why, I'll never understand why I did it. But at the same time I can see exactly why I did it. And I – I can see that I would do the same again, if it all came again as it did.

"I can't tell you. I can't tell myself. Only that it seemed for a long time something I wanted so very much to do."

Calian was silent so long Kanda thought the girl would never speak. Then at last Calian said, "Sometimes when I argue with Sal, I want to hit her. I want.... Sometimes when Morna is being such a pain, when she's spoilt and screaming, and when she was a baby and she cried all night every night and then half the day and you and Dad were so tired by her – I wanted her to die, sometimes. Or just go away somewhere, like she'd never existed. I really did want that. You remember when she was sick and crying all the time and all you and Dad did day and night was worry about her and fuss over her – I thought about going out and finding something poisonous, yew berries or blackcap or nightshade, and giving it to her. Then you'd be sad she'd died but we wouldn't have her crying all the time anymore."

Calian said after a long time, "I gathered a bag of ivy berries, and for three days I had them hidden under the bed. Then I dug a hole as deep as I could by the river, near the grave house, and I buried them, and I begged and begged at the grave house for forgiveness. You thought I was sick as well as Morna, made me stay in bed."

Silence. The rooks had stopped at last. The night was wrong

without the last sound of cattle and sheep. No noise of people far away too far off to be heard but present there in the silence.

"I know," Kanda said. "Sal saw you picking the ivy." She said after a moment, "Why do think I never asked you where your special toy bag had gone?"

"You would have let me do it?"

"Don't be so stupid, Calian. I knew you'd never ever do it, you've loved Morna from the moment I was pregnant with her and anyway you wouldn't do it even to a stranger you'd never met." Also anyway ivy isn't all that poisonous, not enough that three berries would have killed Morna even if she had eaten them. Also I do have some small magic left in me to keep my children safe from harm, remember, Calian. "But I knew you had to learn how it felt to be angry at someone and feel guilt for wanting to hurt them."

Calian said, as Kanda deserved: "Like you did."

Why did the raiders come to steal our cattle, Mum, when they could raise their own without risk of dying, all of us here in the valley could have spared them between us a bull and a breeding cow and a calf, couldn't we, if they'd asked? Why does the headman at Aranth need thirty warriors in his hall, Mother, what in the world do they need to do, swaggering around Aranth like the world's at war, but they didn't do anything when the raiders came, why not, Mum? Why didn't you let that beggar woman come in and eat with us, since you say all the time we should help people and be good? So I go to answer questions that are unanswerable but she looks at me and she knows as I know exactly what the answer is. Kanda thought: that's why she didn't need to ask me why I did it. Because Calian already knows why, my poor wise fierce child. Has known the answer all her life. She had hated the name Calian, fought against it, the worst time of her marriage that time, Dellet so oddly set on it, unmovable, *My father's name, Kanda, and it'll be my child's name and that's that.* The baby kicking in the womb and her horror: an eagle in my belly, clawing to get out: I can't make it that. When the child was born it hadn't drawn three breaths in the world when Dellet said, "Calian my daughter," and Kanda had looked at the child and, yes, that had been the only possible name. A beak and claws and true knowledge, that one. She had been afraid briefly to put the child to her breast for fear she would draw blood.

It was full dark now. An owl hooted: Calian had been terrified of owl cries when she was a baby. A pair of owls raising a brood in the barn the summer Calian was two and she'd screamed every night. Dellet: "Well, what do you expect, she's an eaglet? Corpse birds, owls, death birds, I don't like them either." "But what's wrong with owls, Del-my-heart?" "Everything, Kanda, wife, I don't know, ghosts, death-omens." "If someone died every time anyone heard an owl, Del-my-heart…." "Death birds, Kanda wife, I don't know, there's just something…." "Hoo hoo," she flaps her arms at Dellet, laughs and laughs and they're in bed and he almost laughs back. But she can't tell him she fears eagles far more than owls and she hates her daughter being an eagle because of her first husband.

But everyone has a past, Del-my-heart, she thought now. What did you think, that I was some shy virgin when we married? Yes, I had a husband and a life before we met. Yes, I did things I very much regret, kept secrets from you because I was ashamed of them, yes. Yes! I was well over thirty when I married you. What else did you expect?

Calian said, "But you left them."

Kanda shook herself. Self-defense, self-pitying. I sound like Geiamnyn. What did Dellet expect? Not anyone who has done what I have done.

"Yes, Calian. I left them." I went away, for a long time I walked the world looking for something. I came here, I met your father who seemed like a good man who'd make a good father. Life as a farmer here seemed a pleasant quiet life. That, also – I can't say, it just…. "I made my life here with you four."

"Why did you leave?" Calian said. The question asked as it had not been asked about why she broke her oath and destroyed the Six. And then Calian said, "Do you regret leaving them?"

Regret leaving Roven and the Six? I could pretend that's what I think she means. Kanda said, "I feel nothing but sick shame at what I did then." Horror, revulsion – I did things, no, not 'things', everything I did then was filth and ruin and horror and guilt and regret. When I was pregnant with each of you, the horror of it: I, monster, killer, Ikandera Thygethyn, who has destroyed lives beyond number, I am pregnant with a child, I am creating life, that cannot be right. Terror, horror, looking at her children: I, blood-soaked, wader in blood, swimmer in blood, I am trusted to care for this fragile precious living thing?

"Joining them was the worst thing I ever did and ever could do. Leaving them was the best thing I did in all my life until I had you three, Calian."

Calian thought a little. Kanda saw her thoughts move in her face, surface, sink away. Her lips moved, trying out in her mind her questions. Util the question she asked was not one Kanda had expected.

"What was your name, Mum, before you broke the oath? Your real name, from when you were one of the Six?"

Kanda had to say the truth: "I don't remember what my name was, Calian. I think I do, sometimes, when I'm sleeping, but my tongue can't shape it. Kanda is my real name. Ikandera Thygethyn. That is all I have as a name."

Calian looked long and fierce into the dark. "*Great Warrior.* It's a good name.

"Now you're going to kill them, it's a good name."

Sat here in the dark beneath the apple tree together, and all the darkness and the regret and the horror fled. Kanda said, "Go inside, Calian, go to sleep now. One night and one day and one night and we will kill the monsters. You and I side by side, and Sal and Morna with us. You saw how fierce Morna is becoming."

When the girl had gone Kanda walked down to the place where the hillside fell away steep to the water meadow and the river, where the slope was thickly planted with hawthorns. All the time the owl cried. She went down the slope carefully, stopped sometimes to place her hands on the tree trunks, traced out the bark. The owl cried but there was no noise of sheep or cows or frogs or foxes; even a wolf, she thought, would be welcome. There should be a sense in the air of the noise from Aranth two hours' walk away, where the warriors should be feasting, there should be distant lights and a sense of noise from Ben Apple Tree's farmstead. She broke off a twig of hawthorn. She wondered that they had not burned the hawthorn trees, she saw Ysarene hating them. But, she thought, they would have been afraid of the river and the trees.

Kanda knelt at the burial house at the valley bottom. Round circle of drystone walling knee-high with an entranceway facing the river, the stones worn beautifully smooth where the cattle liked to rub their chins against them. She traced her hands over the smoothness of the stone, it was warm where the warmth of the cows' bodies was held within it. The one who was only *empty* would have stared in fury at this grave. She saw Ysarene running from it too afraid of it to speak. She placed the sprig of hawthorn in the center of the burial house, snapped off a single hair from her head and placed it there like a strand of spider's web. She drew her sword, cut her left palm to draw a thin line of blood.

A fine cloud must have been over the moon and fled now, perhaps. Or a shadow from a tree was changed if the wind blew and shook the tree's branches. And she heard a fox bark. A splash from the river: a deer, a white deer with pool-dark eyes, stood on the far bank of the river, bent its head to drink.

Kanda placed her cut hand on the smooth stone wall of the burial house, squeezed her hand hard to make her blood come.

"You fast-flowing river, and you who lie here buried and resting in peace, you beasts of the field and forest, you birds of the air, earth and stones and pitiless sky: forgive me," Kanda said. "Forgive me for what I once did." The hind raised its head, its body tense to spring in fear. It snorted. It lowered its head, drank again. A great fat moth came blundering in a whirr of dusty wings into Kanda's face.

Kanda walked up the steep slope to the house that had once been her house, and she sang in her heart as she came in to join her family sleeping.

CHAPTER THIRTY-EIGHT

The worst battle the Six ever fought together, and almost the last battle they ever fought together, when they knew all was slowly ending. They rode out together from the Hall Roven with no thought in their heads but enjoying themselves on a fine spring morning. They carried their helmets on the horns of their saddles, they shook out their hair to the wind. They rode back in bitterness and division, wounded. Lord Gallyn had some fine new horse trappings his husband had given him, green enamel and bells set with garnet, had wanted to ride out that morning to show his horse off to the world. He made his horse prance to set the bells ringing, which made Lady Kestre sing and Lord Morren laugh.

Lord Palle, so serious these last years, said, "Those trappings will be no good in battle, Gallyn, the enemy will hear you coming ten miles off, and they'll catch and hold every spearpoint."

"He's right, Gallyn," Lady Erenan said, "though if the ringing of those bells is half as irritating to an enemy's ears as it is to mine, you'll surely win every battle you enter without need for a single sword stroke."

She who was not yet called Kanda, but we must still call her Lady Kanda, she said only, "They are…a little loud, Gallyn. But your horse looks very fine," she said quickly, for Gallyn looked downcast, even angry with his companions, and Gallyn said like a boy, "I like them very much. My husband had them made for me."

"Glittering and noisy," Morren said. And he did not exactly sound now like he was laughing with his friend. After they had ridden a little way, Morren said, "They're making my head ache, now, those bells, Gallyn."

"It's not the bells making your head ache, Morren," Gallyn said. And he made his horse prance and gallop fast away so that it would gallop fast back right up to Morren.

Kanda tried to make it a joke, a game. "Leave poor Morren alone to his headache, race with me, Gallyn, come on then. Kestre can ride and sing along."

"I don't want to race you," Gallyn said. He made his horse prance around Morren's horse so the bells rang.

"Stop your fooling, Gallyn," Erenan snapped at him.

"You'll injure your horse's legs, riding like that, Gallyn," Palle said. He looked around the good summer morning with a deep frown on his forehead, strained his eyes to see the enemy beyond some far horizon. "When the enemy comes, Gallyn, you need to be ready, what if they come and your horse is blown or lame because of your fooling?"

"We shouldn't ride out for pleasure from Roven ever, if you had your way, Palle," said Gallyn, and despite being angry with Gallyn, Morren nodded in agreement with him.

"We should be on the practice field, yes," said Palle.

"You were on the practice field yesterday past sunset, Palle," said Kestre. "You need rest."

"One of us needs to be ready, one of us needs to think about the enemy coming," said Palle, looking at Erenan and at Morren.

"I am ready. Perhaps I don't need to practice as much as you," Erenan said. "And perhaps I have other things to me beyond fighting."

"We fight to defend!" Palle shouted. "To defend!

"Please," Kestre said.

So they rode on in silence save the jangling of Gallyn's new horse trappings, until even Gallyn looked embarrassed.

Then the clouds came over the sun and the rain started, it felt more like a winter's day than a day for maying. "Whose wretched idea was this?" said Morren, whose head still ached.

"Gallyn's," said Erenan.

"Kestre's," said Gallyn.

"Not mine," said Palle. "As I said."

Until it was a relief to Kanda to see a thin trail of smoke on the horizon, white and rising in the rain-damp, and to feel on her skin a creeping like feathers, which she had come recently to feel sometimes when....

"Look!" Kanda cried. "Raiders! A village is burning!"

Erenan looked at her curiously, that she knew so clearly it was a village there burning. "It could be a woodman's fire to keep him warm in this rain," Erenan said, "or charcoal burners, or anything."

Kestre looked at her curiously, that she had sounded almost happy. "A battle would stop us bickering, heal the quarrel between Gallyn and Morren, at least," Kanda said.

They turned their horses and rode fast for the smoke, Gallyn's bells jangling until even Gallyn looked enraged by them. As they rode the country became black with rain, their path led into dead bare fields. A tree stood dead and bare in the distance, with the smoke rising behind it. The path led to the tree. Under the tree a man stood cloaked and hooded against the rain. When he saw the riders he fell to his knees, held out his hands to them.

"Help me, please. I beg. Whoever you are, you have horses and swords. Raiders are destroying my village. Help us, please," he begged.

There was something in his voice that made Kanda look sharply at him.

"My children," the man begged. Sweet, honeyed tones, pleading: "Please. My wife, my children. You may still be in time," he begged.

Erenan shouted, kicked her horse forward. The rest of the Six followed. The path led through empty fields to a stockaded village. The houses and the stockade itself were burning.

The gate of the stockade was open. From beyond it came the sound of fighting. Shapes moved there: horsemen. On the gatepost a human head was set on a pole. "Beware! Beware!" it shouted to them. The Six rode through into village with their swords drawn, ready to defend the villagers from raiders. A roar of battle broke over them, crash of swords, screams of the dying, thud of horses. It was so loud they cried out, and Kestre clapped her hand to her head. Swords flashed before their eyes, horsemen riding, spears flew at them.

But inside the gate the village was empty and deserted.

There were six houses in the village, a pigpen and a cattle byre and a grain barn, a communal oven in the center of the village, a spring with a carved stone and a painted post set in it that was both shrine and water source. Nothing moved anywhere.

Kestre said fearfully, "Why does this seem familiar to me?"

Kanda dismounted, went to look in the nearest house. She came hurrying quickly back again.

"There is a man dead in here," she called to the others. "Unarmed. His throat is cut. Everything in the house has been piled in the hearth and burned. The ashes are cold, his body is cold. Days, I think, he has lain there dead."

Gallyn was looking in another of the houses. "There is…there are two children dead here," Gallyn said slowly. "And a woman. She is wearing a bronze neck ring. Everything has been smashed in the house, but nothing has been taken."

"There are two cows dead in the byre," said Erenan. "Killed and left to rot. And there is grain still in the barn here. There are bronze tools hanging in the barn above the grain."

"This was not raiders," Morren said.

Kestre went over to the spring. It bubbled up from the earth, the pool it made had been carefully lined with stones. The stone set in it was carved with cranes flying, the post was painted with spirals that were almost eyes. The water was very clear, it smelled cold and good, but when Kanda held out her hand over the pool she felt her skin itch. When she took her hand away her skin was dry and cracked and red.

A hiss. Beneath the broken oven, something moved.

"Come out," Erenan shouted.

Kanda shouted, "You know who we are. Show yourselves."

A small crude oven for a village of six houses. The broken mouth of the oven gaped open. From the maw of the oven teeth gleamed, hands reached.

Morren shouted, "Show yourselves!"

A figure dragged itself out from the broken oven. A man, but a man burned and made of ashes. A child came crawling behind him, its arms were sword blades, its eyes were knife blades. A woman followed, tall and strong, but in place of a woman's head she had the head of a long-dead beast. More shadows, ash and bones and crawling darkness, dragging themselves up from the poisoned spring.

Kestre cried out, "What was the thing we met beneath the dead tree?"

Gallyn cried out, "There are too many of them." Never before had he or any of the Six cried such a thing.

Six swords flashed. Six war cries sounded. Palle met the child with sword blades for its arms. Metal shrieked on metal. Palle drew blood, the child drew blood. Erenan fought the woman with the beast's head. Kanda fought the burned man; Gallyn fought a man of bone and shadows, that flowed and moved and could not easily be hit; Morren fought a woman made of ashes; Kestre fought a child made of stone and old blood. Back-to-back, in a tight circle, more and yet more figures crawling in to stab and claw and spit at them. Six great warriors whirling and hacking, drowning and overwhelmed, the dead too many for them. Sick-brained slaughter, giddy with killing: not since that day on the beach when they saved children from starving desperate raiders had they fought like this, their minds as red as their swords shone red.

"I cannot do this," Kestre cried. "There are too many of them."

"They are the enemy, they are evil," Palle cried. "Kestre, we must kill them."

"I cannot do it," Kestre cried. A woman all raw from burning fell beneath her sword with a baby still clutched to her breast suckling, the baby fell from its mother's arms and it was already long-dead. "I cannot face this," Kestre cried. She threw down her sword, turned her horse to flee.

"These are all those lives we have not saved," Gallyn cried. "There are too many. Too many."

"You must fight," Palle cried. *Calm.* His face was like the death knell. "We must destroy them all, Gallyn."

"I cannot bear it!" Gallyn cried. He too turned and fled.

"Cowards!" Palle roared after them.

A tighter circle now, four warriors so soaked with gore their swords were heavy in their hands and their bodies moved slow like sick old men. Their swords were rain in a drought, falling on the dead to give them rest. Their swords were the burial words. Their swords were mourning grief. Fierce and set their faces, they clenched shut their teeth to keep from speaking, they fought with bitterness. They killed dead men, dead women, dead children, dead beasts.

They fought with pleasure, their swords were the warrior's joy-song of pure killing. That song they had known deep in their hearts since the beach and the raiders. Only Gallyn and Kestre had found no pleasure in its singing.

A mountain of dead they built there, and it must be done. But Erenan also cried at last, "This is sickness worse than my heart can bear without breaking. This is nothing but shame. There are too many of them!" She too turned her horse, fled away.

"Erenan," Kanda cried after her. "Wait. There are endless numbers of them – but wait, Erenan."

The spring was choked with the dead they laid to rest there, the water had stopped flowing. There were no carvings now on the crane-stone, there was no paint on the wooden post and its eyes were closed. Kanda ran to the spring, raised her sword high and plunged it deep into the mouth of the water.

A darkness came to her eyes. Her blade bit deep into something that gave like flesh and howled like life and felt like her own heart. A shadow crawled out of the mouth of the spring, rose up to tower over her. The water of the stream sucked at her sword blade, would not release her sword to her. A great gush of blood burst from the mouth of the spring. Kanda fell beneath it. Felt herself drowning.

Out of good sown earth and red autumn berries and wildfire, she had been made. The earth was drowned so the seeds would not grow, the berries rotted uneaten on the branch, the fire was extinguished. Such weariness was in her bones, such dread, such fear: where is the peace, where is the hope? There is nothing but this fighting this killing. Never anything but this killing.

Palle stood over her with his sword, and Morren stood over her with his sword. Palle's helmet had a double crest of gold to it, it was like two sundogs around his head. He looked like the sun in splendor. Morren's helmet was worked with figures dancing: they danced for joy that Kanda was rescued. His sword was all aglitter, his armor was bright around him, he looked like the summer sun and the harvest moon. Kanda crawled to her feet with her eyes clear of shadows, took up her sword that hung cold and heavy in her hand. A great vast weight to it, beside the swords of light her companions wielded. All three together drove their swords into the curse-beast. Great and terrible their stroke. The shadow rose as high as the sky to crash down in them. They struck again all three together, not three swords but one sword that was *kind* and *wise* and *bright* and *hope* and *strength.*

The shadow was gone, the stream flowed clear, the dead lay healed and at peace.

But Kanda bent her head on Palle's shoulder and wept, as Palle and Morren wept. But Kanda said, "They will come back. Always, always, there will be more and more and they will come back. They will never have peace, and it will never end."

Beyond the stockade Kestre, Gallyn and Erenan were waiting. They looked weary and fearful. They did not look ashamed of running: for that Kanda was grateful for she had herself been near to running.

All six of the Six Swords of Roven were wounded. Never yet had they taken a wound in battle, any of them. Erenan's arms ran with blood as if she wore a crimson gown. Morren's right shoulder was cut to the bone. Garryn had a wound in his left thigh so that he could not walk. Kestre's face was bruised, her teeth broken. Palle was stabbed in the chest below his heart. Kanda had claw marks on her hands and her arms and her face. They tended each other's wounds, bound them, dressed them: the water in the spring ran sweet now, clear and singing.

"We will purify the village," Erenan said. "We three."

Kanda shuddered. "Burn it, raze it to the ground, rather, Erenan."

"No," Erenan said. "We will purify it then we will leave it be to rot away or to be resettled."

"And then what? Death will come to it again."

"We will fight then," Erenan said. "Again, again, again." Though Kanda knew deep in her heart that Erenan would leave them soon in her anger, would not be there to fight again again again.

Erenan waded into the pool with the water to her thighs. Her walking sticks splashed in the pool and their reflections in the rippling water looked like trees on the bank of a lake. With trembling hands, her wounds hurting her, she set her sword point to the stone and she called the cranes to fly back to the stone. She set her sword point to the post, called the spiraling eye to open.

Erenan tried, Gallyn tried, Kestre tried. Between them, one crane came back to the stone, one painted spiral that was almost an eye opened. That must be enough. That was not enough.

"We will fight whenever we need to fight," said Palle, and his knuckles were white and bloodless on the hilt of his sword. Already he looked to the far horizon for an enemy to come. "Tomorrow, if need be, we will fight here. Now, if need be."

They rode out of the village, making for Roven with their horses very close together as they rode. They spoke eagerly of peaceful things together, of the good weather, of the crops in the fields and how long till the first hay mowing, of Erenan's Eluisa and Gallyn's Tobelef.

They reached the dead tree: the tree was green in first full leaf, green-golden, a tall beautiful elm tree. The man stood beneath the tree, cloaked and hooded.

"Rejoice!" Morren cried to him. "Evil is defeated." But the words fell heavy. And a fear grew on all of them. The man stood beneath the tree without speaking. They kicked their horses, rode fast away from the tree.

Kestre whispered, "What was that thing beneath the tree there?" Kanda alone turned her head to look back and it was gone. But it seemed to her that something was hanging from a high branch of the elm tree. It seemed to her a sweet voice in her mind was calling.

Gallyn's horse trappings jangled all jaunty music, bright and merry as a may-month morning lust in the green meadow. "That stupid stupid noise," Morren shouted. He rode up to Gallyn's horse, and he ripped the trappings from its head. He threw them to the ground and urged his horse to stamp on them.

"My husband gave me those!" Gallyn shouted. Morren had reopened the wound in his shoulder reaching for the trapping, and now Gallyn reopened the wound in his thigh twisting in his saddle in anger striking at Morren. Palle stared with mad eyes at the far horizon as he searched for the enemy to come.

"Tomorrow, today, now, if need be, we must be ready, we are the Six," Palle whispered. Again again again. He whispered until his voice was dry and cracked and harsh. "We fight, we protect." He whispered, he clenched his hands on the horse's reins, he whispered again again again.

They rode back through the gates of Roven. They feasted. They slept. The next morning indeed the trumpet rang to call them.

Such a horrible story. Kanda closed her eyes tight in the dark, pressed her arms tighter around Dellet. He stirred and grumbled in his sleep.

There were good stories. So many good stories, noble deeds that were great and good without a stain on them, if they were painted on a wall they would be dazzling to look upon. No questions and no horror: stories that were safe to remember in the night while her family slept. But this story and the story of the beach and raiders came back to her. There is no *hope*. There is no *peace*. There is only endless desperate fighting.

But…those stories…they are no more true than the bright stories, she thought then.

She thought: I have found peace here for a little while. I have borne three children, and hoped for them. They will suffer and die – but now they live. And at times it has been so very good.

In golden fire once she and Erenan had saved the city of Samaneth from destruction, an army of fell monsters had come down upon Samaneth and the two of them alone had driven it away; in the monsters' wake fear and falsehoods gripped Samaneth so that its people began to quarrel amongst themselves, take up arms against each other, mother against daughter, father against son, Kanda and Erenan calmed the people, persuaded them to lay down their weapons without a drop of blood shed. A young man came to Roven in despair, fated to pine with love for a woman he had never so much as cast eyes upon, who lived imprisoned at the top of an invisible mountain in a tower with no windows and no door; Kanda and Gallyn found the mountain, rescued the lady, she gave the young man a single kiss and rode away to live her life; he rode away happy to live his. Kanda listened to Calian's quiet breathing, to Morna's soft snores, she thought: those bright stories also have great truth to them. The woman had wept for joy when she was freed, the man had wept for joy: those tears were as true as Kanda's tears of grief. When peace had been restored to Samaneth, the people of the city had embraced in the streets.

She remembered suddenly Dellet's sister saying one day when she came close to saying she was afraid to be a mother: *"Yes, Kanda, Goodsister, I know exactly what you mean, I felt exactly that. Like the world would laugh: you, feckless fly-by-night selfish, to be trusted with a life? It's all right, Kanda, it passes, you'll see. Eventually, it does." And she says in return, "I've done things, in my past, that weren't good things. Before I came here. How can I...how can I be a mother, raise a child well after doing bad things?"* She must have been drunk when she spoke to Dellet's sister, to say that? But she must have been pregnant so she couldn't have been drunk. Just pregnant, Kanda thought.

"I cheated on my husband two days before I married him, and I mostly married him because he isn't a farmer like my brother. No offense, Kanda, obviously. But that doesn't have much to do with how I raise my children,

though, does it? You just do what you can to raise your children as well as you can manage. That's all you can do. It's thankless and endless and…a lot of the time it feels bloody hopeless, I'm telling you now, it does. It feels like it's never enough. Sometimes it isn't enough. Most times it is."

Sometimes the deed is bright as stars. Sometimes the deed is too terrible for the heart to bear. But sometimes it must be met even so.

She thought: let them do all they dare – I am stronger, I was the greatest of the Six and I was far greater than Geiamnyn or Ysarene or that empty one my husband. They looked at me as I fought with awe and with fear. I mocked them even as I fought beside them.

She thought: why would they have left me alone if they had known I was here?

Because they are afraid of me.

She thought: why have they taunted me, haunted me, 'only wanted to talk to me'?

To try to make me fear them so I will not fight them.

She thought: we fought on Calian's island and I defeated all three of them. Why have I forgotten that?

Why have they taken my children?

Because they dare not face me.

A few days of quiet dull life before the dark returns howling – is that not worth any amount of pain and grief?

These also are words that must be said.

CHAPTER THIRTY-NINE

A day, a day, a quiet day. A normal summer farmer's day. Cook food, mend clothes – Morna, I swear, you've grown a thumb's length at least! – tidy, clean. Morna played with her dolls, no mention of swords or war cloaks now, no mention of Ty, she was home safe and a child, the hall fading in her child's mind a dream. Calian with a new calm to her, working at the chores Dellet set her without complaint though she saw how pointless they were. Dellet and Calian sorted stones for the walling, sorted wood for the fish weir. Dellet drew a picture of the fish weir in the soil with a stick, "Here, you see how it works, Cal-bird, yes? Good, eh? Neat." Calian dutifully and truthfully nodded: "Neat." She sorted wood, she sorted stones, she said, "It will be a great thing, Dad, more good tasty fish to eat." Dellet hummed he was so happy, "Lots and lots and lots of good tasty fish!" He said uncertainly later, "I was going to mow the hay meadow...." He said, more certain, "Tomorrow morning, I'll mow it. A better day for it, tomorrow." A day, a day, a quiet day, planning, sorting, gathering, not doing. Because nothing he did today would come to pass, there was no point in doing anything, deep hidden in his heart he knew it. "I'll build the byre up bigger, you think, Kanda? A floor above, for storage? I'll replant the vegetable garden, we could try those good runner beans old Ben was growing, you think, Kanda?" He frowned: "Old Ben.... I wonder," he said, "how Sal and her husband are getting on?" He sang to himself as he went about his business:

"The cows are come in, and the fields they are sleeping.
The cows are come in, and the evening wakes.
The cows are come in, and the children are playing.
At the table the bread and the beer, the fruit, the good meat.

"Now where've I got that from?" he asked, puzzled. "Sure I've heard it before…."

"I think you must have made it up, Dad," Calian said. "It's a nice song."

A night, a night, a quiet night. Morna went off to sleep well before the sun set, cuddled up in her bed with a grin of happiness. Dellet yawned and nodded his way through telling her a story, "Tell you what, mad as it sounds I might get off to bed myself."

"You do that, Del, love," Kanda said.

Kanda and Calian went outside, sat beneath the apple tree in the dark a little while sharpening their swords. The rooks argued and a blackbird sang a last joy-song to the evening. Blocked out the rasp of whetstone on blade.

"I can hear sheep," Calian said suddenly.

Kanda listened. "And cows," Kanda said. "Someone has returned to the valley."

"Perhaps they'll live in this house," said Calian. "Do you think? I'd like that. I think. The monsters rebuilt it, we can't live here, but it's still a good house for someone."

Kanda said, "That would be a fine thing."

Calian turned her sword over, inspected the blade. "That's done, then. Good." She looked at the darkening sky. "So: tomorrow morning, we hunt them down, then." She frowned. "We go to…that hall? Geiamnyn's hall. Break it apart and burn it, like they did with our real house." She said after a moment, baffled, "How do we get there?

"Was that hall ever a real place, Calian? Could a battle be fought there?"

Calian thought. "No. It was an evil place. I would not want to fight there, to shed blood, even that *Burning*'s blood."

"Indeed. I do not think we could go there again even if we wanted to, anyway. Not after the way you and Sal humiliated Geiamnyn there. He'll have destroyed the place by now, I expect. Burned it, smashed it down, screamed at it. Then regretted it."

Calian snorted. "Even Morna doesn't do that anymore. Or not often."

The girl leapt to her feet, raised her sword high: "You monsters! Hoo! Hoo! I am Calian the Eagle, you have stolen my sister away and I curse you! I am Calian the Eagle, I challenge you. Come and fight me if you dare! I challenge you, I will kill you!"

The valley was silent, waiting. Then a sheep bleated somewhere, such a stupid self-satisfied noise in answer that Calian burst out laughing.

"That's the way, sheep. You answer for them. Baaa, that's what those monsters say." The owl hooted, made Calian laugh more. "Baa twit twoo! That's it!" She waved her sword around: "Just you I'm waiting to hear answer, Geiamnyn, *Burning*, you pitiful one. What's a good noise for you, eh? A cow mooing? An ass braying? No, I know: a duck, Geiamnyn, *Burning*, an angry duck, quack quack quack! Or has my sister gelded you already so you're too ashamed to speak at all, Geiamnyn?

"*Burning*, *Hunger*, *Empty*: I challenge you, all three of you!" Calian shouted.

The sheep baaed in answer. The owl hooted.

Calian said, "Come on, then?"

Kanda said wryly, "You thought they'd appear here before us immediately with Sal in chains their prisoner, run straight at us? '*You challenged us, we come*'?"

Calian said, "Well…yes?"

"Is that what you'd do?"

"Well.… Yes."

"That's what I'd do, too. Appear, run at them screaming, *No one challenges me!* Put my foot in a hole, do my ankle in, leap up, slip on some sheep shit, limp on at them. Oh yes. Sadly, Calian, our enemy are rather more cowardly."

"Cowardly?"

"You tell me they are not cowards?"

Calian said thoughtfully, "I keep thinking they'll come and attack us. But actually… they don't, do they? They follow us, they taunt us, but they only fight if we fight them first." She said, astonished and delighted, "They really would leave us alone here forever if we ignored them, wouldn't they? They really are like bleating sheep."

Kanda laughed. "They are, yes. They are terrified of defeat, of others' strength and bravery. They are afraid of what they are, and of what we are. Of what you are, Calian. That…that fear of being defeated…that is why they fight." Kanda too leapt up, raised her sword, raised her face to the night: "And oh, they are afraid of me. Even when I fought beside them, they were afraid of me, I think." Kanda, too, shouted: "Geiamnyn. Ysarene. You *emptiness*, you who are *nothing*. You who were once my companions. You have stolen two of my three children, you have stolen my life away. I am Ikandera Thygethyn, the greatest of the Six Swords of Roven, I am she who broke the oath and destroyed the Hall Roven and all that dwelled there. Matchless, I am. Undefeated. Queen of Battle, Great Warrior. My daughter stands beside me here, and she alone is my equal, she has already challenged you.

"I am Ikandera Thygethyn and I challenge you. Geiamnyn, Ysarene, you who are only *emptiness*! I challenge you to fight me!"

The cow mooed in answer. Calian shouted, "Quack! Quack! Quack!"

"Hush a bit, Calian, you'll wake your sister. Right, now we're ready with our blood up: how do you think we should hunt those cowards?"

"I think…." Calian looked around. "Actually, thinking about it, I'm glad they didn't come yelling at us right away. It would be too horrible, wouldn't it, fighting in our fields and our house? But then…. But what if they just leave us here? What if they just…don't ever come? They think we are happy here, they've given us our house back, Dad's happy, Morna's happy…what if we did just stay, and they, they left us alone? We sit here, and Sal's gone forever, we curse them, challenge them, *Come, Hunger! Come, Burning! Come, you empty one!* and they never come and never come?" Calian groaned and laughed together. "Oh no! Oh Mum! Dad'll kill us. He'll be so angry. Oh, Mum, how absurd. How stupid. Oh, honestly, my legs will drop off soon, Mum. Dad's arms will drop off from carrying Morn." She said, "We came…all that way, and all that way back, and…."

"We came back," Kanda said, "because Geiamnyn made us. Two days we walked, simply because he told us to. So now we walk it again."

She thought: he gave the order, I jumped to it, scurried at his bidding, thank you thank you sorry sorry, whatever you want Geiamnyn. I could have refused his messenger. I could have refused to kill the bull.

A man orders it, I do it. Even I!

"Yes, but, Mum…. Oh it's too ridiculous." Calian jumped and cursed, stretched her hands to the sky to the west. "Walking walking walking! Another reason to hate you, you monsters! But that would be the way of it, yes, you're right there. But what will Dad say?"

Once, twice, three times, four times, five…how many times can I break my oath? *Promise me. I dreamed I was lost there. I'm sorry. I promise.* But he will say…he will say nothing, Calian, he will not speak.

"Geiamnyn led us away from Mal Anwen because he was afraid to face me in battle. He wanted us to come back here to our house and to…forget. Once he was a man – but he has forgotten so many things. All three of them – they remade this house for me thinking I would stay here away from them. Be grateful to them, rebury my sword, go back to living in peace. '*We gave you back your house and your youngest daughter, what more could you want? You should thank us, Ikandera Thygethyn.*' That's what they would say."

She said quietly, "I once rebuilt a village that had been destroyed. In my arrogance and my folly I thought the survivors could simply go back to living there."

All the laughter died away. Calian did not speak and did not speak. At last Calian said, "But it's…it's such a stupidly long way! All that way back, for nothing."

Not for nothing. To give your father two days of peace, Calian. We walked two days at Geiamnyn's bidding and at the end of it I heard your father laugh again. Kanda said, "It is the sort of thing

Geiamnyn takes some stupid amusement in. Making women do things for nothing. A mockery of a journey for a mockery of a wedding." She said, "I am the mother of three children, Calian. A great deal of my time is spent running to and fro doing pointless things."

"If that *Burning* made us walk all the way back here out of—" Calian shook her fist at the night sky. "You think it's funny to make us run to and fro, you monsters! Curse you! I'd…I'd walk on my hands back to Mal Anwen if it spites you!"

Kanda said, "I had a horse that could outrun the wind and the tide once, Calian my love, and it could have ridden there in less time than it takes for you to climb this apple tree. But it couldn't have carried all four of us even if it was here now hoping you would climb this tree to find it an apple. And it certainly couldn't carry all five of us back." She put her hand to her pocket. "But you do not need to walk on your hands, Calian my love. You'll see." She thought: I was so certain they wanted to drive me to Mal Anwen to fetch my sword, that once I had my sword they would come for me to kill me. But all this time they have been striving to keep me away from Mal Anwen. All that they have done, raising the hodden, taking Sal from me, all of it has been to keep me away and take me away from the mountain. They are so afraid of what I shall do and be on that mountain.

Many oaths I have broken. Many promises, and, look – you, Calian, my eagle daughter, came from out of all of those broken promises!

When thunder breaks the stones of Mal Anwen, that is a sign the world will end.

And a new world will begin.

Dellet was sleeping when Kanda and Calian returned to the house; Calian made a show of yawning, rubbing her eyes, "Oh, I'm so tired, Mum, I'll be asleep as soon as my head touches the pillow, I bet." She got into bed beside Morna and was silent immediately. Kanda lay in bed awake breathing slowly, listening to Calian breathing slowly pretending to be fast asleep. After a while Calian rolled over, made what she obviously thought was a deep sleep mumbling groan. Kanda thought: should I suggest she makes some snores?

Dellet was snoring, Kanda put her hands on his back that was warm and slightly damp with night sweat. Pressed herself up close to him smelling his skin and the warm furze beneath the blanket. Calian did pretend to snore. Kanda kissed her husband's back, ran her hands between his legs. He rolled over, still half asleep, sighed deeply, kissed her back and his hands ran over her, went between her legs. His eyes opened, they looked at each other in the dark and for one terrible moment he remembered everything, loathing was in his eyes, he tensed and drew away. Then he pulled his wife to him, wrapped his arms around Kanda strong and tight.

And morning.

Late morning. A long sleep in her husband's arms in the end. Eased loving peace. But morning, and rainfall drummed on the roof. You could have mended that place in the roof, Geiamnyn. Dellet woke, rolled with a smile to look at his wife. "Good morning."

"Good morning." He gave her a questioning grin, she had to signal with her eyebrows that Calian and Morna were awake already. He mouthed, "Tonight, then." What could she do but mouth back, "I'll hold you to that, husband"? His breath smelled stale of her last night's pleasure, she wrinkled her nose and breathed it in.

"We've cooked this morning!" said Morna, dancing in with bannock and cold meat. "Oh oh thank you, Morn, how lovely, argh, no, careful, hold the plate—" Kanda went scrambling to catch the plate up, pull her clothes around her bare breasts. "No it's all right, look, the bannock's fine, the butter side landed upward, we can just carve some more ham." She tried to dust fluff off the bannock without Morna noticing. "Oh that's tasty, Morna. Well buttered."

"Very tasty," said Dellet. Surreptitiously wiping milk off the blanket where Morna had spilled it. "And in my favorite cup."

"Calian did the ham," Morna said. "I poured the milk and buttered the bread. And got the plates."

"Obviously you did."

"Shall we make the fish trap today, Daddy? I can help!" She came in beside and on top of them, started eating Dellet's bannock. "Too much butter," she said, as if anyone in all the world but she had spread it.

"We could, we could," Dellet said over Kanda's head. "Three changes of clothes be enough for today, do you think? Or all four, maybe?" Morna went running into the living place to replace Kanda's dropped ham and Dellet said, "I'll bet you she gets soaked right to the top of her head." Then he said, "You have butter on your left breast, wife." Then he sighed. "But Morna is coming back with more badly carved ham."

Two days. Kanda thought: for nothing? I would walk from here to Mal Anwen and back on my hands every day of my life for this. She thought: I rebuilt a village after it was destroyed, and the survivors… they tried so hard to go back to living there. They almost managed it.

"Where's your sister gone?" Dellet asked Morna. The child made a face, "She's outside waving that sword around. Told me to go away in case I got hit."

"Sound advice," said Dellet.

"Can I have a sword?"

Dellet said in astonishment, "What do you need a sword for, Morna mine? What does Calian need a sword for now, come to that?" He got up. "I'll tell her to put it away. Do something useful."

Morna said, "She can use it for hunting fish!" She knocked Dellet's cup of milk all over the blanket, or it spilled somehow anyway, "I didn't do it," she wailed but obviously she'd spilled it, who else would have managed to spill it? and Dellet got distracted, and Calian came in quietly to put the plates away.

So. Dellet dressed, took Morna out to the river to look at where tomorrow or the next day he would make the fish weir. "Wasn't I going to mow the hay meadow? Tomorrow, yes…." Shook his head.

"So.... Come on then, Morna, let's go and think about catching fish."

So. Calian said, "I wish we could leave them here."

"We could. The two of them together, and they'd forget...Sal off and married, you and I...if we left them here, they'd forget." Just the two of them, forever, safe from all harm, never leaving the valley until Dellet got old and died and at last his daughter would be alone, grown old herself.

Kanda thought: but they'd be happy, in their way. And safe. But I...I cannot bear to leave them. The horror of it: going off into the dark with Dellet and Morna left behind, forgetting. So selfish, so cruel and heartless to them. "We could go now, without them. Or— You could stay too, Calian, I will go, you— Stay here, the three of you, in this house, safe, in peace! Please, Calian!"

Calian said, "I know what Dad would say if he knew you were thinking this."

"Calian—"

"Do we need to pack food and things? Cloaks, I suppose. A whetstone. Dad and Morna will be back from the river soon, Mum, we need to be ready to go when they do. I gave you your two days," Calian said, remorseless. "Two days of pain I've endured for you, Mum. It's time now."

Just a little...a little longer. Another day, Calian. Half a day. The time it takes to walk to the river and back, give me that, Calian. I was wrong, I could stay here forever even knowing I left Sal to Geiamnyn. This is my home, my heart, this is who I am, this house, this place, these memories, my loves. Let me stay here just one more day.

As long as it takes for a cloud to pass over the face of the sun, Calian, give me that. As long as it takes a sunbeam to move across the wall above my bed. As long as it once took for me to break an oath, Calian. Give me that time here in my home, at least.

Less time than a single heartbeat, to break an oath. Kanda strapped on her armor, took up her sword, took up her helmet. Took up the satchel containing the wooden bowl, the piece from the quern, the cracked clay cup and that third *empty* one's broken finger bone. In the pocket on her belt her horse's hooves thundered. She went out of the house with Calian following her, she did not look back and Calian did not look back. Though a thousand peals of children's laughter followed her. Though a thousand shouts and arguments and wails rang in her ears. Though the shadows of children's hands reached out to grasp her, and slipped away half-unseen.

I will forget, she thought. Those memories of their childhood, I will forget. No laughter and no shouting tantrums, I hear only death.

Kanda strode down the hillside where the land ran steep to the River Wenet. There on the bank of the river Dellet and Morna were playing. She came among the hawthorn trees some human hand had once planted. She took up her sword, with one stroke she felled the tallest and the most beautiful of the trees. It fell without a sound, lay stricken with the grass very green about it. From the stump there came a thin frail trickle of blood.

In the garden there was a pile of sticks that Morna collected – Calian's stick collection had only just been dealt with when Morna's collection appeared in its stead. Kanda went back to the garden, found four strong sticks that were about equal in length. One of them was the branch of the apple tree, she noticed as she returned to the hawthorn: Morna had been awake an hour at most before she found and claimed it. Apple and hawthorn, that was good, they were good trees. And this here from a beech tree, where Morna had found it she had no idea. And this from an oak tree, and this from the aspens with their music day and night behind the house. Kanda placed the four sticks against the trunk of the hawthorn, four good legs. She sighed, she winced, she snapped off four of her hairs from the crown of her head. Two were red as wildfire, and the beechwood sang to them. Two were gray-silver.

The aspen stick for one of the gray hairs, she thought ruefully.

She laid the hairs over the sticks and the hawthorn trunk. Thus the sticks were bound to the trunk as firm as if they had grown there.

From her pocket, Kanda took the horse's tooth and the piece of the horse's skull. She knelt and studied the fallen tree very carefully, looking for the best place. She drove the tooth into the wood; it sank in as easily as she had felled the tree. Beside the tooth she drove in the piece of skull. She thought, and she felt guilt and grief at what she was thinking, she took the splinter of rotten wood from her pocket, she drove it into the trunk beside the piece of skull.

Kanda touched the trunk with her sword point. She touched each of the four stick limbs.

The hawthorn had been green with leaves and fuzzed with the first red berries. One branch now was white blossom, one branch was green for summer, one branch was autumn yellow and red. One branch had the leaves just budding. One branch was black and leafless, its last berries withered and shrunken, dulled and frost-blighted. The beech stick was blazing fire in cold midwinter, the oak stick was cool shade on a hot day. The apple stick was sticky scrumping faces, the aspen stick was song and light.

Kanda touched the earth with her sword point. She cut her hand with her sword point, let fall one drop of blood. There were no words she could find that could be said.

The hodden rose in a clatter of sticks and bones and teeth champing. Oh it was beautiful. Oh it was shameful.

Kanda said to the hodden, "Henef. Swiftest and bravest of horses. Countless times did you carry me into battle. Never did your heart fail you. Countless times did you carry me for sport and enjoyment, never did you grow weary or refuse to carry me. I betrayed you and I let you die, I could not save you. I fought you, on the slopes of Mal Anwen I killed you, I saw you die for a second time. On the slopes of Mal Anwen I gave you peace, Henef, best of horses, I saw in my heart that you ran free on the wind. Here in the ashes of my life I summon you, I imprison you, I condemn you once more to this life that is no life. Henef, Queen of Mares, I have made a hodden of you just as my enemies did, I am ashamed of it and my heart breaks. Henef, Queen of Mares, bravest and swiftest and best and most trusted of horses: carry me and my family now in safety to Mal Anwen. Carry us back to the very spot where I killed you. Henef, my companion once – only do this last one thing."

The hodden neighed its horrible gobbling neigh. It gnashed its teeth at Kanda: there was foam and blood on its teeth. It whinnied, the way Henef had whinnied in greeting when Kanda came to the horse field with an apple for her. It was a long high horse with wooden bones and a mane of white flowers, its hide was green leaves, its hooves were teeth. A bridle and reins were around its head. It whinnied, and Kanda pulled herself up onto it, kicked in her heels. Horse and rider leapt.

"Mother! Oh how beautiful! Oh!" Calian came running, hands clasped to her chest. "Oh! Wonderful! Mum!" Kanda stretched out to her, caught her and pulled her up before her. Calian threw her arms around the hodden's neck. "Oh! Oh! Henef!" Calian cried. "Henef! *Swiftest*!" They rode at a gallop down to the valley bottom, in the water meadow the flowers were up to Henef's hocks. They rode in great bounds into the River Wenet, for the sheer pleasure of seeing the hooves kick the water up. Dellet and Morna were sitting on the bank downstream in a place Morna liked because there were bees living in a hollow tree. They rode down the riverbed with the water coursing around Henef's legs; white petals floated on the water, as they did in the spring. The petals flicked their tails and they were darting shimmering little fish, they were dragonflies large as Calian's handspan with iridescent wings.

"Morna!" Calian called. "Dad!"

The two were looking away downriver, deep in conversation about something. They turned – Calian called, "How can you not have heard us coming?"– their faces were a wonder. Dellet had to restrain Morna from wading into the river and throwing herself at the horse's legs.

Kanda nudged the horse onto the riverbank. Dismounted, helped Calian down, looped the reins around a branch.

"Fine, hey?" Calian said.

"Fine," said Dellet. He patted Henef's neck. He was not a tall man and the horse towered over him. It whinnied, flicked back its ears, then settled itself to grazing.

"I like the sound it makes when it eats," said Morna.

"I do too."

"Like cows. Only better. Sleepy sound."

Dellet said carefully, "What are we doing with this?" His face was stretched. He watched the horse, he watched Morna watching it delighted. No telling what he thought he saw: a beaten-down old carthorse, a shaggy pony? A lord's warhorse, a gift from his rich new son-in-law? His hand had wavered when he went to touch it, as if he was uncertain how big it was. "Found it, did you? Lost on the hills?"

"I found it," said Kanda, equally carefully.

"Well, the girls seem to dote on it." Dellet relaxed, smiled. A fat pony for the children to ride on.

"It's having a wee, look!" Morna shrieked in delight.

Kanda closed her eyes a long long time. Sucked in her breath and sucked all this last of this world in.

If I could stay here. If we could stay. We could stay. All we have to do is stay.

Ah, Geiamnyn, *Burning*, you think you hurt me by making me come back here for these brief days! The light behind her closed eyes was so good and warm and hearth-fire-red.

Dellet said, "This is all broken, this life here, isn't it, Kanda? Broken beyond any repair."

Kanda opened her eyes. She did not answer. She got up, stroked Henef's nuzzle. The horse curled her lips. Kanda pulled herself up onto the horse, helped Calian up.

Dellet got up. He called to Morna. The child trotted over, delighted. Dellet lifted her, Kanda and Calian between them caught her, they wrestled her to sitting behind Kanda with her arms gripping Kanda's waist. Dellet pulled himself ungainly up behind.

"I thought it could be fixed," Dellet said. "Like a field wall that a storm breaks. I'm good with my hands at fixing things."

Kanda kicked in her heels. Henef snorted. The hodden stepped.

The hodden raced. Vast and strong as a tree falling, with Kanda's family clutching on it. Beautiful and absurd thing. A song, a song, Muss once made, of the three mighty horses that bore three mighty burdens, so long was the list of the people the mightiest of those three horses bore as its burden that Erenan booed and Gallyn walked out and Morren fell asleep. But never I think did a horse bear a burden as absurd and as terrible as this. They reached the field wall that was the end of their farm's fields, the hodden jumped it; as they crossed the wall all the knowledge of what had passed came back to Dellet and he let out a groan so great even the hodden started, and the tears ran down his face unchecked.

Three days going, three days waiting, two days returning, three nights and two days in the house that Geiamnyn had remade for them. So great was Dellet's groan that the hodden started even as it jumped the field wall, its back hooves caught the top of the wall and the stones of the wall were shattered. And thus for the second and the last time they left that place.

CHAPTER FORTY

A path stretched out before them. Over the hills and the valleys, the high rocks, it ran straight without barrier, a smooth flat surface made for the horse's hooves. Visible but invisible, the eye traced it, cautious, not quite seeing, yet so very clearly it was there. As straight and as vivid as sunbeams stretched across the land in early morning or in the last fire of evening when the sun and the sky cut deep. As straight and as vivid as a shadow thrown sharp across the grass. Droveways ran across the wild hills, paths made by men to lead their cattle. Henket paths ran there, made by warriors marching to die and to kill, the paths of the dead. Cursed, to be avoided, fearful places where the dead might wait. Wilder paths made by beasts, wolf path, deer path, fox path too narrow for human feet; paths made by the dead walking who cannot rest and are not buried, traced in the sky above by the cries of the wild geese. Travelers wandered lost in the high hills; men fled from a battle for wise fear of dying; a woman might wander abandoned in the high wild places seeking her peace. False paths, listen, voices laugh there, mocking, the traveler turns in circles weary until he falls, the traveler strides on confident, a light ahead is welcome, food, shelter, human voices, until the mire rises to drown him without trace. Joy paths, bridal paths for a true wedding journey, a woman leaving her distant home in the wilds for a new hearth. The hodden trod a path that was none of these and was all the paths that ran there in the wilds. So safe a child could walk that path at night without fear. Over crags, over black mire, smooth and straight the path ran. All day the hodden walked with Kanda and her family silent on its back. The sun set, the hodden walked on straight and smooth, one by one the four fell asleep. Even Kanda slept, the reins loose in her hands, cradled safe on the hodden's strong back.

No hunger. No thirst. By the side of the path things might walk or might be crouching, far above things might fly and cast a shadow beneath. Bright flash of pain as a hawk dives for a mouse in the heather, the glory of the hawk's wings, its fierce eyes, the swiftness of its prey's death. Long drawn-out pain as a wounded beast dies alone of old age and hunger and injuries unhealed. The choking unvoiced pain of a beast that dies at birth. The hodden walked without harm, without seeing; the path was the sun's path and the moon's path. Uncaring as the sun and the stars and the moon, and the moon indeed was waning.

Kanda thought in her sleep: let this, also, never end. Not once did Dellet speak to her, though he spoke haltingly to his daughters, tried to talk as a father to his daughters while Morna babbled on and on younger than she was. But he was there near her, his arms had to hold her because he rode behind her on the hodden and they must keep Morna safe wedged between them; she could hear his breathing, smell his breath.

When they had crossed the field wall a scar had appeared on Morna's forehead. Deep and puckered against her luminous brown skin. Then, briefly, Dellet had spoken not to Kanda but not to his children either: "My curse on the sword that did this," Dellet had said. Then he said to no one or to himself, "It was the only thing she could do. The child bit me, and we had to get her out." His head shook, he was silent a long time trying to understand anything. "How did this come to be?" he said to no one and to himself. "What did she think I was when she married me?"

Kanda said then, "A good man and a fine one, and a good husband and a good father, Del-my-heart, I thought you were. And I a good woman, I hoped and wanted to be a good woman, at least, and a good wife to you and a good mother to our children, and nothing less and nothing more."

But Dellet ignored her as if she had not spoken. And perhaps he could not hear her now, whatever she said to him. And on the edges of the hodden's path all the time things were dying and things were being born.

The hodden stopped walking, suddenly so that Kanda was jerked awake. She felt disgusting, dew-damp soaked into her bones, she had forgotten, for a kindness, how disgusting the feel of sleeping damp in armor was. Sweat-damp and dew-damp both. Her eyes were ragged, her mouth tasted clagged. Her body and her mouth must stink. Shallow sleep all confusion – where am I, where are we? The dark still – first dark, last dark before sunrise, where have we been, what direction do we face, an hour I've slept, or a thousand years, what and where is this?

She said with a croak, "What's up, Henef?" Her lips were stuck together with dried spittle, she cleared her throat, "What's this?"

The hodden snorted.

The path stretched before her. She caught her breath because it was beautiful beyond all things. Deep bronze in the moonlight, flowing on from beneath the hodden, grass and rocks and trees cast in bronze. To the left and the right of the path the world was wild and alive for men and for beasts. The path was for a Sword of Roven alone. In the distance it was still liquid.

"Well," Kanda said to the hodden, "that's a fine thing."

The hodden whinnied.

"Shall we stop here, Henef? Get these sleepers watered and fed?" The hodden snorted, stamped. "Yes, Henef: you'd gallop five times as far as it is to Mal Anwen without stopping to draw breath. But these sleepers here need to stop, I think." The dizziness of waking from her own sleep was fading; Kanda could see the mountain close ahead, the path running straight and steep toward its peak. She said, "I would like to stop a bit myself, Henef, *Swiftest*, at least to take off my armor to let my sweat dry, maybe if I'm very lucky there's a stream here so I wash the drool off my face? And there are times, Henef, when a woman of my age does very much want to wash between her legs. Would it astonish you to hear that my bleed has come early now I'm riding into battle on Mal Anwen? Who could have thought such a thing as my bleed coming early as I ride to battle, hey, Henef? And thus perhaps it's not too much to ask even that I could reach Mal Anwen with a clout cloth between my legs, is it?"

She shook Calian gently on the shoulder. Then she shook Calian rather more firmly on the shoulder. Calian mumbled, "What, Mum?" She got all three of her family awake blinking and shaking their heads, got them sleepily down from the horse's broad back. Morna simply curled up in a huddle on a hump of grass, went straight back to sleep. She might in fact have got off the horse in her sleep.

Calian stretched and said, "I was dreaming about something." She said after a moment, "Where even are we?"

"We're...." Ah, the hodden had chosen a good place, look, they were in the cleft cut by a stream between two rolling hills. The path gave bronze light to see by, crossed the stream and the water there was bronze. Kanda washed her face there, when she plunged her hands into the water it was warm. It tasted of metal, but it tasted fresh and good.

"Ugh, I could sleep for a thousand years," said Calian. She too washed her face and her hands, rubbed water over her hair. "Oh that's better," she said. She stretched her back. "Oh I'm stiff."

"A soldier in an army can sleep on the march," said Kanda. "Never mind on horseback."

"I refuse to believe that."

Now Calian was awake she was ravenously hungry. Kanda got out the wooden bowl, the quern stone, the clay cup. She squatted in the mud, the power came so easily: bread, meat, milk. Between them, she and Calian got Morna awake enough to drink some of the milk.

All this time, Dellet sat where he had first dismounted, his arms wrapped around his knees.

Kanda said, "Will you not eat something, Dellet?" She wanted very much to say 'husband', but she did not dare.

"It's tasty, Dad," said Calian. "Come on." Her father raised his head, and Kanda saw his eyes meet Calian's, saw Calian frown.

"Fine then," Calian said. She went a few paces up the stream, sat down, leapt up, ran back to her father.

"Just stop it! Stop it! Stop being so stupid! We're doing this for Sal."

Dellet only shook his head.

"What have you done?" Calian shouted. "You've done nothing. Just sat about in pain because Mum…because Mum…."

"Don't call that creature your mother," said Dellet. "Or if you claim her as your mother, don't call me Father, Calian. That creature, that woman…what has she done these last days but lie to me? A woman? A mother? A monster like those others, that's what she is." He turned his face to Kanda with a look of such loathing she recoiled from him. "Lying, lying," he sang in a parody of Ty's song.

"That's it." Kanda had been about to go off a bit downstream to do the necessary things. Always, when she needed to go off for a little while to do these private things. "Dellet, my husband," she said. "Hate me, blame me, curse me. Fine, yes. Say our marriage is over, yes. I don't want that, but yes, yes. When this is done and over, I will go a thousand miles away from you, or you are welcome to go a thousand miles from me. Never speak my name, tell anyone who asks you never had a wife, yes, yes. A hard thing indeed it is to cope with a woman who is changed!

"Sometimes I am not so sure I want to be married to you now either, Dellet my husband.

"But Sal is lost and taken from us. The darkness is all around us. Blame me – yes, I take the blame for it, yes, yes, every moment since first all this befell us – I blame myself and curse myself, Dellet. But Sal, your daughter, is lost and in need of us, and Calian and Morna need us. Need you.

"So just stop, Dellet. All this, the ruin of our life together, all your distrust of me – if Sal can endure marriage to Geiamnyn, I think you can endure a few more days of being half-civil to your own daughter and to me. I think, Dellet, that if Sal can do what she did for Morna, I think you can do…something. Anything. I think you can speak to your daughter, eat and drink, stop your crying.

"Yes, I lied to you. Yes, I am not what you thought me. Yes! But, Dellet….." She threw up her arms, her mind was red, her eyes were red, her tears were so hot they burned her, her right hand was burning. "I don't know, Dellet. At least look after your children for a few moments while I do something I have to do."

She walked off to do her private necessary business. She shouted to herself the whole time. She struck her hands together in rage so that her palms hurt. She wept. What Dellet said or did while she was gone she did not know; when she returned with her mind still red but her body more comfortable he was getting Morna washed while Calian sharpened her sword. The food needed clearing: when Kanda went to do it, Dellet said sharply, "Leave that! I'll do it once I've finished with Morna," he said more gently. That was all he said the whole time they were stopped there. A part of Kanda thought with bitterness: he could at least use my name when he speaks to me.

"I am the same person you married, Dellet," she said when the girls were out of hearing fussing over the horse.

The man only muttered, "I don't know."

"Well, pretend you do," Kanda said, and went over to the horse. She remembered again him saying when he first saw her in her armor, "It sounds mad, but when I think about you, in my head you've always looked like this." She thought: well, that lasted long, didn't it, Dellet?

They got back on the horse's broad back, a very little while now they must ride, though the path stretched on over the mountain. The path went straight up the stream valley, straight down a hillside beyond, through a wood around another stream where the trees drew back from the path to let them through, and the trees were made of bronze that glowed to light their way in the light of the waning moon.

"When will the night end?" Calian asked.

"When we reach where we are going," Kanda said.

The path came out of the wood, there was the mountain ahead of them, it was vast and dark and steeper than it had been, it was grown so high Kanda could not see its peak. The moon was behind them, shone full on the flank of the mountain before them where the path ran, all over the mountain there was a movement and a twisting and a writhing. Smoke rose from the mountain.

On the edge of the wood a single tree stood dead and bare before them. A man's body was hanging from the tree. The rope around his neck creaked and groaned, the branches of the tree creaked. "Beware," the hanged man called to them. "Come no closer." The hodden snorted and Kanda drew her sword. The rope snapped and the man fell in a clatter of bones, and there were green leaves on the oak tree. Beyond the wood there were two great stones as tall as the hodden's withers. A headless man stood against one stone, on the top of the other stone was his severed head. "Beware," the head called to them. "Come no closer." The hodden neighed and Calian drew her sword. The headless body fell in a clatter of bones, the head rolled from the stone and was gone.

A silver bird flew toward them, the moonlight was white on its metal wings. "Beware," the bird called. "Come no closer."

Kanda was about to raise her sword when Dellet shook his fist at the bird, shouted, "Be gone! Leave my family in peace!" The bird shrieked, but it flew away.

A living bird with brown feathers and a living bird with black feathers and a fox and a wolf and a deer were beside the path, "Go on! Go on! Ride on quickly to the mountain!" they cried. "Do not fear! Ride on!" A black dog ran beside the path, blood-slaver on its muzzle, its eyes were red. Whip marks and welts covered its thin body, around its neck was a metal collar that cut and chafed it. It barked at the hodden, raised its hackles, its teeth were bared. But it did not and could not speak, and Kanda only had to wave her sword at it for it to flee. The wolf and the fox ran after it, in a little while behind her Kanda heard the wolf's snarl and the dog at bay.

The path rose, and they were at the mountain, and the path ran straight up the sheerest steepest flank.

Calian said, "This is not Mal Anwen."

"Is it not? Look closer, Calian."

"It's huge, it blocks out the sky! Its sides are sheer as a wall. It is nothing like Mal Anwen." Calian frowned. "And yet…and yet…."

Morna said, "There's the blue lake, look! And the mine caves are up there, we'll see them soon!"

Dellet's voice was sharp. "You've never been here, Morna."

"Ty showed me. His mummy took us. All the children in the mines were there to play with. But they're not really children like Ty and me, you see, so Ty gets bored of them. They don't like to play with him."

Calian said, "What are you talking about, Morna? Stop babbling." Ah, there was so much fear in Calian's voice.

Dellet's eyes were fixed on the mountain, the hodden stepped up the mountain's sheer steep flank and the sun rose and lit the highest peak. Dellet screamed, "It is Mal Anwen! It is the mountain as I have seen in it my nightmare!"

He tried to leap from the horse's back to run. His terror was so great he could not move, or perhaps the hodden held him trapped there.

Dellet screamed, "The peak! The peak of the mountain! See! See! It is gone and broken!"

It was broken, yes, the spearhead of black stone that had risen from the summit of Mal Anwen since first men had come to the high hills and the Wenet valley. Halfway off, it was broken, clean through. The rising sun lit the black stone and made it golden. It was no longer a spearhead, it was a golden sword broken.

"I cannot go on!" Dellet screamed. But he sat on the horse and did not move. Only he held Morna close and he wept, for he knew.

The hodden stepped careful up the path. So steep was the slope that Kanda and her family had to bend forward, grip themselves together against the hodden's strong neck to stop themselves from falling. The mountain was bare stone, gray and lifeless; Kanda blinked and looked close with her real eyes, she saw the mountain rich with green life growing. Hawthorn trees and oak trees and apple trees all heavy with autumn bounty, full of birds feasting before the winter; dark sweet-scented pine trees running with squirrels, "*Ratatatusk*," the squirrels shouted. The wind blew the trees; almost, almost, the shape of the trees made the shape of a woman with the face of a bird and a deer's antlers.

The hodden stopped on the path. Neighed, snorted. The ground leveled out, the lake Elelan Mere lay before them. Its banks were ringed with yellow irises, purple heather, yellow gorse, but the flowers were all crusted and paled with frost. The water shone clear. The stream that ran down to feed the lake was fierce. Behind the lake the mine workings yawned huge, not tunnels for children to crawl down but vast caverns in which an army could be lost.

"Here we are, then." Kanda dismounted, helped the others down. She stroked the hodden's nuzzle, pressed her face into its mane. "Thank you, Henef, Queen of Mares, for this last journey. I'm sorry," she said, "that I had to do this, take you from your rest. Kindly have you borne this great cruelty I have done you. Go now, Henef. *Swiftest.*"

The hodden snorted, stamped its hooves, rubbed its head against Kanda. It pricked up its ears, whinnied, it sank down on its haunches, fell away to pieces. The pieces crumbled away to nothing, all that was left was a horse's tooth and a shard of bone. Kanda bent and took them up, put them in her pocket. "Thank you, Henef."

Calian was watching something on the sheer height of the mountain. Her hands were clasped in joy at her breast. "She's racing! She's leaping!" Calian said in wonder. "How beautiful she is. The most beautiful horse." Calian waved to the invisible thing high on the mountain. "Goodbye, thank you, Henef." She sighed deeply and contentedly. "And there's the gyrfalcon."

It was very calm and cool up here on the winter mountain. The sky was a clear pale blue, the sun pale and bright. The ground beneath their feet was metal-hard with the frost on it; the taste of that hard cold earth hung in the air, welcome. The best ground for fighting on.

"Now, Calian," Kanda said.

"Now?" The girl had to tear herself away from staring at the gyrfalcon circling.

"Unless you want to wait longer?"

The girl gave a snort very like the way Henef had snorted. "We've already let them be far too long." She drew her sword, Kanda drew her sword, both raised them. The broken sword of the mountain peak was between the two blades. A black sword, a bronze sword, a sword of golden light.

"I am Ikandera Thygethyn, that is *Great Warrior*," Kanda cried. "Come! Fight!"

"I am Calian, that is *Eagle*," Calian cried. "Come! Fight!" She brandished her sword. "You pitiful pathetic cowards! Fight!"

"Fight!" both cried together. They brought their sword blades together, the broken blade of the mountain met their blades, one sword it made of shimmering blazing light.

A peal of thunder rang out, so loud the water of Elelan Mere was churned up in waves. A silence, long and terrible, waiting, the silence before the signal is given to join battle, the silence before the front ranks meet. The silence, Kanda thought, before a new-birthed child cries for the first time, when it might have been born living or been born dead.

"The mines," Kanda said. "That will be the beginning."

They all looked toward the yawning cavern mouths, huge enough to swallow the world away.

"So," said Calian. She strode toward the mine workings. "Come on."

Morna shrieked. The lake Elelan rose in a single wave toward Calian. Broke over Calian, over Kanda rushing to join her. The water was so cold Kanda could not hear or feel or see. She gasped: the water was in her mouth, clawing at her throat. And it was clawing at her eyes, it had fingers like ice pulling into her. She spat, choking, the weight of the water was cold hands crushing her. Swung her sword, punching and kicking at the water; she was falling she was floating she was sinking down the water here was so cold so deep. She spat and cursed. She shook off the water like a dog. She trampled the water of Elelan Mere down beneath her feet.

"Go wide," she called to Dellet. The man snatched up Morna, edged round the lake never letting his eyes leave its surface, keeping a good distance between himself and the water's edge.

Calian was shivering uncontrollably, water pouring from her hair and her clothes. She staggered to dry ground, sat down, pulled off her boots. Water poured out of them.

"My sword!" Calian cried out in horror. "I dropped it in the lake." She leapt to her feet, barefoot and soaking.

"Don't go near the water." Calian's teeth were chattering, her hands had the shriveled look of skin that had spent a long time submerged in water. "I will get your sword in a moment, Calian," Kanda said. She put her hands firmly on her daughter's shoulders, gripped her tight. "You look like Sal did that time she fell in the river in her best dress," Kanda said, trying to make her daughter's body soften. She drew in a deep breath, held it, let it out in a cloud like the fug of Dellet's morning breath over Calian.

A cloud of gold, breathed over Calian. The warmth came back into her. The cold sweet good water of Elelan Mere had only washed the night's ride from her.

"Now your sword," said Kanda. She went to the lake, splashed out a few paces until she was up to her knees. The sword was in a deep pool with a smooth green-veined rock beside it. A shoal of fish darted around the hilt, in the shadow of the pool Kanda thought she could see a trout.

It was a perilous thing, to take back a sword that had gone to the water. Kanda waded deeper until she was up to her waist. Ah, the water was so cold!

"I can see it," Calian shouted. "You're almost on top of it, Mum. Just grab it."

"Yes, thank you, Calian." Kanda waded to the edge of the deep pool. Any farther and the water would be deeper than her head. But her hair like Calian's hair was already dry as if she had never been soaked by Elelan Mere.

"Elelan. *Joyful.* The sword was cast from ore from this mountain, in your depths perhaps you hold the spoil from that ore's mining, or the bones of the one who dug it out. The sword has gone to you. But the sword was given into my daughter's hand from another pool. It was given well. It is a beautiful sword, the finest sword I have seen for a long time, I myself would be happy to wield it. But it is my daughter's sword, *Joyful,* Elelan, and I must ask you to give it back to her.

"I know you did not mean to fight us just now, Elelan, *Joyful.* I know why your waters rose and at whose command. Elelan, *Joyful,* I took the poison from your waters, you are joyful and beautiful now indeed."

The lake was very still. There were a lot of fish flitting around the sword hilt. More and more. More and more. A big trout. A pike.

Kanda said, desperate, "Elelan, *Joyful,* the sword has gone to the water and it is yours forever if you wish it. But I beg you, *give me back my daughter's sword.*"

"Just pick it up, Mum!" Calian shouted.

A pair of ducks flew down quacking at each other, landed on the lake. Then three, four, five, three ducks and two drakes. They splashed and quarreled, quacking. Calian began to laugh. She shouted, "It's Geiamnyn, look! Quack quack!" Kanda laughed, she bent down, the water was so shallow her arm was wet only to just above her wrist. She lifted Calian's sword high, it too had only been washed and cleaned by the bright sweet good water. A pattern showed that she had not noticed before, etched lines feathering the blade.

The ducks flew off in a great mad splash, quacking furiously at each other. Kanda returned the sword to Calian.

The entrance to the mine workings. The largest of the tunnels. So high a horseman could ride through with his spear brandished above him, eagles and ravens flying overhead. So wide six horsemen could ride through abreast. The stone of the entrance was sharp and jagged, as dragon's teeth. The world outside the cavern was day and pale washed sunlight. The world inside the cavern was darkness absolute. This great yawning cave mouth, so wide and so tall, with the green grass tall outside it, the plashing of the stream.

Dellet cowered. "It is my dream," he whispered. "All my life have I feared this."

"They're waiting!" Morna said. "My friends!" She stepped lightly across the threshold and was gone into the dark, her voice came singing, "Ty! Gella! I'm coming."

Calian went to follow her. As Calian drew nearer to the cave mouth Morna's voice came again screaming in fear. "I'm coming, Morna!" Calian cried, running forward, but at the very mouth of the cavern Calian froze. Her lips moved, the darkness into which she spoke swallowed her words away. From the darkness, Morna's scream came.

So near. So distant. Kanda tried to force herself through past her daughter. She who had been a part of darkness beyond even this dark. The cavern's mouth was closed to her also. The cavern entrance was a dragon's jaws; the cavern was a dragon's gaping stinking mouth. In a moment the dragon's flames would come. Twice, Kanda had fought dragons. Her courage failed her, she moaned aloud, cold sweat ran down her back. You are an old gray-haired woman with a clout cloth between your legs, Kanda. Go back to cow shit and sheep shit and mending your children's skirts. You need to be changing your clout cloth soon, anyway, don't you? She swayed, gasped out struggling to breathe, for the dark was choking. She was lost there, no above no below no backward no forward. *Flee*, her mind screamed to her. She could speak enough to command Dellet and Calian to flee. The darkness in a weight like hands pushing on her to drown her. The darkness an emptiness that stretched forever into exhaustion, a whole life could pass before any end had been reached. I cannot go in! I will die if I go in.

She said, her voice as thin as old women's hands shaking, "This is not right. This is not meant. We must go in." She said, "Come. Keep on."

The cavern mouth opened before her and Kanda went in. Calian and Dellet followed her. At the threshold a breath of wind touched her cheek. After a few steps Morna stood in the tunnel waiting for them. "What happened to you?" Morna only said.

Kanda said gently, "Nothing."

Kanda held up her sword, Calian touched her sword point to Kanda's sword point. The two blades shone with black light. Slow footsteps together as they went in.

Kanda thought: this is the mine as the children who worked it felt it. Suffocated in the dark and lost.

"My sword was made from ore dug here," said Calian. In the black light of their blades there were marks of tools on the tunnel walls, picks, hammer stones, and sometimes the marks of little clawing fingers, nails scraping to dig ore from the rock.

"It was," said Kanda. "How do you think any metal is mined, Calian? Or stone quarried, or salt made? The swords that hung on the walls of the Hall Roven, that the Lady of Roven herself placed in the hands of the Six, shining, gold-wearing – how else was that metal mined but like this? How was the gold mined, that the Lady wore around her neck?"

"But—"

"This is an evil place," Kanda said. "As your father has seen in his dreams. I swore to him that I would never come here. Another promise I broke and wish that I had been able to keep. I would that you and I never had to know the cost of the swords we carry to kill the monsters."

The tunnel ebbed and flowed over them. Their swords black light against the darkness. Faint whimper now in the air, currents of sound drifting at the edge of hearing. Almost at the edge of vision as cobwebs move half visible in dim light in the corners of a house. Whispers, high thin cries. As birds circle the reeds of the marsh at twilight, as bats flit above the marsh. And the flicker of candle flames far down in the darkness of the tunnel, snuffed out before the eye fell clearly on them.

"What is it?" Calian whispered. Frightened, yet awed by it. For it was melancholy indeed, and yet – there was no malice in it toward them.

"The mine children," said Dellet. He spoke as one long dreaming. "This is an evil place."

"The silly children here playing silly games," said Morna. She stamped her foot. "Stop it!"

Dellet said, "Leave them be, Morna. Don't make them angry."

But Calian said at the same moment, "Leave them be, Morna. They mean no harm to us. Sal is waiting." She walked on into the dark with her sword so bright before her, she shone like the sword now, and her shadow fell huge on the tunnel wall. "Let us go on," she said. Then she said, and Kanda could hear her smile, "The mine children are pleased. They recognize my sword. They know what I will do with it."

All the air was movement around them as they walked. As they walked deeper the tunnel narrowed, the roof grew low, the floor rose. Water trickled in a stream down the center of the tunnel, cut a channel there like a line traced in the stone. The light of their swords made it gleam bronze. The path the hodden had taken, Kanda thought, stretched on into the bowels of the mountain. For the tunnel led downward, the stream ran not out toward the tunnel mouth but down into the mountain's depths. Kanda's hands brushed the walls now, all but Morna had to walk hunched and bent: water ran down the walls to wet her skin and her clothes, dripped into her hair to trickle down her neck, she brushed a drop of water from her lips and tasted salt.

Narrower, yet narrower, lower, deeper: all but Morna had to crawl on all fours now, and Morna walked bent. Kanda and Calian had to sheath their swords, crawl on in the darkness blind and hoping; Kanda's sword pressed hard into her hip, smacked against her legs, several times Calian shouted at her because the sword point jabbed at Calian's face. "Will you stop doing that, Mum?" "It's hardly my doing, is it? Look, just keep back a bit, some space between you and me, it's not difficult," Kanda said back, then shouted back, then merely mouthed in irritation, then gave up even merely mouthing to merely think: Calian. Morna started on exactly the same at Calian about Calian's sword, Calian started on saying exactly the same thing at Morna.

After a while longer, wet through with aching back aching knees, all three at each other, Dellet right at the back suddenly burst into laughter. "May this tunnel never end," Dellet said. "Thank you, mine workings. Thank you, Mal Anwen. For the length of this tunnel here, I have my wife and two of my daughters returned to me."

Narrower, lower, deeper: a fear rose in Kanda that she was wrong. The tunnel would take them down forever into the mountain, wriggling on their bellies like worms, trapped, the children and her husband starved and dead. A dread rose in her also for Morna, who should be frightened and angry and tired out of her mind now, screaming about the dark and the wet. The girl's screams, she thought, and the evil that had come from them. She drew breath to speak, to say something she knew not what. I still love you beyond anything, Morna, my youngest daughter, my body's last unexpected gift. I still love you beyond anything and anyone. She thought it, but these words she could not speak.

The tunnel widened. It opened very suddenly into a chamber, so that they almost fell together. There was light here, coming from the far distance, the air was suddenly warm. This was not a place made by human hands. A void in the rock. An absence. The mountain at its heart empty and rotted. And the copper there in its rich seams the tracings of that rot. Ah, Kanda thought, no wonder I was drawn to bury my sword here! No wonder Geiamnyn is afraid for me to come here.

The chamber widened, the light grew brighter, the ground beneath their feet grew soft, the air grew sweet. The ceiling was shifting leaves, the walls were tree trunks, the ground was good turf. A glade, pleasant to walk through in the summer twilight, birds sang and bats flitted, now their calls were the melancholy of a day's happiness that draws to an end. The trees leant close around Kanda, a wood where the trees grew thick together untended. The trees were made of copper, cold and dead. The birds and the bats were made of copper. Morna snapped off a copper twig and tucked it in Kanda's helmet. "Pretty Mummy," Morna said.

"Yes, thank you, Morna lamb," Kanda said and she made her voice delighted. When Morna trotted on ahead of them, Kanda threw the twig away.

The trees ended. Another clearing. Morna shouted, "Here we are!" So happy, so confident her voice that Kanda almost wept. At the center of the clearing was a deep round pool. Three women knelt on the banks: the pool was formed from their piss and their blood. The boy Ty sat on the banks playing with a toy boat.

Morna ran to him, caught up his hands. "Ty! I'm here, see! I told you!"

"Hurrah!" said Ty. "Do you like my boat? But what are these doing here?"

"It's very good, can I have a go with it?" Morna pouted and said crossly, "These stupids insisted on coming."

"Hello, Ty," Kanda said, and she tried tried tried to make her voice delighted. "You look well."

"I'm not talking to you," said Ty. "Lying. Lying," he sang about Kanda's words about him.

The two children sat by the pool playing with the toy boat. It was very beautiful, very well made, a real boat in miniature it looked like. Ty made it sail right across to the other bank and then return to him. Then he showed Morna how to splash the water with a stick so that the boat seemed caught in a storm. "It's spinning round and round! It's going to sink!" Morna crowed. "Make it sink!"

"No no no, then it will be gone and ruined." The pool calmed; the boat sailed on back to Ty's hands. "We have to be careful with it," Ty said. He launched it again, showed Morna how to make it sail all the way around the pool one way then the other. But Morna grabbed the stick, splashed the water too hard, the boat rocked, tipped—

"No no no, stupid girl!" The boat sank. "I told you, Morna! Now it's gone!" Ty grabbed the stick, the two children fought over it. Ty had it, struck Morna with it. Morna got it, struck Ty with it. The blow cut Ty's cheek, but he did not bleed.

"Stupid girl." Ty ran off into the copper wood.

"I want Sal!" Morna shouted. "Where's Sal?" She ran off after Ty. Kanda and Dellet and Calian could only follow the two children.

The wood was copper trees. The wood was pine trees, but the pine trees were dead. They were in a cave deep inside the mountain Mal Anwen. They were on the slopes of the mountain that was and was not Mal Anwen. They were in a tunnel so narrow they could not draw breath, the walls running with salt water. They were in a cold night with the clouds low. Always the stream ran before them, a path to guide them, sometimes it was blood running, sometimes it was water, sometimes it was liquid bronze. They were in total darkness, but they were in light as bright as the sun and the full moon and a lamp all shining. All around there came the soundlessness of things creeping. Something seemed to slither unseen almost at Kanda's feet. Morna's footsteps very loud. Led Kanda on. A barren stretch of gray moorland high on the mountain, a great crag rising yet higher before them, the land fell to meet it in a reeking mire. Mud sucked at Kanda's feet. Morna seemed to run above it, float over the mire's surface, while Kanda stumbled. She called out desperately, "Morna, wait!"

In the mire at the very foot of the crag a pavilion had been set up, its walls of thick yellow hide, its poles carved bone. Two guards stood at the doorway. Morna made straight for it. Calian gasped in fear for the guards stepped to meet Morna, but they let her pass unchecked, drew open the doorcurtain indeed, and she went in.

Kanda stopped running. "Here we are, then. Are you ready, Calian mine?"

Calian tried to nod.

Kanda said, "I should have destroyed that tent." She said then, "I… all right, yes, I was and remain very proud of that tent."

The guards had seen them. Being well trained – that training was not Geiamnyn's doing – they stayed at the doorway, but Kanda felt them follow her every movement, she knew they were poised and ready to defend. All around, unseen things waited silent; there was no returning now the way they had come, from the moment they entered the mine workings there had indeed been no returning. Then Kanda laughed: stop trying still to put the dread on me, Geiamnyn. Never since the first morning in the water meadow when I called in the cows has there been any returning from this for me. Never since I broke my oath to my Lord of Roven has there been a returning for me. Many things cannot be returned from, Geiamnyn: sometimes, ah, Geiamnyn, I resent very much that I cannot return from having my children and all the worries my children bring me. So, no, indeed I am quite resigned to there being no returning for me from this place. She stepped bodily up to two guards before her war tent, poor, weak things they were close up, their armor ill-fitting, their bodies weak and ill-fed. They had the faces of her goodsister and her goodbrother in Aranth – Geiamnyn had even rubbed unfired clay under the man's fingernails.

"Do you think this will deter me?" Kanda said with a snort. "What do you think I am, Geiamnyn? Do you think even now this will hurt me more than a scratch? What pointless cruelty, Geiamnyn," she said, "even from you I might have expected something slightly better."

She killed one of the guards with a single sword stroke to the heart before the woman had moved her sword. Calian killed the other with a single stroke.

Morna's laughter came from within the tent. Happy, rejoicing. Kanda and Calian went in. Dellet followed them in.

CHAPTER FORTY-ONE

The tent was newly furnished, as a man should refurnish the marriage chamber for his new bride. Rugs and furs were spread on the floor, they were soaked, they were sinking into the mire beneath them. The bed was hung with red tapestries and spread with cloth of gold and with a great black bearskin. Kanda could not stop herself staring in sick horror at her daughter's marriage bed. Dellet let out a moan. A table and chair stood beside the bed; the table was made of ivory, the chair was of sweetwood and red silk. On the table was a lamp in the form of a seven-headed beast, each head a wick burning; a crystal jug of wine and a winecup half-empty; a dish of apples; a silver gaming board set for the Goose Game with pieces made of gold and diamond. A woman sat in the chair; she was dressed in fine silks of every color, laden down with gems, neck rings and arm rings and finger rings of copper and silver and bronze and gold. A thick veil of silver net covered her face. She did not stir to notice the intruders. She moved a diamond piece to play the Goose Game, moved a gold piece, moved a diamond piece, moved a gold piece. Morna ran up to her, grabbed her hand – Morna was dressed also in fine silks now, hung about with jewels, a little queen. The woman threw up her hands in horror, drew back the veil from her face. She was an old woman, older than Kanda, her skin and her hair and her eyes faded to gray. Deep scars on her lips.

Morna crowed, "Sal Sal Sal Sal Sal Sal Sal! Hurrah!"

So far, so far from *shining*.

"Oh but what are you doing here?" Sal saw her mother then and her sister, her father behind almost hidden by his grief. "No!" Sal shouted, "no, Mother, Calian, no, go away, you – I did this for Morna to get her away," Sal cried out in despair. "So get her away."

The whole tent seemed to waver. They were merely standing on the slopes of Mal Anwen.

"No, Sal," Calian said. Only that. They were in the tent and the three sisters hugged each other as if they would never be parted again.

"But I gave you, I made them give back the farm," Sal said after a long while of silence. "I thought, I wanted— I saw you there, three times I looked and I saw you there, happy, Dad was working in the fields with Calian, Morna was playing, Mum was sewing Morna a dress. I watched you and it was the best thing...."

Sal said, "Help me. Rescue me. Mum."

Calian said fiercely, "Why else are we here, Sal, you stupid? Come on, then."

But: "I'm hungry," Morna said. "Can I have one of these apples?"

"No. Yes. No." Sal looked at her mother. Her mother looked at her daughter. Sal said, "Yes, go on then."

They all watched, silent, as Morna ate an apple and the juice ran down her chin.

"I'm still hungry," Morna said.

Sal clapped her hands. A servant girl appeared at her elbow – there had been no one there a moment before. The servant like her mistress was richly dressed and veiled, but a rope hung about her neck in place of jewels and in place of arm rings she wore heavy shackles. The shape of her head beneath her veil was odd and wrong. The servant girl said in a strange harsh voice that echoed and seemed many voices, "What do you wish for, my lady?"

"A drink of marsh water for my sister here," Sal said, "a crust of stale bread for my sister."

"Would you not rather a cup of milk from a white cow the mother of twin calves, a white cow that has never known a bull but has borne twin calves to the west wind?" the servant asked. "A loaf of bread made with flour that grew on the battlefield where two brothers fought for the sun's hand in marriage, that was harvested with a woman's hair, that was milled by a dragon and a giant and a wolf? These things I can bring you, my lady, if you ask." There was a note of great despair in the servant girl's voice. "A bird in a cage, or a white hind with a collar of human finger bones, or the corpse of a dog that sings as sweet as the starlight shines on a rose, can I bring you?" the servant girl said in her strange thick voice. "The lady your sister would surely like these things more than a cup of marsh water and a crust of stale bread."

Sal said, "What my sister would like most of all is for me to pour her a cup of water from the River Wenet and give her a slice of my mother's badly baked bread. But that will never be."

The servant girl screamed in rage. A cup of water and a plate of crusts appeared on the table. Morna snatched them up as if she had not eaten for days. She ate so fast they were gone in an instant. "More?" she said, but Sal shook her head.

Sal took Morna's hand in hers. "We are going home now, Morna, maybe."

Morna said, puzzled, "But you live here now, Sal. It's so nice here. But I do miss you so much." She said more brightly, "Maybe we can all stay here? All five of us? Can you ask?"

A war trumpet sounded. A war drum beat.

Geiamnyn rose up tall and splendid.

"Uncle Geiamnyn, hurrah hurrah!" Morna shouted. "You can ask him if we can stay!"

CHAPTER FORTY-TWO

All the swords in all the world, a dragon, an army, could do nothing against Geiamnyn, for his arm was around his wife's shoulders and Morna's arms were about his waist. Here was Ysarene, her flayed face very happy; here was that third one, that one who was *nothing* and only *empty*, he prowled in the shadows of the chamber flickering between Kanda and Calian. Armies, shapeless in darkness, roaring seething hate. Gella was there, the three men Marei and Karh and Rit, the boy Ty with the dry wound Morna had given him on his face.

"She broke the thread I sewed her cursed mouth up with," Geiamnyn said, as if that was what Kanda must be staring at in grief. "Gold, that thread was. So I tried again, good leather strips I used from a black bull. But she cut them through with her knife, this bitch. Now she won't let me closer than I am now, and never alone together, and she wears the knife and the leather strips around her neck. And I daren't come near her, because of that." He said with a snarl, "You can have her back, Ikandera Thygethyn, if you want her, this useless bitch. Worse than my last wife, this one."

Gella whimpered. She fawned on Geiamnyn, stroked his hands and his face.

"We have come to kill you," Calian said. "I have come to kill you, monster, *Burning*."

"Kill me?" Geiamnyn was laughing. "Kill me?"

"Not just you," said Calian. "All of you. You, *emptiness*, *nothing*, whom once before I spared, you, *Hunger*, you *Hateful* and *Ruined* and *Grief*, all of you, my mother and I will kill.

"You do not deserve sparing. You do not deserve death, even. If there were a worse thing I could do than kill you, I swear, that I would do to you." Calian said, "Unlike my mother, you *Burning*, you *Hunger*, you who are only *emptiness*, unlike her, I keep the oaths I have sworn. So be ready now, you monsters."

Ysarene too laughed long and loud and frightened. "Two of you. Against us here. And you know your mother loved us three as her family long before she loved you. Her brother and her sister and her beloved husband, we were."

That third one, *nothing*, emptiness where his name was, only hissed at Calian.

"He cannot speak," said Ysarene. "Your daughter has done that to him, Ikandera Thygethyn. That voice you loved, often you told me it was his voice that first drew you to love him, so sweet and so gentle and so yearning with love for you it was, such honeyed words, you said, he spoke to you in that sweet voice of his love! Your daughter let him live out on the mountainside when she spared that pitiful farmer's boy, fool that she was then, and more than a fool – but from that moment on, he has been unable to speak." Ysarene said, "Does that not grieve you, Ikandera Thygethyn? Do you not hate your daughter even a little for that?"

Kanda growled and bared her teeth at Ysarene. "I rejoice at what my daughter did."

But deep in her heart she did grieve, and she did feel in her heart some anger toward Calian.

All these things in the tent, she now recognized. She had once sat at that table playing the Goose Game with that board against her husband: four times out of five she had beaten him. That dress she had worn, those jewels – from the cities of half the world, she had ripped and looted them. From this mire the tent stood upon, her husband's body had once dragged itself back into something like life.

Her former husband hissed again, and there was grief in him also, remembering those times they had had together.

Geiamnyn tried to look as if he was bored and weary of this business. "Well, wife," he said to Sal, "I've let your mother and your father come to visit you again, and much joy I hope you've taken in it. Your mother has cattle dung beneath her nails still. You are reassured? Your father is so afraid of me he does not dare speak. You are reassured? You sister is as ungovernable and stupid as before. I doubt that reassures you. A great show we have made for them, displayed all your new finery, she does look well, doesn't she, Ikandera Thygethyn?" He said pathetically, almost pleading, "You said, Sal, my wife, you said you'd be kinder to me if I let you see your parents again."

Sal lowered her veil back over her face. Her hand went to her breast, where the child's flint knife she had found in the mine passage hung on a leather cord. Sal said gently, "Thank you, yes, such a kind thing you have done for me, my husband. Such a kind good loving man you are to me."

Geiamnyn beamed then. As if he truly believed it. All that he wrought upon Sal, yet he still needed to believe that she would praise him.

Sal pulled at the leather cord around her throat. The leather snapped. The knife came free.

"You did not kill the man whose armor you wear," Sal said. "My mother killed him, she had to help you strip the armor off, even! You did not kill the Lord of Roven, you only sat on his throne after he was dead. You did not manage to sew up my lips. I grant you, husband, you did manage to kill Lady Kestre, who was known more for her song than her swordship." She said with a snort of revulsion, "Let my family visit me? You cowered and wept with fear as you heard the roar of them coming. Begged me to send them away." She said with a laugh of revulsion, "Kind? A good husband? I would rather have married one of my mother's sheep than you, Geiamnyn."

Sal drove her knife at Geiamnyn.

Calian gave a cry of joy, and she sprang at Geiamnyn. Calian's sword was an eagle in truth, flying free and wild. Calian was black light that burned away all darkness. Calian was the dawn when the dark flees and the day breaks.

Kanda leapt, her sword leapt and rejoiced and danced and gnashed its teeth, and she sprang at Geiamnyn.

"Uncle Geiamnyn!" Morna cried. "Don't hurt him! You can't hurt him!" And she threw herself in front of Geiamnyn.

Like a shield she was, standing strong with raised arms before Geiamnyn. Indeed, with her real eyes Ikandera Thygethyn saw there only a shield of fine bronze, worked with the image of a child in gold and white paint.

A flaw in the shield, from where once before Kanda's sword had struck it in Geiamnyn's hall at the marriage feast.

"Morna!" Calian cried, Sal cried, Kanda cried, all three together in one voice.

But it was too late, for Calian and Sal and Kanda were great warriors, as swift in battle as Henef Queen of Mares when she ran across the green field, as strong in battle as the sword Iath, *Kind Strength*. Each blade struck Morna on the forehead, on the scar where Kanda had struck her at the wedding feast.

Morna fell beneath their blows.

A shield of bronze only, sundered from edge to edge.

CHAPTER FORTY-THREE

Dellet did not speak and did not cry. Crouched down by his dead child, put one hand with great gentleness on her painted face. What have you done? Nothing. I didn't mean— None of us— Like a broken cup, a broken toy. An accident.

Again again again, unceasing, the world ends. I am Ikandera Thygethyn. Great Warrior. All I am is slaughter, bloodshed, killing. I thought I could forget? *Promise me, Kanda, that you'll never go to Mal Anwen.* I set a guard on my sword to protect myself and my children. *Kill me, if I ever try to take back my sword. Swear it.* To protect them!

Ikandera Thygethyn let out the grief cry. The earth shook and fell broken. Calian let out the grief cry and the sky was cracked.

A hiss from that third one her husband. That third one, *emptiness*, something in the way he moved toward her – Kanda thought: he feels pity, he feels grief. She stood with her bloody sword lowered; Calian and Sal stood trembling, staring. That third one took one step, two steps, three steps toward Kanda. Or perhaps toward the broken shield that had been Morna. Or perhaps toward Calian. His eagle sword was in his hand, but he held it lowered as the women did. His maimed left hand of broken bones and rotten leather, missing the finger that his wife carried in her belt – he held out his left hand, the peace hand, toward Kanda, toward Calian, toward the dead child there. His left hand, see—

Once, deeply, truly, Ikandera Thygethyn had loved him. And her family was dust and ashes, all she had made here when she was Kanda, all was ashes. And his dead eyes called to her in his dead face and she saw that that time when she had loved him she could go back to, that time could last forever, he and she together loving, if she wanted it. Nothing else for her, nowhere else she could now go.

I killed my own child.

I—

His left hand, his peace hand, he held it out toward her. She raised her left hand, her peace hand, to take it.

But Dellet was crouched unmoving over the broken shield that had been Morna, and now Dellet rose to his feet. He threw himself at that one who was only *emptiness*. *Emptiness* had his armor and his sword Calien. Dellet had his old pocketknife that Calian had returned to him, and his stick.

That third one hissed as Dellet's stick struck his left hand, his peace hand. His left hand crumbled, bones fell from it, rotten flesh and grave worms fell from it. So rotted it was, the slightest touch would destroy it.

Still that third one reached with the rubble of his left hand toward Kanda. Yearning.

Then the third one's right hand, his sword hand, came up.

One stroke, no more, that empty one needed. Dellet was down with his life's blood flowing out of him. He had looked like a man already dying as he ran at the one who was *empty*. He fell now dead.

Kanda let out one long wail of grief.

Again again again without pity the world is ended.

But the red rage was in that place then. Calian's sword flew up killing. Sal's knife flew up. Geiamnyn roared as Sal spun at him, cut him with her flint knife from the mine. Ysarene shrieked with joy to fight.

Kanda hesitated, howling in her mind. Calian shouted, "Mother!" and all the life came back into Kanda with that shout. She flew at that one who was only *empty*, her husband's murderer, she hacked at him. His hood fell back showing his corpse-face. He hissed and spat black bile and black marsh water and old rotted blood. Met her stroke for stroke, warded her, she fought with hate, he fought with hate.

Calian shouted over and over, "Destroyers! Murderers! I will kill you!" She was bright as a thousand suns. Rit and Karh and Marei, *Hateful* and *Ruined* and *Grief*, shouted together, "Let us kill these women." Gella and Ty were shrieking together, "They killed Morna. Kill them. Revenge." Every man in Geiamnyn's army came running, in Ysarene's army, in the army that was sworn to that third one *empty* and *nothing*, that had once been sworn to Ikandera Thygethyn as her war host. A thousand men there, and ten times a thousand. The dark came rushing up to fight them, unseen things that crawled and crept and slithered, in a mass as one great shadow the dark rose towering, it broke and sought to drown the three women. But the three women did not hesitate, no fear was in them now only the joy of killing that which must be killed. They had no fear, they had no mind of it. Scarcely did they see or hear as they killed.

Their backs were set against the sheer rock face that rose to the broken peak of Mal Anwen. Kanda in the middle, Sal at her left hand, Calian at her right. Their swords moved as one sword. In less time than it takes for a child to run five paces to its mother's arms, the bodies lay above them twenty deep. The red rage was in that place boiling as vast as an ocean, the red rage was as vast as the sky. All was murder there, all was slaughter that the heart rejoices at seeing. The cries of the women were as eagles, as wolves, as the north wind on the hilltop. The faces of the women were as butchery, as music, as the earth rent.

Calian fought Ysarene. Ysarene circled the girl as a column of shining silver, no sword could wound her, no blow touch her, she who had once been so gravely wounded by men. She spun, she was too terrible to look at, she cried out and the darkness itself joined in battle with Calian. Men and beasts and shapeless skinless faceless things with nothing about them that was not death. Calian whirled and struck them faster than they could reach her, glorying in her young strength. She was like an eagle as she darted brilliant. Her sword was a whirlwind. Ten, twenty, thirty men of Ysarene's army went down at Calian's sword strokes. A mountain of corpses was at her feet. She leapt, stamped over them. The man Rit was there before her, *Hateful*, his eyes full of lust. Mounted upon her corpses Calian was vast above him, she towered over him, she was an eagle as she came down at him. Her sword went through his chest, opened him up from his neck to his navel, and through into the heart of his brother Marei, *Grief*, behind him. Their brother Karh, *Ruined*, let out a wail, turned to run from Calian. Calian leapt, ran, her sword sank to the hilt into Karh's back between his shoulders, just where the flat of his bones move when a man opens his arms wide to grapple or to embrace. As water flows over smooth rocks, so are the bones and the muscles of a man's shoulders there, a fine thing it is in summer to watch a man in the fields with the bones and the muscles of his great strong shoulders working. Calian's sword sank deep, cut through flesh and bone there: the point of her bright sword, bronze and shining, came out through the meat of Karh's chest just above where his heart was. His arms beat, astonished. He was ruined indeed, he hung upon Calian's sword dead. The weight of him almost tore Calian's sword from her hand, she gave another shout that was both triumph and horror, set her foot to Karh's back to pull out her sword.

Sal fought Geiamnyn. Fought Gella and Ty also. The boy ran at her legs, almost yapping. Gella limped and hit. She who had been briefly radiant, singing at her freedom. She limped and flapped at the woman who had replaced her in defense of her faithless hateful husband. As if it would please Geiamnyn, make him love her, if she defended him. Sal ignored them both. Stabbed at Geiamnyn with the little child-sized flint knife from the mine. Geiamnyn had his sword, his stolen armor, he was so big and strong, Sal was an old woman and a child both. Sal was pressed against the rock face, the hilt of her knife close against her chest. Yet she struck him, wounded him.

The little knife warded every stroke he tried to deal her; warm fire flashed from it bright. Sal cut Geiamnyn's face through the guard of his helmet. His lips were bloody. He cursed, slashed at her, and she met him, her knife cut his hand. He hissed in pain, stepped back. He roared, threw himself on her, Sal slipped and danced to the side, Geiamnyn's sword crashed against the rock face leaving him half-stunned at the impact. Sal threw out her knife and cut his lips a second time. Geiamnyn roared louder. Gella shouted curses, pleaded *don't hurt him don't hurt him.* Ty ran at Sal's legs to trip her. Sal kicked the boy away. Geiamnyn loomed up at her, thrust his sword to take her head from her shoulders in a headman's blow. Sal met him with her bare left hand, warded off the blow. Sal closed her left hand around Geiamnyn's sword blade, held it. Sal drove her little flint knife between the cheekpieces of Geiamnyn's helmet, ground it into Geiamnyn's face.

Kanda fought the third one. Their swords clashed together and rebounded. Many times had Kanda fought him she had married, in war as sworn enemies and in the practice field after they were wed. Where the two blades met, it seemed one sword blade, the metal seemed to flow and join together, it took all their strength to part the two blades and then it seemed as if the two blades fled apart and would not strike. They had loved each other once, those swords, as much or more than their owners had loved. With her sword Kanda could kill her husband *empty* and *nothing,* with his sword that empty one could kill her whom he still loved – both knew it, both feared to strike the other even as each sought to strike and kill and make an end. They circled fearfully, probed each other's defenses, their blades met and rebounded, met and rebounded. They seemed to aim, both of them, to spar together blade to blade, not to wound and kill. Back and forth, round and round, a dance neither wished to end. Nothing on the battlefield dared join them: unlike Sal and Calian, the darkness there left Kanda well alone. Men and beasts and faceless creeping shadows, and none would aid that third one for fear of disturbing that dance between two who once had loved. The third one drove Kanda back until she was pressed hard against the crag, the rock face cutting her. Kanda drove the third one back until he stumbled in the mire, seemed to shrink small. He raised his blade to deal the death blow to her heart, but she parried it, slid away, struck. She raised her sword to strike off his head, but he parried it, struck back. Their eyes were fixed on each other's faces. Each knew the other too well. Kanda reeled back wounded. Her left shoulder, her left arm, and a wound now on her thigh, and now to her chest. She gasped, roared, she must not let him win, she had killed Morna but he, monster, destroyer, he had killed Dellet. Her sword bit into that third one's left shoulder, just where he had wounded her, into his left arm, into his chest. The blood that came out of him now was thick as mud. She hacked at him. A hole where the third one's face was, but he hissed through shattered fragments of jaws and teeth. Shreds of meat where his body was, but his arms moved, his legs moved, he scrabbled in the earth and his hands reached. Frail, broken, pulling together. Filth and meat rising. His sword blade, undamaged, dragged itself at Kanda. Kanda's whole body was red with that third one's blood on her, from the top of her head to her feet she was bloodied and panting. Her sword that he had once given her as a love gift, that sword could kill him. His life was bound to wretched coward Saem Ben Apple Tree's son whom Calian had spared; until Saem died nothing could kill him. All eternity, she would fight him and kill him. Ikandera Thygethyn, *Great Warrior*, greatest, most powerful, destroyer of all that lived. The sun would grow cold, the sea swallow the land, the sky would be extinguished, and she would fight him and kill him. She was Ikandera Thygethyn. She would kill him kill him kill him kill him kill him kill him kill him. No woman was she, only death was she, only killing, only hatred of that which must be hated and destroyed before it killed with hate.

A voice screamed. Like a dream. On the battlefield, I am used to voices screaming. Kill this thing before me, kill it, crush it rubble and maggots and walls fallen, wasteland where life never was and never would be. And still she struck and struck. All eternity I will fight here, wound it, break it, kill. I am Ikandera Thygethyn. I killed my own daughter. I broke every oath I swore, every promise. All I deserve is to fight here, to kill. All I am is to kill.

Sal was against the cliff face, and now she tired and she was losing. Geiamnyn threw himself into her huge just as Ty wrapped himself around her legs to hold her prisoner and Gella thrashed out at Sal, kicked, punched, spat at Sal. Sal staggered, trapped in the coils of Gella's body. Gella ripped the little flint knife from Sal's grasp. Sal punched, tore at Gella's maimed face. Gella screamed, dropped the knife. Sal struggled to rise. The little knife lay just beyond her reach. Sal screamed.

Distant. Voices scream on a battlefield. Let them scream. Kill kill kill kill kill kill kill.

Her daughter. Her child. Screaming.

If I try to help her, Ikandera Thygethyn thought, I will only—

I don't trust myself to help my own children. I am death and killing. If I try to help them, I will kill them too.

Calian saw but could do nothing, Ysarene a column of silver fire around her, shadows and beasts and faceless men beating her down with swords and teeth. Ysarene gathered her every part of herself, drove her sword hard at Calian. Struck hard and deep. Calian screamed.

Her daughters. Her children. Screaming. With this sword, I can kill the monsters. Yet I am wasting myself killing this worthless thing. My former husband. What does he matter one breath, one hair of my head, one turd on the dung heap? My daughters need me to help them. Kanda leapt. Left that third one lying there, only emptiness where his name was and never had anyone been better named than he, for he was nothing. Kanda cried out to her daughters, "Be strong!" They saw her in their despair. They were heartened.

Silver light all around Calian. A column of silver fire spinning.

Calian parried Ysarene's blow. Calian struck back.

Murder was in Calian's sword, in the movements of Calian's body, in her breathing.

No skin on Ysarene's face. No lips, no eyelids.

No skin on Ysarene's throat where Calian's sword bit deep.

A column of silver light shot into the sky. Ysarene's body beat upon the earth, her hands thrashed and clawed. Tried to hold herself down to the earth, keep herself fighting; frantic, senseless, desperate, clutching at the world like drowning. Calian's sword came down again. Ysarene's body jerked. Vanished. A bird flew up on ragged wings. It cast no shadow, no sound came from it. It flew upward into the east rushing to meet the sun. It was gone as if the sun had swallowed it.

Sal reached for her knife, struggled for it. Her hand touched it. Ty bit her hand, knocked the knife out of Sal's reach. Gella kicked Sal in the belly. Geiamnyn raised his sword.

The knife the mine children had given Sal moved. Rolled toward Sal's flailing hand. Sal's fingers closed around it. Its point was very sharp. Sal threw her hands up as Geiamnyn's sword came down and the knife sank into his right arm. Cut very deep. Geiamnyn dropped his sword, his hand hanging useless. Sal staggered to her feet, drove the knife into his chest. It went through the fine armor he had stolen from Lord Morren. Sank into his heart.

He fell like Ysarene. A column of red fire shot up from him. Kanda strode over, stood over him. Handed to Sal her sword that could kill the monsters.

Geiamnyn's mouth opened. He gaped like a fish. Tried to speak.

No point in speaking. Not worth saying one word to, that one. Not worth wasting one moment listening to him.

Sal cut off Geiamnyn's head.

No scream, no fire, no great blaze of hate or pain or rage or joy or light.

Sal just killed him.

CHAPTER FORTY-FOUR

Silence.

Sal and Calian and Kanda stood on the flank of Mal Anwen, in the place Kanda and Calian had fought Saem and the third one and the hodden. Sal's bridal flowers were strewn at Calian's feet.

All those great armies Geiamnyn and Ysarene and Ikandera Thygethyn had gathered to them, armed men and men who fought with their bare hands and their teeth bloodied, beasts, monsters, mere shadows, formless shapeless mindless things of pain and dark and hate, they raged at Sal and Calian in gray silence, they gibbered like dead leaves and like dust on a cold wind, they were gone. Marei, Karh and Rit: dead and gone. Only the body of that third one lay on the ground, very small and crumpled it looked, a sad long-dead shriveled thing. A dried-up dead toad, found with a cry of disgust by a woman cutting peat in the marsh for burning, "Peat's bad here, no heat no fuel here," she says, "peat cut here's no good for nothing."

Like a toad, he tried to hop away. He mouthed and dragged at the blood-soaked earth. He was so small and broken that Kanda could pick him up in her cupped hands. A toad in truth. She took the pocket from her belt, dropped him into it. He and his finger bone reunited.

"I had forgotten your face, I had forgotten that you ever existed, until you came here," Kanda said.

She sang in her mind: lying, lying.

She walked down the mountain following the stream until she could see Elelan Mere spread before her. Dark silver water, purple irises, purple heather, yellow gorse. The lake was like a round eye with the clouds running. The wind made tiny waves on the lake's surface. A flicker of movement in the water: a trout catching a fly, she saw its tail with the rainbows on it. A flash of movement on the far bank: a deer, panicked at the sound of her approach, that fled in a bolt of white.

Kanda searched the stream banks until she found a round gray pebble. She rubbed her bloody hands over the pebble until it was no longer gray but red. She put the pebble in the purse beside the finger bone and the toad thing. She plucked a hair from her head. Gray as the pebble. She bound the purse shut with the hair.

Inside the purse, the third one squirmed horribly. In her mind, she heard him begging.

She dropped the purse into the stream. It sank without a sound or a ripple. The stream carried it quickly away. Singing laughing leaping down the mountain into the lake.

"Elelan Mere, you took my daughter's sword and you returned it. Guard this now, this evil thing. Keep it hidden there, this evil thing." The blood must go to the stone and the stone must go to the stream and the stream must go to the lake. "If I have any power left in me for good or ill – even this dead thing this evil thing can have peace. He was drowned a thousand years in the mire. May your bright waters now take him. A thousand years, Elelan Mere, you will hide him. Elelan Mere, children suffered beside your waters. Elelan Mere, children were given comfort by your waters. Elelan Mere, guard this dead thing this evil thing and keep him safe and keep him hidden. Thus do I, Ikandera Thygethyn, thus do I bind you."

In a tree above her a squirrel quarreled *ratatatusk*. A dragonfly darted three times around her head. Briefly, she thought she saw a light on the water, she thought she heard children's voices whispering.

But now it was done, it must be faced. Sal and Calian knelt injured beside their father's body, looking at him unable to speak. He was tall and strong and broad in the shoulders; broad in the waist too, from good peaceful living. His face had no peace in it.

One wound, that third one had dealt him.

One wound! Kanda's body was covered in wounds.

She heard Sal say, "We should bury him."

She heard Calian say, "Where's Mother gone?"

She could not approach them. She did not dare. She turned away. Her children were a wall between her and any chance of hope. When she looked at her children she saw the Lord of Roven dead, the Hall Roven burning.

They knew she was there without her needing to speak or them needing to see her. They turned, two faces one old and weary one so young, both soaked with blood. They hesitated. They came to her running. Slowly, and then fast and eager and desperate. Like two milch calves, they came running.

Hug them tight, hold them tight bury your face in their hair, kiss them so they can't see your face and your tears. Squeeze them tight so they can't feel you shake. Breathe them in.

After a little, Sal said, "He – Dad – he can't have thought he could kill him?"

"No. But he wanted to kill him."

Calian, furious, trying to blame: "He should have stayed out of the fighting. Stupid!"

Kanda could say only, "Yes, he should have done that."

"Stupid! Stupid!"

"And Morna?" Sal said.

There was nothing where the child had fallen. When they looked close, there was only a single drop of red blood.

"She was here. Just here. I remember. I saw her – it's hardly like I could make a mistake about where she— It was an accident. She leapt—"

Silence.

Just here, had she seen…a dead dried-up thing like a toad, clawing and mouthing at bloodied earth, trying to grasp hold of something…?

Your daughter, Ikandera Thygethyn.

Silence. Don't speak.

Calian said, "Why did he do it?"

"Because…because he was angry, Calian."

Calian said, "No, obviously. I mean, why did Dad—?"

"Calian: because he was angry at me."

Silence.

"It was – an accident—" Sal said again.

Calian said, "She—"

Calian screamed, "Stupid! Stupid Morna!"

Silence.

Silence.

Silence.

The two girls beginning to draw away from Kanda. From each other. What we did, the three of us, what we have lost, we cannot go on from that. All things end, our family is scattered and gone.

But no. From grief, desperate despairing righteous furious deluded hope. I have Sal back, I have Calian, I have my own life. I will not let this be how we end.

Kanda stepped back from her children, stood over Dellet's body. A belly wound, that third one her husband had dealt him, deep to the core of him, but belly wounds could be slow to kill. Kanda said slowly and weakly, "I am *Great Warrior.* I am the greatest of the Six Swords of Roven." She said, more fiercely, "I am *Great Warrior.* My enemies are defeated."

She knelt, put her hands on Dellet's shoulders. "Dellet. Husband. There are many things I want to do with my life, still, Dellet, great fierce wonderful things. I am no longer Kanda the farmer, no, you are right, Dellet, those years, that life, that world, all of that is done. I am Ikandera Thygethyn again, a warrior. I am not the woman you married.

"But, for this new life I will lead now, Dellet, Dellet-my-husband, I would like very much for you to be here beside me."

She heard beasts, birds, the wind in the corn before the harvest. She felt spring rain on her hands and on her husband's shoulders, his wound drank in the good rain, rustled like the corn in a summer wind.

He fought it: he was cold and still and heavy. He did not want to live.

She shouted to Dellet, just as she had shouted to him to hurry up and do something in the house, "Dellet! Husband! Get up. Stop lying there dead and cold. Your family needs you. I'm sorry I shouted at you: hate me, ignore me, leave me, if you want to. But look, Dellet, your children need you. Get up, put your arms round Calian, put your arms round Sal, be a comfort to them. Morna is dead. They need you."

Nothing.

She shook his cold dead body. She shouted, "Your daughters and I have just fought an army. Your daughters need you more now than they have ever needed you in their lives, Dellet." She shouted, "I am exhausted beyond exhausted! And you, Dellet, lie there like you're sleeping!"

It was that last shouting, not her magic, she would swear, that made Dellet jump up. The wound in his belly was raw, half-healed, his face was gray with no blood in it. So much grief in him it ran down his skin. He was blurred like a man seen in winter mist on the hillside, a shadow in the trees and the clouds as the light moves and the birds circle, a trick of the eye, a fear of a stranger coming that is only blown cloud and blown leaves. He held up his hands as if he was still fighting that third one, he spun around in panic. He cried out, "Kanda! Children!"

He fell down again, sat down staring at his hands. His eyes narrowed in anger. "Morna— You— Him—"

He sighed deeply. He looked at his own hands with his blood on them, at the wound on him.

He said, wondering, "I was—"

He said, "Cal-bird. Sal-flower. Daughters. I'm bloody furious with the pair of you. Don't you either of you ever do anything like that again. You could have been killed, the both of you."

He said to Kanda, "You're exhausted? Try being bloody murdered, woman. That's exhausting."

Never any good at fancy words, was Dellet. But it was not for his honeyed words that Kanda had married him.

They would have hugged and embraced and laughed together, awkward as they were with Sal an old woman older than her parents, Dellet back from being dead, Morna murdered. So they tried to hug and embrace and laugh, for all that they were frightened of each other, strained, awkward, but it was a strange hard thing.

Sal, what she was now: that was the worst thing.

The memory of three blades together striking Morna down: that was the worst thing.

So they tried to hug and be glad they were all four alive.

That was the hardest thing.

Sounds. Crack and whimper, grind of stones, creep of feet. Calian spun around. "Who's there?" A relief to them all, if there was more fighting, more killing, no thinking.

"Who's there?" Calian, sword drawn, poised ready for killing killing killing killing.

A woman shrieked in fear. A boy shouted, "Murderers."

Gella. Ty. The woman was creeping down the mountainside toward the lake Elelan Mere. Her son crawling behind her. Still she was whispering on and on *I'm sorry I'm sorry I'm sorry, husband.*

"Gella," Sal said. "Oh, Gella."

The woman looked up, terrified, cowered from Sal. "I didn't mean to hurt you, Lady Sal, I didn't, I—"

"I freed you from him," Calian said. "But you went back to him."

Gella's face was fierce then. "You did free me. But – where did I have to go? You tell me, girl: where could I go but back to him?"

"Anywhere in the world," Calian said. "Anywhere but back to him."

But Gella laughed and Calian fell silent.

"He'll come again," Gella said. "Worse and more angry. Always does."

Sal said, "He's dead, Gella. Dead."

"He might be dead for you, Lady Sal. I don't believe he's dead. I'll never believe he's dead, that one. He might be dead for you here, but he always comes back to hurt me again."

She crept on injured limbs, where Sal had wounded her. Creeping away. *I'm sorry I'm sorry I'm sorry, husband.*

"She's one of them!" Calian shouted. "She doesn't deserve to live. What are you doing?"

Sal said, "Wait, Gella. Please." The woman looked at Sal. She was very young now compared to Sal. A long time the two looked at each other. The grass seemed to grow up thicker and greener and sweet with flowers in the line of the sight between them. Gella stood tall like any woman. She took Ty's hand like any mother holding her son. "It's easy for you to judge," Gella said to Calian. "You with your sword there. Look at you. You think, you, that you can judge me?" She said quietly, "No matter what, he always finds me."

"He's dead, Gella. I promise."

"Promises!"

Sal said, "This promise I do not break."

Gella looked straight at Sal.

Nodded.

Sal said, "There's one place, Gella, where you can go that's safe. One place you can raise Ty safely. You know where I mean?"

"What are you doing?" Calian shouted. "She's one of them!"

"Be well, Gella," Sal said. "Be safe."

Gella walked away down the mountainside, past the lake Elelan Mere, holding her son's hand like any mother walking with her child. After a little time the boy jumped and played, they heard his voice crowing. As they passed the lake the water sparkled, the children were laughing. Ty pointed up, glorious, amazed, because the gyrfalcon was circling high overhead.

They walked away together east towards the valley of the Wenet.

Kanda thought: nothing can last forever. And sometimes that is a good thing.

Calian spat where Gella had been crouching. "Murderer! You should be dead! Crawling to him! I hate you, I'll kill you!" Calian screamed.

Terrible to see Calian's face flushed and screaming after a wretched harried bent broken life. Anger rose up in Kanda. "Don't say that, Calian, stop that," she said, shouting also, almost, almost, her hand was raised.

Dellet said, "Look at your sister, Cal-bird. Think about your sister, hey?"

Calian sat quiet with her sword drawn. After a little while she sheathed her sword. After a long while she went to the place where she had spat at Gella, wiped it up with a leaf.

CHAPTER FORTY-FIVE

"What's this?" Sal bent over something in the grass. "Oh! Your sword, Mum." She picked it up. "I must have dropped it. After I killed.... It's horrible! Oh!" Like a slug in her food, like when she put her foot in dog shit. The beast on the pommel bared its teeth. The third one's blood on it. Geiamnyn's blood. Morna's blood. Sal threw the sword down. It fell at Kanda's feet.

Kanda's right hand burned. A thrill inside her, an eagerness, still, looking at the black blade, thinking of what she had done and could do with it. Powerful and glorious, triumphant beyond all things! She thought: I had another sword once, a better sword. Very like Calian's sword, it was. A good sword – this sword is not good. Let it lie here on the mountain where I killed my own child.

Kanda said lightly, "Look at the state of it. The first thing you do after a battle is check your sword and clean it. You certainly don't leave it lying around." She said, more desperately still to be light and easy, "I thought your father taught you to take care of your tools, but it seems I was wrong."

Dellet grunted, also desperate, "I tell them all the time, but they don't listen to a word of it. They learned that well enough from you."

Dellet looked at Kanda. Kanda looked at Dellet. So tired of grief and pain and greatness. Let us have ordinary strained bickering. You don't do enough with the children, husband, you can be a right pain at times, wife. In a moment I can say something rude about your sister, you can bring up that time six years ago at the Sun Return Feast.

Thank you, with all my heart, Dellet.

Silence.

Kanda said, "He gave it me."

Dellet said, "I'd guessed."

Dellet said, "I gave you a cow byre and a milking stool and a butter churn, woman. And I made those myself with my own hands, which I'd bet is more than…than he did."

Morna's death was there in the sword. Her right hand burned to touch it. Her vision swam red. Who in the world has the strength to carry the sword they killed their own child with? Who could use such a sword for anything? *Kill me, if I ever try to take back my sword. If I beg for it, plead, weep; whatever the reason – do not give me back my sword.* I remember, she thought, the joy I felt, the day I buried this sword. Even birthing my children was not as good a day.

Dellet said, "It suits you, that sword. Looks good hanging at your hip. Now I look at you, you look kind of odd not wearing it."

Calian said, "Stop fussing, Mum. Come on. Then we can get off this stupid mountain."

Not a good sword, no. Shameful. Evil. A constant reminder of what she was. So: she picked it up, put it on.

Dellet said, "That's better. Like…that's how I see you. Always have, which is a bit odd when you think about it. Also, if you hadn't picked it up, I'd have ended up having to lug the wretched thing until you changed your mind. You know I would.

"It really does suit you, Kanda, that sword. Good eye that…your first husband had, choosing it for you. Very slimming on your hips, that black color, too."

Trying too hard, those words. Awkward words; not his way of speaking to anyone. But he was almost smiling. Her sword felt wrong and terrible by her side, and it felt strong and good.

The family walked down from the mountain. West into the setting sun, away from the valley of the River Wenet with their old world and their old lives behind them. Walked in silence. *Morna*, Kanda's heart beat in her ears. *Morna*, her footsteps said. The path narrowed, Dellet had to walk close to her, touched her right hand sort of by accident. Kanda drew her hand away. They smiled bleakly at each other. Then they smiled with an attempt at warmth. If they couldn't go back, go onward into new things.

The high hills lowered into soft green fields. Rolling valleys with gentle rivers and gentle woods. The corn had been gathered, the straw was piled ready to be baled. A farmstead showed with lights already in the window, smoke rising where someone cooked the midday meal. The orchard was ripe with apples. A stream meandered fat and contented into a pond. Washing hung on a line. Two ducks on the pond were quarreling. A blackbird sang in a may tree. "Time to come in, small ones!" a woman's voice called.

The family walked on. Kanda shoulders tensed with stone-weight. Her right hand felt hot.

The day lengthened, grew into the gold of afternoon in late summer, haze over the raw fields, flies like mist. Cattle lowed in the distance. There were rooks in the fields following the plow, black on the brown and the gold and the deep-sky-blue. The hedgerows were thick with spider webs.

Kanda found her mind wandering. She'd washed up, hadn't she, before they left? Or had she? She must have, washed and tidied. She must have, yes. The meal crock was full, there was water drawn enough for a day at least – oh, but – the winter blankets – they were on that high shelf in the cupboard she had to stand on a stool to reach, Dellet always said that was a stupid place to put them; would Gella find them? Honestly, I mean, who puts heavy blankets where you have to stand on tiptoe on a stool to reach? And the cups, the one with the big crack in it that leaked if you filled it to the top and they all ignored the leak because Kanda liked it, you just had to sort of hold it not fully upright, what is this? These sheets are threadbare. This floor can't have been washed for years. But look, the beds are very comfortable, Gella, once you've worked out where I kept things you'll see it makes perfect sense. The meal crock's full, there's butter and cheese and ham in the store – thank Geiamnyn for that, hah! – there's clothes I think should fit Ty with growing room, the brown cow's a right pain about being milked but her milk's almost pure cream so do persevere.

Shook the thoughts away. Nothing could be done whatever state the house was left in. She was sure she'd washed up.

Her left hand brushed Dellet's hand. She kept her left hand touching him.

The sun set in a wound that was quickly healed. Already in the east at their backs the twin stars Irulth were shining, red star and bronze star, a gate. The broken peak of Mal Anwen was between the gate. Soon it was full dark, cool and brilliant. The moon was thin. They walked through a soft sweet wood, the trees were aspens, whispered, made music. The family walked on. They waded across a stream that was silver in the starlight. A fine path of bronze stretched before them, led them on.

"Where are we going?" Calian said at last as the dawn was breaking.

Kanda said, "Where do you think?"

Calian shook her head. "I don't know."

They walked on. The day grew warm, pleasant to walk in. The woods were shrouded in sunlight. Birds sang in the leaves. A rain shower, leaving all perfumed. Raindrops on Sal's eyelashes. The first autumn colors, mussed-brown-red-faded-golden, the last colors of long hot sun. Dried stems of summer flowers crowned with damp black seed heads. They walked without weariness, without hunger. They walked almost without grief. The path lay before them, a thread of bronze stretched leading them onward, fine as Morna's hair. Clouds were banked gray on the horizon. Kanda could smell in the distance the first faint trace of the sea.

"Where are we going?" Sal said at last as the day was ending. "What are we going to do?"

She stands on the threshold. The hall is dark, windowless, a low roof. The walls are made of woven hazel packed with straw and mud. The roof is dried bracken. The floor is beaten earth. A bronze cauldron on a tripod but the metal is cracked beyond use or repair, the cauldron is empty save for dust and cobwebs, the hearth beneath the cauldron is cold and dead. Rain has leaked in, lies in a puddle near the hearth. The hall is empty. Not even bats or owls will come here. Not even crows. But at the far end of the hall there is the sound of something moving. A clink of dry pebbles.

The threshold stone before her is worn down to the sea-sky-stone colorlessness, smooth and pitted, deeply worn with use. Three things, once, she had seen buried beneath it. One of those things she herself had fetched.

She steps over the threshold, fearless. Her heart sings with joy. She speaks the words that must be spoken, the words hang on golden threads in the air. She walks into the dark hall, her feet crunch on the rubble. Ashes. Burned wood. Cracked stone. She touches the cauldron as she passes it. Sets the thin metal trembling.

Something croaks in the dark at the far end of the hall.

She takes a bundle of sticks from her satchel. Oak, aspen, apple, beech. Most of the sticks are broken from children's playing. This one was a dragon. This one was a throwing spear. This one was a trumpet. This one was just a very good stick. She takes straw from her satchel; with the sticks and the straw she builds up a fire in the hearth. Flames spring up very high and bright. She holds her hands to the fire to warm them.

Something croaks in the darkness. Comes closer. It is afraid, if she is not. A thin old man, bent and aching, naked. His hair hangs off him filthy and matted; his skin is cracked, covered with sores; his eyes blink, pained by the light, blinded, rimed and red. In his hands he clutches a few splinters of old wood. His belly is swollen with pregnancy. Milk runs from his breasts. She takes off her cloak, wraps it around him.

She lifts him in her arms. He is light and frail as a newborn baby, his limbs and head hang loose in a way she half remembers from her own children. He is warm and fragile, like holding a dried leaf. The firelight shows a jumble at the back of the hall, a table and chairs, cups, plates, thrown down and broken, dusty, cobwebbed. She carries him easily, with one hand she can hold him while with the other she easily picks up his great throne. She sets his throne to rights. Blows the dust off it. It is chipped, damaged, but the seat is whole and smooth. She places him on his throne.

A horn sounds.

A trumpet rings.

She kneels.

The fire blazes up sweet.

He blinks at her with pained eyes. He says slowly, quietly, "I know you. You were.... You are.... You did...."

She is the greatest of the Six Swords of Roven. The bravest, the strongest, the best. She rides the arrowhead, her five companions following, even her companions cannot but cheer her ride. Her sword is gold, her helmet is gold, her skin is the brown of rich fields new sown, her hair is flame-red. Out of good sown earth and wildfire and red autumn berries, she was created.

On the horizon an army is gathered. Men who are no longer men, armed for killing, hateful – the good earth of a peaceful world spreads before these men but they see only bloodlust. Hate that which is gentle, kind, soft. Burn the fields, tear down the trees, choke the waters – turn life to death, turn death to looted wealth. She has no fear as she rides to meet the army. Her courage and her hope, her certainty that she will prevail over such evil, her courage flows from her to her five companions, they too know that this evil can be defeated. The army breaks before her. Runs. Flees. She meets the enemy captains in battle, one, two, three of them against her alone while her companions still ride to catch her wake. Three against one, but she is undaunted, she throws her enemies down, banishes them. Defeated men are at her feet pleading to surrender; one of her companions, the first to reach her, Lord Morren, shouts, "Kill them." But she, the greatest, the best, she will not kill these wretches. She understands as they grovel and plead that they have been tricked, deceived, that despite all they have done they deserve another chance at life, she spares them though she knows some of them will only fight her again.

The battle is won, she rides back at the head of her companions to the Hall Roven, to feast her victory, to rest a little while. Her body and her mind ache for rest. This is futile, she thinks, sometimes; it is so futile, a soft voice in her mind thinks. Peace? Hope? The dark is endless. But tomorrow she will be summoned to another battle and she will ride out without fear, her sword will shine bright.

She is Ikandera Thygethyn. She howls her war cry to make men's skulls crack. She is gore to the top of her helmet, her eyes are two ragged holes in a mask of blood. Her sword is not metal but fire, she brings down a hundred men with each sword stroke. She does not kill them quickly: slow killing, suppurating, are the wounds she gives to her enemies. Open the belly, let a man be days dying. Open the lungs, let a man suffocate on the battlefield. Stride through the killing ground into the enemy's camp, ah, mockery, camp followers here readying ale and bread and bandages, thinking at the least that when the battle ends there will be survivors to tend. Cleave them, wound them, trample the camp here. Piss will be their ale. Dust will be their bread. Not bandages but a winding sheet. The corpses are piled waist-high, the river that flows here is choked up with corpses, never will the earth blossom, never will the river cease from being poisoned. Any who survive will starve.

She shouts in her great war cry. "You who survive here: you will eat the flesh of your own children, you will live by picking bronze from the charnel house I have left you here, selling the swords that killed you to other killing men. That is all the future I allow you, now and forever until the world ends."

She has found a freedom in killing that she has never felt before and will never feel again.

She is Kanda, wife, mother to three daughters, and one is an old, abused woman; one is an angry savage girl; one is dead. Her husband does not trust her, she lied to him, led him to his death, she stood by while another man she loved killed him. She shouts at her children, two of the three now she's wounded. She's neither patient nor particularly understanding with her children. She brought her husband back to life by shouting at him.

She's heavy and sagging in the thighs and the belly, gray-haired, certainly not in her first youth. She snores, wets herself when she laughs, farts in her sleep, sweats in her sleep so the blanket needs washing. Sometimes she farts and wets herself when she comes. Right now, she urgently needs to change the clout cloth between her legs.

She's very fond of beer. She's terrible at baking. She likes sewing her children's clothes. She once got so drunk at a party she couldn't look after her children the next day. She tells fine bedtime stories. Her greatest delight in life is walking over wet grass to fetch the cows in.

She killed her own child. She carries the sword she killed her child with.

She throws back her head now, roars to the sky, "We are going to rebuild the Hall Roven, my beloveds."

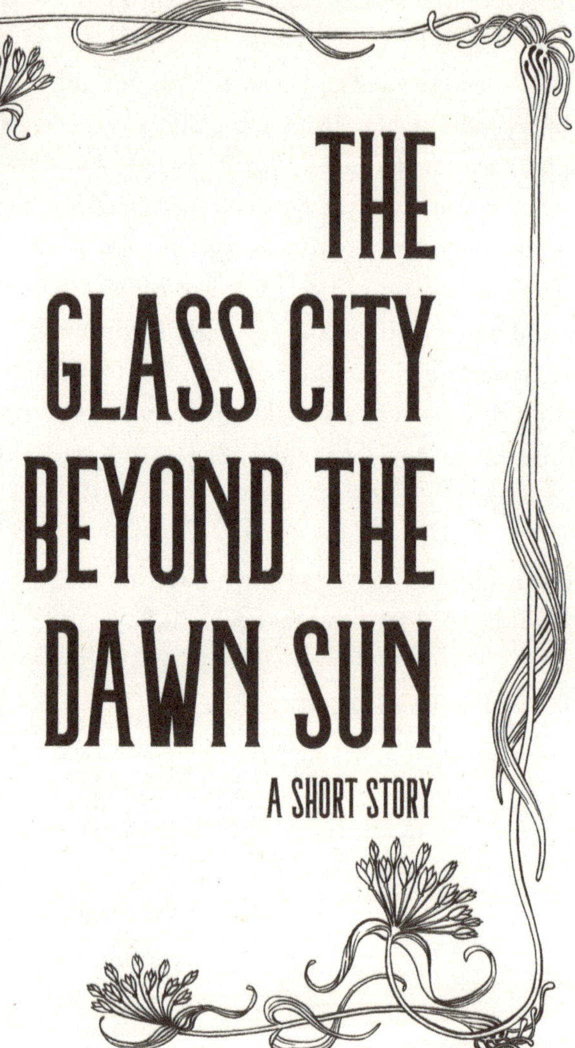

THE GLASS CITY BEYOND THE DAWN SUN

A SHORT STORY

The girl was dancing in a green dress, and Morren was dancing with her. Her hair hung long down her back. She turned, stepped away with green skirts spinning, danced away from him. She turned, stepped toward him and her eyes were gold and silver and the lamps made shadows on her white cheeks. Like leaf shadows when the sun shines through a tree in late-fading almost-faded summer, when the leaves are thick and heavy and the sun is hot and rotting and the sun falls through the trees green and faint.

Ah, Morren danced with her and she was enchanting! So fair she was with her soft hair and her gold eyes and her green dress!

The lamps burned high in the Hall Roven so the shadows were banished high to the far corners of the hall's roof. The hearth blazed bright in the Hall Roven so the winter cold was banished and the dancers' faces were flushed and jeweled with sweat. The meat was roasted and the wine was mixed in the bronze cauldron. The herbs were strewn on the floor and already trampled, the smell of sweet herbs was lost in the hall with the smell of meat and wine and the sweat of bodies, but all these scents too were good and sweet.

In the Hall Roven the lords and ladies feasted the sun returning in the depths of winter, and of all the lords and ladies and fair ones of Roven, Morren was the finest dancer, the finest-looking, the finest poet of love and wine and dancing and of sweated bodies with bright wide eyes and gleaming hair. The lady danced away from him, toward him, tossed back her head so that her hair was as ripe wheat rippling in the fields (such a poet you are, Morren! Yes!), the sweat on her brow from heat and dancing was fairer than any crown.

A young man danced now beside her, red hair and skin like midnight; he too was smiling and dancing at Morren, now Morren was dancing and smiling at both of them. Perhaps, the three of us…? Her hair like ripe wheat laid across his smooth skin…? Her eyes and his eyes and Morren's eyes all laughing, *yes*. We'll dance, we'll feast, we'll tumble together into Morren's great bed. Red hair and yellow hair on his pillow in the morning, red hair and yellow hair shining caught on his clothes and his bed sheets for days. A headache from much wine and little sleeping. A memory to make his heart lift, when…

How it would be, how good it would be, if that was all he needed to be and do.

For this was, as so very often, both a celebratory feast and a farewell feast.

The hearth fire died down to embers. Even in Morren's chamber the lamps were dim. Red hair and yellow hair splayed out on Morren's pillows, beside Morren's own hair that might be made of pure gold. Much wine and, oh, perhaps as much as an hour or two hours of sleep.

A pounding on the door. Loud as Morren's head would soon be pounding. A voice, giggling (she hasn't had much sleep either): "Morren! Sleepyhead! Wake up! Get up! Cela, Gion, you need to get up and kick Morren awake!"

"Go away. Sela, Dion [that must be their names?], you can't kick me out of my own bed."

Jion [?] curled himself beneath the silver covers. Pulled a pillow over his and Kela[?]'s head. "You're riding out, Morren, not us."

"I'm riding out. Oof. Yes." He got up, lay down, got up.

Red hair and yellow hair on his pillow like a storm cloud. Oh, the cruelties of life! The room full of shadow, the sky through his bedchamber windows deepest black.

Too

Early

So

Early.

It's

Still

The

Dead

Of

Night.

Then he thought sadly: well, but it is the second-longest night of the year.

"So get up and get going," Kestre called.

"Yes, yes." Cela was snoring with her mouth open, *put put put* a bit like a puppy smacking its lips. One of them, beautiful Cela or beautiful Gion, farted absolutely vilely, enough to make Cela *put put put* snort louder in her sleep. Beautiful Gion rolled over in a cloud of fart-stench. Beautiful Gion had gnarly hairy feet.

Ah, but beautiful Gion was otherwise very beautiful, yes.

He thought slowly: yes, but, well, Gion and Cela and many others will still be here when I ride back. And Lord Morren of the Six Swords of Roven hurriedly took off last night's shirt and leggings and found a clean set, went out blinking to wash before he rode out on a glorious knightly quest.

The Hall Roven had walls of silver. Its roof was made of gold. The floor upon which Morren had danced trampling down sweet herbs, lavender, rosemary, mint, melissa, that floor was made of diamonds. The windows were of oiled silk dyed red, green, blue, white, purple. Outside the windows white lilies and red roses and golden honeysuckle bloomed. It was midwinter, the morning after the second-longest night of the year, indeed, yes, but still the flowers were in full bloom. Frost lay thick on the flagstones of the Hall's courtyard, quenched the brilliance of the golden roof, but the flowers were untouched. A fountain sang in the courtyard among the flowers. Morren ducked his head into the icy water, shrieked, dunked himself until he was clean. Shrieking whooping jumping about clean.

Roven meant *peace.* As Kestre, sighing, sometimes reminded Morren.

"*Peace* as in: *not war*, Kestre. *Peace* as in: *time to leap and dance and drink and yell and fuck and do all the joyful things.* War is quiet, Kestre. Waiting in the ranks before a battle, staring at the enemy, knowing many of them will die and many of us will die: is that *quiet* enough for you? The whetstone on the blade, the fire that burns a house to ruin, the fire that burns the dead to ash: that's *quiet.* The killing ground when the battle is over: that's the *quiet*est place in all the world, as you and I both well know. Shouting whooping jumping stamping coming with a yell of triumph: that's *peace.*" Then their companion Lord Gallyn of the Six, who does not have Lord Morren's poetry (oh, Morren has a golden tongue – as Cela/Sela/Kela and Gion/Dion/Jion will attest), Lord Gallyn says: "Kestre, you sing. Your name is *Song*. Morren and I, we shout and laugh and jump and whoop. My name is *Great Leap.*" He jumps and kicks his heels together, twists like a salmon in the air. Facing her facing away facing her facing away and his heels click click click. And Kestre shakes her head setting her long yellow hair flying, she laughs, she says, "Yes, true, I suppose. You've convinced me, yes." And Gallyn's clicking heels and the thuds when he lands are a rhythm to set words to, so they all sing together the three of them, a happy song, but Kestre's voice is so beautiful, like birds, that Gallyn stops his leaping, Morren and Gallyn fall silent to listen. And Morren is especially delighted, because he made up the words of the song.

But now, in the courtyard of the Hall Roven in the dark in the snow, Morren whooped and sneezed at the cold water, dressed himself in a fine shirt and leggings, armed himself in bronze and leather, mounted his high horse, rode off into the snow-bound sunrise still sneezing, with Lady Kestre, not now singing but rather laughing at him, riding beside him. A quest, a quest, a fine quest, they were riding out for. Sharp swords and polished, um, helmets, fast-ridden, ahem, horses, to rescue a fair lady from some terrible fate.

Lord Morren of the Six Swords of Roven threw back his head and roared. Caught flakes of falling snow on his tongue. Snowflakes on his long eyelashes. Lady Kestre of the Six Swords of Roven laughed with him.

In the first morning of the world, the Lord of Roven called the Six to him. Out of sunlight and firelight and flowers and birdsong and sweet water, out of soil and leaves and autumn berries, out of salt spray when the wind blows over the ocean, out of mist and rain and frost on the moors and winds blowing, out of all these things and more, he made them. Six warrior knights, great and mighty, lords and ladies of the sword. In days of peace they lived in the Hall Roven feasting, dancing, resting. When word came they rode out to battle, to fight all that was dark and fearful, to help any that were in need.

Of the Six that midwinter feast-day:

One was hunting a fell beast with teeth made of blue fire;

One was battling an enchantress in the wildest of wild woods;

One was riding to defend a city in the desert;

One was riding to stop a kingdom tearing itself to bloody shreds.

Two remained that feast-day idle and impatient in the Hall Roven, staring with longing at the gates hoping a call to arms would come also for them. One was Lady Kestre, her hair was long and golden, her eyes were full of kindness and wisdom, out of birds' feathers and the wind in the trees and green wheat she had been made. Her sword was worked with silver, and the trappings of her horse, and her fine armor; she wore a helmet inlaid with silver, crested with the white feathers of a crane. The other was Lord Morren. Lord *Golden.* His hair was gold, his skin was gold, his armor and his helmet and his sword were trimmed with gold. His face was golden in its beauty, his tongue was the golden tongue of a poet, his nature was golden as a summer afternoon when the world basks in warm sleep.

A sweet singer, a lover of *making-music* and *gathering-flowers* and *walking-in-the-fields* and *baking-bread*. A golden lover of beauty and feasts. It may be, in truth, it may have been that neither Lady Kestre nor Lord Morren had been staring at the gates of Roven eagerly awaiting a summons to ride out to battle. It may be, in truth, it may have been that both Lady Kestre and Lord Morren were very happy to have been left behind to represent the Six at the midwinter feast in the Hall Roven, had watched the days come and go with no summons forthcoming not with impatience but with relief. Morren could sleep for days in his fine chamber. Kestre could sit with her harp by the fountain. Six Swords were raised in the Hall Roven – and of the Six, Kestre and Morren were ever the least eager to fight. Then, alas, on the very day of the feast of the sun-returning, when the longest night was done and their thoughts could turn, distant and hopeful, to longer days of spring – on that very day even as the meat was roasting and the wine being mixed – on that very day, even as Morren was trying on his new shirt and leggings, even as Morren was placing a garland of white roses on his handsome head, even as Morren was dreaming of the dance and the fair faces of the dancers – on that very day, alas! alas! the summons came. A man rode up to the gates of Roven to call the Six to battle, to save a lady from some terrible fate. And as four of the Six were off and questing, ("One of them might ride back today? Gallyn, perhaps?" Morren said hopefully, "He'd be already dressed for questing, could ride straight off again?" "No," Kestre said) why, poor Morren must ready himself to ride out the next morning early when the sky and the sun still thought it not morning early but still the previous night, must kiss farewell to those fair-faced ones whose names he was not quite sure of, must ride out through the great wide high gates of Roven with the snow falling, falling, his head pounding, pounding, hero eyes set bright on the long road ahead.

"Where are we going, then?" Morren asked when they had been riding for perhaps an hour. Riding east into the rising sun. Kestre went to say … something, and Morren said with a laugh, "Stop it, obviously I know where we're going, Kestre."

"East, and then south, and then east, ride hard and fast and long enough, leap your horses, you will come after many days of hard riding, you will come to a city made of glass at the foot of a mountain made of copper in a kingdom that lies behind the dawn sun. In that city, there is a tower. In that tower there is a room. In that room there is locked away a fine fair lady who should and would and could be queen of that city and that kingdom."

The only problems: the city is guarded by monsters, the tower is invisible, the room has no windows or door. The lady has no desire to be queen of that kingdom. Also, um, you may have noticed…the kingdom is hidden behind the dawn sun?

"So we ride, then," Morren said, "we ride east and south and east and south and east, we outride the sun. When we get to the city, we kill the monsters, we find the tower, we break down the tower's walls. We tell the lady she needs to be queen."

"Easy," Kestre said.

The snow came down around them. Like swans' feathers, the snowflakes fell. The sun lit the snowfields to silver fire. "An easy quest for us," Kestre said. She took off her white-plumed helmet, tied it to the horn of her saddle. Her long hair hung like a cloak to her waist. She kicked her horse, it leapt forward racing. Now her hair was flying behind her like a flag. Morren rode behind her to watch her hair streaming. How good it was to watch her horse run! Her horse was dappled brown and gray like a bird's wings. It was not the swiftest of the Six's horses, nor was Kestre the best rider of the Six. The worst rider of the Six, perhaps, Morren thought to himself. But it was a joy to watch a horse race, the muscles of its body, the sun flashing on its silver head trappings, the snow thrown up by its gilded hooves. A joy to watch Kestre's hair streaming in the wind. Then Morren kicked his horse to race also, knowing he could not catch Kestre and she would have to stop to let him reach her, but it was good to feel his horse race. His horse was gray (not golden!), its mane and tail were black. Neither was Morren's horse the swiftest nor Morren the best rider (though his horse had the most ornate saddle and head trappings of all the Six's horses. That pleased Morren greatly. And greatly seemed to please the horse). But it was such a wise horse that his master the Lord of Roven had gifted Morren that he could close his eyes while he was riding, let go the reins, let the sun on his eyelids make the world gold and red. No harm would come to him in this gold and red world behind his closed eyes, he could feel the icy wind on his face, the horse's muscles working, hear the horse's breathing and the wonderful hollow ring of its hooves as they threw up the snow. A crow was calling, the winter geese were calling, the wind shook the trees so that with a slither and a clatter the trees dropped their burdens of snow. There, you see, Kestre? Loud brilliant *peace*.

They rode all day east and south and east and south and east. They rode through the rich fields and woods and meadows around Roven, sleeping beneath the snow. They rode across a bridge over a fast-flowing river where the water sang to greet them; they rode across the ice of a frozen river with their horses' hooves making the ice creak. Through a pine forest, through a beech forest, through an oak forest. Through snow fields where the crops were sleeping, past villages and farmsteads huddled around their hearths. Morren made a song of winter snow, shouted it loud and tuneless. Kestre made a song of winter trees. East and south and east and south and east. The snow stopped, although the earth everywhere was old-snow-crusted-dirty. The sky was pale might-rain might-snow might-clear gray. The wind blew from the west, a warmer softer wind. Fields and forests; signs of homesteads; smoke and noise from a village; a charcoal burners' hut, dirty perfumed; once a cart passed them on the roadway, horse and driver groaning beneath the weight of its load, the horse pricked up its ears, kicked up its hooves, the driver greeted them with a salute. They stopped to eat in an orchard where a brook flowed across the roadway. Old trees, some with rotten hollow trunks.

"Look here!" Morren called to Kestre, delighted. A leaning tree, with a hole at the top big enough to drop an apple through, the apple would roll down the hollow trunk and out at the bottom, where there was a snowy mush of rotten fruit.

Morren had three apples in his saddle bag. Rolled them one two three.

"Can I have one of your apples, Kestre?"

"Can you—? I'm sorry, what? Is that what you said to Cela last night?"

"What?"

Kestre threw him an apple. Moren rolled it down the tree. One two three four apples at the bottom of the tree covered in snow and rotted apple and cobwebs and general muck from inside the tree. He fed one to his horse, one to Kestre's horse, thought about eating one himself but thought better of it. Rolled the remaining two down the hole a couple more times then tossed them away over the brook for the beasts and the birds. A crow hurried down to peck at one. Cawed. "Yes, thank you for thanking me, oh crow."

Morren put his hands on the trunk of the tree. It was alive, faint and sleeping, the cold gnawed at its innards, blight had got in among its roots. The earth was not good here, for all the brook ran nearby. The orchard dreamed of white blossom. Green and red apples, apples like a woman's blushes, apples like a freckled face. Apples that had a star pattern when you cut them open the right way. Apples for cakes and puddings and cider, dried apples to sweeten a winter day. A woman gathering apples to treat her children. A boy eating apples straight from the trees, then washing his hands in the brook so no one knows he's been scrumping. A bride eating apples with honey at her wedding feast. Too many apples for the people to manage, so they feed them to the pigs and the cows and the wild beasts. The trees yearned to blossom, to flourish, to ripen. The earth was poor, the blight gnawed their roots, the blight and the rot got into their fruit. The trees slept fitful, shivering cold, dreaming, dying.

Morren pressed his hands harder against the tree trunk.

Warmth in his hands. Warmth, flowing from Morren into the tree. He could taste apples. Feel apple juice sticky in his lips just like the boy in the tree's dreams. He closed his eyes, breathed in the scent of apple blossom. Then the scent of rotten windfall apples, yeasty, a little like the smell of a newborn baby's head. He could hear the rustle of leaves.

"Grow. Flourish. All your dreams: let them be made not dreams but real. Fruit and flowers beyond counting. Cool leaves to shade a weary traveler. Beauty for a traveler's eyes to delight in."

He pressed his feet deeper into the frozen ground. Warmth, flowing from Morren deep into the soil.

"You are poor and thin, you earth here. The brook runs sweet, but you are dry and thin. Why are you dry and thin? Stop!" he said to the soil. "Stop being dry and poor and thin. Be rich good earth for these trees to grow fat and feed the people here so they are fat also." He scolded the brook: "Make the soil here damp and good, you brook! You run so careless, sing so thoughtless; so heartless you are, brook! Stop being heartless." He scolded the blight: "You are living here in the roots of these trees! Gorging on the roots of these trees! I forbid it. Leave these trees." He whispered, because such words should always be whispered in sorrow and in shame, even to such things as tree blight: "Flee, die, vanish from this good world, you blight."

The trees smiled in their sleep. In their dreams they saw it real: apple cakes and apple puddings, stewed apples with honey, apple cider, wreaths of apple blossom, wreathes of apple leaves. The soil smiled with the trees.

The brook shrugged on carelessly thoughtlessly but chastened.

The blight screamed in fury and was gone.

Morren took his hands from the tree trunk, looked about him, laughed aloud. His feet were sunk ankle-deep in snow slush and rotten apples and cold mud.

"That was a fine thing," Kestre said. She threw him a last apple from her saddle bag that she had been saving for herself, for him to eat.

"It was such a fine thing," he said.

They remounted their horses, rode on. Morren sang and sang of harvest dances, of wassail night games among the trees. The smell of apples drifted with the wind.

In the afternoon when their shadows were long before them trampled beneath their horses' hooves, they came to a great marsh. Sedge running to the horizon, gray to meet a bleaker, grayer winter sky. The day was fading, the wind was rising, the sun was weaker and the snow clouds building. But in the west behind them the sky was gold and blue. They drew their horses to standing. A single trackway ran across the marsh, twisting sometimes east, sometimes south. It was raised about the water, a wooden causeway so narrow they would need to lead the horses through on foot. There was a great sound of birds, ducks and geese, snipe, herons, cormorants.

Kestre shivered. "I have never liked marsh lands." She had fought a beast almost a man on the edge of a great marsh like this, once. Three long days, she and the beast had fought.

East and then south and then east. South was across the marshes. East was across the marshes. In the north and the west there were woods and the last of the day's light. The sedge grew as high as Morren's shoulders, leaf blades like spears crusted with frost. A smell of rot and growth, the mud and the water glistening dark as dark metal. The water shining pale as pale gray eyes.

"In the summer..." Morren said. "For hunting..." He too shivered. "I would not want to still be out on these marshes when the sun sets," Morren said.

"No..." Kestre dismounted, stroked her horse's neck. "Well, then, girl, we had best go on." She led it forward, it shied from the trackway but at her reassurance went on. Its hooves rang on the wet wood of the track. The sedge hissed around her. A crowd, hissing, booing. Or – as if she was walking step by step onward into the sea. Morren stood his horse where the earth was still dry, grass and nettles, whitelace stems all winter-dead. Kestre was farther off, deep in the marshes, almost gone. He drew a long breath. It is not that this is a dead place, he thought, it is alive with bird life, plant life. Fish, frogs… I feel them, know them. But…but… He looked out to the horizon, gray on gray on gray. Birds were wheeling out over the marshes. Lacing the sky. Rushing toward the dry land, toward the gray sea. He heard a gull scream. So much life here. But…

"Morren!" Kestre called. "Come on!" Her voice was immense. Two ducks started up in panic; Morren's horse neighed. Moren too dismounted, led his horse onto the causeway. It snorted as its hooves met the wooden planks. Colder, suddenly, and the sedge hissed not wanting him near. But, but, he thought, so much life in this place.

He called as loud as he could, "Coming!" Shook his reigns to make the horse trapping ring.

They rode through the marsh for many hours. The track was narrow so that the horses' flanks pushed through the sedge. At last, when the sun was sinking to evening, they came out of the marsh onto a low headland, the sedge and the mire rising to gorse and heather and thick coarse grass. Small tangled trees, may trees, bare and black but with the last few haws standing out in the branches. Black bark, red berries, yellow lichen, white snow. And then only scrubbed grass, and then only bare stone. The sea beating there at the end of the headland. Gray cold sea on gray cold snow-crusted stone.

Low cliffs like an altar, at the end of the world where sea and sky and land met. If the marsh had been a bad place to Morren, the headland here was a terrible place.

Kestre pointed, shouted, "Look!" A building, or the remains of one, on the top of the headland. Tumbled walls waist-high at the most, what might have been the lintel of a doorway. A stone hut that would be too small for a privy in Roven. Morren dismounted, picked his way over to it. On the lintel, a carved face stared up at him. There were bird droppings everywhere. A dead gull in a corner, bones and a few feathers clinging to one wing. But the bird's head had been mummified by the salt. One black eye stared like the carved face at the doorway. Both the bird and the hut watching him.

Death, watching him.

This, he thought, was a dead place.

"Someone lived here."

He jumped, caught his foot on a piece of rubble, cursed.

"Someone lived here," Kestre said again. She shivered, looking around her at the emptiness. "It's tiny. There can't have been room to stand upright. When the storms come, it must have been…"

"…Unbearable. No one could live here, Kestre."

She pointed to a darker place in the rubble. "That's a hearth. See?"

"No." The rubble Morren had stumbled over was a spindle-whorl. He nudged it with his foot. "No one ever lived here, Kestre. A lookout, maybe, at the most. Fishermen watching the sea." He turned quickly away, hurried back to his horse. It snorted at him, pleased he was going back to it. It did not like this place. "There's nothing here," he called to Kestre. She was standing at the very edge of the headland looking down into the sea. A sudden mad fear that she would jump. Lady Kestre, Lady *Song*, called from birds' feathers and the wind in the trees and green wheat to be one of the Six Swords of Roven; a lover of music, of poetry, of flowers and good food; she hated fighting, she would weep sometimes when the Six were called to ride out, but in battle she was the bravest of them, would throw herself into the thickest part of the fighting, when battle came she was always the first of the Six to draw her sword, the last of the Six to sheath it. And she would jump now, leap from the headland here to be broken and drowned between gray rocks and bitter gray sea.

"Kestre!" Dread filled him. "Kestre! Come away!"

"What?" Kestre turned to him. The wind blew her hair around her, light – what light? Light from where? It was cold winter evening in this wild empty place – light caught her hair brilliant gold. She stood on the farthest east of the world, and her hair and her kind face were the sunrise at evening.

"Are you all right, Morren?" Kestre said.

What a fool I am, Moren thought. If there is evil here, it cannot touch Kestre. If there is pain here, Kestre will heal it.

If there is death, he thought – everywhere in this world, there is death.

He went back to join Kestre in the ruins. They stood together and looked into the sea. They threw the dead gull down into the sea. They made a fire in the place where the hearth had once been, got out food and water, tended their horses. When Kestre was busy with her horse, Morren dug up the spindle-whorl. It was made of bone, felt warm when he touched it, was pleasant in his hand the way old made things can be.

"I told you someone once lived here," Kestre said.

"Visited here," Morren said stubbornly. "Sat spinning thread while they waited for a ship to come in."

"You'll never accept I'm right and you're wrong, will you?"

He gave her his most golden smile, that only ever made her laugh and roll her eyes at him. "No. Wait, yes, no, I mean: you're wrong, I mean…"

He threw the spindle-whorl away. "I'm right and you're wrong, I mean." He looked out to the west where the sun had vanished. A last bar of red marking the sun's death. "I can really feel the days growing longer, can't you?" he said.

The fire they had made spat and a few twigs tumbled down sending out sparks. "Even the fire knows what to say to that joke," Kestre said. She pulled her cloak around her, curled up against the tumbled wall. "I'm going to try to sleep."

Sleep?

A great gift, their Lord of Roven had given Kestre: wherever she was, whatever danger and discomfort faced her, Kestre of the Six could quickly and easily fall asleep. Morren sat hunched in his cloak with his eyes closed. The ground was very cold, the air was colder, the tumbled stone wall (cold) dug into his back. His left leg began to ache from the way he was sitting. He moved it, the ache stopped, but an agony of pins and needles in his left foot. His right leg began to ache. The sea was very loud. The gulls were very loud: deep dark winter night, but the gulls did not seem to need to sleep. He needed a piss. He shifted his right leg, agony of pins and needles, his right foot sent a stone clattering off.

"Go to sleep, Morren," Kestre said in her sleep.

"I'm going for a piss. Then I'll sleep."

All excuses. This place was not a place for gentle sleep. If he slept, he'd see nightmares. The gulls screamed and they sounded like men on the battlefield dying. In the dark when the fighting was over, walking in the mud holding a torch, searching out the injured and the dying among the cold and the dead. Holding a man's hand, granting a woman a last sip of water, trying to bring healing, hands cupped over a wound, hoping, whispering charm words...dealing the death stroke, teeth gritted, hating it, staring down unblinking into a man's eyes as he killed him to give him some little peace. The only possible peace. We try, we try, but we can't heal them all, we can't save them all, sometimes the best thing we can do – the only thing we can do – is...is... We fight against the darkness, we are victorious, but – the cost... We are the light against the darkness, but sometimes – sometimes death is the only tiny last light.

He leapt up, crying out like the gulls cried. Cold and dark, snow in the air, below against the rocks the sea broke in heavy waves. The sea was darker and colder and deeper than the darkest longest night. His mouth tasted vile, his face puffy, damp on his clothes from snow and spray, salt crusted on his hair and his face.

Kestre leapt up beside him, sword drawn. The blade shone in the dark. "What–? Where–? Danger–? Morren–?"

"Nothing... I...I was asleep. Dreams." His voice was thick, his lips thick and dry. He thought of the dead dried gull they had thrown over the cliff. "Nothing...nothing..."

He had been asleep a long time, he realized. A faint luminosity to the sky out over the sea. And the sea...it sparkled with color, like stars, a hundred thousand stars rising from the deep. Like colored glass when a cup is thrown down, breaks with ring of sad music, the lamplight catches and catches on the fragments, the floor of the hall is made brilliant. Like jewels from a woman's necklace, scattered and floating on the waves. And the light – in the east – the stars falling – and the sun – the dawn light—

He thought: I see—

"Quick!" Kestre shouted. "Quickly! The horses! The horses!"

Morren leapt, his horse already running to meet him. He mounted up, Kestre mounted up. The gulls were shrieking overhead, he thought suddenly that their cries were not sad but wild and beautiful.

The sun rose, the first breath of the sun's light as the sun cried out its birth. The wound in the sky as the sun tore itself into being. The sky was the purple of crocus flowers, the sky was the yellow of crocus flowers, the sea was solid darkness, the sea was a liquid living thing all made of light. The gulls, the rocks of the headland – silver with light!

Into the sunrise, up into the sunrise – the two horses carrying the two of the six of Roven – leapt!

Through the sunrise—

And the light—

And there was nothing but the light—

And all that was or is or will be, of gold and silver and the color-that-is-no-color of the dawn rising of the sun's birthing, all that ever was or dreamed of being, the light was all that ever was or will be, and all that was or is or will be, all the world of light alone was made.

And leapt forever in that breaking morning, through the wound in the sky as the winter sun was born.

And all was light, all that is and was and ever will be, all of light was all the world new made.

And all was light.

And all was light.

And all was light.

And landed, on the other side of the sunrise.

A green field, the horses stood upon. A green field where the earth was deep rich mud and the horses sank to their fetlocks. Wheat growing knee-high, green and not yet ripe. Blue sky, not the cold blue of snow-and-winter but the warm blue of babies' eyes new-opened, marbled with high cream-white cloud. Their shadows fell silver before them now. A wind blew from behind them, smelling of green growing things. Morren turned to look back. Green fields, green trees that might be apple trees just past flowering. Leaves shivered in the breeze, and he thought suddenly for a moment that the trees were made not of wood and leaf-stuff but of brown and green glass. Poured, molded, dead trees. The wheat in the fields was a month perhaps off harvesting. He had thought earlier of Kestre's hair as like ripe wheat in the field; now suddenly, for a moment and a moment longer, he thought that the wheat here was only silk cloth silvery pale, spread out over the cold earth. On the far horizon, barely visible in the morning sun, might be a line that was a distant sea, and he thought for far longer than a moment that it was the edge of a blade, with the metal gleaming and sun and sweat and tears gleaming on it.

A bird called. A cow lowed. How foolish! Ahead of them, a road ran through the fields toward a high-walled city. Towers, thin as grass stems, that must up close be high and huge.

Kestre's smile was so huge her face must be hurting. She shook her head to make her hair fly out around her. She said, delighted, "Well done, my horse." She said with a laugh, "Well done, Lord Morren." She said, looking around her, "If it hadn't been for you, I'd still be curled up in that hut asleep."

"My nightmares." Morren's face felt filthy with salt damp and sleep. Thickness to the skin of his face. He rubbed his eyes. "Or am I dreaming still?"

"Would you like me to pinch you?"

Kestre took her waterskin from her saddlebag, drank. Passed it to Morren, who drank then poured water over his head.

"Oh, that's better." He gave her back the empty waterskin. "So, that must be the city?"

"I assume so. A city, certainly." She looked to the right, that here in this place beyond the sunrise might be the north or the south or the east or the west; looked to the left; looked behind her; looked half-eager half-afraid straight ahead. "And the only city I can see."

Then she said, "And if that's the city…that is—"

A nightmare.

One of the monsters.

It was huge, twice, three times as tall as the horses. It, too, was made of light. Wings, eyes, a long curling tail. Three wide-mouthed heads. One head was the head of a woman with long flowing silvery hair. One head was the head of a cat. One head was the head of a goat.

Its body was like that of a firedrake, scaled green and silver like the wheat in the field; its wings, bird's wings, were green and gold. Cat eyes, goat eyes, woman's eyes. Eyes also in its three foreheads, on its wings, on its scales, on the knots of muscle on its legs. Blue eyes and green eyes, beast eyes and human eyes both clear with hate and knowing.

Kestre drew her sword. Morren drew his sword.

The monster launched itself to meet them.

If all had been light so recently, so long so briefly bright light blinding – if all had been made of light and light the air they breathed and light the air they leapt through – now all was shadow and strange dark and weight of fighting. The size of the monster like city walls, slick with muscle, reared up on its hind legs, its front legs clawing at Morren. The cat head mauled at Kestre, its breath stank and she cried out, her horse skittered backward already wounded on its neck. Its tail lashed and beat the earth, drumming. Claws on a human hand as big as a shield raked across Morren's chest. The woman's face was up close to him, holding his gaze while the hands ripped. Morren thrust his sword, felt the blade connect with hard scales. Felt the blade thwarted, glance off. He slashed again, harder, shouting; Kestre was shouting, her sword stabbed again and again at the cat face. That was wounding it: blood splatter on Morren, stung him. The woman's face and claws all over him, he couldn't see Kestre fighting but he felt the blood she drew. Her horse reared. The monster's tail lashed around Morren's horse's legs. Like hacking stone. Pointless. Its claws caught him, opened up a wound in his right arm, a wound in his right leg.

The goat head spat out black fire. Dry sour heat, like a cauldron boiled dry, burned hair, pain and stench and pain and stench.

Oh but…I mean…come on! Morren was the best poet of the Six, the best poet in all the Hall Roven, gold and silver, master of words, Morren's tongue. But poetry, beauty, riddling cleverness of spell-words, charm-words…love and joy and grief and wonder, sorrow in a man's death in battle, glory in a woman's pursed lips – nothing, no words, for this monster, no words but – *come on! It's not fair! I mean…come on!*

Morren's sword was gleaming almost molten. Sweat dripping from Morren's forehead hissed in steam on the sword blade. The hairs on his arms shriveled up crisped.

He struck with eyes closed at the fire. Again, felt his sword meet but not cut. The world was red behind his eyelids, as it had been that morning on the other side of the sun. Claws met and cut his body. White woman's teeth met and cut him. Black fire – goat fire! – and the lashing of its tail making the earth tremble, and the beat of its wings blowing the fire like bellows, choking him. Pain pain pain pain heat pain. Wounds dried to dust. Blood boiled away. Its claws as they rip him, they are burning, blazing hot. If he opened his eyes, in this heat and this pain he would not be able to see. His horse was screaming. Bucking, twisting. He was screaming something, and the fire was in his mouth and his throat.

He felt his blade slide over scale and heavy muscle. Fail and fail and fail and—

Cut!

Bite!

His horse reared and crashed forward. Shock of its hooves stamping down into scale and muscle. Cracking bones. Monstrous eyes beaten down, put out. His sword jabbing, hacking, wild – and it caught, and it sank in, and it tore flesh.

The fire was gutted. Like a candle, his sword the fingers snuffing the flame out.

Eyes open. His eyes, blue and handsome, seeing the monster's thousand eyes close and die.

Hate, as the monster slowly died. The woman's face spitting curses without language. A sword wound running from its chin to its forehead.

Joy!

Relief!

Exhaustion.

Morren slumped in the saddle. The horse, wounded and weary, staggered. Morren slid off, knelt on the ruined earth gasping. Kestre sank down next to him. Dropped her sword with a moan of disgust. Bloodied to the hilt, reeking. The cat head lay severed at her feet.

"One of the monsters. Yes," she said.

The great bulk of the thing stretched before them, a hill of meat and bone. A river of blood.

"You killed it," Morren said at last.

"I think I probably did, yes," Kestre said. She said after a pause, looking at the cat head, "You helped."

"It..." The woman's head was turned away from them, so Kestre could not see the sword wound he'd made in it. But the front legs and hands had cuts on them also. He'd done that.

Kestre rubbed the back of her neck. A thing she did when she was angry, trying not to be angry. "One of the monsters." Her hair all crusted with soot. Her skin raw red. She prodded it carefully with the toe of her boot. "What was it?"

Morren said, "The worst of them?" He brushed his hand down his arm, watched with some interest as the singed remains of his arm hairs floated off. "Nothing else that's fire-breathing, at least." They were sitting in its shadow, its wings spilled around them, feathers scattered and themselves scorched. Hurt itself, in the end. Just colored feathers, the thousand hating eyes that had stared from its wings. He felt something like sorrow now for having killed it.

They cleaned themselves up a little, rubbed the worst of the blood and the soot off their armor, their faces, wiped their swords clean. Before they got mired in blood and ruin again. Neither said this, exactly. Met each other's gaze while working, sighed, looked away. Kestre a creature of more even spirit, look on the better side of things, don't fear the worst – Morren trying to draw comfort, and he was – he liked – to be a hero. She doesn't care for bravery, he'd think of her before a battle. She could be a quiet creature at home, doing good in other quiet ways. But now here she smiled, rubbed the back of her neck, patted her horse's flank, looked ahead of them toward the city rising distant, more monsters would be there guarding the city but she hummed to herself now getting herself ready for another battle. While Morren the *golden* hero – hoped it would all somehow – go away.

Enough!

Drew his sword.

Kicked his horse to ride.

Charged!

At nothing!

At everything!

Run of color sound feel taste his heartbeat in his ears the hoofbeats in his ears his hair flying eyes watering mouth open teeth clattering to the horse's jolt. Heat and cold, wind rushing sun rushing wind and world his mouth tastes blood and spittle and the joy in it, fire-flashing breath-shrieking crash onward panting straining run at nothing run and the sheer joy and the pleasure and the madness of it hooves thundering heart thundering breath in his head like drums and his eyes water and – the sky, the light, the colors, racing through it, racing past it, the world exploding, running with him panting sweat drips I am I was I will be I too am light and color and fast wind onrush and no frail slow flesh thing. And run, and running onward, and can run forever, and the horse is winged as birds as clouds and he the rider running winged. And his sword – the wind-rush makes it singing! And the wind is cut and dances ribbons from the blade. Horse hooves run the earth, breath gasping cuts the sky open. Rainbows from his sword blade, from his tears, his spittle, crowd his half-closed wide wild eyes. Shouts – roaring! Oceans – roaring! Storms – roaring! Thunder of hooves, thunder of heartbeats, his skin his hair his beauty raining down crashing down gold. Fearless. Dauntless. Determined. Spark flash. Fire flash. He is – only joy – and run – and breathless onward forever race. And run. And run and race. And race.

And halt. Where the walls of the city rose forbidding onward running, and another beast rose forbidding – him.

Bone beast.

Bones its eyes. Bone its hands that reached. Limbs, face, made not of flesh but of bone. A woman, if a woman was tall as two women standing one on the other's shoulders. If a woman had four arms each ending not in fingers but in bone-knives.

Yellow hair, rippling like a cornfield on the harvest morning. Red clots of blood, like poppies mixed among the golden wheat.

Naked and beautiful as all women, even though it was only made of bone.

Morren's horse pulled up hard, skidded, hooves clutching into the earth. Morren sawed on the reins, pointless, the horse quicker to react than he was, but…trying.

Swore as the monster ran fast as his horse straight toward him.

His sword hit bone. Clicked like knitting needles clicking, he thought. A hand closed around his horse's neck, five puncture wounds opened red where the finger-blades cut in. Another hand jabbed his face, fingers closing as five knife blades, groping to get inside the eyeholes of his helmet to stab and scratch. Blind with knives he hacked down, splintered bone. Strike to his throat, hard making his head jerk back, teeth chatter, hard making him gag and choke. Too many arms, too many blades, too much bone. He struck: sword on bone, left hand on bone. Smashed bone and hurt hand and hurt it. His horse reared, he heard and felt its hooves trample down with a crack. The hand pulled away from his face. Blood in his eyes now, his helmet askew awkward. He thought: I still…can't…see. His head was ringing. Beneath the metal of his helmet he could taste and smell bone. The weight of the monster lifted from him. He thought: killed it? Then a flash of yellow hair, ripples, waves: no! There! The beast! Lashed out, yelled in triumph. Shining sword on shining hair.

An arm caught his arm. Kestre shouted: "Stop! It's dead! It's me!"

Shining hair and Kestre's sweated face.

"Ohh." Morren removed his helmet, wiped his eyes. Kestre, dust on her face, her horse standing in a pile of old yellow bones. Bird bones. Thin, frail bones from small creeping beasts. She gave Morren a half smile.

"It's over. Just…"

"Lots of tiny bones."

"It was huge. When I was fighting it."

The city walls rose in the distance. Morren blinked, shook his head. "It was huge… Everything… Look! Look at the wounds on my horse's neck here. Huge claws. And, look, my face…"

Stinging pain. A sudden wind blowing sharp, blowing on the scratches. Blowing dust into them. Sweat and tears into them. He wiped his face again and his hand came away bloody.

"See?"

Kestre said slowly, "I'm not sure I see anything." She said then, "I'm not sure I like this place."

"It's beyond the world," Morren said. "Beyond the earth and the sun."

Kestre said after a moment, "We should not like this place."

The city walls were so distant still. High towers. See the drift of banners. Like reflections on water. Like pollen drifts. Strain to hear the peal of silver bells. A beautiful city, it must be beautiful, Morren thought. Strange and full of wonders. Marvels even my eyes have not seen; my mind, even, one of the Six Swords of Roven and formed out of flowers and the warm hearthstone and evening light, but even my mind that has seen such things will never have seen beauty such as this city must have, nor thought of the wonders that must dwell within it. And there, lit behind it, the gleam of copper that was the mountain, beautiful indeed, and it gleamed like skin. The birds that circled that far mountain were not birds but dragons; the water that flowed in cold streams from the mountain peaks was not water but liquid metal. The sky above and behind the mountain was pale and colorless. There is no eye could see, no mind conceive, of such a strange and beautiful thing.

Kestre said, "Your wounds are healing. Let us ride on, then."

Night came as they rode, but there were no stars. Morren looked up and said with wonder, "The Hall Roven, our companions…they are beyond the sky somewhere, while we are riding here." He tilted his head back until it seemed he would fall from his horse and drop a thousand miles into the night sky. Down and down and down through the night, falling or swimming down, until he fell home to Roven, and the quest left failed. Kestre shuddered, reached out to grab his arm, hold on to him. In the dark around them they heard the moan and cry of monsters.

Once, up close, they heard footsteps running. For a while something ran along beside them, off to their left. Flopping feet, panting breath. It tired, they drew ahead of it. It wailed, or something wailed. Another wail, like to the first, came from far off ahead of them. A little later they heard the crash of something large running toward and past them, something smaller and faster running after it. A little later they thought, both of them, that they saw a dark shape in the darkness, it seemed to them both that it turned its head to look at them. Once, far off, they heard two things fighting. They could not see their own hands holding the reins, or the ground beneath them. But as they rode on to the sound of the two things fighting, one from the sound must be dying, two yellow stars appeared overhead. And then all the sounds and the feel of the monsters ceased. Even the sound of their horses' breathing, their own breathing, ceased.

In this strange silent darkness, they came to the city walls.

Lamps and fires and candles lit the city brilliant. Outside the walls it was night but inside the city it was light as day. The walls were made of glass indeed. They were as high as cliffs, but they were clear glass and the city showed through them. But the buildings of the city too were made of clear glass, and the people inside were clearly visible moving about. Layer upon layer of people, looking through and through houses, workshops, storerooms, streets. A troop of guards seen through the walls of a house where a woman was rocking a cradle; two merchants deep in discussion over their scales, while as if in the air above them a man was in bed asleep. Layers upon layers of people, like rock carvings layer upon layer. A child seemed to run through a cookfire where a spit was turning. The guards hefted their spears as if challenging the woman shushing her baby to sleep. Mice in the attic; rats in the cellar; swifts nesting in the eaves; foxes in a butcher's midden. A pack of dogs chased a cat; a cat stalked a bird; a bird pecked at a piece of fruit. The woman threw up her hands to rage at the sleepless baby. The merchants shook on their deal. The running child twisted an ankle and made a face. Two lovers quarreled and kissed. All layered and mixed up together, the child's face between the merchants' clasped hands, the spit turning in a hiss of fat and flames before the baby beneath the lovers behind the mice above the rats, all seen in silence through the city walls. Look through and through and through, more people more color more movement, layer upon layer of people living seen through wall upon wall of glass. Blurred to a distance, a hundred thousand people houses workers beasts and birds, hair colors skin colors clothes fires lamps torches metal furs silks satins trees flowers through and through to the heart of the city, to the walls of the city, to the mountain and the sky beyond. A woman in a blue dress caught his eye, he could follow her in and out of buildings, lost behind a crowd, appearing again and again. Growing smaller, smaller, lost to him in an endlessly visible world. Like…seeing each thread in a tapestry moving. Seeing each individual hair spread on his pillow, and each warp and weft of the cloth the pillow is made from, and each mote of dust in a beam of sunlight in the air stirred by his lover's breath; seeing each and every tiny detail there, all living moving being, all at once. Seeing everything in the city, every life there, all at once.

Dizzying. Morren's stomach lurched. Too much to see. Too much life. Too much beauty. Too much movement. Too many stories unfolding all at once.

After a long time, Kestre said, awed, "It's like…it's like looking into…into a deep clear river, and you can see all the life there, the flies above the water, the beetles in the surface, the shoals of fish, the crawling things on the riverbed…" She said, "This must be how birds see a city. See us, in the fields around Roven, in the practice ground and the orchards. Don't you think, Morren?"

He was supposed to be the poet. Morren only nodded dumbly, closed his eyes but the light and the movement was still there behind his eyelids fierce and red. A man playing with children, a woman combing her hair, two young men talking, two young men fighting, a youth eating an apple, a youth with a tray of cakes… Watch them, follow them with his eyes, try to see all of them at once…

He thought: now we just need to find an invisible tower, break our way in, persuade the woman inside to come out and be queen.

"Or how dragons see," Kestre said.

"Not the way the dragon I last fought saw," Morren said. "I cut its stupid head off and it didn't see anything."

He felt wrong, ashamed, as he had said that, and Kestre looked at him sharply. "There's a gate, there, look," she said. She pointed to their left, exaggerating the gesture as you might with an angry child. Her kindness in hurrying over his awkward frightened crudity. It made Morren smile.

He felt a little better, because or in spite of his awkward frightened crudity.

They rode slowly toward the gate. The people in the city must be able to see them, through the glass walls, surely? Then he thought of dark windows and lighted feast halls, the dazzle of looking from a campfire out into the night. Never look at the campfire when you're on watch. The people in the city could not see out of their glass walls, he thought. We can see them, but they can't see us outside looking in.

Strange.

He thought of listening to a story. Listening to the hero's thoughts and feelings. The hero has no idea he is overheard.

He thought: how can the people in this city live like this?

The gate was there before them. A fine gatehouse, a red banner proud above it, torches burning, soldiers on the walls looking down, soldiers at the gateway watching the people filing in. Strange people: richly embroidered robes, neck rings and arm rings of gold and silver, jewels and gold in their piled hair. Gold and silver paint on their faces. Bells at their ankles and their wrists. Beards dyed red as rubies, green as emeralds, or plaited and oiled and hung with pearls. Fingernails as long again as their fingers, enameled blue or white or black, tipped with feathers. Some rode great white horses; some walked with a strange swaying skipping gait.

Each stopped at the gate's threshold. A soldier stepped forward. Each spoke one word. The soldier waved each in through the city gate. Morren strained to hear what was said, but could not hear what was said.

A long road led out from the gates into the empty night, and the road was crowded with people as far as Morren could see. All of them were utterly silent.

He looked at Kestre. "We…join the queue?" He looked at the endless line of people. "We can't…join the queue?" He said, "If we join that queue, we'll never leave this place."

Kestre said nothing. In the torchlight, her eyes were wide and dazzled by the beauty of the city and the people, and her eyes were full of fear. The people had horns like goats, and antlers like stags, and cats' paws, and birds' beaks. They had long tails, or dragonfly wings. They had scales. Fur. Tusks. Their arms were made of chipped stone or wooden sticks. Each spoke one word to be permitted to enter the city, and now Morren could hear the word, but he could not hold it in his mind to repeat it. He saw from Kestre's face that she too heard without hearing, the fear grew and grew in the face of that one of the Six who loved singing, who was Lady *Song*.

The singer and the poet. All this beauty and rich strangeness – so worthy of song and poetry, the best singer, the greatest poet, but neither could hold this one word in their mind. And all the time the people who could speak this word were filing in through the gates of the city, some had wolf-fangs, some had boars' snouts, some had the multi-faceted eyes of insects, some had long necks like twining snakes, and each person was more beautiful than the last. And so many of them passed in through the gates of the city that Morren began to think that the city must be filled to overflowing, for not one person walked out of the city through that gate.

And through the glass walls he could see the life of the city, men and women and children, beasts, birds, workers, traders, lovers, enemies, those that ran and jumped and those that quietly slept. More and more and more people, and Morren could see all of them, through to the very heart of the city and out to the walls of the city and to the copper mountain and the night sky beyond.

Kestre said nothing, said nothing, said nothing, for she was so moved and so frightened by this beautiful terrible place. Morren said nothing said nothing said nothing, for there was nothing he could find to say. And the night was so dark that they could see nothing except the city with its lamps and fires and torches blazing. And in the night sky overhead there were only two yellow stars.

The queue of people went in through the gates. Morren saw a woman with six green eyes in a silver face, and he thought that she was the most beautiful thing he had ever seen. Her hair was black, her dress was green. She wore a green jewel the size of a human heart at her throat. She was so lovely that Morren almost stepped forward to speak to her. She spoke the word, passed in through the gates. Morren saw a man with black bull's horns and white hair and huge white eyes. He was dressed in red from his boots to his cloak. He was so lovely that Morren reached out a hand to touch him. He spoke the word, passed in through the gates.

A great anger swept over Morren. He drew his sword – watched himself draw his sword. Watched himself ride straight into the line of people.

Watched himself kill them.

A woman in a red dress. Killed her! A man cloaked in yellow. Killed him! Two three four five six seven, killed killed killed. They threw up hands with birds' claws or the soft pads of kittens, they tried to run on their crane-fly-legs. Beat at him, cried surrender. Shouted, begged, gnashed tusks, gnashed teeth. Their blood was very red in the dark night. Smelled not of metal, as blood should, but of jasmine flowers. Some few of them tried valiantly to fight against him, struck at him, punched him; some very few drew weapons, small pitiful weapons, pretty jeweled daggers, sharp jeweled hair pins. They rustled around Morren, very tall; those on horseback were twice his hight, at least. But the rustle was like leaves in the wind when the child fears it's raining, "unfair," the child says, "I had such plans to play out in the fields all day," then the child realizes it's not rain she hears but only a strong wind in the trees behind her mother's farmstead, the trees she loves to play in, and she dances to the music the leaves make and is glad and wild in the wind, and Morren like the child was not fighting and was only dancing. Yet with each stroke of his sword he killed and killed and killed them.

They rushed at him all together, a hundred of them, silk and jewels and shining hair, all that was left of them. He threw up his sword. He killed them. They were gone, flown, nothing, like fallen leaves on the strong wind.

The gates stood open. Waiting. Soldiers at the gate. Through the glass walls Morren saw the people of the city going about their business, merchants, craftsmen, slaves, nobles, beggars, children, Morren watched a woman throw crumbs to a flock of sparrows, a child run away from a barking dog.

Sound of footsteps behind him. Bells jingling. Morren spun round and there behind him out of the dark more people were coming to enter the city, beautiful and stately and bejeweled, some riding great white horses, some walking with their strange swaying skipping gait.

"Quickly!" Morren shouted to Kestre. "Help me!" His sword felt heavy in his hands, as though it was made of lead. He kicked his horse, Kestre kicked her horse, they rode fast to the gateway. A soldier stepped forward to question them, Morren felt a great fear and tried to shape the impossible word in his mouth, but Kestre said simply, "We have business in the city, may we enter?" and the soldier stepped back, waved them in.

Don't look back, Morren thought as he rode through the gateway. So then he must look back over his shoulder into the dark. He saw the night sky with its two yellow stars, the peak of the copper mountain. A great crowd of people was moving toward the gates. Flowing toward the gates. Rare and beautiful they looked, seen from inside the city now, and a great yearning rose again in Morren to go among them, touch them, speak to them. Indeed, he might have turned again his horse, ridden back to join the crowd, had Kestre not called to him in alarm. For even as Morren hesitated, the soldiers in the gatehouse shouted an order and the city gates shut with a crash.

The gates were made of bronze. But the crowd pressed up against the walls on either side of the gates, staring in, holding their hands to the glass. More and more and more of them, pressing closer and closer, until the people at the front were crushed against the walls and Morren saw the terror in their faces, their mouths open screaming.

"Open the gates!" Morren shouted to the soldiers. "They're dying out there, can't you see?"

But I just killed them, he thought. And his sword was like a ruby, stained to the hilt with their blood. And no one inside the city saw or cared what was happening outside the walls.

"Come away," Kestre said. "Come away, Morren. Don't look."

"How can you say that?" She was the one who wept for their enemies after a battle. *"Remember, see what we have done; for shame at what we have done, such shame,"* she would say after a battle, when all Moren cared for was to wash off the filth and celebrate. "They're dying!" Morren shouted.

"Come away!" Kestre said again, more urgent. "Morren!" And outside the walls there was nothing, only the dark and the cold barren mountainside. And Morren's sword was clean as if he had only just drawn it from its sheath. And the gates stood open.

"We should leave the horses," Kestre said.

"What? The—? Yes… Yes." The clamor of a great city, crowds and noise; the stink of a great city, all its perfumes and enticements. Two soldiers patrolling, they chatted together, nodded and smiled at a passing fair lady (a passing, fair lady; a passing-fair lady), stopped to buy skewers of meat from a trader's stall. Burst of flame then from the meat grilling over hot coals, the fat dripped down, the succulent juices, the fire burned up with a roar, the smoke smelled of spice and heat in a way that made Morren's eyes water and his mouth water both. A flock of goats, little ones, smaller than the goats they kept at the Hall Roven, gray silky things with stubby legs and curved white horns. Herded bleating and flooding underfoot, like a flow of goats getting everywhere Morren looked, herded somehow ragged toward an alleyway by a young man his face very harassed, the soldiers with greasy meat-stained faces and a woman vivid in green velvet and many others glaring get those goats going at the poor young man herding them. Pushed them on, a flow of goats, to the alley and a yard entrance, gone inside, soon they'd be meat skewers, candles, soap, knife hilts. A peddler selling silk flowers to wear as ornaments, and a peddler selling charms made of pebbles, and a peddler selling real limp faded flowers. A wineshop doorway yawning open, three off-duty soldiers, still in armor, stumbling through the door yawning. Waved and shouted greetings to the greasy-faced soldiers their colleagues, the on-duty soldiers, dutiful, quick-waved and acknowledged and ignored them. A gang of children. A woman with a bale of clothes. A dog shitting right in the middle of the roadway. A man playing the flute.

"What? The—? Oh, yes, we should leave the horses, yes," Morren said. Now in this bustle and chaos, let's see – the slaughterhouse; the wineshop; the fair maidens and the music and the children; the beggars in the corners one even now rushing to scrape the dog's turds up. (What! Disgusting! Is there nothing sane and safe here? But wait – admire Morren's own good leather boots.) The music of the flute, and bird shit, goat shit, a young man's sweaty shitty perfume, a woman reeking perfume, until his head was spinning and he could barely see. A tall building around a courtyard, rooms on the upper floors stabling for horses beneath. In one of the bedrooms two people were – three people – look away quickly – there, look, better thing to look at, a dining room— stop looking— where diners— stop looking— were – stop looking— dining.

Four people????

"We can leave the horses there," Kestre said.

Morren said quickly, "Don't look up."

A pause. "Goodness. Well. Glass buildings. Yes."

That was me, yesterday, Morren thought. Sighed. Yesterday, or tomorrow, or a thousand years ago or a thousand years away. If this quest is ended, if we can ride home again, ride and leap out from behind the rising sun. How, how can we ride and leap like that, back from behind the rising sun? A city made of glass and a mountain made of copper, an invisible tower with neither windows nor door, a woman to persuade of something she has no wish for, then we ride, we ride, and we leap – through from behind the sun?

Somehow the horses had to be stabled directly underneath the bedroom Morren was trying not to look into. (Only three people. He was sure of it. Only! Three!) If they returned in a few hours they would find their horses watered, groomed, fed. "Such fine horses," the stable girl said, wistful, dreamy, her smile and her praise surely not for Morren's horse but for golden gleaming Morren.

"We should ask her what she thinks about living in a city made of glass," said Kestre. "She seems…good at not looking up?" The girl's eyes smiling were beautiful, like diamonds, but her head was bent low with the weight of her hair and the long tusks in her mouth. Kestre and Morren walked back past the slaughterhouse, they heard the goats begging not to be killed in sweet childish voices and a woman's voice saying, "But you must be killed and eaten, all of you, alas, my little ones." From out of the slaughterhouse came a woman with a goat's horns and goat's hooves, but inside the slaughterhouse the little gray goats now were screaming for mercy as they were slaughtered. The goat-footed woman bought fruit from a stall and ate it as if nothing was happening, the red juice of the fruit ran down her chin. Morren thought of apple juice on a boy's face in an orchard. Felt sad and sick. Let this quest end soon, let us ride home out from behind the sun. I don't care, he thought, whether we succeed or fail. Let the fair lady stay a prisoner in her tower – I must get away from this place. He was very small compared to the people of the city, felt low and weak beside them. Beneath them. So beautiful. So brilliant.

Their footsteps rustling and whispering. He thought: this city is a terrible place. He thought: I am hardly surprised the lady does not want to be queen of it.

"But it's a beautiful place," Kestre said.

"Too beautiful."

She raised her eyebrows. "You, Lord Morren the poet, call something 'too beautiful'?"

There: a great hall far larger even than the Hall Roven that was the seat of six deathless matchless peerless warriors, that had walls of silver and a roof of gold, a great hall with columns and arches and balconies soaring to the skies, a hall made of glass worked so cunningly that is seemed to move, be alive with light and rainbows, like a woman's hair when she dances in the moonlight and her hair is wet with summer rain. There: a glass tree hung with fruit and birds in ivory cages, the birds were made of metal, they flapped their wings and sang like real birds. There: a courtyard where a fountain played, the water in the fountain changed its color to the rhythm of a heartbeat from green to blue to yellow to red. There: a gateway leading through into a garden of white flowers. The sky was dark, night with only the two yellow stars there like eyes, but it was bright as full morning. Fairer than the lilies of the field, fairer than the taste of sweet water, fairer than any man or woman born, this city is.

"I hate it beyond words," Morren said. Like a pain, like teeth, between his legs.

"Poor Morren." He thought Kestre was mocking him, which she did seldom but was very good at when she did. But when he turned to defend himself, Kestre's face was grave and full of understanding. "I dream sometimes that I can no longer sing," Kestre said, "that all the words come out of my mouth dry until my mouth is full of pain and I feel a sickness from the dry taste of the words. It takes me a long time sometimes, days, to forget the dry taste." She squeezed Morren's hand. "This quest will be over soon, Morren, I'm sure, and then we can go home."

Fairer than lilies, Kestre's words. But a great despair and fear, that she knew and he knew she was lying. Fairer than lilies and more fragile than lilies is my hope of fleeing this place. Morren closed his eyes on the city's beauty, and in the dark behind his eyes he saw again the night's vision by the sea in the real world he had leapt from so thoughtlessly, in the dark when the fighting was over walking in the mud holding a torch to search out the injured and the dying among the cold and the dead. Saw his hand golden splendid holding a dying man's hand, his hand granting a woman a last sip of water trying to bring healing. His hand dealing the death stroke to man and woman, teeth gritted, hating it. The man dying had red hair and skin like midnight. The woman dying wore green armor, had hair like a field of ripe rippling wheat.

Morren snapped his eyes open. The city rose around him, glass houses, glass walls, a glass world. Torches and the sky black behind them. The two yellow stars that were almost a woman's eyes.

"End this." He walked left down the street. Turned right, then left, then left, then right.

Kestre hurried after him. "Where are you going? Morren?" She shouted, "Slow down! Where are we going?"

To find an invisible tower. Everything here is too visible, is it not? Morren turned right, then right, then right, then left. A wide street, an alley, a street that curved like a bow, a street as straight and narrow as a warp thread. Not quite running. Not quite walking. Twisting dodging turning through crowds in the packed streets. And he thought with a sudden roar of laughter as he wove his way through the crowds: dancing!

Without stopping, he said to Kestre: "Sing."

"Sing?" But she without stopping almost running almost not enough breath to sing, she sang while Morren danced. Through the city, step and step, through the beauty, all the layers of glass looking into the city's heart. Rushing, running, pouring, being, hand-in-hand how fair how fragile small soft golden song thread. The city is vast; the world is vast; the sun, they say, is vast, if one could climb or swim or fly up to the sun. A warrior king once boasted he would lead his army into the sky to conquer the sun. Tiny Morren.

Tiny Kestre. Fragile in hard cold glass with only human faces, human hands, human limbs. Sang and danced through the cold clear glass city to its heart, its heart before them beating, and the sound when they reached the city's heart was the sound of waves beating on a cold cliff. Moren looked at Kestre. Kestre looked at Morren. Hand-in-hand, the singer and the dancer

leapt.

A room with closed solid walls. The ceiling very low. Furnishings: a table on which stood a white dish of yellow apples; a narrow bed with bright coverlets; a tapestry on the wall; a stool set cosily before the hearth.

In the chair, a woman sat, the firelight hiding and stroking her face. She was dressed in gold, her long hair hung silver down her back. She was spinning a skein of gray wool.

A small room. Not much room, now Morren and Kestre were there as well. Morren's elbow was almost in the dish of apples. It was warm and clean, the hearth fire burned sweetly and with little smoke. But in the distance the wind howled around the walls cold and sea-spray-salt wet. And Morren knew that behind the walls of the room there was never a sunrise or a sunset.

The Queen of the Glass City put down her spindle. Took her distaff from her belt. The distaff was made of gold, the spindle was made of gold, the wool she spun was gray and it had a light in it so that it glowed as bright as the flames in the hearth, but the spindle-whorl was old chipped bone. The Queen of the Glass City turned yellow cat's eyes on Lady Kestre and Lord Morren.

What to say?

We're…here to rescue you?

Her shining hair, her yellow eyes so full of kindness, her clever fingers working spinning the gray wool. This warm room, pleasant, sheltered, the roar of the sea and the scream of the gulls outside far away. No reason for her to leave this place. Morren shifted his elbow out of the fruit bowl. Which unfortunately left his elbow pressed against the tapestry on the wall. The man in the tapestry crumpled up, Morren's elbow in his ribs. The tapestry showed a man killing a great three-headed beast, and now it looked as if the beast had triumphed and killed him.

No words. Nothing worth speaking of or for or about. A fair lady imprisoned in a high tower, we have quested so far and so hard to rescue her from…to bring her back to…

Goat's horns, bird's wings, cat's eyes, horse's hooves, boar's tusks. She shook her silver hair that was sweetly perfumed with musk rose. She stared at Morren, Morren stared back into her yellow eyes that were almost like stars. I would love to dance with you, my lady. Roll in a warm bed with you. Above all things, my lady, I would love to see you seated on your throne as a queen.

(For then, a part of Morren thought, and he hated himself for thinking it, for then, lady, I can – go home.)

But this room has no windows and no door.

But you sit here and cannot be reached by any human words.

But the world outside is cold.

Kestre reached out, touched the woman's arm as she had touched Morren's arm, the same kind reassuring gesture. "My lady. My companion and I have traveled a great distance to find you. We are weary, we are heart-sick. My companion has not enjoyed this quest." Kestre paused, said ruefully, "In truth, I have not enjoyed this quest. We were feasting and resting happily before we were summoned to ride to your rescue. I was looking forward greatly to going out on a sledge. And now I am not sure what it is we have ridden to save you from. Yourself?" Kestre paused, said fiercely, "I think…we have ridden out of the world and behind the rising sun to rescue you from…nothing."

The Queen of the Glass City said nothing. But her eyes flashed with such anger that Morren would have stepped back frightened, if he had not been pressed again the wall with a sleeve buckle caught in the tapestry and pulling a thread from the man's embroidered face.

The Queen of the Glass City said in a dry voice, "I do not want rescuing. You are right in that, at least: there is nothing to rescue me from."

Morren thought: that's true, yes, let's go home, the quest is done.

But Morren and Kestre together looked around the room, so warm and comfortable but with no window and no door. And Kestre said, "No?"

"I do not want to be rescued," the Queen of the Glass City said again.

This time Morren said, "No?"

"I will open the door," Kestre said.

Kestre drew her sword, stuck the blade hard against the stone wall. A door opened there. The towers of the glass city showed brilliant against the night sky. Through the open door came the sound of hooves galloping toward the city, the sound of feet running toward the city, the whisper and rustle of a crowd. Though the land around the city was bare and empty, flawless as if it was merely a picture woven of fine cloth.

"I will open a door," Morren said.

Morren drew his sword, touched the blade against the stone wall. A door opened there, to a low headland, gorse and heather and thick coarse grass and May trees in the first furze of spring. Beyond the headland a marsh spread gray-and-green and waking, the sky gray-and-white-and-colorless-pale. Sea birds and marsh birds, like dust motes in a shaft of light.

The Queen of the Glass City took one step toward the door Morren had opened. One step. Two steps. Three steps. Four steps. A hope rose in Morren, for she was fair indeed, this lady he could rescue, he would love indeed to dance with her, to roll with her in a warm bed. She stood right on the threshold with the sea wind blowing her silver hair. Morren though – hoped – feared – that she would leap. She was all silver and gold against the gray and green and colorless pale of sea and rock and marshland, her hair was the silver of clean water when the sun catches it dancing, her dress was the golden joy of the first warm day of spring. She reached out one hand through the door.

She turned away, crossed the room. One step. Two steps. Three steps. Four steps. She stood right in the threshold of the door Kestre had opened. The glass city rose before her. She reached out one hand through the door.

She turned on the threshold. She smiled at Morren, sadly, as if she would have loved to dance and roll in a bed with him. Morren would swear it, anyway, that that was how she smiled at him. She nodded at Kestre (didn't smile). She stepped through the doorway into her kingdom, all gold and silver with a copper crown on her shining head.

A cheer rang out, so fine, so joyful. Fairer than lilies. Fairer than all the birds of the air. "Returned! Returned! Our lady!" And trumpets rang, and horses neighed, and the little gray goats bleated bleated bleated. Even the lovers laid off their kissing, even the children ceased to run and play and shout and found their peace.

She sighed. Deep her sigh, and weary. Her glass city guarded by monsters, that lies hidden beyond the dawn sun. Such a work, to rule such a city! Such a trial, such weariness, that rule must bring.

The cheers rang, the air was sweet with music. The Queen of the Glass City sighed, and sighed – and stepped.

And the city was like a star, so bright and shining.

And the Queen of the Glass City was like a star that sinks at last and fades, and once – had brightly shone.

The door to the glass city closed.

Through the door to the marshes, the sky was drear and gray.

On the spring noon when the day and the night are exactly balanced as equals, Lord Morren and Lady Kestre of the Six Swords of Roven rode their horses along the wooden trackway through the marsh. Such a racket of birds and frogs and buzzing insects, such a roar of the wind in the reeds, such a plashing of life in the waters of the marsh. Hidden in the reeds, the life there, bursting, flashing, flickering, vanishing again. Empty and writhing with life. After a long time they turned at last into drier land, firmer footfalls, rode through rich meadows, rode through a great apple orchard. Through fields stubbled with the wheat growing, people in the fields working. They rode their horses fast across a ford, the ford turned out to be deeper than they had realized and they were both soaked to the waist. They rode through an oak forest, through a beech forest, through a pine forest. Kestre made a song of spring. When the sun was sinking in its first wounded fires, they saw far before them the flash of a golden roof. The road turned, ran down into a woodland; anemones and celandines were in flower beneath the still-sleeping trees. There! A deer! There! A fox! There! A racket of pigeons greater than the racket of marsh fowl! There! A – girl! A girl in a green dress with hair like ripe wheat. Mud on her dress, in her hair. Mud and green-stuff on her hands, for she was gathering the flowers in a basket.

She looked up, laughed in delight when she saw Kestre and Morren.

"Four of the Six Swords are sitting warm and well-rested in the Hall Roven. For days now we have feasted them every night. But two of the Six Swords have long been absent from the Hall Roven, and they have been sorely missed." The girl Cela threw a flower up at Morren. "Cold nights, we've had, some of us, in the Hall Roven. At tonight's feast, my Lord Morren, perhaps Gion and I will dance with you again."

Morren threw back his head, shouted a laugh back to her that sent the birds panicking up from the still-sleeping trees.

Oh, the joys of life! Oh, the beauty of life!

He said to Sela, "I would like that very much."

"You'd best hurry back to Roven, then," Gela said.

Kestre looked at Morren. "Come on, then!"

"I'm coming! Will you come with me, Kela my pretty one? A fast ride with me on my strong and mighty mount?" He helped Cela up behind him. "Hold on! Hold tight!"

Leapt. And the sun and the trees and Khela's laughter – leapt! And Lord Morren and Lady Kestre kicked their horses to a run, ran and raced and rode the sheer joy and the pleasure and the madness of it, hooves thundering heart thundering breath in their heads like drums, throwing up mud and green-stuff and flowers, breathless roaring racing running riding, until they came to the gates of the Hall Roven, at the end of the quest.

ACKNOWLEDGMENTS

As always, there are an impossibly large number of people to thank for the making of this book. The usual suspects thanked in previous books – consider yourselves all thanked again. Special thanks as always to Adrian Collins at *Grimdark Magazine* for his amazing support for my writing over the years. Also Adrian Tchaikovsky, Allen Stroud, Michael R. Fletcher, Peter McLean, Peter Philpott, Steven Poore.

Stas Borodin and Quint Von Canon, who between them drew this story before I wrote it.

Nick Wells, Don D'Auria and the team at Flame Tree.

But the real thanks for this book go to the women who inspired Kanda: Judith Katz, Kate Byers, Jo Feagan, Kate Dalton, Jo Connor, Karen Fishwick, Sammy K Smith, Charlotte Bond, S Naomi Scott, Beth Faulds, Jo Gibson, Rosa Watkinson, Jenny Hannaford, Hayley Spencer, Francesca Barbini, Linda Ketley, Shona Kinsella, Jo Hall. And above all my mother, the strongest and the best.

ABOUT THE AUTHOR

Anna Smith Spark is the author of two critically acclaimed fantasy series, the grimdark epic fantasy *Empires of Dust* trilogy and the folk horror high fantasy *The Remaking of This World Ruined* series, as well as the standalones *A Woman of The Sword* and *In the Shadow of Their Dying*. She writes lyrical prose-poetry about war, love, landscapes, and war. Her writing has been described as 'a masterwork' by *Nightmarish Conjurings*, 'an experience like no other series in fantasy' by *Grimdark Magazine*, 'literary *Game of Thrones*' by the *Sunday Times*, and 'howls like early Moorcock, converses like the best of Le Guin' by the *Daily Mail*. Her favourite authors are Mary Renault, R. Scott Bakker and M. John Harrison.

Anna has a BA in Ancient World Studies, an MA in Cultural and Social History and a PhD in English Literature. Her particular areas of historical interest are ancient Greece, early Medieval Britain, and ancient and medieval Central Asia, with a particular focus on women's lives in ancient and medieval societies. Her writing is very influenced by her studies, with many references to the literature and culture of these periods.

FLAME TREE FICTION

A wide range of new and classic fiction, from myth to modern stories, with tales from the distant past to the far future, including short story anthologies **Beyond & Within**, **Collector's Editions**, **Collectable Classics**, **Cothic Fantasy Collections** and **Epic Tales** of mythology and folklore.